Rose Blood

The Phantasmagoriad Book One

An Anti-Verse Tale by
Peter Guy Blacklock

This KDP Paper Back Edition
Published by the 451 ePublishing Haus
ISBN: 9781549898426

Acknowledgements

Designed & Published by the
451 ePublishing Haus

The author of this work is
Peter Guy Blacklock.
Cover image is by
Peter Guy Blacklock.

- Permissions -
Permission is freely given to quote or reproduce a line or two of text for review or reference purposes in your or another person's publication or web-site so long as the following link back to this publication's web-page is incorporated in the review or reference with the publisher's and author's name clearly stated.
Please use this link **http://harbinger451.co.uk/antiverse01.html**

- Disclosure -
The novel represented in this book is a work of fiction. All names, characters, and settings are there-fore fictitious. Any resemblance to actual events, names, locales, organisations, or persons living or dead, is entirely coincidental.

- Author's Dedication -
With undying love and gratitude this book is dedicated to Mia, my wife, my Priestess and my Goddess.
Thanks must also go to my family for their support in everything I have done.

Foreword

There have always been tales - in fable, legend and myth - of other worlds; running side by side with our own, and yet somehow within, beyond or beneath it. Whether we call it the Netherworld, the Underworld, the land of Fairy or the land of the gods – whether it be a place of dreams or a place of nightmares, or even a place of the dead. Ever since humanity has had the capacity to imagine and to wonder, there has been an 'other' world – and that otherworld is the Anti-Verse.

Modern science has made great leaps in explaining the observable universe but there is so much that is still beyond our ability to observe. Though we are constantly expanding the limitations of our perception with advances in technology and even, some may argue, with 'mind altering' drugs, it is estimated that the matter (in the form of mass & energy) that we can see, or is illuminated, represents only four percent of the universe in which we live. Another twenty-three percent or so, is thought to be composed of what is termed dark-matter. That is, matter that we cannot see - meaning that it is not being made evident by either its own light or by the emitted or reflected light of other, more conventional matter such as stars or galaxies. Generally, it is assumed, the majority of this mysterious dark-matter is locked up within black-holes, dead stars and planets, or is simply present in vast, diffuse clouds of none illuminated dust. Spiral galaxies, like our own Milky Way, are now thought to exist within roughly spherical halos or cloud bubbles of dark-matter particles.

So, what of the other seventy-three percent? I hear you ask. Here, we are forced to consider the even more mysterious dark-energy: the unexplained, and possibly inexplicable, repulsive or inflationary energy (force or quality) of the vacuum of space. Which must exist to explain the apparent acceleration of the rate of expansion of the observable universe and that is somehow counteracting the force of gravity. Its fundamental nature, however, is anyone's guess! The possibility that dark-energy may involve interactions between the standard three spatial dimensions that we see (the classic x, y & z) and extra spatial dimensions that we don't, may go some way to account for the strange properties of otherwise empty space.

String theorists have suggested there may be many more dimensions at play in the universe than the standard three of space and one of time, which comprise the four-dimensional space-time continuum in which we, and the observable universe, exist and interact. String Theory relies on the supposition that the basic quanta of sub-atomic particles are not so much a point, as they are envisioned in our space-time continuum, but are in fact line-like strings running through our continuum along an extra dimension we cannot, as yet, perceive.

The related M-Theory follows on from this and postulates that the different properties of quanta are defined by the harmonies of these strings. They vibrate within extra-dimensional planes (or membranes - composed of two extra dimensions) or are even resonating within other multi-dimensional continua (composed of three, four or possibly more extra dimensions). M-Theorists suggest that there may be at least six extra spatial dimensions beyond our mundane three, and therefore numerous planes and continua are potentially operating in conjunction with ours, but about which we may never know more of than their existence by inference.

Since the production of antimatter quanta in particle accelerators, the possibility of an antiverse has been suggested, a universe the exact opposite (sub-atomically at least) of our own. We could never physically travel to such an anti-verse of course, for as soon as an ordinary particle comes into contact with its anti-matter counterpart; they annihilate each other in a burst of energy. Perhaps this anti-verse exists within its own extra-dimensional continuum running parallel, or more accurately parallax, with ours. If we are not able to physically travel there, perhaps a shift in consciousness or perception is all that is needed to experience this other world... in fact, many of us may have already done so. There are numerous unexplained phenomena that may simply be a case of altered states of consciousness or perception that have allowed us glimpses of another, essentially alien but somehow strangely familiar, aspect of our own universe. This 'otherworld', and one may assume potentially many others, has always been there - out of sight, but not necessarily out of mind.

Perhaps, hypothetically at least, extra-dimensional gossamer threads link positive quanta at one end to negative quanta at the other. Likewise negative quanta in this world links to positive in that, the polar ends of these invisible strings mirroring each other. By these fundamental bonds of nature the two mirror worlds would be inextricably bound.

So the Anti-Verse is a dark mirror image of our own universe, in many ways very similar to it, manifesting as it does along the same dimension of time as ours - but its three spatial dimensions are not the same as those that form our continuum. It is an otherworld which operates in a continuum that is, in effect, a reflection of our own – opposite and yet beside us, beyond and yet around us, poles apart but less than a hair's breadth away. Throughout history we have been provided with glimpses of this otherworld; in our myths, legends and folklore, our fantasies, dreams and nightmares – even in our encounters with ghosts, fairy folk, cryptids and other unexplained phenomena... through these, the Anti-Verse has been revealed.

The Chronicles and Testaments of Citizen No Name Kane

Peter Guy Blacklock

Prologue: Lilith

Mikael.

The mists of deep slumber slowly faded away. Someone had called his name and disturbed his sleep, cutting through the dreams. He was being summoned into consciousness.

Mikael, wake up. He woke with a start. It had been a woman's voice, but no one was there!

Mikael looked around the room – it was strange to him, he did not recognise the plush new surroundings, it was all very different from his own humble home.

The large four-poster bed, in which he lay, with rich curtains draped about it, was totally alien to the simple bunk he usually slept in. The deep pillows and thick heavy covers, spread tightly over him, were so incredibly comfortable and warm – *surely fit for some great Prince or King of Old.*

An open fire blazed on his left, casting flickering shadows across the room; and many small candles, arranged around on a variety of holders and candelabra, added to the wild dance of light and shade. The only area of calm was under the steady light of the bright moon that shone in through the many panes of the tall windows opposite the fireplace.

Pulling the covers aside he swung his legs around and sat on the edge of the high bed, facing the huge hearth's warming glow.

Where am I? He thought. Mikael could not remember how he had got there and he certainly did not recall falling asleep in that bed.

Becoming conscious of his nakedness he stood up and searched for some clothes, but there were none to be seen and the only piece of furniture, apart from the bed, was a giant chest at its foot; looking inside he found it totally empty. The chest, like the posts of the bed, had all manner of wondrous creatures carved into its dark hard wood: dragons and unicorns, as well as many beasts unknown to him, were intricately depicted. After easing the heavy lid back down Mikael turned and, looking about himself, a very strange fact was slowly unveiled.

There are no doors! The thought idly dawned into his still sleepy head – *At least, none that can be seen.*

The walls were hung with large, faded tapestries illustrating what seemed to be scenes from folklore and old historical tales. He moved to inspect one.

More words, soft and quite, came to him. "You will not find a door hidden behind any of them." They said, spoken just at his shoulder. It was the same beautiful voice that had so suddenly awoken him from sleep.

There IS someone else in this room! He thought with growing rationality and alertness, spinning round though he still saw no one.

Mikael ventured toward one of the windows, intent on looking behind the drapes that were suspended from the ceiling; their deep red, dappled by candle light, providing a dazzling contrast with the pale blue moonbeams shinning steadily in.

Approaching the curtains the full moon caught his gaze and held him in its beguiling glow. Its large orb hung in a cloudless sky that exposed the deepest black of space and an immense scattering of apparently tiny stars; below, from beneath the window to the hazy distance of the horizon, spread a huge dark forest both silent and dreadful.

"Beautiful." Those same pleasant tones, tantalisingly close. "Is it not?" They asked "So... wild and brooding."

Turning, more slowly this time, he glimpsed a figure in one of the darker corners of the chamber.

An enchanting vision evolved as the young woman gracefully approached him. Dark brunette hair, long and rich, framed a pale creamy – *almost elfin* – face and neck; she wore a white silken robe tied at her slim waist, the swell of her ample breasts stretching the close fitting material. Mikael perceived the curves of her shapely legs as the angelic girl moved in front of the fire place, its burning light shining through the translucent lengths of her garment, and the dance like motion of her limbs hypnotised him to the point of veneration.

As she came nearer he marvelled at her large hazel eyes, they seemed to catch the flickering candle light as if they were ablaze, and her searing, impossibly red lips glistened with delectable moisture. A delicate hand lifted from her side and gently untied the simple knot at her middle, the tenuous gown parted to reveal her delightful naked form and she pushed it from her shoulders allowing it to fall to the floor. An unmistakable charge of attractive tension amassed between their naked bodies. Mikael would swear that the hairs on the back of his neck were standing.

A transformation of living human flesh, with the spirit of fire dancing over it, into an animated statue of an immortal goddess bathed in brilliance took place as she stepped into the moonlight. The sight took his breath away as she came and stood before him, her skin now radiantly white; the only colour was that of her lips. She looked up into his eyes and touched his shoulder with talon like finger nails, her hand spread, she gently but firmly traced the five points down his chest to his stomach muscles which involuntarily flexed at her touch.

Mikael, heart beating fast and hard, leaned in to bring his face toward her's, his mouth closer to her's, the heat of her body palpable in its closeness to his. Her lips parted, barely revealing sharp white teeth, as she met his kiss head on.

He woke with that same sudden heart stopping shock that had plagued the ends of dreams when he was a child – like he had fallen from a great height, fearing for his life for a brief but terrifying instant of pure panic. His rapidly beating heart and extremely exited body slowly calmed as he realised that the dream had come again. Mikael, having been haunted almost nightly by the same vision for nearly two weeks now, usually only caught a glimpse of the girl before waking; yesterday she had approached, this morning though she had touched and even kissed him.

Oh, how I had longed for that kiss. He thought with a passion he could hardly contain, the traumatic awakening now entirely forgotten.

He knew not who she was, never seeing her outside of the dream; his only wish was to meet her in life and to make her fair beauty his own.

Mikael Feraiyn, aching and weary, allowed his tall lean body a rest, leaning on his battered axe he looked at the small amount of chopped wood at his feet. His mind wandered, as it often did these days, to his family. All his chores seemed so hard now, each familiar task or tool summoned a multitude of memories, both happy and sad, of his caring parents and loving sister. The tears flooded into his eyes once more as the knowledge of their deaths again wrecked his heart and mind with grief.

Emma had been the first to go, he had loved his sister dearly and their parting had been terrible, growing weaker day by day her strength had been sapped by some strange and uncanny illness, her mind becoming delirious. She died in her sleep, too weak to fight, pale and thin like a withered rose.

His mother was broken-hearted at the loss of her daughter, so young at only seventeen years. While mourning she seemed to lose the will to live and soon Mikael and his father helplessly watched the essence of someone close weirdly ebb away once again.

Mikael's morose thoughts were suddenly interrupted by a distant voice calling him, hauntingly familiar, more sensed than heard.

"No!" His whisper seemed to shatter the silence that had just fallen like a shroud over the forest where he now stood. "It cannot be!" He dumbly mouthed.

The notion of madness crept into his brain, was he then to suffer as his father had before him, or did fate have an alternative end in view.

Mikael.

There it was again! It was her, he was sure of it, the girl from his dreams. But he still could not be sure if he had heard it for real or whether it was but a figment of his anguished mind.

He remembered his father's last tormented days, falling into madness and raving of beautiful phantoms and hideous demons that plagued him night and day. Would she be the phantom to usher him to the grave – just like his father before him – or ... *or what!?* He dare not think of his desires for her, after all she was just a dream and *she* did not exist.

He looked into the dark sombre trees surrounding the now shabby cottage, once kept so clean and tidy by his mother and sister. Everyday noises of the forest and of the few animals that Mikael still managed to keep began to replace the eerie silence. The tending of their livestock had been neglected somewhat since his father's death, he guiltily ignored his only living dependents however as he searched for the source of the voice. He peered down the only lane leading from his home but nothing could be seen. He had not really expected to see anyone, the nearest village, almost an hour's ride away, was full of superstitious peasants convinced, since the deaths, that a disease or curse hung over the Feraiyn family and their s*tead*. For they lived relatively deep into the Great Forest – too deep for supposed civilised people, too close to the Old Forest – at least that's how *they* figured it.

Sometimes I'm not entirely sure I don't believe them – he thought, maybe he *was* cursed or maledicted in some way! But he refused to let such thoughts jeopardise his sanity and fog his mind now. From nowhere the memory of his father's last, inexplicable words came to him, *rose blood* he had said as he drew his last breath, but Mikael still could not fathom their meaning.

The day was drawing to a close and, convincing himself the voice was imagination and that there was no one about, he collected the firewood together and carried it into the little family cottage that had seen much better days.

It will be enough to keep me warm tonight – he thought as he crossed the main room and piled it near the fire place.

The hurried knocks on the hefty wooden door that he had *just closed behind him* sent Mikael's heart leaping. He stared at the entrance incredulously, nobody could have covered that distance, from the invisibility that the forest afforded, all the way to the door, in such a short time – his family had cleared the forest back a good two hundred yards from their s*tead* generations ago – and he was sure that there could not have been anyone in the more immediate vicinity. Quietly he approached the door, listening for any sounds outside. He knew before even touching it that a young woman waited beyond. It all seemed so inevitable – though he refused to believe in such things as Destiny or Fate.

Slowly opening the door he was met by a dark figure tightly wrapped in a large black cowl, silhouetted in a burning haze as the sun buried itself in the distant tree line behind. Mikael watched as the spreading twilight shade of woodland crept towards the cottage, reaching the door and slowly rising up the mysterious hooded figure before him.

With the disappearance of the sun she raised her hands and lowered her hood revealing the lovely face that he had longed to see, a half smile playing on her familiar blood red lips.

Hello, Mikael. She said simply. It was the *witch* voice he now knew so well, not physically spoken but heard within his mind.

Unable to speak himself, he could only watch as she entered and passed him, with her cloak trailing the floor it was almost as if she glided into his home. She turned to face him and removed the garment in a way reminiscent of his dream, as it fell to the floor he noticed that it was faded and worn with great age.

She stood in his modest home glorious in her beauty, porcelain skin clothed in an emerald dress of rich velvet brocade. Clasped in her hands, held against her tight low cut bodice, was a single rose mirroring the colour of her lips exactly. Holding it out, she offered him the rufescent flower.

His head was full of questions; he looked into her dark, non blinking eyes, they seemed to penetrate deep into his soul as she gave the answer he sought most.

Lilith. Her name echoed through his mind.

Mikael stepped forward, impulsively reaching out to take her gift, and a long, wide thorn pierced his skin, sinking into the pad of his finger tip. He quickly pulled his injured hand back.

The wound was deep and dark crimson blood soon filled it to overflowing. His finger throbbed with an increasing dull pain as she raised the offending stem to her mouth and eagerly lapped at the thorn with a single stroke of her delicate tongue, a drop of his precious blood quickly spreading onto its moist surface. She placed the barbed, bloodied rose on the table by her side and then took Mikael's wounded but unresisting hand in hers, first kissing and then licking at the deep cut on his finger.

The warm healing touch of her lips and tongue thrilled him greatly but he wondered at the tears appearing in her eyes. Her grip grew incredibly strong as her teeth pressed either side of the small laceration, forcing more blood into her mouth. He knew she was drawing his blood – *drinking it!* But he did not care. With his free hand Mikael caressed the soft lengths of her rich, dark hair and then brushed the salty tears from her cheek. Sucking now she drew his finger full into her warm mouth and began to milk the wound with gentle persistence, easing the pain and slowly rendering it numb. They stood in that same position for what seemed an eternity but could only have been minutes. Eventually she let his hand go, his finger stiff but devoid of hurt, a weakness in his hand and arm.

He believed he knew her true nature now; she was not human but vampire and witch, heralding only death. Mikael's love and desire for her eliminated any hate or fear he might feel as he realised all he had to live for was her and the enchantments she commanded. From that moment he knew he would do anything, even die, to satisfy her needs and fill her hunger.

Lilith smiled knowingly but not without compassion, "I want your love Mikael, not your life." She said. "I am still human, a sapien like you. Different – yes... better – yes. You would not believe some of the things that I am capable of... and some of the things I can *do* for you." It was the first time he had actually heard her spoken voice. "I am not a demon or a witch." She added.

"But..." He was confused. "But you can hear my thoughts ... and my dreams – how is it possible for you to be in my dreams?"

"Join me Mikael, become like me and you will see how. You will be able to do these things and more, much more." Her eyes now pleading,

"I need you... please... let me change you – make you as I am. Together we would be – almost invincible!"

Staring at her he declared, "You must already know that I would do anything for you." His look was akin to worship.

"Yes – yes I know it." She spoke quietly, and still with a strange melancholic air. "Come, we must leave this place."

Taking his hand she led him out of the cottage into the forest, a garden of delight that was her own. His love carried him obediently after her, their flight from his past lit by the waxing moon and a multitude of bright stars.

They were deep into the forest, closer to its more ancient heart, and had been walking half the night before finally coming to a stop, enabling Mikael to rest. He was amazed at how Lilith's deft and graceful movement had propelled her so easily through the dense undergrowth. She seemed to have been able to find trails and openings where he could see only darkness and the speed of her travel had him thoroughly exhausted while appearing not to affect her at all.

She now stood before a large stone monolith, covered with moss and lichen it was laid on its side and at a slight angle, the massive roots of a giant oak gripping its base and holding it forever in the earth. Her body was deathly still as he approached, gradually getting his breath back. He stopped at her shoulder and looked at the ancient stone, he was just able to make out the primitive markings of simple cup like indents, patterns of lines and spiralling rings cut into its surface.

"Can you feel the power Mikael? This is Natures realm and here her forces are collected; here we begin your transformation." As she spoke Lilith cast her cloak aside and, walking up to the stone, she gently, almost lovingly, stroked its weathered surface.

Mikael noticed the rose in her hand for the first time since leaving the cottage, if she had not now been laying it on that imposing, altar like slab before him he would have sworn it was still on the table back at his home.

He could imagine her the vision of a faerie queen, an archaic divinity tending her woodland shrine, preparing it for a mysterious sacrificial rite. She gestured for him to come forward. He obeyed with head bowed, for the first time feeling fear, not of her but of the unknown, of what this transformation might bring. Hand in hand they knelt facing each other, her emanating warmth reassuring him in the cold night air.

Lilith kissed his hands and released them, he watched her deliberately raise a delicate pale forearm over the stone and bring it down hard on to the stem of the rose, a thorn burying itself deep into her flesh. Mikael flinched but was silenced from protest by her subtle remonstration voiced in his mind. The small hole in her upper wrist bled freely, spattering the flower, and the stone on which it lay, as she lifted her pierced limb. Standing, she hurriedly pushed her arm to his mouth.

"Drink," she exclaimed. "You must drink my life's blood to gain the power and strength you need!"

He knew he should feel only revulsion but passionate desire and thirst overwhelmed him at the first taste. Holding her arm to his lips he eagerly consumed her sap as it pumped into him; hot and sweet, it was nectar he could now never forsake.

"I instilled the thirst when feeding off you," she whispered while stroking the back of his neck with her free hand, her lips close to his ear. "Do not gorge yourself, drink slowly and only enough to invigorate your mind and body. You will not need to feed this way often – but the more you do the less you will need to eat and drink as was normal."

She released her arm from his grip. "Enough!" She said. "Too much may cause delirium and sickness, especially before succumbing to the vampirism fully."

Lilith smiled at the look of shock that had appeared on his face; she wondered what erroneous tales he had heard concerning her kind and tried to reassure him. "I did not lie when I said I was human Mikael, I am mortal like any other woman, but I will live longer and I do possess some so called supernatural powers – though once you understand them, you too will see that they are just as natural as breathing. You must forget all those superstitious myths made up by fools to hide their ignorance. Many people grow to hate what they do not understand – they hate it so much that it must be destroyed by any means possible – by violence, by treachery, but especially by lies.

"You must dispel all those deceitful legends from your memory... wipe your heart clean and let me teach you the truth anew."

As he got to his feet she embraced him. "Love me," she pleaded, her hot breath stroking his cheek. Her entreaty was impossible to refuse as she kissed him with a passion none could ignore.

That night, beneath the canopy of early autumn leaves, they vowed eternal love and fidelity, swearing to shield and succour each other till after even death had claimed its prize. Naked they consummated their secret marriage of blood on a bed of stone and moss. Oblivious to the cold and discomfort, their lovemaking – at first intense – became a playful game and then a joyous exploration of shared sensual pleasure.

Lilith's chosen minions, her *lilim*, watched and waited in the shadows of the night. They watched and waited for their Dark Mistress to summon them... for summon them she inevitably would. Each almost as ancient as their mistress they had learnt the sweet art of patience a long, long time ago. The time would come when her archaic eldritch progenitor would call to her – then, she would cast aside her plaything... and it would be time for the lilim to have *their* fill.

Chapter One: Rebekah

Rebekah Beddoes came closer to tears the more her situation worsened; bravely fighting them back she continued her weary trek down the isolated forest road. Her exhausted body gained no relief in the stifling heat, even the breeze playing with the long curls of her ruddy-chestnut coloured hair could do nothing to alleviate the high temperature.

How she longed to leave the ominous cover of the forest behind, it seemed to trap the midsummer warmth and amplify it to an almost unbearable degree. *Oh, midsummer*, she thought wistfully. There were only a few days of Fallowmonth left so it would soon be Litha's Eve. *Please let me get home before then* – she begged of the gods dryly. Rebekah's youthful good looks and normally pale complexion were transformed by tiredness and worry, her skin now flush and uncomfortably damp with sweat; the clothes she wore, totally unsuitable for such a long walk, were becoming heavier and more cumbersome with every step. She had wanted to look her best for her father when arriving home so had dressed in her finest clothes and most valued shoes. Although she could not have foreseen what was to befall her on the journey she wished dearly that her chosen apparel had been cooler and much more practical for travelling in.

If only those stupid horses hadn't bolted and that damned carriage overturned, thought a now bitter Rebekah, *I would be with Luwsiy and Papa, telling them tales of my time at finishing-school and of the new friends I had made there.* She would not be thirsty and hungry but would be comfortable and relaxed, looking forward to a peaceful night in her soft cosy bed and at the days of celebration ahead.

Nightfall was not far off she realised, and home still seemed a great distance away, the surrounding area was not familiar to her and she had met with no signs of life since the accident. Her anguish grew at the thought of spending the night away from home, alone with only the trees for shelter and the earth as a bed.

Rebekah thanked the gods that misfortune chose to hit her in summer and not on some frozen wintry evening through which she would not be likely to survive. A distant thunder storm was brewing though, so perhaps adverse weather would not leave her entirely unmolested. She prayed it would pass over, leaving her well alone.

As her imagination pondered other various hardships that could descend on her; wild animals, thieves and bandits; she approached a lane that turned off from the road she now tread. Rebekah stopped at its entrance and peered into the distance, trying to see where it might lead, but the shadows of the crowded trees frustrated her efforts. The track was overgrown but it looked as if it might have once been wide enough for a carriage to pass, now though only a narrow trail remained bare, worn by a single horse or man on foot.

Her intuition awoke within her a strong feeling to follow this new path, shelter and safety would be found at its end and whoever it was that used this trail would bring her no harm, of that she was sure. Rebekah could not explain these feelings and thoughts that manifested themselves in her mind, she just knew they must be heeded; after all, they were hardly ever wrong and she had no practical alternative. She followed her intuition.

With the sun low in the sky, the forest had become uncannily dark and gloomy; straining her eyes she carefully tried to follow the track, her hurried steps carrying her rapidly on. Heavy, sombre clouds had collected overhead; the air grew oppressively close and was still very warm despite the rapid approach of dusk.

Rebekah fantasised of a long cool bath, using its promise to spur her on to her destination, wherever it may prove to be. She dreamt of slowly peeling off her damp, grubby clothes, relishing the removal of each sweaty garment in turn, gradually getting cooler.

Once naked she would step into the bath, stretching and wriggling her toes, letting the fresh water tickle her skin. Within her fantasy she held herself in a sitting position just over the water then leisurely lowered herself into it, allowing its cool mass to thrill her flesh inch by inch. Cupping the delightful liquid in her hands she splashed her face and neck, the droplets trickling down her chest and back causing a tingling cooling ecstasy.

Her fancy then saw her totally immersed in the chill pool, looking up through the trembling water's surface, her body cool and rested.

The surface became suddenly still, delicate crystals appearing above her... sensual pleasure turned to horror as the biting water froze solid above and around her, icy daggers cut through flesh and bone towards her heart.

The impending doom snapped her out of the suddenly nightmarish daydream as she almost ran headlong into the large forbidding gates that loomed up before her – she hadn't even realised they were there. Rebekah stopped sharply in front of them, the confrontation with their uninviting facade causing her to forget the upsetting and entirely unbidden finale to the vision she had just conjured up for herself.

Formidable old walls extended out into the forest on either side of the gates, cracked and crumbling they were covered with all kinds of climbing plant and ran a gauntlet of mighty trees that would, inevitably, bring the artificial barriers to ruin, slowly destroyed by nature's imperceptible but relentless advance.

Grotesque dragon-like statues were mounted on two columns flanking the gates; Rebekah could see that their eyes shone as if alive.

Some form of precious stone – she rationalised. *Embedded into the sockets and reflecting the fading sunlight.*

Expecting the rusty iron gates to jam, or at least be stiff, she gave one a hefty push and prepared her ears for a nauseating screech that would disrupt the uncannily quiet forest.

The heavy gate glided open, smooth and silent. With some trepidation she passed through the portal.

A hill, covered with woodland of oak and beech, rose up before her. The trees were more widely spaced and the air cooler than in the forest proper back through the gateway.

Rebekah followed the trail to the right, it ran parallel with the wall for about a furlong and then turned away around the base of the hill, it twisted through tranquil glades and gentle rolling slopes until, widening ahead of her, it circled the most pleasing sight she had ever seen.

A lake! A cool breeze brushed her skin.

The sinking sun reflected in its calm, mottled surface, an orange blaze framed by the greys and blues of ominous clouds and a bewildering range of greens from the woodland all around. On the far shore a large mansion lay, the dark silhouette of its towers against the sunset cut a black mirror image into the myriad colours of the watery expanse before her. Even from this distance though she could see that it was deserted and in ruins; like the wall surrounding its grounds it had been mastered by nature and would eventually be destroyed by it.

Rebekah began to skirt the lake, enchanted by the soft broad shapes of the weeping beech and willow trees that grew along its shores and kissed the water with their delicate hanging fronds. She had been sure she would find someone here that could help her, now she realised her intuition had been very wrong. The house did not look as if it had been lived in for centuries.

At least it will provide shelter, she thought, *and a place to rest for the night.*

As she came nearer the almost castle like building the sound of gushing water came to her ears.

Maybe it's a stream flowing into the lake? Desperate for a drink and a wash she rushed towards the noise, hoping it would be fresh and clean.

As Rebekah approached an incline she became aware that the land on which she tread was probably once a large ornamental garden, now wild and unkempt. Surrounding her she saw in the shadows and undergrowth, life size statues of strange eldritch creatures, their detail worn, and in some cases, lost forever; only ghostly contours remaining to define their shape. In the fading light she could see imitations of more common kinds of man and beast.

Where a hillside came to meet the shore a couple of exquisite figures caught her attention. A handsome, well built young man knelt before the waters, his hand stretched out and a bewitched look of helpless adoration on his face. Rising from the lake and reaching out to touch his fingers was a beautiful elfin girl, too fine and delicate by far to be a sapien like herself. The face was that of an innocent child, her body a blooming form of virginal purity.

Rebekah guessed the pale naked sculptures, which appeared to be almost as perfect as the day they were made, depicted the legendry Haiylas, companion to the great hero Herakliys, falling in love with the elfin maiden charged with the care of a holy spring. The beautiful elf girl had pulled him into the water where, some say, he drowned. Rebekah preferred the version that ended with them becoming lovers in her aqueous domain. Of course people now know that elves do not live under the water – *not even sea-elves, but those myths were written such a long time ago,* she thought condescendingly*, when superstition was more powerful than fact.*

She was fascinated by all aspects of history and folklore, she had learnt about the ancient Hellenik myth at finishing school, and was beginning to get very curious about this house and its gardens.

Haiylas and his elfin lover – *what was she called again* – were situated at the bottom of some wide stone steps that rose up the side of the hill; fast water flowed down a channel that ran through the middle of this cracked and weathered stairway. She began climbing to try and find the water's origin.

About thirty steps up an open grotto had been hollowed out of the hillside; its floor, level with the top step, was a pool of crystal clear water. Another set of stairs, an echo of the outer ones, could be seen descending into the cool depths.

The walls, lit by the setting sun behind her, were striking indeed, an intricate structure of many nudes, some coupled together. What seemed to be the main figure, directly opposite the channel, was that of a graceful woman holding on her shoulder a large ewer with sparkling water pouring from it. One of this statue's knees was held up, almost pointing straight to the sun, and a torrent of water fell onto her thigh, dispersing in all directions and splashing noisily into the pool.

Rebekah's hot sticky body was worn out, her mouth parched and her stomach empty. The pool was the most inviting thing she had ever been tempted with. After looking around tentatively she quickly and carelessly undressed herself. It was a glorious feeling to remove the heavy, sweat-damp and stifling clothes

She let the slight breeze furtively stroke her body; its soft caresses excite her tired skin. The air was becoming cooler and the clouds beginning to disperse, causing the sky to slowly lighten again.

She pushed her hair behind her shoulders and entered the pool, slowly moving down the stairway.

Oh... so cool. It was just enough to refresh and not to freeze her, as she had half expected it to.

With every step the water gradually rose up her lithe legs, the rippling surface rousing her – especially as it ascended and licked at the soft and sensitive skin of her inner thighs. She paused when it reached their apex and cherished the enjoyment she felt as it lapped against her most private flesh there.

The indulgence only half shaming her she then rapidly descended the last couple of steps.

At its deepest the water came to just above her navel so she went to the cascading source and stood beneath the wild shower. She let it wash away the sweat and tears of a very toilsome day, its refreshing fall making her feel alive once more.

As the water smacked and tumbled down her body she climbed the stone figure and sat astride its cold, smooth thigh, there she drank directly from the ewer, gulping down as many mouthfuls as she could. Once her thirst was satisfied she carefully turned on her perch and sat with her back to the flow, arching under its revitalising force.

Her revelry was interrupted by a truncated exclamation of surprise followed by a rather polite but hurried cough that could only just be heard above the sounds of splashing water. Taking a few seconds to realise what the muffled tone was, Rebekah looked down. Startled she saw a man, she guessed in his late twenties, standing just to the right of the grotto's threshold, he was watching her, obviously entranced but with a veneer of undeniable embarrassment.

Panicking, she immediately slid from the statue into the pool, crouching down to cover herself entirely with its waters.

As she looked up through its shimmering surface, darkness seemed to cross over her; the sudden, alarming memory of a not-too-distant daydream pushed her back up to the air. The man had moved to the centre of the stairway, the sun at his back.

"Lady, you have no need to hide yourself," he said, "or to be ashamed of your body. You are very beautiful." His voice was restful and melodious. Rebekah was unsure how to act, whether to be indignant or contrite. She ended up simply staring suspiciously, all her words lodging in her throat.

"I am sorry I startled you, but I was not expecting to find someone in my pool." He added with a smile, "Especially one such as you."

Rebekah blushed deeply but finally managed to speak, opting for indignant. "Who are you, Sir? And how long have you been watching me!" It was all she could think of to say.

"You are the trespasser," he laughed. "I should be asking you the questions. Never mind though, my name is Mikael, Mikael Feraiyn, I live here." He held out his hand, as if for her to shake in greeting.

She ignored it, keeping the water line strictly at her neck and her hands and arms tightly wrapped about her naked breasts and groin. "But I thought this place was deserted! It looked so... derelict."

He chuckled softly. "Yes, it does. How did you get here? You are miles from anywhere."

"My carriage, it... it overturned. The driver was killed!" She could feel tears beginning to well in her eyes again, she forced them back. "I did not know what to do, so I walked as far as I could – to get help... get home." Rebekah was beginning to shiver; the water seemed much colder now that the sun had almost gone. She was losing her patience too.

"Please," she said forcefully, "you must help me. Help me get home." She knew he was her only hope and, although it pained her, she had to rely on his help.

"I will," he said kindly. "But you will have to stay at my home till morning, it is nearly dark and we cannot very well travel at night. And besides, I think you need some sleep, and probably something to eat as well... do you not?"

His smile was very engaging and despite everything Rebekah found herself smiling back.

"You had better get out of the water, you do not want to get a chill... you look freezing." He sauntered over to where she had first seen him and picked up a couple of towels he must have left there. "They were to have been for me," he explained. "Come... you must get dry." He held them out for her, inviting her out of the water.

"I can manage thank you..." she said briskly, "please, Sir – leave them... put them down and turn around."

Smiling pleasantly he gave a slight nod and complied with her request, moving away a good few steps down.

Rebekah rushed up the underwater stairs and out of the pool, she quickly rubbed her body down and pulled on her dress, packing her underclothes into a little bundle. She kept her shoes off. "I need some clean clothes and some... all my things are in my luggage, back with the coach..."

"Just use the clothes you have for now, I will take you to my home first, put you by a fire with some food and blankets... and then I will find this coach and bring you your luggage."

Rebekah smiled and said "You can turn round now, I'm dressed." as she draped a towel round her still damp hair.

He obeyed and approached her. "Give me your hand." He said looking into her face, obviously appraising her features, causing her to flush. She was tall, only a few inches shorter than he. "How old are you... sixteen... seventeen?"

"Eighteen... nearly nineteen" She replied a little self-consciously and then with more confidence "Not that it's any of your business!"

He smiled again, very engagingly. "I apologise for my impertinence, madam. Now, shall I guide you to my home?" He held a hand out for hers.

Not entirely letting her guard down Rebekah put her hand in his and walked with him; carrying her shoes in her other hand, and the bundle of underwear as unobtrusively as possible under her arm.

They silently walked through the increasingly strange and spectacular gardens. Statues became more numerous, seemingly less infected by corrosion the nearer to the house they were situated, and were sometimes grouped together to make up scenes from fable and legend. Most of which seemed to be either violent or erotic in nature, though all had a definite beauty and grace. Skirting an absolutely huge maze, which was mainly hidden in darkness, Rebekah finally got to see the house close up. Even the fading twilight could not detract from the blaze of floral colour she was now a witness to. She gasped, unable to hide her amazement. The sweet smell of roses was overwhelming.

Chapter Two - The Scent of Roses

Rebekah sat on the carpeted and slightly dusty floor, by a large fireplace in one of the old sitting rooms at the archaic mansion, in a considerably wilder part of the Great Forest than she was entirely comfortable with – *a little too close to the Old Forest* – for her liking she was sure. The cracking and whistling of the burning wood seemed to echo about her. She had taken off her dress again and was now wrapped in a wonderfully soft, warm blanket, leaning forward to try and dry her hair near the flames while combing it through with her fingers.

It will be hellish when the time comes to use a brush on it, she thought to herself.

She was alone now, Mikael had left, following her directions, to find the carriage and retrieve her luggage. She only felt slightly ashamed that she didn't volunteer to show the way and help him.

Mikael, Rebekah smiled, *he IS very handsome... in a brooding sort of way – but also quite strange... in a curious sort of way.*

"Mikael." She said his name aloud, trying to get the feel of it. Thinking her hair to be about dry she sat back into a great leather armchair, it seemed relatively new or at least in good condition – as did some of the other furniture she had seen. There were plenty of antiquities around but only occasionally could they be said to be anything other than dusty and broken relics of a past time.

He must be fairly wealthy though. She speculated. *But why live in such a dilapidated old house?*

Mikael had told her that he had found the place a few years ago, she remembered that he had paused before saying how long – as if he had to consider how long it was – *had he forgotten...* or was he deliberating what to tell her. *Had he lied?* She thought to herself. He went on to tell her that he had just decided to stay despite its dilapidation. He had liked it and therefore acquired it.

Standing up Rebekah went to the window and peered out, all she could see were the constellations and the bright crescent of the moon watching over the very faint glow of the eastern horizon. Below that was total darkness except for the few pale roses, lit from the inside, which framed the window. Nearly all of the outside walls of the great castellated house had seemed to be covered with climbing rose bushes of many different types. The ones she now observed were a delightful example; the soft white petals were tinged with a deep pink at their edges, almost as if each one had been partially dipped in blood. The scent of roses was all pervading.

She shivered. It was cold away from the fire so she returned to its warm flames, pushing a couch, which had seen better days, nearer the welcoming glow. Mikael had left two blankets for her, as well as apples, cheese, bread and butter, a pitcher of water and a bottle of wine. He had said he would make a proper meal on his return but that these would have to do for now. Rebekah insisted that they were quite enough and would definitely serve to fill her hunger.

Laying on the couch and spreading the second blanket over herself she began to eat. The meal was simple but very satisfying.

Staring into the fire and sipping the wine she began to feel very tired, her mind becoming drowsy and blurred.

The day must finally be catching up with me, she thought wearily. Her leaden thoughts managed to find some hidden reserves for turning to consider Mikael Feraiyn again. *Will I ever be able to figure him out, get to know him properly?*

She wondered how old he was; *he looked in his late twenties, twenty seven or eight at the most.*

His manners and character seemed to be that of a much older man though.

And his clothes... they were of the finest materials and most up to date fashions... but again for an older man, a sober man like my father – or grand-father even. She smiled at the thought. *He was certainly no foppish popinjay.*

Finally she started to nod off and slowly descend into a deep sleep. *Dryope, that was her name, the elfin nymph that seduced Haiylas into the water –* was the last thought that entered her mind as she slipped into unconsciousness.

He gazed at her sleeping face, the bright blue eyes now hidden. Her heavy eyelids gently flickered as the orbs moved to and fro behind them. Mikael wondered what she now beheld, what illusionary lands her feet now tread. Carefully probing her mind, entering her dream, he saw... a lake.

She was standing on a lake shore. Surrounding it lay a vast desert, nothing but barren sand that stretched out to the horizon under a deep blue sky and a blazing sun.

She was terribly hot and very thirsty. Rebekah knew the lake to be pure clean water but could not drink of it, something inside held her back, she did not know what – or why – but she was prevented from approaching it.

A small distance from the shore she saw a slight disturbance in the lake. Something was slowly rising up out of it!

First the head, shoulders, and then the whole figure of a young man rose to stand on the water's surface. Mikael recognised the features as his own.

His semblance beckoned her forward. She obeyed without question for all reluctance to approach the water had disappeared.

Mikael withdrew from her sleeping mind.

So, she is already dreaming of me. In a small way the thought satisfied him.

He looked at her beautiful face once more; compared to the deep coppery reddish-brown of her soft hair the young woman's skin, apart from a small but distinct bruise on her forehead, seemed so pale but invested with a subtle inner warmth. Her locks had appeared very dark, almost black, when wet – but now seemed to shine with a brilliance of their own. Mikael could see the curve of her breast gently rise and fall beneath the blanket covering her, the regular motion of her breathing a hypnotic relaxant that eased his troubled psyche.

Pulling the blanket ever-so delicately – her neck, shoulders, and one slender arm were revealed to him.

He touched her cheek with fingertips.

So smooth – so soft!

Her lips opened slightly, pulling the air into her sweet mouth. Rebekah was very much like Lilith, different colouring and slightly taller perhaps, but her features and figure were remarkably similar.

She looks so young, he thought. *Would she be too young to understand what I need from her? Was she too young to be able to help me?*

Her body and mind are strong though... and she has a hint of the sight. She could become very powerful once turned to the Blood and taught the old eldritch-ways.

Already she feels for me... she could grow to love me quite easily. I may have no choice but to use her.

Rebekah woke and stretched, letting out a low prolonged moan as she did so; looking to the window she saw it was still dark.

Her luggage had been lifted into the room.

"Mikael?" She spoke up. There was no reply. "Mister Feraiyn." She said louder.

She was alone.

Surely he could not have moved my trunk unaided! But there it was, sitting in the room with her few smaller bags. Although she had not seen anyone else Rebekah assumed there must be servants – at *least one, surely?*

Mikael must have woken his helper after leaving me. She decided.

Discarding the blankets she opened the trunk and dressed herself. The soft clean clothes, including one of her favourite summer dresses, filled her with a blossoming freshness. She yearned to search the house; eager to find Mikael, now that she was attractively clothed and the fatigue that had jaded her earlier was gone.

Rebekah pulled a hairbrush from her vanity case and stood in front of a large mirror that did its best to cover the whole wall opposite the fire, she paused only momentarily before subjecting her tresses to its cruel strokes. They did not resist as much as she had feared and soon she had her curls arranged in a carefully orchestrated tumble of confusion that spread from her head and shoulders almost to the small of her back.

Using the mirror to check her appearance from every angle Rebekah caught sight of a faint glow through the window. Breaking from her preening she advanced towards the panes; the glow, like that caused by flames, was on the hillside by the lake, near the pool where she had bathed.

Her curiosity had been baited so she grabbed a shawl and headed for the doorway. Before passing through to the corridor though she shouted. "Hello, Mister Feraiyn," then paused, listening. "Is anyone there?" Still no answer, the house was perfectly quiet. She could only assume that Mikael, and whoever else that lives there, was at the pool and must be responsible for the light she saw.

Rushing from the house Rebekah was surprised by the warmth of the air outside. The chill she had felt earlier was probably just a mixture of her tiredness and being damp.

The short summer night was beginning to retreat as a band of light pushed from the east. Dawn's first faint advances lit the grounds and hillside as Rebekah worked her way to the place of her first meeting with

Mikael. The stairway leading up to the pool was bordered by woodland that thinned out as it neared the lake, Rebekah crouched in the thick undergrowth at the top, only a couple of yards back, though she did not know it, from where Mikael had watched her earlier that night.

She could see him in the pond bathing and then standing beneath the spring as she had. A number of torches set into the hands of some of the statues circling the pool were to blame for the eerie glow she had seen from the house, their flickering light making the stony sculptures seem almost alive.

Rebekah marvelled at Mikael's naked form as he climbed out of the water, she had never seen a man fully unclothed before and the sight filled her with an inquisitive desire and excitement that, till now, had been largely foreign to her. The overpowering feeling far exceeded any subtle sensations she had experienced before.

Guilt battled with curiosity but she could not pull her eyes from his alien form.

She wanted to be nearer, to touch him... and to be touched, to feel his tall slim body next to hers.

His physique looked strong and supple, and his movements so graceful as he mounted the top step.

She now longed for him to love her. The strength of the desire surprised and, in no little measure, it scared her too.

She wanted so much to make her presence known to him, to confess her desires, but she dare not move.

Mikael's legs and arms were covered with fine hairs, darkened and matted against his pale skin by the wet. Rebekah had expected his chest to be similar but it appeared to be bare, unlike his flat stomach on which the hairs seemed to form a faint cross with his navel at its centre and his pubes its base. Though his thick shaggy growth put her soft wisp to shame it still drew attention to, rather than hid, his loins and Rebekah was finding it increasingly difficult not to stare solely at them.

Mikael turned away from her, much to her dismay, and revealed a sinewy back and firm buttocks as he bent and picked up a large towel and began drying himself.

She wanted to stay and watch him dress but she realised he could probably get to the house much quicker than her, so dragging herself away she rushed as quietly as she could back to the old mansion.

As Rebekah sat in the room waiting for Mikael's return she chomped on one of the apples left from the night before and pondered on the sensations she had felt while watching him. She wondered why the sight of his body and the thought of his touch should stir her in much the same way as the kiss of cold water from the pool on her loins. Somewhat shamefully she also remembered how the close touch of her sister had sometimes stirred these feelings within her. Even since the approach of their adulthood they had shared a bed – they had many close nights, especially during the cold winter months – often hugging, frequently playful – making little jokes about their budding forms. It was just childish play really – just young girl talk, sisters fooling together. She knew that what she felt for Mikael was *a whole different kettle of fish* – somehow more serious, more adult.

"Oh Luwsiy, I wish you could be here now." She'd forgotten herself and spoke aloud. "I miss you so much!" She then added smiling, "I wonder what you would think of him?"

"Who are you talking to?" Mikael's gentle voice made her heart jump. Rebekah turned to see him standing in the doorway, his hair still damp.

"I... was, eh... just talking to myself." She said with a feeble smile, trying not to stare at his body now clothed in dark breeches and a baggy white shirt, much less formal than those he wore the previous evening. "I was thinking of my young sister and how I have missed her."

"Oh... how long have you been away from her?" He entered the room and stood before her.

"Three months. It was my first term at the Kingsburg Academy School. My father arranged for me to attend before I start properly after the summer, he knows the school master you see. He wanted me to see if I would like it there."

"And do you... like it?"

"I liked it well enough, but I missed Luwsiy and Papa though. I do not think I will be able to spend *so much* time away from them, especially Luwsiy, I missed her so much – she's my best friend." Rebekah stopped, she realised she was beginning to chatter like a child and did not want to make a fool of herself. *It's probably too late for that!* She thought dryly.

Mikael picked an apple up from off the table but before taking a bite he said, "Surely you can make new friends there, you will not be half as lonely then. Will you?"

"I suppose not, the girls there all seemed nice enough and the master and his wife were kind to me. I have already made some friends there in fact, but none could be as close as Luwsiy, I think I would always miss her."

"Well in that case I think we had better get you back to her as soon as possible, the sun will be up soon and I am sure your father and sister will be very worried about you."

"Oh yes... they will! I wrote to them, to tell them when I was coming, we must hurry back – they will have been expecting me yesterday!" She stood up as if to leave that second, obviously distressed.

"Hold on," he said laughing. "We should have some breakfast first, and you have not even told me where you live yet."

They were now standing very close, looking up into his eyes she said, "I'm sorry, I did not think. My father owns the inn at a village called Meadengiat. The Unicorn's Rest – do you know it?"

"Yes, it is only a few miles or so from here. It will not take us long to get there."

"Oh, good." Rebekah was relieved but also a little sad, once home she may never see him again. "You must come to dinner one evening... as a thank you for helping me." She was surprised at her own tenacity and could feel her cheeks beginning to blush again.

"I would like that very much; I would hate to think I may never see you again."

She turned away as her blushes deepened, *could he possibly know the thoughts I have entertained about him, how I... want him?*

"We can take some food with us and eat breakfast as we travel if you like. It should be very pleasant, like a picnic." He smiled as he spoke and Rebekah turned back to mirror his expression.

"Yes, that would be nice."

Suddenly serious he said, "I think there is one more thing you should do for me first though before I agree to take you back."

"Oh, and what would that be?" She asked hesitantly.

He leaned toward her, bringing them even closer so that their faces almost touched. "You could tell me your name." He said as his smile returned.

"Oh... yes, my name," she laughed, remembering that she had deliberately withheld that piece of information when he had introduced himself the night before. "Rebekah Beddoes." she said.

"Rebekah... what a lovely name."

"Thank you." She liked the sound of her name on his lips and she hoped he would have cause to use it often.

Rebekah's heart was full of joy, her bliss two fold, not only would she soon be reunited with Luwsiy and her father but she felt she had found a new, very special friend and was greatly looking forward to introducing them all.

She sat by Mikael's side as he deftly guided his speeding trap down the twisting road and engaged her in conversation both interesting and amusing. It was a warm, summery morning; they had left the forest behind and were now travelling through a pleasant landscape of meadow and coppice that suggested to Rebekah they were nearing her home. She was confident that the distance travelled was in fact a lot more than a few miles but she said nothing. The hood of the light carriage kept the sun off them as it rose in the sky to their left. Her luggage was strapped to the rear, precariously she thought – though Mikael had insisted it was all perfectly balanced and safe.

He had moved all her bags himself, although she had given a hand with the trunk she knew he had taken all the weight and could easily have lifted it alone. His strength amazed her, but she kept silent and did not praise him, not wishing to sound foolish. He must have retrieved her things the night before alone as well for she had learnt from him that he had no servants and was the sole occupier of the house.

As they neared a sharp bend in the road the sounds of a fast approaching vehicle and horses assailed their ears. Mikael quickly pulled his trap over to the side of the lane to avoid an accident and they watched the curve ahead, waiting for the other carriage to appear. Almost immediately two horses came into sight, pulling a heavy cart with two men sat upon it.

They thundered round the high hedged corner and were intent on speeding past when Rebekah suddenly stood up and hailed "Father!" She jumped from Mikael's carriage and waved to the occupants of the cart which were pulled to as rapid a stop as was possible for the two sprinting cart horses. One of the men, the oldest – but only by a few years – leapt from his seat and ran to her; he was surprisingly agile for a rather rotund older man.

"Beky!" he shouted. "Oh, Beky, where have you been?" Hugging her he lifted the young woman off the ground and spun her half round – much to her chagrin.

Laughing though she kissed him, "I'm all right father, I am well. We had an accident but I'm all right... Mister Feraiyn here helped me." Rebekah pointed to Mikael, eager to get them introduced and the awkwardness over with. Mikael alighted from his carriage and approached her father with his hand held out to shake – in the time honoured fashion of all Saxanglish men meeting for the first time.

"An honour to meet you sir," he said, "I can assure you it was a privilege to aid such a delightful young lady."

He nodded to Mikael curtly and abruptly turned back to his daughter without shaking the proffered hand, "What do you mean an accident, what happened?" Pushing her fringe aside he looked at the dark bruise on her forehead. "Tell me what happened, Rebekah. Where is the coach?"

"Oh, Papa," tears began to fill her eyes, as she was quite incapable of holding them back before her father, "it overturned, the horses panicked or... or we hit a stone – I do not know. I was half asleep, I just remember it turning over and I was being thrown about inside. The driver was killed Papa – killed! I saw him, lying there, still and lifeless." Loud sobs burst from her as she hugged her father even tighter.

"His neck was broken, in the fall from the carriage I think." interjected Mikael gently.

Rebekah's father eased her over to his cart and sat her down on its back end, prompting and encouraging her to tell him what had happened. She recounted her tale between sobs and sniffles, diplomatically leaving out certain episodes, and gradually regaining control of her emotions, recovering her demeanour by telling the story and establishing her version of what had happened to her.

Mikael took careful note of what she told her father – and of what she did not.

When she had finished, Mister Beddoes comforted his daughter lightly then turned to Mikael and said, "I have much to thank you for sir, you helped my daughter when she was in a most needy and defenceless state." The older man now took the hand of the other to shake. "I believe she has already invited you to dinner one evening so I would like to second that – and hope that you may join us tomorrow, if that is convenient?"

"Assuredly so, I look forward to it a great deal."

"Well Rebekah, we must get you home, Luwsiy was greatly distressed when you did not arrive yesterday. She swore something awful must have happened to you, she even claimed to have dreamt you were drowning – gods know where you would drown in these parts at the height of summer?" Then with a little chuckle he added, "We will have to do something about that girl's fanciful imagination."

After standing up and holding her father's hand she said in a quiet coaxing voice. "Papa, can Mikael drive me home, his trap is much more comfortable than your bumpy old cart... and I do still feel a bit shaken."

"Oh – Mikael is it, eh?" She reddened at her father's playful whisper and looked to the ground. "Well all right," he said, "if he does not mind. We had better look after you till I can get the physician to check you over; gods know what this accident could have done to your system."

"Oh it is nothing serious father, it's just a knock."

"Well Mister Feraiyn?" He said to Mikael. "Would you let my Becky ride with you again?"

"Of course, I would be delighted to take Miss Beddoes to her home."

Mister Beddoes turned his cart around and headed home with Mikael and his daughter following in the trap behind.

"Who is that man with your father?" Mikael asked. "He seemed to be staring at me the whole time."

"Oh, that's just Bodkin; he works for my father at the inn. He never says much, just looks at people." She giggled. "I don't know why, but Papa seems to like his company. He always strikes me as being a bit strange – though harmless I think, my father seems to trust him implicitly."

"How long has he been with your father?"

"I'm not sure, for as long as I can remember and probably since before I was born. Come to think of it, I'm not even sure if it's his birth name, his family name or if it's just a nickname – I don't think I've ever heard of him being referred to as anything other than simply Bodkin."

"Does he always look so stern and mistrustful?" interjected Mikael.

"Yes, mostly," she replied, "he's an old soldier like my father; they were quartermasters – or something – in the Army, the Lord Protector's First Infantry," then mimicking her father's gruff voice, "the finest fighting force in the land and Bodkin was one of the finest."

They rode mainly in silence after that, Rebekah would furtively glance in his direction to study his profile then quickly look forward again. She did this a couple of times before realising he was glancing at her as well; they smiled and laughed softly when they caught each other's eye.

She moved gradually closer till she leant on his arm and could feel his heat.

As they entered the village of Meadengiat he seemed to contemplate her, when she returned his gaze he merely enquired the time her family usually sat for dinner.

"At High-Eight," she replied, "but please come a bit earlier," Rebekah smiled, "I want time to introduce you properly to Luwsiy."

The village looked so small and quiet after her term of schooling in the busy market town of Kingsburg, she wasn't sure which she preferred, the small and quite of the village or the constant bustle of the crowds in the larger town.

Meadengiat was actually the most sizeable village in quite a large area, situated at a confluence of main roads, between Kingsburg to the north, Oakdial to the west and Albiyon City to the south-east; Albiyon was the capital of Saxangland and the economic and cultural hub of the burgeoning Free Commonwealth states, so The Unicorn's Rest was perfectly placed for an inn. They would often have travellers stay the night, either on their way to or from the City, and every few days the coach would come through with passengers seeking lunch and refreshment; if it was late, as it often was, they too would spend the night before continuing their journey. She had seen western Britanniks and Atlantean sea-elves as well as the occasional northern Pikt or goblin Bogart staying at her father's establishment. The lounge bar at the inn was a very popular place too, regularly attended by Meadengiat's villagers as well as people from steads, farms and smaller villages in the surrounding area – there was even a small community of the notoriously insular halfling hobbs not too far away, somewhere within the Great Forest, the braver of whom would, from time to time, visit her father's well stocked bar. Rebekah had seen a dwarf once, but had never seen a troll... she'd always wanted to see a troll – her father had told her once that troll women were called trollops, but she was pretty sure that he had been joking. All in all, she considered, the small village of Meadengiat was really quite cosmopolitan – more so than its size would at first suggest.

The sign heralding her home came into view. The words, THE UNICORN'S REST, were depicted in richly decorative gold letters beneath a rather fanciful picture of a noble unicorn, laid with its head resting on a young maiden's lap. With one hand the maid stroked the unicorn's neck and with the other she gripped its single horn, her fingers encircling it.

The sign was hung at the entrance to the forecourt of the old timber-frame inn and as they passed Rebekah could see Mikael studying it, a knowing smile formed on his lips. She knew the legend of the unicorn held some secret meaning, as did most myths and fairy tales depicted in the painted signs of inns, but she did not know what it was. Her father would never explain the painting to her, though she was sure he knew its deeper, hidden message. Hidden messages annoyed her – *why are they hidden? I must look it up when I'm back at school.* She would ask her father, but she doubted that she'd get a straight answer out of him.

Mikael drew his trap to a halt beside her father's cart in front of the palatial Coaching Inn. Rebekah could see her sister eagerly waiting in the large doorway; she immediately jumped down from the small carriage and rushed towards her. Luwsiy ran to meet Rebekah with an excited screech; their embrace was but a brief prelude to the intense asking and giving of questions and answers, a heated and whispered exchange that only they heard in full – or even understood.

Mikael was happy to see Rebekah and her sister reunited. Luwsiy was slightly shorter than her older sister; she had striking ash blonde hair - like that of the sea elves. He edged his light trap forward until he was level with them and said. "Miss Beddoes." The two sisters looked up to him. Two pairs of piercing eyes, one pair blue the other green. "I am afraid I must hurry away," He said. "I have many things to see to."

"Yes," said their father. "We have kept you away from your home long enough but please accept our thanks; it would seem we owe you a great deal."

"High-Eight, remember!" Rebekah exclaimed.

"I will not be late," he smiled, "till tomorrow then." Waving, Mikael drove out of the forecourt, picking up speed as he went.

Unobserved, a furtive feminine face in an upstairs window watched him leave and tracked the trail of his fast moving trap till it was out of sight.

Rebekah was somewhat taken aback by the suddenness of his departure but soon forgot as she turned to Luwsiy and knew an instant desire to tell her all that had happened, especially everything she knew about Mikael.

Chapter Three – The Unicorn's Rest

Mikael paced the long dusty corridors of the house, searching.

"Lilith?" he cried with frustration. "Are you there?"

The muted whispering of the wind, channelled through hidden cracks and fissures, was the only response in the dusty, cobwebbed halls. Clouds of fine particles rose as his motion disturbed the restful blanket of centuries, his steps clearly discernible in the layer of dust behind.

At one corridor's end large double doors greeted him; twisting the stiff handles he pushed and opened them. A strong breeze immediately blew through, driving the dust at his feet away from the doorway. The room he entered was free of the dirt that had soiled the corridor, though dust-sheets covered all the furniture. Delicate sweeping curtains were billowing inwards from the open windows as brilliant sunlight streamed in and reflected off the gleaming, chequered floor.

Mikael was reminded of a chessboard by the flooring and the thought alone triggered a dreamlike transformation of the cloaked furnishings into giant white chessmen and pawns. Trying to ignore the shifting transmutations of the surroundings, for of course he knew that he was in a dream world, he approached the doors in the opposite wall and quickly passed through to another room.

Except for the moonlight that shone in through the windows and the much diminished breeze, the new chamber was identical to the previous one. In this one the chess pieces were black.

"Lilith? I must speak with you, are you here?" He heard the childish giggles of a young girl in the shadows.

"Lilith?" He said moving to the centre of the room. "Is that you?"

"Hello Mikael."

Turning toward her voice he saw a girl of about ten years sitting in a large chair which had been a Rook when he had passed it. Though younger she greatly resembled Rebekah's elfin haired sister.

"Lilith?" He repeated, quizzically.

She smiled. "Yes." It was the girls voice this time, not her own.

"Why have you taken that form?"

"She was already here Mikael. I just took her image over."

At first he was puzzled by Luwsiy's presence but then, he realised, he should not be so surprised, whenever he let his dreams take their own course something, or someone, unexpected always appeared.

"Who is she?" asked Lilith.

"A girl I saw today, though she was not as young as this, she was about seventeen. She must have made some sort of impact on my subconscious."

Lilith seemed to muse on this a while then the girl began to transform and grow into the beautiful womanhood of Lilith. Mikael was suddenly struck by how similar they looked – more so than Rebekah – Luwsiy could easily be Lilith as a child, except for their contrasting hair colour and the girl's deep green eyes.

"Will she be the one for you to share your life's blood with?" said the woman as she stood and faced him.

"No. At least I do not think so; but I don't know her all that well. She has a sister though, Rebekah, she is older and seems to be gifted with the sight, though in a raw and primitive form. She *may* be the one."

Lilith pulled her eyes from his and bowed her head. "Is she beautiful?" she asked wistfully then returned her focus to him, her now watery eyes cutting into his heart.

"Yes," he replied softly. "Very." He immediately regretted adding that last word, "But you know I love you Lilith, I always will."

His hushed tones were followed by her gentle weeping.

"I am sorry" she said, and then added, "I know you must find someone. I never doubted your love, but things are changing. It is getting harder for me to come to you – he is trying to stop me Mikael – I'm sure of it."

"But how can he?"

"Please do not underestimate him, he is very powerful – more powerful than you or even I could ever have been." She moved to him and held him tightly, then sobbed "Will he never let me rest?" Her tear streaked cheek dampening his shoulder where it lay.

"You will be avenged Lilith. I swear it. I will find him one day... and I *will* destroy him."

"Be careful Mikael, do not rush into it, you cannot go against him alone – you must find help."

"I know... and I will. I promise you." Caressing her chin he brought her face up and kissed her tenderly on the lips. "He will never part us. Even in death we are together." Gently he stroked the tears from her face then, bending slightly, picked her up and carried her in his arms toward a door which led to a room that they both knew well.

They entered a chamber with a large four poster bed surrounded by candles and tapestry covered walls. The door closed and disappeared behind them as he laid her down on the soft bed.

"Are we in your conscious or subconscious mind now?" she said with a more mirthful aspect.

Mikael laughed. "Very much my conscious mind, I cannot leave a dream totally to chance when it is the only time we can be together."

The sadness came upon her again and she said "I can't bear to be apart from you, my heart seems to freeze as it hungers for the warmth of your touch. My existence is but a nightmarish wandering of a god-forsaken wilderness... that I can only escape from when you dream and join me."

Mikael pitied her greatly, he sat beside her supine body and, leaning over, said "Then we must waste no more time." He kissed her passionately. Both mouths opened and their sweet slippery tongues vied to caress the succulent and fleshy underside of the other. Mikael drew Lilith's tongue into his mouth as he gained mastery and gently suckled on it. Breathlessly they parted.

"Soon we will be together forever," he said. "Once that foul Bäliyl Samiyl is dealt with I will be free to join you. Nothing will then hold me to this life."

"Forever." She whispered dreamily as his lips caressed her white neck and his gentle hands untied the delicate lacy bodice of her dress.

"We will enjoy an eternity of sensual bliss." His murmured words were only just audible to her as he kissed her lips again and eased the dress from her shoulders.

He began to pull its lengths down her body, slowly tugging it from her curves. Lilith revelled in his attention and savoured his touches as he unveiled her naked body.

Her nipples hardened as the cool material brushed away and his gaze fell upon them. Wanton urges and desires built up in her as he pulled the dress down past her stomach revealing a deep elongated navel. He then edged it round her hips till the downy triangle of dark pubic hair appeared. The garment gradually descended her delightful shapely legs until he drew it from her bare feet and cast it aside.

Mikael stood at the bottom of the bed studying the nude he had just uncovered as an artist appreciating the perfect form of true beauty.

Lilith smiled and thrilled at his expression of obvious love and adoration. She watched excitedly as he undressed his own, masculine, figure; her legs involuntarily parting as his newly naked phallus swelled to become firm and rigid. Lilith was becoming very moist between her legs and she desperately wanted him to enter her.

He sat by her feet and began to kiss her toes, she knew immediately what he was about, it was a game they had played often, so she lay back and relaxed with her arms above her head, ready to enjoy his kissing and fondling as his mouth slowly rose up the length of her body.

Mikael woke with the memory of their dreamy lovemaking still fresh in his mind, he could still hear Lilith's ecstatic sighs and moans climaxing as her womanly juices flowed.

To be separated from her again filled him with a terrible bleakness that he knew he must transcend, at least until he had avenged Lilith's death with that of Bäliyl's, *for then I can be with her for all time.*

He forced his thoughts from Lilith to Rebekah, but his mind lay troubled there too. He must use Rebekah, and her love, to strengthen and protect himself; they must share each other's blood and become lovers to create a powerful bond. His love for Lilith though would always outweigh anything he could feel for anyone else and this would weaken that bond. It would be a weakness Bäliyl could exploit and use against him.

I must be as honest as I possibly can when dealing with Rebekah.

Stirring from his contemplation he became aware of the setting sun. He could not see it but he sensed the light fading and the air cooling outside. Mikael rose from his bed, walked to the dark heavy drapes and drew them apart. The window revealed the fading crimson orb sinking into the forest beyond his mansion house. As he breathed he mouthed Rebekah's name.

Rebekah stopped brushing her hair. *Had someone called her?* Staring at her reflection in the mirror she listened intently. The solicitation she had dimly heard was not repeated.

Sitting before a large dressing table, in her old bedroom which she shared with her sister, Rebekah suddenly felt guilty. Luwsiy would now be busy with her chores downstairs, in the lounge serving drinks or in the kitchen helping her father cook any late meals.

She studied her clear face and looked into the cool, sapphire like eyes. Rebekah had told her father she was tired after her ordeal and so he had let her rest the whole day through, even though the physician had assured him she was perfectly well. She had a lot to think about though, and needed the peace and quiet to do so.

The chimes of High-Nine had sounded; the midsummer sun was setting and the evening quarter over. Soon Luwsiy would be able to retire for the night and join her while their father and Bodkin would stay up until the last of the customers and guests had either left or gone to their rooms.

Rebekah had noticed two new faces enjoying the hospitality of The Unicorns Rest, one was an old though stalwart looking man, the other a young woman, pretty despite her plain clothing. She guessed they were waiting for the coach to the City, the one she had been on. Rebekah wondered what they would do now.

The door suddenly opened and in from the dimly lit corridor came Luwsiy, the joy she felt at the return of her elder sister was clearly displayed on her face. She closed the door and rushed forward.

"Oh Becky I have missed you so!" She said sitting lightly on her sister's lap. "I am so glad you're back." Luwsiy hugged her tightly.

"And I too," said Rebekah softly, kissing Luwsiy's cheek. "I wish I could be here with you always."

Luwsiy broke the lingering silence that followed. "He is very handsome... do you love him?"

Taken aback by the suddenness of the statement Rebekah hesitated. "Yes, very much." she eventually answered.

"But does he love you?"

Rebekah laughed at the mock seriousness on her young sister's face. "I do not know... I wish I did."

"Would you marry him if he did?"

"We must both marry eventually Luwsiy."

The light-hearted expression dissolved leaving only the glumly serious features. "So you will leave me again."

"Luwsiy I would never go far from you... you know that. I love you. We are sisters – that will never change."

Luwsiy stood and moved from her saying, "I know... I'm being foolish. I'm sorry."

"You will find a young man soon; then you will not care so much about me."

"Do not say that!" Interjected Luwsiy turning, "I will always care about you – no matter what."

Rebekah watched silently as her sister undressed and prepared herself for bed. She was very beautiful, smaller than herself – but her form was perfectly proportioned. She had that kind of comely but delicate frailty that begged for protection and tenderness. *No... Luwsiy would have no difficulty in finding a lover.*

As Luwsiy climbed into their large bed Rebekah asked her if anyone had been waiting for the coach.

"Yes," she replied, "a girl. Ann she's called. She was going to the City to start working as a maid. I don't think she wanted to, but her family needs the money."

"What about that old man, was he not waiting for the coach too?"

"No, he's been here a few days. A very strange man to say the least, he arrived looking like some sort of vagabond. Father was not going to let him stay but when he produced a week's money in advance, well... you know Papa, money means everything."

Rebekah imitated her father's gruff voice. "Gods, it is money that feeds and shelters you girl!" They laughed at the words he had used often in reply to their taunts about his liking for money.

"Papa seems to be really taken with him, they stay up all hours with some of the regulars talking and drinking; Bodkin seems to be the only one not affected by him. He has got a really strange name too... Arturom or something... Arturom Kast-onin? Something like that anyway."

"But what do they have to talk about?"

"As to that, I do not know, I think it is the old man that does most of the talking, the others just listen. From what I can gather he has travelled a great deal and has many tall tales to tell. So long as there is ale in his tankard and some *weed* in his pipe he will recite his stories – and there always seems to be a sufficient audience to ensure that both are full to the brim." Luwsiy had forced the last few words out through a prolonged yawn. "Oh I am sorry, you must forgive me but I am so tired. Since you have been away father has been working me constantly, I must have some sleep." With that she turned onto her side, facing away, and mumbled a good night.

Rebekah stood and walked over to the bed, removed her dressing gown and got in bed beside her young sister. Moving close she whispered "Do you really think he is handsome?"

"Who... the old man?"

"No" laughed Rebekah, "you know who I mean – Mikael."

"Yes, yes I do. He is rich too... father will be pleased." Smiling she turned to face her sister and they both laughed.

Rebekah was enjoying the sun, its warmth and its brightness. The air was heavy with pollen and spores; hundreds of small insects lazily drifted to and fro providing a constant low hum. She knelt in an isolated glade picking flowers from the multitude that surrounded her as all her senses were charmed and overpowered by rich beauty.

She was conscious of the many woodland animals around her but was also aware of something watching, something intelligent. Looking up she saw an equine ideal, a pure white stallion with a single proud horn. He approached, leaving the shimmering foliage in which he was hid, and entered the glade.

Rebekah stayed perfectly still, not wishing to startle him. The unicorn began to circle the small clearing and soon moved out of her sight. As she listened intently the pattern of his hoof falls seemed to change.

The touch of a large human hand on her shoulder made her quickly glance round – the face of the beast stared back at her but now its maned neck was joined to the shoulders of a massive, and naked, sapien male. His body was as perfectly proportioned as the horse's before it, his body-hair as white as the unicorn's own.

The creature walked up to the stunned girl, nearing he knelt and then lay with his head on her lap, pushing his snout into the folds of her dress and between her legs. Excited by his naked presence and the sensation of his hot contented breath rushing onto her inner thighs as he breathed – she looked up to the skies and gasped as her body thrilled.

Bringing her eyes back down Rebekah saw that the creature had changed again, it was now totally sapien in appearance and of more natural proportions. It was Mikael.

Lifting himself up he kissed her forcefully on the mouth, pushing her back and laying her out on the grass, her knees were forced up and her dress folded onto her stomach leaving her legs bare.

As his sweet fervent tongue probed her mouth one of his hands stroked her thigh, circling and running up the underside till his fingers reached her bottom. He then brought his hand back round under her dress and rested it on her stomach. Slowly his fingers were pushed down onto her pubic mound and gently began to stroke her there, getting lower each time.

Mikael lifted his mouth from hers and began to kiss her neck and then her breasts through the light summer dress that still covered them. Wetting the thin material with his tongue, making her nipples tingle and burn he began to rouse them with his teasing bites and kisses.

Rebekah's chest heaved as she drew each breath in; her whole body was aglow with passion. Moans and sighs escaped her uncontrollably as Mikael's gentle fingers explored between her legs, probing and delving into her innermost secrets. Her heart beat faster, her genitals seemed to tremor and flush as... as – she woke to find herself in her bed with only a sleeping Luwsiy by her side.

Rebekah pushed the covers away to let the air cool her inflamed, perspiring body. *Gods!* She thought – *these dreams are becoming way too real!*

Once Rebekah was awake, Mikael pulled his mind from hers; she had been very responsive and was obviously a very sensual young girl.

He sat in the darkness, perched on the inn's roof just above her room, waiting for his libido to subside. He let his mind wander through the other rooms and corridors below.

A single guest slept in their room and the rest of the inn was practically deserted except for the lounge bar where about ten men were gathered. He recognised Rebekah's father and Bodkin; the others, he guessed, were patrons of the bar.

One among them caught his attention, a large man with long white hair cut at his shoulders and a close cropped beard. It was not his outward appearance that made him stand out however; it was more his bearing... it was his spirit in fact – *very powerful!* Mikael recognised a kind of kinship between them and by a subtle change in the aged face he knew the old man had sensed him too. Arkturon Kustenin – the old man allowed Mikael the knowledge of his name. The name meant nothing to Mikael and he felt no threat from the stranger.

Despite his surprise at finding an apparently kindred spirit – and at being detected at all – Mikael's attention stayed and listened awhile. The old man had his audience enthralled but this was due to a simple mind trick rather than interesting conversation and Mikael soon grew bored of his tales. He could see the gentleman was disturbed only slightly by his presence so he left him to milk his congregation of admiration and ale in peace. It seemed clear the old man had no intention of interfering with Mikael's activities.

His mind's eye returned to the sisters' bedroom; Rebckah was drifting back to sleep while her sibling seemed to be in the throes of a growing nightmare. Fitfully she pushed at the covers and distressing groans formed at her lips. Mikael was again struck by her likeness to Lilith and took pity on her.

He entered Luwsiy's dream in the hope of easing her sleep... but Mikael was horrified that a girl so young should dream such things.

Terrified, Luwsiy was tied spread-eagled to her bed, Rebekah was nowhere to be seen. Huge spiders were crawling about her naked body and two obese, evil looking snakes were slowly winding their way up her legs, one coiled on each pale limb. The black, unearthly worms glistened with a slime that left a foul trail on her pale skin.

At the bottom of the bed stood a shadowy figure that giggled dementedly and held a viciously curved knife in a twisted, deformed grip.

Luwsiy was becoming hysterical as the fat heads of the serpents reached the top of her thighs and thin tongues protruded and flickered on her delicate flesh. The two heads began to combine between her legs, the snakes twisted about each other to become one hideous body. The writhing oozy mass pushed up against her crotch and Mikael knew he must act quickly before it enters her and splits the screaming girl apart, even though it was but a dream he knew it could cause untold damage to her mind, such a horrendous obscenity could fracture her sanity for good.

Materialising his astral body into the dream room he lunged at the figure, taking the knife and pushing him aside, then grabbed the slippery head of the now single snake, pulled it from between Luwsiy's legs and threw it at the sprawled and still giggling stranger. Mikael cut through Luwsiy's bonds with the knife, threw it aside and grabbed her shoulders.

"Wake up!" He shouted – urgently shaking her, "wake up!"

"Wake up," Rebekah said shaking her sister, "it's just a dream – you're all right."

A shocked Luwsiy stared back at Rebekah and started to cry "It was so real... so frightening." She was shivering and still seemed scared, looking about the room as if someone might be hiding.

"It's all right, Luwsiy – you're safe now." Rebekah reassured her in as calming a voice as she could muster.

Mikael watched and listened to them through his mind's eye as Luwsiy told Rebekah about her nightmare.

The elder sister was clearly disturbed when Luwsiy had finished and Mikael too was concerned. The strange shadowy man had all the hallmarks of an intruder in her dream, it had been him controlling it not Luwsiy's subconscious. Mikael felt himself lucky to have surprised him in that way – though Luwsiy had been the luckier – and he couldn't help but wonder if the intruder was in fact Arkturon Kustenin... but he dismissed the idea – the old man was harmless – of that he was sure.

"I too dreamed of Mikael tonight," said Rebekah, "but in far happier, though just as strange, circumstances."

Though he knew Rebekah just wanted to help Luwsiy forget her nightmare Mikael was surprised and even a little embarrassed when she shared every intimate detail of the *their* dream with her young sister.

Mikael found himself greatly aroused by the retelling though and he could see the two girls were too – though *they* would deny it – adding to his excitement.

As the girls hugged and wished each other good night again they kissed and Mikael saw that they both lingered hesitantly before pulling apart.

Watching the sisters he began to lust for a woman and he could feel the thirst for blood build within him too. He could smell it in their young bodies as he realised he had not fed for some time. It was a dangerous time for him – the vampirism diminished his soul and only the taste of blood could nourish it. The longer he went without a blood feast the weaker and more debased his soul would become. More like a ravening beast his thirst for blood would drive him... to commit unspeakable depravities – he would indeed become a true monster.

Mikael did not want to use Rebekah or Luwsiy... *Not yet. But there is someone... someone I can use.*

Ann Benwik slept a grateful sleep. Every day and night she had before getting to the City was, in her eyes, an extra day and night of freedom. Although sorry for the coach driver she was glad when she heard of the accident, and at least the innkeeper's daughter had not been hurt. Anything that prevented her from becoming a servant to a rich family in the City, even for just a short time, was to be welcomed.

The innkeeper had allowed her to stay until a replacement coach could come despite the fact she could not pay.

She was thankful that there were plenty of free rooms, as he had said she should be. He could not hide his kindness though, no matter how hard he tried.

Mikael crossed the roof with the ease of a prowling cat and opened the latch of the window with unseen hands despite the pane of glass between. Creeping through into the corridor he silently moved to the locked door of her room.

He could hear her breathing within that room. Feel her pumping heart. The scent of her sweet juices made him fantasise of Luwsiy and Rebekah making love. It made his thirst more urgent – his thirst for her.

The key was in the lock on the inside. Causing it to turn he opened the door. Mikael locked it again behind him.

Passing a hand over her temples he lulled her into a deeper and sounder sleep. Pulling the sheets away he saw that her night-dress had ridden up to her waist, he removed the encumbrance.

She was healthy, clean and, from the thoughts and dreams he was able to detect, he deduced she was no longer virgin. A quick inspection of her memories proved this to be so.

He could prevent impregnation with his will alone so did not have to worry about her conceiving a child.

After stripping himself he brought her into a semi-conscious state so, although still asleep, she would be responsive to his lovemaking and remember it as a passionate dream.

Mikael spent his lust inside her and quenched his thirst as the throws of orgasm raged through her body. Nipping the soft flesh above her breast between sharp hard teeth he broke her skin and sucked the hot blood that flowed from her. Her sexual energy pumped it into him and filled him with new life and vitality.

Once Mikael was satiated, he bathed the small wound with his saliva, repeatedly kissing and licking it – so it would heal quickly and cleanly.

He lay beside her, held her to him and eased her back into an untroubled slumber.

Ann woke suddenly as morning came, a horrible laughter still echoing in her mind.

"It was a nightmare," she reassured herself, "just a dream."

She saw that in her sleep she had pushed the covers right back and had tossed her night-dress aside. *I must have had a restless night.* The memory of her nightmare was already fading, though she recalled an earlier dream with perfect clarity. It had been so real, so... *fulfilling.* She actually felt as if she had copulated that night.

Looking down at her nakedness she saw a small scar above her left breast, it was where he had been kissing me... *I must have nipped myself when pulling off my night-dress, probably when dreaming of his carnal advances.*

It was obvious she had been thrashing about during her dreams, *I hope I was not calling out too,* she thought. *My last coupling had been a very noisy affair.* She smiled at the memory of those screams and moans of ecstasy in the hay loft just weeks earlier.

Her phantom suitor had been the young man who had brought the innkeeper's daughter home after the accident. She wondered if he would visit the inn again before she would have to leave for the City.

Lilith was beginning to get hysterical; he should not have mentioned Luwsiy's dream.

"It IS him Mikael, I am sure of it!" She said.

"You don't know that." He said wearily.

"I know him – how he thinks – what he takes pleasure in... what amuses him. We have just run out of time Mikael, he's going to use that girl to get me back."

"You're panicking, he cannot bring you back – it's impossible."

"No Mikael - NO, you're wrong. I told you, he is more powerful than we could ever imagine."

"But why would he want to bring you back – HE killed you."

"Yes, in a fit of anger and jealously; he had plans for me Mikael. They were ruined when I ran away – when I met you." She fell silent awhile then continued in hushed, thoughtful tones. "You are going to have to watch this Luwsiy very carefully from now on, you must guard her as she sleeps and monitor her dreams."

Mikael knew Lilith was right and he realised the moment that would decide if they could spend eternity together was fast approaching.

They held each other while they could; laying in their dream bound bed and daring to hope for a future together – without the ominous cloud of Bäliyl constantly hanging over them.

Chapter Four - Murder by Troll

Luwsiy was waiting with her sister for Mikael to arrive, the meal was almost ready but it seemed he would not appear until the hour of High-Eight had actually chimed on the tall clock in the inn's lobby. There had been a silence between the two girls all day, a coldness in deep contrast to the warmth of the night before. Luwsiy could not rid herself of the images from her nightmare... and also of the dream Rebekah had described. She could not decide which was worse – for she felt a jealousy growing inside her that made just the thought of her sister making love to Mikael unbearable. *It's wrong, I know... but I just can't help it.* She chided herself.

Her musing was suddenly interrupted.

"You two mopers will have to snap out of whatever it is that's bothering you and get on with setting the table." Both girls jumped at their father's voice and hurriedly got on with their tasks. "Our guest will be here soon." He continued.

Luwsiy glanced at Rebekah and wondered what thoughts he had disturbed in her.

It had been an awfully long time since she had seen their private dining room looking so grand, the last time must have been when that rich merchant had refused to eat in the public dining room, insisting on privacy. Allowing herself a secret smile she remembered her father's bowing and scraping.

When the table was set, he let Luwsiy and Rebekah go to the front door to await Mikael's arrival. On the way they peeked into the smoky bar room, it was much fuller than usual and both Bodkin and Martta, the barmaid, were busy serving so they decided not to bother them. Martta was one of two local girls employed at the inn as maids but whose duties seemed to include anything Luwsiy's father could throw at them. Complaints were few however for they were both well paid.

As they reached the main doorway Mikael's horse and trap pulled up in front of them, accompanied by the sound of eight chimes from the clock behind them. "Good evening, ladies." he exclaimed, "I hope I am not late."

Dismounting, he handed the reins to the stable lad who appeared from the side of the inn at almost the same instant Mikael had arrived.

"Hullo Danny" said Luwsiy brightly.

The youth looked up timidly. "Hello Miss Luwsiy." He nodded a smile then turned to her sister and with a second, even more timid nod he said, "Miss Rebekah." Head bowed again he quickly led the horse and trap away. Rebekah, her forehead furrowing for just a second, gave Luwsiy a quick reprimand in the form of a lightning nudge with a sharp elbow. Not pausing to even blink she immediately turned back to Mikael. "Of course you are not late, you are right on time."

"Good." He said with a soft laugh.

"I know you have already seen her once but let me introduce you properly. My little sister Luwsiy," she said waving her hand toward the now annoyed girl. Luwsiy hated it when Rebekah called her little sister, it was so child like. "Luwsiy – Mikael." Rebekah concluded brusquely.

He took Luwsiy's hand and kissed the back of her fingers. "An honour." he said simply as he let go of her hand.

Luwsiy was at a loss, not quite knowing what to say in reply, so saying nothing she smiled as sweetly as she possibly could.

They ushered Mikael into the inn, through the entrance hall, past the stairs and the doors to the bar and public dining rooms, to the private part of the house where their father waited.

"I am glad to see you again Mister Feraiyn, please – come through." He said.

"Thank you, Sir."

"Dinner is ready so I think we should sit at the table straight away." Mikael was led to the small dining room and seated, with Mister Beddoes, at the table. While the men talked Luwsiy and Rebekah served the meal then sat at their places, Luwsiy next to Mikael and facing her father with Rebekah opposite Mikael.

Luwsiy, initially pleased to be sat next to Mikael, soon came to realise that Rebekah was better situated by far.

Her father had been asking Mikael about where he lived and had received his reply. He seemed quite surprised. "The old Rose Mansion! But that house has been deserted for centuries surely – certainly for at least as long as I can remember. It must have needed a great deal of work doing to it."

"Oh it did – and still does; I only live in a part of the house at the moment. I will expand my living area a bit at a time as I tame its many rooms and corridors. The grounds are greatly overgrown too so it may be a while before it will gain some of its former glory." He paused a moment as he ate some food. "I must admit though," he then added, "its wildness at the moment appeals to me enormously."

Luwsiy saw her father suddenly smile before he spoke out.

"You know, when I was young, there used to be many rumours and dark tales about that house and its former occupants... a little too close to the *Old Forest* if you get my meaning – there was talk of witchcraft and sorcery..." He gave Luwsiy a truly wicked look. "They even used to say that it was now haunted by those evil, dreadful people. But of course that was when I was young... and was probably just talk."

She was surprised that he seemed to know so much about the house and its past, *I had never even heard of the place before Rebekah had returned.*

"I had heard such tales," uttered Mikael. "I gave them no credence – though I found them interesting. They gave the old place a certain character."

"But were you not even slightly scared when you moved in?" interjected Rebekah. "Were you so convinced the house was not haunted?"

"I must confess to having second thoughts when I woke on my first night there – to total darkness, the wind blowing through the rafters and the trees outside, the old floor boards creaking. It took all my will power to dispel the irrational notions running through my mind."

"Well I am glad I had not heard the place was haunted before I spent the night there," admitted Rebekah. "I would not have slept a wink."

"I wish it had been me" pronounced Luwsiy. "I would have loved to spend the night in a real haunted house, even if they are just stories it would still be exciting."

"Do not be silly Luwsiy," her father said. "You would have been scared out of your wits."

"I would not." She said defensively. She hated it when her father teased her in front of other people. It was something he seemed to get a great deal of pleasure from though.

"Well I can assure you," intervened Mikael, "my house is no more haunted than this inn. I, for one, cannot believe in such things as ghosts... you must agree Mister Beddoes?"

"Oh – undoubtedly." he replied.

"Perhaps you, and your daughters, would like to come and visit one evening and I can show you all around, show you what I have done so far and tell you of my plans for the rest of the house."

"We would be honoured but I'm afraid I could not leave the inn unattended in the evening."

"But father" blurted Luwsiy before Rebekah could even open her mouth. "Bodkin can easily look after this place."

"I am sure he can but I prefer to be here as well." The older man was enjoying the looks of disappointment on his daughters' faces for he knew it would soon be dispelled. "However," he added, "I see no reason why my two loving daughters may not visit your home so long as you can ensure their safe journey there and back within the hours of daylight."

The girl's delight was obvious when Mikael said "I will look after them as if they were my own blood."

When the meal was finished and the girls were clearing the table their father asked Mikael if he would like an ale or cider, the wine they had been drinking was almost gone.

"Yes" he replied. "Ale would go down quite well I think."

"Good; Rebekah... go and get two tankards of ale from Bodkin."

Rebekah nodded and was just about to leave when Mikael said "Perhaps we can all go through to the bar and have the drinks there, I have not seen your bar-room yet and I was thinking I might begin to visit it on a regular basis if it proves to be congenial."

The innkeeper seemed very pleased at the suggestion and conceded with a laugh, "Very well, if it promotes future business I will agree to almost anything." Looking at his daughters he then said, "Leave the table for now and come to the bar; I will treat you both to some mead."

The girls looked at each other as their father and Mikael left the room, they smiled at the look of pleasant surprise on each other's face. Usually he did not like them in the bar except when working and normally, apart from some table wine on special occasions, he would not let a hint of alcohol touch their lips.

"It must be the midsummer festive cheer getting to him." whispered Luwsiy in Rebekah's ear, forcing her to stifle a faint giggle.

The bar had emptied somewhat since the sisters had earlier looked in, though there was still a considerable amount of customers available. The various conversations seemed to quieten down as the four entered; Luwsiy was gratified to see Bodkin's raised eyebrow and she also noticed the way Martta looked appreciatively at Mikael then enviously at Rebekah who had moved up to his side. Luwsiy suddenly felt a hint of jealousy herself and moved to Mikael's other side.

The majority of the inn's patrons were grouped, as usual, around the old traveller who seemed to have just finished another tale, he was staring at them as they entered, or at least at one of them in particular.

He's staring at Mikael, thought Luwsiy. *How incredibly rude!* She looked at Mikael to see if he had noticed, just in time to see him give an almost imperceptible nod in the older man's direction. Luwsiy quickly looked back to see the man return the gesture.

Very mysterious, she thought. *They must know each other.* No one else seemed to have noticed the exchange.

"Bodkin..." Her father barked loudly, "two tankards of ale and two piping hot cups of mead for my darling daughters."

Gods – how embarrassing! Luwsiy opined to herself.

Rebekah uttered under her breath "He is trying to show us up again."

Luwsiy mockingly looked at her sister with an air of resigned acceptance; the elder sister again had to hold a giggle back.

"Here you go, girls." They looked to their beloved patriarch as he handed them a steaming cup each. "Now Luwsiy – do not gulp it down, it is hot and strong so just take your time and sip it."

"I am not a child father."

He glanced at her as if to say – *oh yes you are*. "You two go sit in that alcove over there," he pointed. "We will join you in a minute."

They moved over to the shady alcove that he had indicated. Luwsiy became aware that many eyes followed them; a lot of the men in the bar were watching them with secretive comments that caused many wide smiles to appear. She could feel herself beginning to blush and was glad when they sat down.

"What do they think they are all looking at?" She whispered harshly. "It is not as if they have never seen us before."

"Yes – but we are all dressed up and looking our best, they have probably never noticed us as women before – just little girls." Rebekah then slyly added "Especially you Luwsiy, you have grown a lot lately."

"Oh." Was all the dumbfounded girl could manage to say. From the burning in her cheeks she knew she was still blushing so she brought her cup up to her mouth with both hands, hoping to hide as much of her face as possible. Luwsiy sniffed the mead and took a sip, it was sweet and spicy.

Reminds me of the hot spicy buns we have during Eostre, she thought, *how delicious.*

It was also very strong.

"You will have to get used to men looking at you like that, you are a beautiful young woman now."

Luwsiy was so absorbed in the taste and smell of her drink, she was unsure if Rebekah had actually spoken the words or if they had spontaneously formed in her head, before she could decide though her father and Mikael arrived with their ales.

Just as the men were sitting down a piercing, unnaturally loud scream shattered the bar's tranquil atmosphere. Everyone, it seemed to Luwsiy, froze as the horrible sound lingered causing the small hairs on the back of her neck to stand icily straight. She felt the colour drain from her as the scream stopped abruptly. The utter and complete silence that followed was worse by far than any scream. An uncontrollable shiver surged through Luwsiy's body.

Her father barked something at his daughters then he and Mikael were gone in an instant.

Luwsiy scrambled out of her seat but was grabbed by Rebekah. "No! Father said to stay." But Luwsiy pulled free and went after them. Rebekah followed her closely.

The sisters fell in behind Bodkin as he too followed Mikael and the innkeeper who were now running up the stairs out in the entrance hall. When Bodkin reached the top of the stairs and turned left, Luwsiy could hear a heavy pounding ahead, he sprinted down the corridor and turned left again, out of her sight, to the sounds of a splintering crash. When Luwsiy reached the turn she still could not see him, just another corridor. She walked slowly down it with Rebekah close behind. There was no sound to be heard.

The last door on the left was broken in. *It's that girl's room... Ann... Ann Benwik.*

Luwsiy slowed to a halt before the doorway. Bodkin was standing in the threshold of the room. She looked past him and saw her father crouched on the floor; Mikael was just beyond him bending over. They were staring at something.

Papa is crying... why?

She peaked round Bodkin's bulk to see what they were looking at. Her father was holding Ann Benwik's hand – she was sprawled on the floor naked. Mesmerised by the girl's pale beauty it was some time before Luwsiy noticed her throat, it was covered by something. *A scarf?*

No... she suddenly realised. *Blood... Dark crimson blood – her throat has been ripped out!*

The girl's head was at an impossible angle. It was twisted toward her and seemed to be looking directly at her but with dead staring eyes.

She's staring right at me!

Horror was etched onto the young woman's face...

Staring at ME... No – stop staring...

"Stop it..." Luwsiy shouted. "Stop staring at me! STOP!" She screamed at the top her voice and did not hear her father shout at Rebekah to get her out of there and take her to their room.

Rebekah grabbed her young sister's shoulders and guided her back down the corridor. Luwsiy had fallen silent and could now hear Rebekah crying too. They turned left and came to their room; Rebekah opened the door and guided Luwsiy in.

A massive hand grabbed Luwsiy's wrist and pulled her through toward the hulking man that it belonged to, he embraced her with his other arm, almost squeezing the life out of her and then sent the shocked Rebekah flying back through the doorway with a ferocious back handed slap to her face. Luwsiy started to scream again but was silenced by a pungent cloth that was forced to her face – it was in her mouth – blocking her nose... she tried to breath but could not.

A heavy darkness overwhelmed her.

Mikael stared at the dead girl's features – *Did I bring this fate upon her?* A dawning pang of guilt slowly stabbed its way into his conscience. *Was it my taking advantage of her that caused this doom? Drawing attention to her?* He had used her purely for his own pleasure and satiation. He jumped involuntarily at Luwsiy's foreshortened scream and looked at Mister Beddoes shocked face. *Was Luwsiy still suffering from shock or... or...*

Rebekah's yelling answered him.

The old innkeeper was on his feet immediately, barging past Bodkin who ran after him. Mikael was fast on their heels – his thoughts in turmoil. They sped through the narrow, low ceilinged corridors once again – to see a giant of a man lowering an unconscious figure out of a window at the end of the passage leading past the girl's bedroom.

Rebekah was leaning heavily on the doorframe and shrieking Luwsiy's name. There was a large and angry red mark on her cheek and jaw, her lip was swollen and bleeding.

Mister Beddoes rushed toward the stranger who, having dropped his burden out through the window, span round – a manic grin on his primitive face and a long lethal dagger in his hand.

"It's a troll! Bodkin exclaimed in panic, but the innkeeper's momentum was too great for him to stop and the hulking troll simply stood there – hardly needing to employ any force to push the deadly blade deep into the old man's oncoming abdomen. Bodkin and Mikael came to a halt as the intruder then forcefully ripped his weapon up and out – and let poor Mister Beddoes' gaping and lifeless body just fall to the floor.

Rebekah's shouting stopped as she gawped at her father's collapsed, bloodied corpse and his shocked – frozen features.

Mikael dived at the troll and, grabbed his bulging knife arm, managed to push the brute against the wall – the murderer was obviously surprised by Mikael's strength. Bodkin was straight on him too, repeatedly beating the stranger about the head with his furious balled fists. Mikael had to physically stop Bodkin's savage punching as the overpowered troll slumped to the floor unconscious.

"See to Rebekah," Mikael said pushing him toward the girl. Bodkin came to his senses and led her into her room. Mikael went over to the window and looked out. Leaning over the sill he could just make out hoof marks below the window.

But no horse, no Luwsiy... no one. Damn! He cursed himself. *It's happening too quickly!* He span round to see a crowded corridor – the barmaid and half the customers from the bar had appeared.

"The innkeeper and a patron have been murdered and his youngest daughter kidnapped," Mikael shouted. "We must quickly search outside, check the whole village – she must be found. Call the Watch!"

The shocked faces swiftly parted with the old traveller organising them into search parties. Soon only the barmaid was left, staring at the wound in her employer's chest with tears welling in her eyes. Mikael put a hand to her shoulder, she was trembling. "Look after Rebekah," he said. "She is in shock – she needs you to comfort her."

Martta looked at him, at his grey-blue eyes, and with a dazed expression nodded silently. She went into Rebekah's room.

Mikael stepped over the innkeeper and crouched beside his murderer, he looked into the badly beaten face. The grey-green tinged skin was already beginning to darken and bruise. A stream of blood had spilled from the *caveman*'s bulbous nose. *That Bodkin can certainly pack a punch,* thought Mikael – for this blackguard was big, even for a troll. *Is this one of Bäliyl's minions?* Deep down he knew the answer to be yes. A footfall behind him made Mikael look up sharply.

"Bodkin," he said. "We will need some strong rope to tie this bastard up before he comes round – can you get some."

"Yes – of course, I'll be right back."

Chapter Five - A Whiff of Magik

Arkturon Kustenin stooped over some fresh hoof tracks that ran through the soft earth at his feet; they disappeared into a muddy stream then came out the other side and headed off toward the forest. They matched those left on the dusty ground beneath the window back at the inn.

He was both relieved and saddened. He stood on the outskirts of the village, looking across fields and meadows toward the forest. The Great Forest was indeed great – still covering at least half of the landmass known as Greater Britannika. Large portions of it had been mostly tamed now – *as if something so wild can be tamed at all* – but the primeval heart of that forest, known as the Old Forest, still had a malingering persistent and substantial presence. The alarm bell was ringing flatly in the village – *the Watch will be here soon, and then there will be the Truth Seekers, asking their questions and writing their reports.*

Brooding thoughts crept into Arkturon's mind. *Mikael knows something of these events – he's involved somehow.*

He is young and inexperienced though – probably does not know what he is doing – what he's involved in. This ancient power struggle is beyond him.

"You saw fit to bring me here." Arkturon said wearily, seeming to address the forest. "I pray that I am still able to serve your wishes for even I am getting old and tired."

The forest, a long dark smudge on the moon-lit horizon, did not reply.

Mikael and Bodkin had dragged their still unconscious prisoner roughly down the inn's stairs and were tying him to the stout solid oak support at the centre of the sprawling building's structure – when Arkturon came in through the main entrance followed by two officers of the Watch.

"There is no sign of the girl," the old traveller said gruffly. "Whoever took her was on horseback – and a fast horse you can bet; there were tracks beneath the window and some more heading across the meadows toward the forest."

Bodkin spoke out as he finished tying the stout rope round the troll and the massive supporting beam "– how can you be sure they were from the same horse – it's pitch black out there!"

"They *were* from the same horse," the old man stated. "– of that you can be sure."

"Then we must be after them!" shouted Mikael, "We're wasting time here!"

"No one here now is going anywhere just yet!" The Sergeant-at-arms of the Meadengiat Watch stepped forward with the authority of many years service and the innate confidence of a man who believed he could handle any eventuality. "The Watch Inspector will be here soon and word has been sent to the Priory Chapter House requesting the attendance of a Truth Seeker. When they arrive they'll need you ALL to answer some questions – but first, I need someone to tell me – and show me – exactly what happened here tonight." He approached the slumbering troll and kicked the massive hob-nailed sole of the creature's booted foot. The troll did not stir, "This, the culprit?" he asked of them all.

Nursing his now sore knuckles Bodkin volunteered himself to reply and said "He's one of them – he killed Danderik Beddoes the innkeeper – and a poor girl up in her room – before we could do anything to stop him! Another one has taken Beddoes' young daughter – surely we should be after them!"

"Another troll?" asked the Sergeant.

"Yes – well no... I don't know, we didn't see the other one – he was waiting outside. This troll dropped Luwsiy from the window upstairs." He indicated the mass of bound and unconscious muscle on the floor.

"Come," said the watchman – indicating the stairs "– show me." Then, to the young constable that came in with him, he said "Edgarson – stay here while I go upstairs... but let me know when the Inspector or the Rangers arrive – they'll want to get on the trail as soon as possible."

Before heading up the stairs with Bodkin, he addressed them all – as if reassuring them. "We sent our fastest constable over to the Ranger Station near the forest. If *anyone* can track and find the girl *they* can – they know that forest like the back of their hand!"

Rebekah sat in her room in a total daze. Martta was still trying to comfort her – though her tears had stopped now – but neither woman could find the words to say anything... what could they say. The right side of Rebekah's face burned fiercely but her mind was occupied with the sight of her dead father's face... *Oh gods he's dead! He's dead – he's dead!* The thought would just not go. *What's to become of us... How can we go on –*

how can I cope? What am I going to do – what am I going to do? Poor Luwsiy depends on me now... Poor Luwsiy – Poor Luwsiy!

"Luwsıy!" Rebekah exclaimed aloud causing Martta to jolt up-right with shock. "We have to get after Luwsiy" said Rebekah urgently "– that *thing* dropped her out of the window – she's out there somewhere now!"

"The men will be after her Miss Beky," reassured Martta, "they'll find her I'm sure."

"We should be helping!" Rebekah stood suddenly. "I've got to see that she's alright!" She moved to leave but Martta caught her arm.

"Miss! The men will see to it... it might be dangerous!" Martta was alarmed that Rebekah should even consider such a thing as leaving the room – there was at least one murderer and a kidnapper in the inn not minutes or even seconds ago – *who's to say there aren't more of them loose out there – waiting to grab the first woman they see!*

When Bodkin had left, Martta had immediately locked the bedroom door – for the sisters had always kept the key on a ribbon hanging from the inside handle. To unlock it, was unthinkable in Martta's eyes – *why would anyone do that – it's crazy!*

But that's exactly what Rebekah did. She shrugged off Martta's tenuous grasp on her arm, strode boldly to the door and unlocked it. She was through the door before Martta had even stood and stepped forward to follow.

Directly outside of her room Rebekah came straight up against the Watch Sergeant, with Bodkin who explained. "Watch Sergeant Tanner needs to inspect your room Miss Rebekah."

"Why?" She said automatically.

"Lady – was not the troll hiding in there," said the Watchman, "waiting to grab your sister?"

"Yes." she said. "He was."

"Do you have any idea how he got into your room – was there a window open, or could he have just come in through the door... was it locked?" He moved his way through into Rebekah and Luwsiy's bedroom, quickly but thoroughly scanning and appraising everything his wandering eyes laid their gaze upon.

"I have no idea how he got in there... but the door wasn't locked." Rebekah answered truthfully, and then speculated "He must have snuck in while we were having dinner downstairs?"

"Yesss," said Sergeant Tanner, as if cogitating hard, "this is all very strange... and it definitely has the whiff of magik."

He considered a little longer before announcing "Everybody downstairs please." He then addressed Bodkin, "Is there anyone else in the inn? I want everyone in the entrance hall as quickly as possible."

"Just Danny – the stable lad – I think everyone else went out to help in the search."

"Good – please bring the stable lad to the entrance hall, as quick as you can." The Sergeant then brought his attention to Rebekah and Martta, "Ladies," he said, "please come downstairs with me now."

Arkturon turned to Mikael, away from the capable but distracted constable who was staring suspiciously at the unconscious troll, and whispered "We must be after Luwsiy as soon as possible, I think you know *we* are the only ones who have a chance of catching *whoever* it is – especially if they go deep into the forest. The Rangers probably won't be much good if the *situation* were to lead them into the *Old Forest*... though they say some of them know a great deal of the *Arcane Arts* – so it is possible we may get lucky."

Mikael's thoughts were in turmoil. *Should I trust this Arkturon...? CAN I trust him?*

They both sauntered a little further from the constable. Mikael whispered in return, "Who *are* you – how do I know *you're* not in league with..." Mikael almost blurted Bäliyl's name... and it showed. He continued his sentence belatedly "– with these kidnappers?" He of course regretted his hushed outburst immediately. Arkturon stared icily... reading him like a book – or so it seemed to Mikael.

The older man speculated "You know who is behind all this... don't you!"

"I... I *suspect* someone."

"No! You *know*."

"I didn't know *all this* was going to happen," said Mikael defensively. "I *swear*!"

"But you *should* have – you *should* have seen it coming." Arkturon was scanning Mikael's open and confused mind as he spoke. "You *were* warned, you should have known what *could* happen – *you* brought *HIM* here!"

"Look – I'm sorry about everything – but it happened so fast... I'm sorry I ever came here! But that doesn't help us now – it doesn't change what's happened and it doesn't help us get Luwsiy back!"

"You're right – you're right!" said the old traveller, "Recriminations don't help us – what's done is done and all that – but we need to come up with a way of dealing with the consequences – fast!"

The thundering noise of riders and horses approaching the main doorway of the inn and coming to a hurried standstill outside caused Mikael, Arkturon and Constable Edgarson all to glance over to the front doors in expectation.

Arkturon quickly whispered to Mikael "This'll probably be the Rangers – I know how to deal with them so let ME do the talking – you just go along with whatever I say!"

Before Mikael could utter a response the heavy doors thrust inward and four dark hooded and heavily armed Rangers stepped through into the previously spacious but now increasingly crowded reception hall. As they made their overly dramatic entrance the Sergeant of the Watch was coming back down the stairs, followed by Rebekah and an extremely nervous Martta in tow. Rebekah was staring at him and Arkturon with savage intensity.

"Ah, Lieutenant Lethbridj," the Watch Sergeant addressed the leading Ranger, whom he obviously knew, and got straight to the point as he approached them, "we have two murders, the first murder was a distraction, and may be magikal, to allow for the kidnap of the young woman – which, it seems, was the primary aim. The second murder was probably an unintended consequence of being discovered mid-kidnap. One intruder has been caught," he gestured to the bound troll, "there is however, another as yet unaccounted for – who is probably skilled in the use of magik... and of course there is the kidnapper, who was waiting outside, and is at this moment fleeing with his captive into the forest. We don't know whether the other perpetrators of the crimes are trolls too but it may be a fair assumption."

"The one fleeing into the forest is definitely not a troll!" said Arkturon forcefully. "With the weight of the girl, the depth of the hoof tracks suggest a rider much lighter than a troll – probably a small man, a goblin or maybe even a dwarf – and the distraction murder was most definitely carried out with the use of magik, as the Sergeant said – but probably done at a distance by physically manifesting a Fetch... but I can't be sure of that as yet."

"And what makes you such an expert in the tracking of horse sign AND in the arts of magik?" The unphased Lieutenant asked blankly of Arkturon.

"I'm the District Agent for the Parliamentary Occult Intelligence Service." He replied just as blankly.

Of course everyone there had heard of the that particular Service, the Lord Protector's mysterious and secretive magikal defence force and advisory – everyone in the Commonwealth knew of their existence – but very few knew anything more than that. There were not many people alive who could say that they knew a member of the Service's Ministerial Council – let alone any of their secretive agents – personally, for its membership was a secret sanctioned and guarded by the highest authority in the land. More commonly referred to as the Protector's Cabal of Wizards, their inherent secrecy meant that they were regarded by many with suspicion and even fear. Mikael had always suspected, and he was not alone in this, that their supposed influence was an exaggeration – *if not a downright deception*, propaganda designed to scare off the enemies of the Commonwealth while encouraging the citizenry to be loyal and lawful. He could not believe that Arkturon claimed to be connected to them in some way. *Surely he's just some sort of vagabond trickster, travelling from one mark to the next,* Mikael thought – *getting free drinks and smoking like a druidic shaman of old. He couldn't possibly be one of the Cabal's agents!*

The Lieutenant simply said "Do you have the proper Sigil?"

Arkturon delved into an inside pocket of his long overcoat and after some searching pulled out a small, beaten leather box about two inches square and half an inch thick. He opened it and removed a shiny bronze button or disk that had some sort of complicated glyph embossed on its surface, then presented it to the Lieutenant.

Lieutenant Lethbridj looked at it carefully and then nodded. "We're lucky to have you here, Sir." He said. "What are your orders?"

Arkturon asked "Have you sent out any Rangers after the kidnapper and the girl yet? That's got to be our immediate priority."

"When we got word at the station – of what happened here – I sent a four man unit to the north of the village and another to the south in an attempt to intercept any fleeing miscreants or find and take up the trail. We've come here to gather information and follow any trails from the source of the incident – we'll start the pursuit now Sir – if you can tell us where exactly you found the tracks."

"Excellent," said Arkturon, "they head north-west, crossing Blueberry Beck just south of its northern ford, beyond Old Kobb's windmill – you'll pick up the trail easier than I did I'm sure." He then continued before the Lieutenant could reply "But I must ask you to leave your occult specialist with me, I may need him – for I have an alternative, shall we say more magikal, trail to follow."

Lieutenant Lethbridj turned and pointed to one of his men. "Corporal Villovürt." He ordered. "You aid the good Agent here as best you can. The rest of us are going hunting." He turned back to Arkturon and saluted him by forcefully bringing his right hand to his breast and sharply clicking his heals together. Lethbridj then promptly marched out the door with his two Rangers in tow. The remaining Ranger stepped forward; lowering her hood to reveal her olive, hawk-like face and her thick black, green-tinged hair... she was a dark-elf, one of the Svaart-Aelfa from the continental Blak Forest. "At your service, Sir." she said – her black eyes shining.

Arkturon nodded and turned to Mikael. "We should set off straight away; we need to get to your Rose Mansion as soon as possible."

"But why," said Mikael, "We should be after them with the rest of the Rangers!"

"If I remember rightly, your adopted home will provide us with a quicker and more... let's say surreptitious – route." The occult agent said mysteriously, "But we must leave now."

They were stopped by a sudden shout from the stairs. "I'm going too!"

It was Rebekah, her eyes red and puffy; the bruise on her face had darkened to a purple-blue. Martta hovered close behind.

"No!" Both Mikael and Bodkin said in unison. Bodkin had entered the room from the rear with a bewildered looking Danny only moments earlier.

"I AM going." She insisted. "If not with you, I'll follow you alone."

"Do not be a fool!" Bodkin bellowed. "You don't understand..."

"I am going, Bodkin, and there is nothing you can do to stop me – you work for me now, remember!"

Bodkin stared with teeth clenched, but for the moment silenced.

"She WILL come with us." Arkturon spoke softly but with authority. "There is a strong bond between her and her young sister, we might need that, it can only help us."

"But she is just a child," protested Bodkin. "You cannot lead her into that forest... that hiding place of villainy and evil."

"Either we lead her," Arkturon said, becoming angry, "or she tries to follow... getting lost... and alone amongst all your so-called evil."

Slowly the emptiness receded. First came the pain, dull and aching, and then the noise – a constant pounding – at first both were distant and indistinct, but they were rapidly growing to a hateful intensity. The noise became unbearably loud and the pain jarring her to the very core as she was being jolted up and down mercilessly. There was a strong musky smell and a great pressure on her back.

Gradually Luwsiy opened her eyes... it was dark.

She was laid face down, across a sprinting horse, a stranger's rough hand holding her down.

Memory slowly filtered into the pain; she remembered a massive, noxious hand tightly clamped over her face; she saw Rebekah reeling and falling to the floor... and a dead girl laying there with her throat ripped out.

Luwsiy swooned and the comforting blanket of emptiness mercifully returned.

Four horsemen galloped along the edges of the Old Forest. The lead one hunkering low on his mount, scanning the ground ahead – despite the thunderous pace – looking for signs of passage across their path. Suddenly he pulled up and raised his arm – silently messaging the others to stop.

"Found anything, Sarge?" whispered the first to pull up beside him.

"A single horse heading into the forest – very recent, not following any obvious track ways – seems to be coming straight from the village – so it seems likely that this is our kidnapper and the young woman."

"How young exactly are we talking, Sarge?" said the handsome Ranger with a lecherous grin that made his upper lip and well groomed moustache arch up to the right.

"Shut it, Wellnap – now's not the time to be thinking with your todger. We've got work to do."

"We goin' after 'em, Sarge?" Asked another of the Rangers, he wasn't the brightest of the four men, but he was by far the biggest in both height and breadth. He was clean shaven on both his head and face.

"Yes we are, Sinkhoal. There's not much of a trail but it's pretty overgrown in the forest so the signs o' passage should be easy to spot – keep close behind me, the lot o' ya." The Sarge looked into the faces of each of his men. "Stay alert lads, the tracks are heading into the Old Forest. We could be coming back heroes if this goes well." He felt like adding, *or not coming back at all if it doesn't*, for the Old Forest was not a place to be taken lightly, but he didn't want to spook the men before they'd even made contact, so he said it silently in his head. *Nothing good ever came out of the Old Forest... and nothing good is ever in a hurry to get back in there.*

The Sergeant nudged his horse toward the tangled wall of trees and the others fell in line behind him.

The deeper they went the darker and more tangled it got, but the tracks that the Sarge was following were obviously made by someone who knew where they were going – for they followed a trail through the thick boughed growth that he would never have known was there otherwise.

The small unit of soldiers travelled like this for a good fifteen minutes until the Sergeant stopped once more.

"What's up, Sarge?" asked the Ranger directly behind him. He was the rookie of the troop; he was barely old enough to shave so he sported sparse fuzzy blond facial hair in a haphazard fashion all his own.

"I'm not sure, Gudrun. Something doesn't feel right about the trail ahead. Looks like they stopped for some reason about seven yards in front. See that little pile of sticks?" He pointed.

"Can't see anything in this light, Sarge." The diffuse moonlight was getting paler and more diminished as the cloud cover slowly thickened.

"Well take my word for it. There's a pile o' sticks that's been placed there... an' I don't like the look of it."

The two other Rangers came up beside them.

"You think it's some sort of trap?" asked Wellnap suspiciously.

"I do." said the Sarge. "Sinkhoal?"

"Yes Sarge?"

"Can ya see that pile o' sticks?"

"Yes Sarge."

"Do you think ya can hit it with a rock or something from here?"

"I think so Sarge."

"Then do it lad – but don't get any closer."

Sinkhoal dismounted and rummaged around for a suitable stone. He picked up a decent sized one and weighed it in his large hand before taking aim and lobbing it. The stone crashed into the little pile of sticks and scattered them. A puff of green-brown smoke billowed up from where the stone impacted and, in a most unnatural fashion, the strange cloud quickly formed tendril like arms that settled in to the ground vegetation and out toward the neighbouring trees.

"Oh – that's not good!" said the Sarge. "Get ya *Dragons* ready lads, it's some sort o' elemental trap – this could be messy... I'm guessing golems – or possibly spriggans."

It was spriggans.

Five gnarly and sinewy spriggans noisily tore themselves from the roots and shoots of the surrounding vegetation and from the barks of the four nearest trees to the magical trap that had been left on the trail.

The four well-drilled soldiers frantically loaded their large bore, short barrelled, flintlock blunderbusses with powder and iron shot. The guns were affectionately called *Dragons* after the carved dragon heads that decorated the flared muzzles. They each had two of them – one for each hand.

"Once you've expended your shot," said the Sergeant, "it'll be hack 'n' slash with your sabres... so make 'em count – an' wait till I give the order."

The spriggans freed themselves from, and formed themselves out of, the surrounding tree and vegetable matter. Taking roughly humanoid form they came at the soldiers in lanky and sporadic strides, their long knobbly branch-like limbs and digits clawing spasmodically at the ground and the air as if to get at the men quicker.

"Take aim at the legs," the Sergeant ordered, "and... FIRE!"

The thunderous retort of all eight Dragons firing at once was deafening and the flash almost blinding. The devastating volley of shot splintered and shattered the lower limbs of the oncoming spriggans. The magically animated, but now lame and mostly legless, creatures stumbled and faltered – but continued forward, dragging themselves toward the Rangers, determinedly clawing at the undergrowth and the surrounding trees with their upper limbs to propel themselves on.

The Sergeant holstered his two guns and, dismounting, drew his razor-sharp steel sabre. "All right boys," he said almost gleefully, "it's hack 'n' slash time. I want 'em cut to tiny pieces!"

The soldiers obeyed his command.

Chapter Six - Of Vampires and Wizards

Rebekah was squeezed between Mikael and the old man; all three were being shaken piteously by the trap's rapid passage toward Mikael's home. The constant jarring with the thundering of hoof and wheel on baked ground would not allow Rebekah's thoughts to settle. Questions repeatedly tumbled to the forefront of her mind, only to be quickly replaced by other more urgent ones.

Why would someone take Luwsiy like that?
And why kill poor Ann Benwik?
Who is this so called Agent Arkturon...
And what does Mikael have to do with it all?

She had seen Mikael and Arkturon arguing heatedly before the Rangers arrived, Arkturon was questioning Mikael with – what seemed to her – absolute suspicion. She wished she could have heard their whispered exchange for she swore their demeanour became strangely conspiratorial toward the end.

Can I trust any of these people? She thought darkly.

Then she remembered her father's face at the moment of his death and her mind became gnawingly empty and achingly cold. She tried to remember him alive but she could not, his death mask forever before her, never letting her mind concentrate, leaving it open for the questions to start again. Her head, it seemed, was beginning to implode and her jaw burned with increasing intensity.

They sped down the road with forest rushing by on either side, the moon was hidden behind thick clouds above and Rebekah thought it like travelling through an impenetrably dark tunnel. She wondered how Mikael could possibly see the road clearly enough to warrant such haste; he was hunched forward, peering over the sweating horse, with concentration manifest in his face and manner. The dark-elf Ranger was somewhere about but Rebekah could see no trace of her or the large powerful horse that she had leapt upon before they left. It was all just darkness before and about her.

Her life had seemed so perfect, it had promised so much when she had arrived home yesterday... *was it only yesterday?* It seemed an age ago.

Now, she thought, *I am being pulled by a nightmare into a black labyrinthine hole... with no possible escape in sight.* The forest seemed so thick about her yet she knew this was just the outskirts of a vast ancient wood that sprawled down the length of the country, civilisation existed on its boundaries but never ventured deep.

How deep would we be forced to go? How far would safety and security be left behind?

She tried to ponder on many things as the barely visible trees slipped past; her father, Mikael, but most of all Luwsiy.

Why Luwsiy, she asked again. *Why?* She waited, but no answer came.

It does not matter why... she's been taken, that's what matters. That is all that matters.

They suddenly veered right, off the road and onto a lane that ran through an immense gateway; the entrance to the grounds of Mikael's house. The walls on either side were overgrown like the ones through which Rebekah had originally entered, but the lane itself was free of all vegetation and was obviously used more often.

Mikael slowed as they approached the side of the house, a black mass that loomed in the darkness, and he pulled to a stop at the rear, by the entrance to the kitchens. Corporal Villovürt appeared out of the blackness behind them, astride her massive black horse, and came alongside.

"You three go inside and start to look for some provisions," Mikael said nodding to the door. "I need to tend to my horse – she's done more work today than she has done in a long time."

Arkturon and Rebekah dismounted from the carriage as the Corporal nimbly alighted from her powerful steed. Mikael led the trap and its exhausted horse away toward the stables while the Ranger tethered the reins of her mount to a post near the doorway.

Rebekah and the dark-elf followed the old man through the door, their heavy riding boots clumping on the stone floor. Rebekah stopped short though and stood perfectly still – for beyond the doorway was total darkness – she could not see, nor hear, a single thing. Villovürt was forced to stop mid stride behind her. Rebekah was just about to shout out when a light flared before them, the old man was lighting a lamp on a table in the centre of the large kitchen. *How had he seen that?* She asked herself as she continued in.

He was wearing a very long and shabby overcoat that seemed to be covered with pockets, *or are some of them holes?* Rebekah saw a tinder box quickly disappear into one of them. There was a short cape attached to the shoulders of his coat, Rebekah guessed it doubled as a hood when it rained. She could see why her father was not going to let him stay at the inn, and to add to the general state of his scruffiness their horse drawn journey had left his white hair blown about his head like a pale fiery halo.

"I suggest we find something to eat now," he said, "then collect suitable foods to take with us." He put the bulky pack that he had been carrying down on the floor by the sturdy kitchen table and rested his tall staff beside it. The Ranger silently availed herself of one of the chairs at the table.

Addressing Arkturon, Rebekah said "How long do you think it will take us to catch up with them?"

"Catch up with them?" he pondered, "That depends on when and where they stop to rest, and how often, also on where they are going. A couple of days maybe – but it is impossible to say for sure."

Days! She had envisioned a quick chase through the forest, overtaking the criminal and rescuing Luwsiy. *But days!* Rebekah suddenly wondered what she was doing here. *Maybe I should just leave it to them... they know what they are doing.*

The old man moved toward one of the far doors leading from the kitchen and looked through. "This smells like the pantry." He said and walked in.

Rebekah followed. "What do they call you – what is your name?" She draped her heavy, red cloak over a chair.

"My name?" She heard him say. "Arkturon Kustenin."

"Arkturon Kustenin?" She whispered to herself. *That really is a strange name.* Rebekah peered through the door he had disappeared into. *But then he really is a strange person.* There was a short corridor with two further doors in the left hand wall and a third straight ahead, the nearest was open and sounds of movement were emanating from within.

"Why did you agree to let me come along with you?" She called through. "How can I help you, I'll just slow you down?"

"Not necessarily." He said. "You are young and fit; I am just an old man." Arkturon came into view carrying a large tray full of food. "You are the sister of the girl we seek, you are close to her and you love her. That will help us find her."

"But how?" she asked as she moved aside to let him back through. "I don't understand."

He set the food down beside the lamp on the table. "When our friend Mikael returns we will talk and I will try to explain."

"Talk? But should we not be out there looking for her – this is all time wasting!"

"No, the Rangers on her trail have a better chance of catching up with Luwsiy – they are her best hope of rescue at this point – but I'm more concerned with the bigger picture, getting your sister back will not be the end of this, not by a long shot. Mikael knows something of what is happening – he must share his knowledge with us before we can proceed. I think he might know where your young sister is being taken." Arkturon had pasted a large piece of crusty bread with butter while talking; he now began to cut some cheese off a chunk he had brought through. "I think you should eat as much as you can now, once we set off it may be awhile before we stop for another meal."

Rebekah's head was beginning to ache again and a great tiredness was threatening to engulf her. *So many questions.* Back at the inn she had seen Mikael almost mention a name. *Does he really know who is behind all this? Is he involved?* She sat at the table and began to nibble at some hazelnuts while eyeing the salted ham.

Looking very distracted Mikael entered. "I've saddled three fresh horses for us and tethered them outside." He said, "I am going to change into my travelling clothes." He walked across the kitchen toward another door.

"Do not take long," Arkturon said, "time is precious and we must talk before setting off."

Mikael looked blankly at the old man, but saying nothing he left the room. Rebekah went over to a large basin set beneath a window; she filled a pitcher with water then returned and placed it on the table. After looking for some mugs she offered the vessels to Arkturon and the Ranger, they took them gratefully and filled them. She did the same for herself. The old man had consumed his cheese and bread almost immediately and was now cutting at the ham. Rebekah accepted some when he offered it to her.

The three ate without speaking and waited for Mikael's return.

Luwsiy was fully conscious now and wished heartily that she was not. She was aching throughout the extent of her body and was desperately uncomfortable for she could not move and her arms seemed pinned to her side.

"So... the pretty girl is awake," a rough voice sounded in her ear, above the noise of the horse's galloping. "Don't be afraid – but don't struggle – or I might drop ya... now, Pretty wouldn't want that – would she. WOULD SHE!" His sudden shout was punctuated with a punch to the small of her back.

Luwsiy flinched but could do nothing but let her tears flow and listen to his maddening laughter.

She knew her father would be following... *and Mikael – he would help.* She was sure of that. *After all, he had saved me once before, even if it was just a dream.*

"Oh have we got plans for you, Pretty," her captor whispered coarsely. "You'll have a fine time before ya die – but that won't be the end of it, OH NO... it won't stop there... it won't stop!"

He followed these mutterings with another loud maniacal laugh.

Luwsiy tried to ignore him, ignore everything. She withdrew into her mind where it was safe and warm. She stopped struggling and stopped crying, for both were futile. Luwsiy thought of Rebekah and silently called her name.

Rebekah had just bitten into an apple when Mikael came back into the room; he was dressed much more practically now for a journey into the wilds. He reminded her of an illustration of a highwayman she had seen in a pamphlet once; a mask was all that was needed to complete the picture. She noticed he even carried two flintlock pistols holstered to his broad belt and had a tri-cornered hat clasped in his hand.

Mikael directly addressed the old man immediately. "You wish to know who and why... and how I am involved."

"It would be a start."

Mikael sat down at the table, opposite Arkturon, with the lamp directly between them. Rebekah and Villovürt faced each other between the two men.

"It started a long time ago," the younger man began, "about thirty years." He then told them of his meeting with Lilith, hesitantly at first but as the memories came clear his tale became more confident. Arkturon listened silently without even moving, his head slightly bowed and his arms crossed on the table.

Rebekah watched Mikael as he spoke; he stared into the light and seemed lost in his story. *But it is not a story,* she reminded herself, *it is true*

– it happened! Impossible as that seemed, thirty years ago he could hardly have been born... *surely?*

Mikael told how he and this woman named Lilith became lovers deep in the forest, taking strength from each other, living an ideal. But Lilith was on the run and her past eventually caught up with her, and it was a cruel and vengeful past that instinctively destroyed her in its raging anger, and left Mikael alone and grief stricken.

Although Lilith was dead, through time he learnt she was not departed; she remained by him and haunted his dreams, guiding and loving him. Mikael travelled about the land, back and forth, till he found a place to settle, somewhere secluded, somewhere to be alone with his wraith-like lover.

In the course of time Lilith's murderer became aware that her spirit was still tied to this world though, and he began to pursue her in death as he had in life. His name was Bäliyl an ancient and evil vampiric sorcerer who had wished to use Lilith – his own daughter – in some dark and secret rite before she fled. Mikael could not fight him alone, he needed help, he needed the strength and succour of a lover, a living lover. That was what brought him to the inn... and that, it seems, is was what brought Bäliyl too.

Dumb struck Rebekah listened, how could she have thought he had loved her, she felt cheated and ashamed. She could not understand how he could go in search of a lover when it was obvious that he could not love in return. Surely any strength he could hope to gain from that would be false and useless.

Arkturon seemed to be of the same opinion, "You have been a fool," he said bluntly, "surely you can see Lilith's love is the only love that you need, it gulfs even death... a stronger love you could not hope to find."

Mikael hung his head and glared at the table's wooden surface. "But Lilith told me that you must feed off another – she told me that it is the rite of blood that gives the necessary strength and power..."

"She is wrong – what she knows of such things she has learnt from her father, her view of the world is warped, through no fault of her own; and so, therefore, is yours. She was brought up amongst evil and corruption – she will have been deceived in many things."

"So what can I do to fight him, Lilith said he is much too strong to be faced alone."

"You will not be alone... we will help you." Arkturon indicated himself, the Ranger and Rebekah. Rebekah was tempted to say, why should she, but then remembered Luwsiy and realised it could be her only chance of rescue. He then added, "And of course Lilith will help us."

"But she is dead," said Mikael. "How can she? She only comes in my dreams."

"No... in dreams you enter the threshold of the next world, but she can come here, to this world... she just does not know the way. Her love for you has kept her from moving on to the higher planes; she drifts in a kind of limbo and can venture into either side while she remains tied to you. We must guide her spirit back to this plane."

"How?" Mikael said in a perturbed and puzzled voice.

"It is relatively simple. You come to her in the usual way, in your dreams, and you tell her she can come back to the physical world, that the path she is on not only leads forward but back as well. You see, it is the simple matter of not knowing this that has held her where she is for so long. Not wanting to move on and leave you, but not knowing she can come back."

"How can you know all this?" Mikael asked.

"How, how, how... is that the only word you people know?" replied Arkturon exasperated. "I have travelled this path, and others like it, many times and I have entered many worlds and planes, both higher and lower than this one that we live in. But we do not have time to discuss this now, we have work to do." He then turned his head rapidly to Rebekah. "Do you now see how your love for Luwsiy might help us?"

She was surprised by this sudden question directed at her and she could only shake her head.

"You have heard what love can do. It strengthens and bonds people. It makes them do things that should be beyond them, it pushes them past limits that cannot otherwise be passed. It is the strongest force in the Universe and can even bridge death."

Rebekah nodded quickly then forced herself to ask, "Why did he take Luwsiy... if he is after his daughter's spirit – why take Luwsiy?"

"I do not know." Arkturon said after a pause.

"Who *are* you?" She suddenly blurted. "Both of you – *what* are you?" She looked rapidly from one man to the other. "Vampires – warlocks – wizards... what?" Rebekah had led a relatively sheltered life and her father had always told her to beware of vampires and wizards and the like... stay away from magik, he'd say, for it always spelt trouble with a capital T. Now she found herself in the company of a rogue vampire, a wizard agent of the state, and a dark-elf Ranger who specialises in the occult. Her father dead – murdered by a troll – and her young sister kidnapped by a probable dwarf! Rebekah began to get hysterical, the confusing talk and the shattering events of the past day were wearing her patience very thin indeed. "TELL ME!" She screamed.

Mikael began to speak but was silenced by Arkturon with a gesture of his hand.

"Very well," the older man said calmly to Rebekah. "I can imagine that you are puzzled by a lot of what has been said... you deserve a detailed explanation but, I'm afraid, it must be brief. You will have to take what I say in good faith and just believe it." Arkturon paused a moment to think. "There have been many stories and legends concerning those of our kind... we have been named many things; wizards, vampires, angels and daemons; every supernatural being from the gods to faeries we have been labelled. All these names have certain characteristics attached to them, some can be applied to us and some cannot." His rapid words were soft and persistent. "The name nearest Mikael's nature is vampire, especially when applied to the more evil individuals like this Bäliyl that he spoke of, but the terms wizard or sorcerer can also be applicable to a larger or lesser extent – depending on the individual concerned.

We are not immortal; though we do have a longer life span than most – and we are certainly not the dead come back to life. Although we can be sensitive to bright light and heat we are not the nocturnal beasts of myth – indiscriminately sucking the blood of poor innocents... at least we need not be!" He stated the last part with a glaring glance to Mikael. "A true vampire takes the blood of his chosen mate, and she of him. Through this they grow and become strong in mind and body; and power comes to them. Mikael has told how he became a vampire, which is the only way – through the consumption of a vampire's blood. Think of it as a kind of virus that is transferred through this exchange of blood, a virus that is largely beneficent though, one that brings a kind of transformation into a higher and more complex form of being. Magik comes easier to a vampire, which is why many magik users choose to become vampires.

As for myself, I am more than just a vampire... much more. I am, indeed, what's known colloquially as a wizard... but a wizard is born, not made. You cannot become a wizard – unlike a warlock, witch, sorcerer or any other user of learned magik – you either are... or you are not – and that is the end of it. Wizards are a very ancient breed – it is said that we all belong to an archaic familial line – naturally infused with magik ability by a sole progenitor thousands of years ago. I know that we were many once, but now we are few.

Of course, as with all things, there are evil vampires and there are evil wizards, using their powers viciously or for criminal gain; some vampires can get corrupted, acquire a taste for blood – any person's blood – a literal blood lust overwhelms them. Blood need only be necessary to begin with though, to cause a person to turn into a vampire and to bring the full nature of what that means to its zenith; although many continue well into the relationship there is no need to feed off each other's blood indefinitely. Eventually they can feed off each other's love alone, strengthening each other through the phantasmic exchange of their vitalizing life-force."

"I know nothing of such things," said Mikael confused. "I know only of blood... you must show me how to forsake it."

"You do not need me, you need Lilith... you must teach yourselves. If you love each other, you *will* succeed."

Silence followed while Arkturon cogitated.

He then announced, "A plan is beginning to formulate; I suggest Mikael that you stable the horses again and then we will get in touch with Lilith and bring her back to us."

As Mikael stood to do this, Corporal Villovürt stood too and announced, "I will tend to my own horse... his needs are very particular."

Mikael nodded and led the way.

Luwsiy watched her captor light a fire in the centre of a small clearing that was run through by the narrow trail that they had been following. The forest was incredibly thick and overgrown all around them, the trees were so tightly packed that the trail was the only means of passage through it. She assumed this would make it easier for anyone in pursuit.

But what if they do not find the path? She thought. The kidnapper did not seem unduly worried about being followed and he had not even bothered to tie her up so the possibility of her escaping had not even entered his mind – *if he has one.* She allowed herself a secret internal smile, only briefly though. *If I were to escape, where would I go?* The forest was definitely out of the question and the only routes she could possibly follow were back along the trail, or forward to where she was being taken to anyway. *Back along the trail it would have to be...* if she were to escape.

A small spitting blaze was soon under way in front of the hunched figure of the dwarf-like man... *was he a Dwarf?* She pondered. He had the long arms, short legs, prominent brow and flat nose typical of that Race but he was thinner and more wiry than any Dwarf she had seen or even heard of before. Their break-neck flight had been in almost total darkness and this was the clearest look she had of him so far. Hunched up seemed to be his natural posture and his appearance in no way betrayed the great strength he obviously possessed. He had held her down with ease while they were on the horse and on stopping he had bodily picked her up before throwing her to the ground.

Luwsiy had stayed where she fell, watching him continually as she waited for the stiff numbness to leave her limbs. His monkey-like features occasionally glanced in her direction, the small glittering eyes looking straight into hers, the cruel smirk never leaving his cold lips.

Once the fire was burning he stood up and slowly walked towards her. "It's a shame... such a shame," he whispered in his debased excuse for a voice, "that the Master must 'ave you all to 'imself."

Crouching down beside her he put his face before hers, his foul hot breath invading her senses. She began to pull herself away along the ground but his spindly hand grabbed the back of her neck and pulled her face to his. "When I first saw you I thought it were the young Mistress come back to 'aunt me... but no, you're far too young. I loved 'er – she were pretty, like you... will *Pretty*, give me a kiss then?" Saliva dribbled from his open mouth as it closed around her lips. Luwsiy kept her mouth tightly shut as his putrid tongue pushed against her; he then pulled it up across her face with an exaggerated licking noise, over her nose and rapidly closed eye the tongue left its sickening, salivary trail.

He tossed his head back and laughed as she frantically wiped her face with her fingers and made her sounds of disgust as explicate as possible.

"Oh... don't be like that." He said as he straddled her stomach. "I like you... and really, you like me too – don't ya... not like that Lilith... she 'ated me... always so 'igh and mighty - she never even looked at me!" He ripped the bodice of her dress wide open and exposed her breasts, giggling he roughly fondled her as she struggled in vain. Slobbering he began to kiss and lick her chest, she beat and kicked him furiously but he held her down with ease. He started to lay himself on top of her, his legs holding her legs down, his hands gripping her wrists; there was nothing she could do to stop him.

"My Pretty... you're my Pretty now... "

The hideous little man was rubbing his groin on her lower stomach; she could feel his erection push onto her. Weakening Luwsiy could not fight for much longer. His ugly, twisted face hovered above hers; he licked his lips and whispered hoarsely, "You're my Pretty."

He suddenly stopped his quickening motion and stared at her. "NO!" He shouted frighteningly. "You're not mine... you're the Master's – you belong to 'im!" He pushed himself off her and got up. "You tried to trick me!" He yelled accusingly.

Luwsiy tried to calm her breathing and her heartbeat as he walked away. She decided silence was her best option at that moment and covered herself as best she could with the ripped dress.

Without warning the vile demon turned toward her and, pointing, he screamed, "Don't you ever do that again!"

Chapter Seven – At the Shores of Sopor

Rebekah was confused, she had been told to wait, so she did, *but wait for what?* Mikael and Arkturon had gone in search of Lilith, or at least their senses had – *in search of her spirit or some such*; they were actually both still sitting there at the table, in a kind of trance.

Arkturon had given the younger man some-sort of fine powdery snuff to snort – the old man had scooped it from a small tin that he carried in one of his many pockets using a tiny, long handled spoon. Mikael fell into an immediate stupor. Arkturon gently pushed him back in his seat while mumbling something incoherent. Then Mikael was asleep. After telling her and Villovürt to wait, Arkturon sat himself down and he too took a deep sniff of the fine powder – then fell into a deep slumber himself.

Both men now seemed totally oblivious to the waking world – oblivious to the two women who were sitting across from each other in silence. Rebekah awkwardly avoided the dark-elf's penetrating gaze.

Rebekah wondered where Luwsiy was now, *what is she doing, what is happening to her – what is she being put through?*

A drop of water hit the table where she stared; she was hunched over it, and was at first puzzled as to where it could have come from. She studied the little pool it formed and another drop fell by its side.

She was crying.

Rebekah stood and wiped her face, sniffed, then searched for some candles in the drawers and cupboards around her. Finally she found some and took a hand-full, lighting one from the lamp and, putting it in a holder, she consigned the others to her jacket pocket.

"I'm just going for a walk... to look around the house." She said, wiping her face.

Corporal Villovürt stared at her intently. "Don't go far." she ordered softly. "They may wake at any moment."

Rebekah couldn't bear the waiting. She nodded and set out to explore the house, hoping to forget for a short while at least.

It was neither cold nor warm, neither light nor dark.

There was no indication of up or down, left or right.

There was just forward.

The sensation of motion was overwhelming and uncanny for he could not see, hear nor feel anything; there was no physical evidence to prove he was moving at all.

With difficulty he remembered how he had got there, he had fallen asleep... and had dreamt...

Mikael had been alone in his kitchen when Arkturon had materialised in front of him. They had stood and the old man had held out his hand toward him. At first Mikael was perplexed but when he looked into the sage-like eyes he saw a distant memory of his late father. Mikael became as a child again and without a thought he placed his hand into that of Arkturon. The warm security and safety the hand had offered soon dissolved though into the bland, monotonous world where he was now trapped.

He slowly realised he could still feel Arkturon's hand holding his... *but I cannot see him... I can't even see myself!*

Am I blind?

Mikael had always imagined that blindness would be total blackness... *not this, this is much worse... it is nothing! Oblivion!*

No... He could still feel Arkturon's hand... and there were shapes forming, dull and indistinct – but definitely there.

They're getting clearer.

Gradually Arkturon formed beside him; a cold breeze began to blow in his face, gaining in strength. Mikael looked down and saw his own body again – and ground beneath it.

They stood in a windswept wilderness, it was night and just above the horizon before them the full moon shone strong. A golden path trailed into the hilly distance where it was flanked by two incredibly tall towers. The howling of wolves or dogs could be heard. A huge body of water lay behind them, a lake – *probably* – disappearing into the mist and its black waters were, for the moment, calm. Mikael could see life, teeming and primal, swarming beneath the surface and he felt compelled to hurry away, he did not know why.

He noticed a hooded figure huddled by the side of the road about a furlong from where they stood; Arkturon pulled him by the hand toward the stranger. Mikael allowed himself to be led like a child for it was as if he had never known anything different.

Sorrowful crying could be heard as they approached and a rain began to fall; large and unnaturally slow – the dark drops descended.

The pitiful figure did not notice them until they were beside her – Mikael guessed it was a woman by the sound of the sobs. She looked up at the two men and her hood fell back... Mikael was stung by the shock of recognition and memory. "Lilith!" He gasped, letting go of Arkturon's hand and kneeling beside her. They hugged like the long-lost lovers they were.

"Finally," she said emotionally through her tears. "We can move on together now... and forget... forget about Bäliyl – about revenge. We are free!"

"No... no Lilith, I am not dead. I have come to bring you back."

"Wh... what do you mean, how did you get here... you cannot go back from this place... this land of the dead."

"Yes I can – we can. It's not just my dreams that you can return to, but to the physical world too... you can cross back over to the living world. You are free already."

"Mikael... I...." her voice wavered and she was trembling, obviously very confused.

"I have to go back Lilith, to destroy Bäliyl. I need your help, you must come with us." He indicated Arkturon and she looked at the old man as if noticing him for the first time. "Please," Mikael added, "come with us."

They helped her to her feet and, one on either side then led her back along the path toward the ominously undulating waters. She did not protest or struggle but accepted the situation passively.

When they reached the lake shore Mikael could feel apprehension building up inside himself, almost panicking at the thought of those waters. He could see that Lilith felt the same but in a much more pronounced way, actually shaking with the growing fear inside her. Mikael held Lilith tightly while Arkturon's purposeful steps and the sheer power of his silent presence drove all three of them forward.

There was a little wooden jetty with a small boat tied to it, Mikael wondered at the fact that he had not noticed them before. Arkturon directed them into the boat; it was just big enough for the three of them. He untied its securing rope. Almost immediately the craft drifted away from the shore, the waters churned about them with primeval life, crustaceous and piscine limbs and bodies seemingly propelled them along and away from the shore – out into the endless expanse of forbidding waters.

Mikael and Lilith sat down and huddled together as Arkturon stood behind them like the psychopompic ferryman of fable. The land receded into the distance and a thickening fog materialised about them. Sight, sound and orientation were soon obliterated.

Mikael became conscious, he was back in the kitchen again and sitting opposite Arkturon who was also just waking up.

"Lilith," Mikael said looking around. "Lilith!" He shouted this time.

"She is not here yet," the older man said, "it will take her a little longer to return to us, she has not got a physical body to be drawn back into. She will need time to adjust... and then to find us – find you."

Mikael looked around again then said "– and where is Rebekah?"

Corporal Villovürt, still sitting in the same position they had left her, informed them that she had gone for a walk. "I told her not to wander too far." she added.

"It is probably for the best," mumbled Arkturon, "she may find it alarming when Lilith appears."

Mikael was lost in thought for awhile – then he asked, "That place... where was it – where were we?"

"It was the Wasteland... the road to the Otherworld, to the world of the unconscious. The two towers we saw were the gate into the first Realm of the Astral Plane where the Koventiyna, the Divine Maiden, rules. If we had walked that path we would have entered a land of dream and fantasy, the domain of Moon and water. Remember what you saw and meditate upon it for I have never seen the path laid so clearly before."

"This Astral Plane; is it where we go when we dream then – and who is this Koventiyna that rules there?"

Arkturon smiled. "You have a great deal to learn." He said. "Our sleeping dreams are but a base form of the Koventiyna's realm; they are echoes, a shadow even of her blessed land... but the Koventiyna's rule covers only a part of what is the Astral Plane. It is hard to explain."

Arkturon stopped talking and, showing no signs of continuing, Mikael was forced to prompt him. "- and who, or what, is Koventiyna?"

The older man sighed. "Koventiyna is a title, it means Divine Maiden. Her names are many... but Sul is the Britannik name which was imparted to me. She is the goddess of inspiration and she is ever virgin. Her Saxanglish name is Idunna, but you may also know her as the Hellenik goddess Artemis, or the Romannik Diyana."

"The more you tell me the more questions I have." Said Mikael irritated. "You just make things more complicated."

At first Arkturon looked annoyed, then his face suddenly lightened, he delved into a pocket deep inside his enveloping coat and brought out a rolled up parchment. He untied the faded ribbon binding it and unfurled and gave it to Mikael. It showed a confusing diagram made of different sized circles and criss-crossing lines, words were written all about it in an ornate and delicate hand. The title of the page, written in the Saxanglish common tongue, read 'The Gates of Anuuwn'.

"There are nine states of being above this one – so ten all together," Arkturon pointed to a small circle marked 'Kear Britannik' at the bottom of the chart, the nine others were arranged above it. "They are split into four overlapping groups or planes; the Physical Plane is the first group," he pointed to the lowest of the four large circles in the diagram. "The next up is the Astral Plane 'Avalon', and then there is the Ethereal Plane 'Logrea' and finally the Spiritual Plane 'Sarras'." In turn he pointed to each of the four stacked and slightly overlapping larger circles.

He now pointed to the upper of the two smaller circles within the lowest of the large ones. It was labelled 'Kear Widiyr'. "This is the realm of Sul, the Koventiyna, as you can see; it bridges the Physical and the Astral Planes.

"Many of the paths have gods, or more precisely demigods, connected with them too; the path on which we found ourselves earlier is ruled by Nudd." He pointed to the two vertical parallel lines that joined the smaller circles marked 'Kear Britannik' and 'Kear Widiyr' – the path was labelled 'Lleuada – the Moon'. "He is the demigod of Sea and river, and is the guardian of Avalon; for this reason he has influence on the other two paths leading from this world as well. Like Sul he too has had many names given to him by many peoples. The Helleniks and Romanniks call him Okeyanos and Okiyanus, in your Saxanglish he is Nyurd while the other Nordik peoples call him Nyordr. I believe the elfin peoples call him Nuada." He looked to the Corporal for confirmation of this fact.

"The Atlantean sea-elves do," she replied in a soft voice, "we dark-elves call him Nodens."

Mikael studied the ancient diagram; he could not believe what he was looking at. "So are you trying to tell me that this is a map of the nine heavenly abodes... a map to the gods?"

"You could put it like that, but it's more a map of the human psyche – it represents metaphorical ideals that manifest as gods... they are personifications constructed by the beliefs of all the human races. It could also be considered a plan of the lower realms too, where the demonic powers rule – for all the gods have a flip side, a negative aspect to them."

"So it is a map of the nine hells then too!"

Arkturon paused, then said, "Yes... but that is an over-simplification"

Mikael felt a sudden chill, it was as if the existence of the nine hells had just been proven; previously he had never given the notion of the hells a second thought – or of the heavens for that matter – he had always dismissed them as fairy tales. He tried to forget it, pushing it out of his mind with questions. "The top most circle is blank, it has no title, why is that?"

"Because even I do not know what lies there, no one has ever returned from that plane... perhaps it heralds the beginning of the whole process again, but as a form of higher existence... or maybe it represents the achievement of some form of godhood or paradise... I do not know."

As he spoke Arkturon was searching his coat for something. "You see the titles given to the paths?" Mikael nodded in reply as Arkturon added, "They are the titles of the twenty-six trumps in the Tarot pack of cards... are you familiar with them?"

"Vaguely." answered Mikael.

Arkturon appeared to find what he was looking for and again pulled something from inside his coat. "Study them." He said and handed it to Mikael.

It was a pack of cards wrapped in a black cloth.

Rebekah felt like an intruder as she walked through the corridors and looked into rooms, but it was not that which made her feel guilty, it was Luwsiy.

Should we not be out there looking for her, she thought. *Trying to find and save her.*

The walk had not stopped her tears coming and images of her young sister kept appearing in her head – horrible and irrational images.

What if Luwsiy has died – been killed in some terrible way, and her mournful ghost is at this moment watching me, hating me for not trying to save her – or even help her!

Rebekah chided herself for having such foolish thoughts... but she could not get away from the feeling that they should be out there physically looking for her sister... not doing all this talking and sleeping!

She decided to go back to the kitchen and tell them that they must set out after Luwsiy straight away, she turned around but abruptly stopped, she had heard something... a sigh – *or was it a moan.*

Looking around she slowly walked back along the corridor towards where she thought the sound had come from. It came again, louder this time, but Rebekah still could not decide whether it was a sigh of pleasure or a moan of sorrow. She approached a door at the end of the corridor, sure that the noise had come from behind it.

Torn between rushing back to the kitchen to get the others and opening the door to see who was behind it, Rebekah found herself laying hesitant fingers on the handle, gripping it and turning... she jumped as the moan repeated, louder and longer than ever.

Rebekah pulled on the handle... the door stayed shut. She paused, thinking... then pushed it slowly open.

Inside was a richly furnished bedroom and Rebekah could not help but wonder if this was where Mikael slept. Cautiously she entered.

There was a rapid and almost passionate cry to her right and she quickly glanced round to see its source. A swirling mist of beautiful colour greeted her, peach and emerald surrounded a bright, shinning core, and milky vapour fell cascading to the floor. A delicate female figure was amidst the filmy dance and the shinning core was at her heart.

Rebekah looked into the elfin face and the life seemed to drain from her. "Luwsiy... Luwsiy – is it you?" Her mouth uttered the trembling words as it suddenly went dry and she came over all hot and dizzy.

The figure glided towards her, a hand held forward. It touched Rebekah's cheek and gently stroked the bruise that lies there.

"Luwsiy... Luwsiy forgive me." Rebekah cried, convinced that it was the phantom of her young sister.

The ghostly hand lowered and held hers, it was like warm silk brushing against her skin but still it sent a sudden chill into her, causing an uneasy clamminess to ripple through her flesh.

The spirit spoke with a dove like voice. "Luwsiy is not here... she is far away, in the forest... but safe for the moment."

Rebekah felt her hand go free.

Mikael placed the Tarot card down on the table, it was entitled 'The Moon' and the illustration was easily identifiable with the path he had seen in his induced dream earlier. Most of the other twenty five trump cards had illustrations of people on them and he assumed that these were purely symbolic or were pictures of the deities associated with their respective paths. He was just about to quiz Arkturon about this when Rebekah charged into the room, pale and upset, glancing behind her with apprehension. Out of breath she managed to mention a name... *Lilith*!

Mikael immediately stood up and grabbed her, "Where?" he shouted urgently.

She pointed back the way she had come and eventually managed to speak again. Bedroom was all that Mikael needed to hear.

He rushed out of the kitchen, ran up stairs and through passage ways until he was stood before the open door of his bedroom. Slowly and calmly he entered.

Lilith's naked form was before him in the centre of the room, pastel mists constantly formed and reformed about her in the ever changing shapes of clothing, some simple, some ornate... all beautiful. She span with hands out-stretched and little girl giggles came from her. It sounded like a bubbling forest stream to Mikael... and he was a man who had thirsted for years.

His voice broke through the emotion that filled him, "Lilith."

The fairy-like girl stopped her playful dance and gazed at Mikael.

The phantasmic mists settled and formed an even halo around her nude body. It receded into her, seeping into the pores of her skin, channels and eddies formed as the milky substance rushed into her orifices; ears, nose, mouth and those between her legs. Mikael thought he saw a pulsating light in place of her heart but it faded as the mists disappeared and she became more opaque.

She looked so alive... so vibrant. Mikael went to her speechless and she reached out and touched him... seemingly so solid... so warm. They embraced passionately and she gave such an ardent kiss that he was quite taken aback.

Eagerly she began to undress him... and he let her do so. As she exposed his body she kissed and stroked him, thrilling in the physicality of it after so long living a dream.

Shortly they faced each other totally naked, close enough to feel the other's body heat but not actually touching. Lilith pushed a hand forward and caressed his phallus, stroking with long finger nails that gave both pain and pleasure, until it was engorged with blood and rigid. She pressed it to her belly and rubbed the thick, powerful head against her navel, pressing it to the soft depression there.

Lilith then fell to her knees and kissed him, took him into her mouth, her hard sharp teeth pushing back his foreskin. Mikael thought he would explode with the ecstasy that filled him almost to overflowing. Playfully she fellated him to the point of ejaculation, only to subside and let him recover... and then she began again.

Mikael drew her up to her feet though and pushed her back onto his bed. He lay beside her and kissed her full on the mouth as his questing fingers moved about her exited body. He lowered himself to delight in her breasts; gently he squeezed and kissed them, alternately moving from one to the other. Mikael drew one of her hardened, cherry pink nipples into his mouth, pressing it with his teeth and flicking his tongue over it.

His hand stroked between her legs as he began to suckle strange sweet milk from her. Lilith, trembling and moaning uncontrollably, began to fondle her free breast, teasing the nipple until it too expelled the strange glowing liquid. Seeing this Mikael quickly moved his mouth to that breast, willing to taste the juice of all her fruits.

When he felt Lilith was becoming too broody though he left her succulent nipples and moved his tongue down to her stomach, dallying at her deep navel. She raised her legs and parted them as his tongue cut a furrow in her soft feathery pubic hair; he then lapped at her almost bald, peach like genitalia. Using his fingers and tongue he opened her labia and probed the flowery folds that lay hidden there, he was like a bee collecting nectar from deep inside a scarlet rosebud.

Lilith arched her back with a great sigh and took Mikael's head in her hands as if to hold him there forever while he lightly flicked his tongue over her clitoris. His lips and tongue gradually built up the pressure round the engorged little knob of flesh as it increasingly protruded from the folds above her vulva. Gently he began to suck on it like a nipple, as her juices flowed over his chin he lowered his mouth to collect them. Mikael felt so invigorated that he wondered if he would ever have to feed again.

He eventually pulled from her and rose back up her body. As their eyes met his penis reached her now incredibly moist vulva... the salacious smile that appeared on her lips made Mikael feel so aroused that he pushed into her immediately. Lilith screamed with passion and entwined her legs around him, grabbing his buttocks with both hands to push him further in. They both felt spasms of rapture as they pushed against each other in a licentiously building rhythm of sexual pleasure. Mikael's breathing and heartbeat quickened and became louder the deeper he thrust, causing Lilith to exhale little cries in time with his motion. Her vagina seemed to grip him then loosen, only to grip again but tighter than ever as he drove into her at first hard then gentle, quick then slow.

The complicated rhythm of give and take possessed them both; they were no longer two separate beings but one, the physical union a poor imitation of the spiritual.

Mikael looked into Lilith's face and knew he could never love another, never even look at another. In her exquisite eyes he saw his own spirit... his soul. He could not be without her again.

They stared, spellbound at each other as their lovemaking reached a climax that far exceeded anything either of them had felt before.

They became conscious of exchanging life-force, Lilith exhaled the milky mists of her phantasmic essence from nose and mouth, and they entered Mikael, sucked in by his strained breathing. He knew he was taking from her vitality, but he was also giving. She was receiving his male essence as he received her femininity. One needed the other to exist; they were opposite forces, but complimentary, essential to each other. Mikael now began to understand what Arkturon had spoken of.

As they both reached a point of intense sexual excitement they knew they would never be the same again. The two lovers had now opened a door showing a journey of vast potential, they now knew the true and pure nature of vampirism and love, receiving the sexual essence of the opposite sex to arouse and infuse one's own life-force, to strengthen and to harmonise it.

All they needed was to love and to live, for there is no death, just eternal life, eternal being.

The Sergeant signalled for his men to silently dismount. There was the distant, warm glow of a small camp fire up-ahead, but at that distance he could not discern if there was anyone around it.

"All right, Wellnap – you're up." He said quietly. "We know how good you are at sneaking in and out of ladies' bedrooms – let's see how good you are in the forest. I want you to get up close to that fire ahead. Don't follow the trail – they'll see you coming – go into the trees and don't make a sound... and don't do anything when you get there – just take a look, then get back here and report what you see."

Wellnap nodded and whispered, "Yes, Sarge." He took a piece of burnt cork out of his right breast pocket and started smudging it across his face. "All the better to blend in, Sarge." he said.

"Yes, well – just break up the shape of your face – don't overdo it Wellnap, or you'll be as black as I am." The well built though rangy Sergeant was a dark skinned Aedenite, one of the Naama of Namib, who'd escaped slavery as a youth when the Commonwealth frigate Rinawn had intercepted the Freebooter slave-ship in which he was being transported. He'd been a Commonwealth citizen ever since, and a Ranger for the greater part of that time; although he had kept his given first name, he adopted the name of the ship that had rescued him as his family name when his citizenship was formalised – for it had been his old family that had sold him into the slavery from which he was rescued.

Wellnap slowly and carefully weaved his way through the dark, overgrown forest; it took all his concentration and every bit of his skill to do it silently. He crept up to the campsite, had a good look around and then crept back to the Sergeant and his fellow Rangers.

"Well, man?" said the Sergeant, "What did you see?"

"It's a campsite Sarge – there's a small clearing, a fire, and what seems to be two people sleeping under blankets either side – we could walk in there right now Sarge, and 'av 'em, easy."

The Sergeant uttered a humph at that. "Let's not be so hasty." He said. "Was there a horse tethered there?"

"Er... no Sarge."

"Bit odd, don't you think? Kidnapper and captive go to sleep, all cosy like, round the fire – not a care for the horse that they are making their escape on... or the undoubted posse of villagers, Watchmen or Rangers that are sure to be following... no, this has got to be another trap."

"What do we do then, Sarge?"

"We spring it, Wellnap. We spring it."

About twenty minutes later Sergeant D'Geai Rinawn calmly walked down the trail into the campsite with nothing more than a long stick, which was his unstrung yew longbow, in his hand. He cautiously approached the nearest of the laid out figures beside the fire... from six feet away he used the bow-stave to pick at the blanket, which he could now see was a cloak, and tried to nudge it aside to reveal who, or what, was lying beneath.

As soon as he moved one of the cloaks a little, both cloaks started to rise up – as if standing figures were vertically rising out of the ground beneath them. Immediately the Sergeant started backing away toward the edge of the small clearing, once there he stood his ground and placed his bow-stave carefully on the ground behind him. He then drew his sabre.

Two large cloaked figures now stood on either side of the little camp-fire. They both faced the Sergeant, not that he could see their faces – they were deep in shadow, lost under cowled black maws that seemingly stared right at him. Confident his men were hidden in the trees around the clearing, one on either side and one ahead somewhere, he shouted one simple command of "Fire!" and then dived to the ground as six retorts sent lethal shot flying toward the cloaked figures.

Sergeant Rinawn looked up – both figures still stood there. The cloaks were peppered with holes but what was beneath them seemed impervious to the lead shot. "Damn it to all the hells!" He cursed, as he stood and readied his sabre.

Just as the figures began to advance on him, arrows started flying from left and right. One embedded deep into the chest of one figure while another passed through the head of the other. They kept advancing.

Sinkhoal came out of the trees behind them and picked up a couple of burning sticks from the fire – he set the cloaks alight, both immediately went up in flames. But still they advanced on the Sergeant.

The Sergeant started circling to the right, so that one of the creatures would inevitably be closer than the other. The cloaks rapidly became nothing more than burnt rags and flying embers and finally the Rangers could see what they were dealing with. Golems – magikally called and fashioned from the damp soil of the forest. The Sergeant sliced his sabre right through the neck of the barely humanoid mass of dirt that was closest to him. It's bulbous, uneven head went flying and came to the ground with a dull thump.

Sinkhoal impaled his sabre through the chest of the other golem. It span round before he had a chance to withdraw his weapon and the sabre was pulled from his grasp. The golem's massive, muddy hands clamped on Sinkhoal's neck and immediately started choking him. He grabbed at the slippery and unbelievably powerful arms of the monster – and tried, with all his might and bulging muscles, to prise them apart and away from his throat. They didn't budge. Gudrun suddenly shouted "Watch you're 'ands!" as he sliced his sabre through the golem's crudely wrought wrists. Sinkhoal had just managed to get his hands out of the way before the flashing blade had descended. The golem tottered back a little as if surprised at the loss of its hands. It struck out at Gudrun with its stumps, but the Ranger ducked and sliced it through the middle, causing its upper body to fall to the ground – while it's lower body remained standing and started to kick at him. Gudrun sliced down through the waist of the golem, and it's legs fell apart from each other – both twitching on the ground, desperate to kick out at him but with nothing to use as leverage in order to do so. The young Ranger then set to slicing up the torso which, using its stumped arms to propel itself, was now charging him.

The Sergeant and Wellnap had successfully sliced the other golem into ineffectual pieces, but Sinkhoal was still being steadily choked by the grasping fingers of two amputated thick-set golem hands. Both he and Gudrun were trying to prise them from the big Ranger's equally thick-set neck – but to no avail.

"The gods damn you Sinkhoal!" said the Sergeant. "How many times do I have to tell you – ya don't stab golems, ya slice 'em!"

"Sorry, Sarge." said Sinkhoal hoarsely through his gritted teeth.

"Now, all of you – get your hands away, and Sinkhoal, don't move a muscle."

Sinkhoal did indeed not move a muscle, as the Sergeant's razor sharp sabre came whistling at his throat and stopped just short of inflicting a serious injury. Twitching parts of muddy golem hands, and fingers, fell to the clearing floor.

Chapter Eight - A Plot is Revealed

Rebekah was beginning to regret asking Arkturon about the map... *surely he is not serious...* but of course, she knew that he was.

After he had calmed her down about the appearance of Lilith's ghost and told her how they had found the dead girl's spirit, she had tried to convince him that they must go after Luwsiy immediately. He simply said that Lilith will find her, and smiled – as if reassuring a child that there was nothing to fear from the dark.

"The forest is too large for us to find Luwsiy unaided," he had said "especially quickly... we need Lilith."

Rebekah had then asked him about the map and cards that lay on the table, simply because she could not bear the silence that constantly reminded her that Luwsiy was in peril while she did nothing. Arkturon had embarked on a tortuous explanation of otherworldly paths and realms; and she forced herself to listen to him.

It was a long time before Mikael returned, but when he did he struck her as being different somehow... *he seems so at ease... but also so full of life.* Lilith's appearance was an even bigger surprise; dressed in a simple white gown she followed Mikael into the room. Rebekah's heart missed a beat for she so reminded her of Luwsiy – but more mature and with rich auburn hair... and so perfect. No blemish on her skin or excess on her body... *she's immaculate.*

Rebekah had expected her to be more ghost-like, but what she saw was a woman, radiant and beautiful, and – although pale – more alive than anyone she had ever seen.

Even Arkturon seemed impressed. "You have mastered your material form very quickly," he said to her, "... strikingly so."

Lilith gave a coy laugh and with a graceful gesture ran her fingers through her hair, the colouring changed from deep brown to jet black. "Mikael has told me I have you to thank," she said walking over to him. "That *you* brought me back." She leant down and kissed his bristly cheek as her hair returned to its original colour.

Rebekah could swear that she saw the old man blush slightly before he blustered, "Oh – it was nothing my child... nothing at all."

Arkturon continued. "At the moment you have taken the form that your psyche has imprinted in it, it is your ideal, a representation of your physical body at its prime. In time and with practice you will be able to change your form to any shape you desire. At first it would be wise to stick to the human mould, though eventually you will be able to take on the shape of animals... or anything that your imagination can handle, for you are not flesh and bone, but a malleable phantasmic presence with force and form comprised of pure energy instead of matter – no longer tied to the bounds of a physical body."

Lilith smiled pertly and looked at Rebekah. "Anything that my imagination can handle – that should be interesting." She said, and chuckled mischievously.

Rebekah felt herself redden, for an image of two horses wildly mating had come, unbidden, into her mind.

Contemplating Rebekah, Lilith suddenly became solemn. "Mikael has also told me of Luwsiy." She said softly. "I am truly sorry... believe me when I say that I will do all that I can to help for, in truth, I am in part to blame."

Arkturon asked her if she had any idea why Bäliyl would take Luwsiy.

"He wants me back," she said. "I think he may use Luwsiy to get me in his power again... as some sort of exchange perhaps. His mind works differently from that of most men though, he is pure evil and steeped in dark sorceries. Maybe he just took her because she looks like me – or to get back at Mikael for helping me escape."

Arkturon's bright eyes seemed to study Lilith. "The likeness is uncanny; I admit I was surprised when I first saw you." He then appeared to brood about something, after a pause he asked "Do you know where he might be taking her."

"He used to live far into the forest, in an old castle – hundreds of years old... it is about two days ride from here."

"A castle?" Arkturon seemed to search his memory. "Are you sure he will be taking her there?"

"I cannot be sure. It was where he would have taken her when I was alive... I can go there and find out if he still resides there. I should be able to get there and back in the hours still left before dawn."

Arkturon nodded and was about to say something when Corporal Villovürt suddenly beat him to it. "What is it that he wanted you for?" She asked. "Why do you think he wants you back?"

"Yes" agreed Arkturon. "What were his plans for you when you ran away?"

With an air of hesitation Lilith sat down at the table, she turned very melancholic and Rebekah was sure that she was about to cry with the sorrow that suddenly became evident.

"He is an ancient vampire sorcerer... and a very powerful one." It was obvious to them all that she had difficulty in talking about her father; she was beginning to tremble and Mikael put an encouraging hand on her shoulder. "He – he was going to use me in some sort of ritual... he planned to summon a demon... to copulate with me... conceive a child within me. Once the offspring was born he would kill me and let the demon take my soul as payment – I would be enslaved to it for all eternity. With his magic he hoped to control the child and use its powers for his own purposes."

"How did you find all this out?" asked Arkturon. "I am sure he did not tell you."

"He could not stop dreaming about it. I became suspicious as I was the only one among my sisters he tried to keep a virgin, so I entered his mind while he slept... it was all there for me to see. How close his plans were to fruition I do not know, I did not stay to find out."

"This is unbelievable!" said Arkturon outraged. "A child born of vampire parents is liable to madness anyway but of vampire and demon seed, the child would be a deplorable aberration."

Sardonically Lilith laughed through her emotion. "That explains my father's evil madness... both his parents were vampires."

Arkturon hung his head. "Madness indeed if he thought he would be able to control such a child... thank the gods vampirism seems to make most sterile."

He looked up at Lilith. "I hope you do not mind me asking, but your mother... she was human I take it."

She stared at him indignantly, but then mellowed. "Yes... she was one of his... " Lilith appeared to search for the right word, eventually – and with great bitterness – she said, "... servants."

"Were you born a vampire?"

"Yes." She replied without emotion to Arkturon's question.

Rebekah thought that the old man seemed impressed by Lilith's response, *or was it surprise?*

"Then you are special indeed," he said. "I can see why Bäliyl would be so eager to have you in his power – he was greatly mistaken in underestimating you as he did."

Lilith visibly sagged, racked with undeniably sadness.

"I am sorry you had to tell us those things," said Arkturon. "But it was necessary." He reached out across the table to lay a hand on hers. "You should prepare to set off in search of Luwsiy and see if Băliyl still occupies his castle." Lilith nodded and brushed away her glistening tears – Arkturon continued. "Do not do anything when you are there though, just watch and come back to tell us what you see... and be very careful – really you should take more time to adjust to your new situation, but I am afraid that it would be time that we simply do not have."

Lilith laughed – a delightful and surprisingly carefree laugh, all sadness apparently forgotten. "I will be fine... I have never been better." She stood and gave Mikael an impassioned kiss – Rebekah felt sure that she should not watch this personal exchange, but she could not draw her eyes away from it.

Their embrace over, Lilith backed away from him, she stood still and seemed to fall into a spell of deep concentration. Slowly Rebekah realised the young woman was fading, becoming transparent. Soon all that was left was a shinning iridescent ball where her heart had been. It hovered awhile and then, with a hushed sound of giggling, it shot off through the ceiling, ripples of energy emanated from the point of impact then slowly faded. There was nothing to show for the encounter but Rebekah's loudly beating heart. The room seemed strangely dull and lifeless without her

"Arkturon?" Rebekah asked.

His head turned to look at her. "Yes?"

"My father... could you help his spirit back... he must be so worried about Luwsiy."

The old man smiled warmly. "Dear Rebekah... your father lived a long, good life – he has moved on. Very few people get to come back, or even want too. Remember he will always be watching you and your sister though; until, in time, you are all reunited."

Rebekah nodded gloomily.

"Be happy for him, not sad," said Arkturon. "You know now that there is life after death, so rejoice. He is with his wife... your mother. You cannot deny him that."

"You are right... I know. I'm just being selfish."

"Nonsense – what you feel is only natural." He said gently.

Rebekah had never known her mother; she had died giving birth to Luwsiy. She desperately wanted to be alone now and felt incredibly tired all of a sudden. Standing, Rebekah asked Mikael if she could use one of the bedrooms to rest in until Lilith's return.

He nodded but seemed lost in thought.

She took her leave of the two men and the dark-elf.

Lilith skimmed over the forest, her forest. This was where she belonged. When she had lived, before meeting Mikael, she and her sisters had roamed its length and breadth searching for prey. In out laying villages, lonely homesteads and on the forest roads they had found it... and had quenched their insatiable thirst for a while.

Then it was all she had known, but now she has no need for blood... she is beyond that. Her need is now a much sweeter juice.

Low over the trees she tried her new powers, her new magik. Mikael had given her fresh strength and vitality with his love – she felt she could do anything. She was bathing in rapture.

Lilith tried to put form to the flight she was now undertaking... wings she wanted, an eagle's wings – strong and majestic.

She laughed as her cavorting and lithely body sprouted feathered wings of brown, gold and white from her shoulder blades.

Lilith then fancied herself a fiary queen, wings of gossamer that trail filmy cobwebs behind her sprightly naked figure.

Anyone below would, on seeing her, think themselves blessed, or else that they dreamt, for such a vision cannot be true.

Lilith's nails and canine teeth then suddenly grew long and sharp as her laughing turned dark, her wings became black and leathery – and clawed at the air. Her skin took an emerald tinge and her hair a raven hue.

She headed for her old home and hoped that Bäliyl would still be there.

Revenge will be sweet indeed, she thought.

The trees below were getting taller and more tightly packed, they twisted and entwined around each other becoming grim and foreboding but she glided above them unhindered, her bat wings outstretched. She stroked and embraced herself into a brooding state of sensuality as the night air caressed and flowed over her.

Lilith entered an ancient area of the forest, an area she knew well. There was a shadowy rise ahead of her and she sailed up its incline, heading for a prominent tree that towered above the rest. Lilith settled in the tangled crown and looked down on the wide valley beyond like a carrion crow surveying her territory.

Amidst the time worn wood below, weather beaten walls and towers could be seen; black and grey stonework, battered and overgrown, they sprawled in the maze like complex of a castle so archaic none knew who built it. There were lights in that castle, burning deep within.

Lilith dissolved her physical form and flowed into the valley like a mist, pouring close to the ground, through the gnarled and twisted roots of mighty trees and lowly undergrowth. She surged over long forgotten defences and labyrinthine walls till she came to the battlements and towers of the castle proper. Her shallow fog crept through ominous portals, across deserted courtyards and under heavy doors. Lilith cloaked herself in total invisibility as she sensed Bäliyl's presence; it was unmistakable... but more potent and malevolent than ever.

Remembering Arkturon's warning not to do anything and afraid that Bäliyl may sense her presence as she sensed his, she withdrew.

Luwsiy wanted to sleep, she longed for its solace, but it would not come – *it could not come, not while he watches me!* He sat facing her on the opposite side of the small fire, staring. He made no attempt to rekindle or enliven the dying flames, he did not speak, he did not move. For this, at least, she was grateful, but still she dare not sleep – *not while he watches... and waits.*

A heavy fog slowly rolled out of the forest and filled the clearing, not rising above about two feet from the ground. It swirled about them but kept from the fire, not touching its flames. The kidnapper did not seem to notice, so intent were his eyes on her.

The mist then seemed to build up behind him, raising itself up into a form. At first Luwsiy thought her eyes were deceiving her and that sleep had overcome her, but no, a woman was appearing behind him, though at the moment misty and blurred. The fog dispersed as the figure became clear.

Luwsiy felt sure now that she was in a dream – *sleep HAS claimed me!*

It was a woman that stood behind that hideous little man, a woman that bent and laid her hands over his eyes and whispered in his ear. It was a woman's arms that cradled him as he fell back, apparently unconscious.

Luwsiy watched mesmerised as the figure – whose countenance was so like her own – circled the fire and came to her with a comforting and friendly smile. The woman knelt beside her and laid a gentle hand on Luwsiy's arm. "Do not fear," she said. "Help is on the way." The woman then bent and kissed Luwsiy on the lips with the words "I give you understanding."

The woman that was so like Luwsiy then stood up... and disappeared with a lilting laugh that faded slowly.

Luwsiy quickly looked across the dwindling fire to see her adversary sat, staring at her as if nothing had happened.

Thank you Lilith, she thought. That kiss had filled her mind with pictures and knowledge; of Rebekah, Mikael and of Arkturon. Her fear was far less now that she knew help was on its way, that there was a chance. She had been given hope, though she understood things were still far from certain.

With the strangeness of what had happened it was some time before Luwsiy wondered about her father and why his image had not come to her, why he was not coming to her aid. *Nothing would stop him... unless he was ill, or injured... or...*

The bedroom repeatedly focused and unfocused as Rebekah drifted between sleep and wakefulness. Ultimately, consciousness prevailed and forced the notion of further sleep to depart. She lay there staring at the unfamiliar room, confused. Then memory rushed in and filled her mind like a cruel, unstoppable flood.

Rebekah had chosen a room next to Mikael's, it was smaller but just as richly furnished, she lay on top of the bed still fully clothed. She would have liked to have stayed that way longer but her bladder was full and felt ready to burst. She stirred herself and eased off the bed, kneeling on the floor she looked underneath, a large chamber pot was just within stretching distance of her hand. Rebekah pulled it from under the bed and urgently undid her riding breeches, pulling them down she squatted over the pot and held her shirt up out of the way. The torrent of water rushed out immediately, to her great relief, and noisily splashed into the rapidly growing pool.

When she had finished Rebekah bounced herself up and down a few times to shake off any excess water that may be left on her.

"It reminds me of when you were a child," a man's deep voice said. "You used to do that every time." It came from behind her and made her jump, almost knocking the pot over. Pulling her breeches up quickly she span round. It was her father.

"I used to hold your hand, although you probably do not remember, you were no more than a toddler then."

Rebekah would have blushed furiously if she had not cried "Father! Are you back to stay... "

"No child," he said gently. "I just want to tell you that I am all right... I am happy. Do not grieve for me; you have greater concerns in your life."

"Oh papa..." She sobbed and began to rush round the bed to hug her father on the other side, she caught her foot on a turned up corner of a rug and fell face first – emitting a fearful shout. She involuntarily jolted herself up, almost leaving the bed she was still lying on entirely, and fell back again as she realised that it had been a dream and she had startled herself awake.

She should have known it was a dream; even her father would not use a moment like that to embarrass her... *although?*

Her heart was still beating fast from the shock of the fall that had woken her when there was a knock at the door. It opened and Mikael looked in.

"Are you all right," he said, "I thought I heard you shout out as I passed?"

"Yes, I am fine." said Rebekah curtly and moved onto her side, looking away from him. "It was just a dream." She heard the door close, but she knew that Mikael was still in the room. He walked towards her and sat on the bed beside her.

"I must talk with you," he said. "I wish to apologise for what has happened... for how things have turned out." Rebekah made no sign of hearing him, he continued. "I did love you – do love you... but Lilith is here now, I never thought that I would see her again before my death. I needed you then..."

"- But you do not need me now!" Rebekah spoke sharply then, pushing herself up to look into his face, she continued. "Don't pretend that you loved me – you intended to USE me... that's all it was. Please, do not pretend that it was otherwise."

"I could never love you the way that I love Lilith."

"But I loved you," she cried. "I would have done anything for you, gone anywhere... but what's the point in talking about it now!" Looking away she dropped herself heavily back onto the pillow.

"I am sorry," he repeated, "I just wanted you to understand..." He touched her shoulder lightly. She did not speak, did not move.

Mikael left her.

Rebekah drifted on the borderline of sleep again as she summoned up many images of her life, before Mikael had come into it. As sleep grew stronger images came unasked for. She heard her name being called, as if from a distance. Rebekah sought its source.

Travelling through darkness the calling became louder. Rebekah was in a forest, at night, looking on into a small clearing. A vile, dwarf like man was lifting a girl onto a horse, laying her across its back. He got up into his saddle, behind the girl, and held her down with a totally unwarranted force. It was Luwsiy that he held and it was she that called, yet her mouth remained closed.

The horse reared up and then galloped away at speed down a trail and disappeared into the forest.

Rebekah wanted to follow but she seemed tied to the spot. Unable to pursue them she fretted helplessly as she slowly dragged herself into the clearing through what was like deep and sticky mud... but on looking down she saw that her feet were free and on solid ground – she tumbled forward – and awoke again with an anxious gasp. Rebekah punched her bed in frustration.

"Having trouble sleeping?" Said Lilith, she was stood at the end of the bed.

Rebekah sat up and faced her, "Yes... dreams."

Lilith smiled sympathetically but seemed to be studying her.

Rebekah said "You have not been gone long, when did you come back?"

"Just now, it is nearly dawn – I have been gone a couple of hours."

Rebekah looked at the window and saw the growing twilight, she had not realised so much time had passed. "Did you see Luwsiy – is she all right?"

"Yes. She has not reached the castle yet, but is being taken there at this moment."

"Has that horrible little man touched her... hurt her?"

"No, he would not dare if his master wants Luwsiy alive... but how did you know about him."

"I saw him... in a dream." Rebekah sounded unsure.

"I see." said Lilith, not doubting it. She moved forward and sat on the bed – the same spot where Mikael had earlier. "Mikael suspected that you were gifted, I see now that he was right." She reached out and caressed Rebekah's face with pale fingers. "Not bad for one so young." She smiled.

Rebekah smiled too and relaxed for what seemed the first time all night, she lay back down.

Lilith leant over and kissed her forehead. "Do not hate him," she said. "Love him like a brother for he surely loves you." Lilith then stood and said "I do not know what Arkturon has planned, but we should be leaving this morning so join us soon – for the moment though, lie still." She left the room.

Rebekah did lie a while but soon she stirred herself and prepared to go down to see the others. Automatically she sat at a dressing table and looked into a mirror like she had a thousand times before. Adjusting her hair and examining her face it was sometime before she realised the bruising on her forehead, cheek and jaw had gone, even her lip had healed. Rebekah gently rubbed her face.

It's not even tender, she thought astonished.

Arkturon was very impressed by the size and scope of Mikael's library; after Rebekah had gone to one of the bedrooms he had asked Mikael if the house had possessed such a room and on finding it, his hopes had been far surpassed.

There were many oil lamps scattered about the oaken room so he and Corporal Villovürt went from one to the other lighting them, revealing the full extent of the collection. The walls of the huge chamber were totally covered by shelves; stacked with books, documents and maps; these surrounded a row of lesser shelves that were flanked by two long tables - all piled high with dusty books and other folios. It looked like Mikael had made an attempt at sorting them, but only a half-hearted one. Leading from this main room were two smaller ones, these were thick with dust and cobwebs, and obviously they had been entirely undisturbed for years except for the opening of the doors.

"It seems this long empty house has been saved from plunder by its dark and haunted reputation." said Arkturon idly.

"It would seem so, Sir." replied the Corporal with typical laconicness, a quality in her that Arkturon appreciated greatly. "Is there something specific we are looking for?" She asked.

"I'm looking for works detailing the more archaic arts of magik, or more specifically, the black arts of sorcery. I have a suspicion regarding Bäliyl's intent... and a vague idea of what he might want to do... but these ideas need clarifying." He was quickly glancing over and thumbing through books and papers as he spoke. The library covered an impressive array of subjects and he found himself wondering if Mikael had even the first clue as to the wealth of knowledge it contained. "This house has a rather legendary reputation as an abode of sorcery... I'm hoping there is some basis to it."

"May I speak frankly with you, Sir... and in confidence?"

"Of course."

"Something doesn't ring true about the ghost's story."

"Lilith's story – you doubt it?"

"Not entirely, Sir. But I think she's definitely holding something back... and I can't get the idea out of my head – that it might be something important."

Arkturon stopped leafing through books, as if thinking for a moment. "You might be right." He finally said. "A vampire born of a mortal woman – I've never heard of such a thing before... but, that doesn't make it impossible. Corporal, see what you can find in this library regarding the history and origins of vampires. Also, if this Bäliyl fellow is as ancient and as powerful a sorcerer as Lilith suggests, then he must have been recorded in the historical record... see what you can find out about him."

She nodded and started her search.

Arkturon returned to what he was looking for; he wanted a detailed view of what Bäliyl could be planning so he can combat it effectively with his own magik.

In searching the older quarters of the library Arkturon realised the dark rumours of the house were probably founded more in fact than he cared to think about, some of the books he saw, and the rituals therein, would be dangerous indeed in the hands of a sorcerer powerful enough, and fool enough, to use them.

Eventually Arkturon found the works he now knew he was looking for, the most powerful texts ever written compiled into a set of nine volumes. They were small and insignificant looking when placed against some of the larger and more beautifully bound tomes that also occupied the library but Arkturon knew none could compare to these books of shadow. They were bound in plain black leather and the title, 'Grimorium Verum Samielus' followed by successive numerals, was embossed on the front of each. Arkturon carefully took them from their grubby surroundings and carried them into the relatively clean main library.

He sat at one of the tables and began to read the books, page after page, volume after volume, blowing off dust and wiping off grime as he went.

Treating them with the care and respect that such knowledge demands he did not have time to wonder how circumstance had brought these most sought after records of magikal ritual and practice in history to this house and into his hands. In fact he had long since stopped wondering about such occurrences of chance in his life, *they happened and that was that, why try to explain it?*

Through the rest of the night he and the Corporal studied their various finds, and as dawn approached they consulted with each other. They discussed what had been learned, and then they discussed what should be done about it.

Sometime after dawn Mikael came into the library to see both Arkturon and Corporal Villovürt seemingly buried in books and lost in thought. "Have you found anything that might help us?" He asked of them both.

Startled Arkturon looked up then nodded an affirmative. "I think I may know what Bäliyl is planning to do with young Luwsiy... he'll use her to get his hands on Lilith again."

He looked very grim as Mikael asked what he knew.

"It is not good," he said. "There is a ritual whereby he can invest a living body with a spirit of the dead. It would be like inducing a possession. With the correct knowledge he could force the dead spirit, willing or not, to push out the living spirit of the body he wants possessing."

"What are you saying?" Mikael asked, "That he can put the ghost of Lilith into the body of Luwsiy."

Arkturon just nodded.

"But what will happen to Luwsiy?"

"She will become the ghost and move onto the next plane, she will die... though her body will live on with Lilith vitalising it – and Bäliyl controlling her."

"Then Bäliyl will use Lilith as he originally planned." said Mikael with fatalistic tones.

"Probably."

"But why could he not just use Luwsiy... without Lilith?"

"Because he wants the subsequent child to be as powerful as possible, he needs Lilith, for not only is she his daughter, she was born a vampire and..." Arkturon hesitated and glanced at the Corporal before continuing, "We think she may also be the daughter of a demoness. Lilith may well have been the product of a similar rite to the one he had planned for her before she ran away, though instead of a demon fathering a child on a human, it involved a human – Bäliyl himself – fathering a child on a demoness, or at least some sort of vessel possessed by one. We think he's trying to propagate power upon power through successive progeny. If he succeeds, the resulting child would be his grandchild... so would be bound to him, just as Lilith herself is – in a metaphysical sense at least... and according to his ancient Kanaanite beliefs."

"But, that is crazy!" said Mikael, a little shocked. *Lilith's mother was some sort of demoness.* The thought lingered uncomfortably.

"He is crazy... and don't underestimate the magikal power of a belief... especially if it has transcended into gnosis." Arkturon said quietly. Then, shrugging, he added "I could be wrong, I may be assuming too much."

A feminine voice then exclaimed, "You are not wrong... he can do it and he will!" Lilith materialised through the closed door. "He has the gnostic power, he has the sorcerous knowledge and he certainly has the will!"

"Then we must get to him as soon as possible!" Mikael cried. "This cannot happen!"

"Calm down," said Arkturon. "We must not lose our heads. Lilith, I take it that Bäliyl is at the castle?"

She nodded.

"And how long before Luwsiy is brought there?"

"They should get there sometime around sunset tomorrow, depending on how fast they ride and on how often they rest, but certainly no later."

"Midsummer's eve, of course... well, we still have plenty of time."

"But his castle is at least two days ride from here!" Mikael said annoyed. "How can there be plenty of time if Luwsiy will get there before us."

"We are not going to the castle, at least not yet anyway, we are going to stay here and bring Luwsiy to us. Then Bäliyl will be forced to come here after her, and we can deal with him on our own ground and in our own time."

"What are you talking about old man?" Mikael shouted angrily. "How can we bring Luwsiy here without leaving ourselves?"

Arkturon smiled calmly, "With magik." He said simply.

Chapter Nine – A Plan is Proposed

Rebekah had been surprised at first, but then, she thought, why should they all still be in the kitchen. They could be anywhere. So she left that deserted room and began looking for them.

She was walking down a long unlit corridor when she heard their voices, Mikael's was raised. Rebekah came to the door behind which they were, she heard Mikael shout about bringing Luwsiy here without themselves leaving. She could not hear Arkturon's reply very well but she certainly heard Mikael say, "I hope you know what you are doing!" as she pressed her ear to the door.

Rebekah then opened it, and entered what turned out to be a library; all four occupants looked round at her and silence fell. "What is going on," she asked impatiently, "how are we going to rescue Luwsiy?"

"Ask him!" said Mikael and pointed at Arkturon who remained composed and spoke steadily.

"With Magik;" he repeated, "I will call upon the help of certain elementals to get Luwsiy back to us. When the time comes it will have to be done with lightning speed for Bäliyl is sure to be watching the progress of his prize through the forest. Once he suspects there is something wrong he will send a horde of his own agents after her. For this reason we must prepare a place here that will protect us from such evil spirits and other sorceries that he can send against us. I plan to do this just before dawn tomorrow so we have a full day and night to get ourselves ready."

"Get ready – how!" Rebekah asked. "How can we protect ourselves from demons and sorcery?"

Arkturon put his hands up to still her worries. "I will chart a magik circle about us; while we stay within that circle we are safe from all evil. There are many other protections we can employ for outside of the circle... that little silver amulet you wear round your neck -" he pointed to the pendant of Woden upon the tree, which her father had given her on her sixteenth birthday, "is one of them."

"A magik circle?" Mikael said, seeming to ponder on something. "What exactly does a magik circle look like?"

Arkturon looked at Mikael quite brusquely at this request for what he obviously thought was unnecessary detail, but he answered in his usual cool and lecturing manner. "It is two circles, one within the other and a purifying spell written between them. Within the inner circle is a hexagram

– a six pointed star – and maybe smaller symbols of power placed around that."

"The six pointed star – is it made from two intertwined triangles?" Mikael asked.

"Yes, it is." confirmed Arkturon, now curious at Mikael's apparent knowledge.

"There's one here, carved in stone!" said Mikael. "It's upstairs in the observatory, a huge circle with a six pointed star just like you said – mapped out on the floor. It's more like a temple up there than an observatory now that I think about it."

Arkturon stood up immediately. "Show me – quickly!" he said.

So Mikael, with a lamp in his hand, led Arkturon and the three women out of his library and into the maze of passageways and rooms that sprawled throughout the house. When they reached the main entrance hall Mikael ushered them up the widest staircase Rebekah had ever seen, dust was thick on the floor and it muffled their footsteps making everything seem strangely eerie.

"I only live in parts of the house at the moment," explained Mikael, "so it is only those parts I keep clean."

At the first floor the staircase split in half and swept back on itself, rising to the second floor. Here the dirt was worse and huge cobwebs hung everywhere. All the furnishings and paintings were stained with age; the wallpaper had yellowed greatly and was peeling and mouldy all about.

"I hardly ever venture up here." Mikael confessed. Carefully he led them down further hallways. "Some floorboards may be rotten so watch your step."

They came to a small unobtrusive door that almost seemed to be hidden in a dim and shadowy corner. Mikael opened it and led them through to a very steep and narrow set of stairs. Climbing them he came to a trap door in the ceiling above, with a shove he opened it. As he lifted himself through the others were momentarily left in darkness but they managed to climb up after him.

"This is the only room in this part of the house that I had started to explore and clean... curiosity I suppose; it was so different from all the other rooms."

As Mikael talked, the others stared at the room, almost in disbelief. The walls and dome like roof were made from panes of glass that looked out over the roofs, chimney pots and turrets of the house and on into the dawn. The sun was just beginning to climb over the horizon and slowly the light crept into all six corners if the hexagonal room.

Mikael blew out his lamp.

The trap door was at the side of the north facing wall and the entire floor around it seemed to be of solid, polished stone; a raised circular platform filled the centre of the room and an altar like cube was raised in the middle of that. There was a hexagram cut into the circular platform, its six points met the inner of two huge circles which had curious words and signs carved between them. Outside of all this were four tall pillars, marking the four corners of an invisible square whose sides, facing north, south, east and west, would touch the circumference of the outer circle.

"This is the weirdest room I have ever seen." Rebekah said.

"It is perfect." stated Arkturon. "We will have to give it a thorough cleansing first though... and get rid of all this rubbish!" He waved his hand expressively at the huge assortment of bric-a-brac that cluttered the room and was piled in some of the corners.

Arkturon bent down to examine the carvings on the floor, they were not cut deep but they were roughly hewn so they contrasted greatly with shiny smoothness of the top surface, making the designs stand out extremely well. Mikael and Lilith went to the centre of the room to sit on the cube. They watched the old man. Rebekah walked over to a long telescope that pointed out through the glass, she swivelled its brass length round on the heavy tripod and looked out over the bits of forest she could see between the architecture of the house.

Rebekah had no idea what she might see, or even why she bothered to look. It gave her a sense of actually doing something though.

Luwsiy felt they must have ridden for miles and was sure that her stomach and chest would be covered in bruises for she ached terribly.

"Where are you taking me?" She yelled. "How much further... I can't take it much longer – it's hurting me!"

He laughed and pulled up the horse. "What's the matter?" He said feigning concern, "Saddle sore?"

With a laud guffaw he slapped her backside so hard she screamed with pain. "My... that's a nice arse you've got there." He then slapped her again, even harder this time. "Let's 'ave a look at it!" he whispered coarsely and lifted her skirts.

Luwsiy struggled but he held her down easily with one hand while with the other he pawed her roughly, rubbing her bottom and the upper parts of her legs. "No... No please – stop!" She yelled but he took no notice and tried to push his fingers between her tightly closed thighs, failing that he moved his fingers up toward the gap below her buttocks. She suddenly shouted "Wait till I tell the master what you've done." His fingers paused, trembling while she continued, desperately shouting "He will make you pay for what you've done – pay with more than just your life!"

He pulled away and screeched "NO!" sending birds scattering out of the trees. His voice then became a whimper. "Please... my Pretty wouldn't do that... Pretty likes me."

"I am not your pretty, I am the master's, and when he finds out what you did to me..."

"Please... don't tell 'im... I won't 'urt you - I like you - will look after you." Gently he pulled her skirts back over her.

"Let me sit upright... and give me some of your food." She tried to invest her words with some authority

He lifted her up and let her bring her leg over the other side so she could sit astride the horse. Luwsiy tucked her skirts beneath her to give herself some padding, *and protection from prying fingers*, she thought.

The now mild and meek man delved into a bag he carried over his shoulder and gave her some biscuits and a hard baked bun. He then let her drink some water from a large animal skin pouch that was over the other shoulder. The food was stale and the water foul, but she thought it better not to complain now that she had him in an apparently harmless mood. He was obviously insane and Luwsiy thought that maybe she could try to charm and trick him. She gently leaned back onto him and, even though it made her stomach turn, she spoke to him with her softest, sweetest voice.

"If you take me to my father first" she said, "I will tell your master how kind and thoughtful you were."

His arm gripped her waist tightly and he chuckled coldly in her ear, "I may act crazy sometimes, but I'm no fool!" He spurred the horse on again.

Through the course of that day Arkturon and the others cleared the observatory of everything that he decided was not needed. Anything that Mikael thought maybe of value, or of later use, had to be taken through the trap door and down the stairs, everything else was taken through some glass doors that opened out onto the roof and thrown over the side to form a heap below. Among the things Arkturon decided to keep in the room with them was the telescope which he lifted, with Mikael's help, onto the platform.

Arkturon insisted that all the dust and filth had to be cleaned away from everywhere and everything inside the outer circle carved into the floor, including all objects, surfaces, nooks and crannies, no matter how small or difficult to get at. They then washed down the windows, inside and out, so Arkturon could have a clear view of his surroundings.

When all this was done the better part of the day was gone and they all retired back to the kitchen to get something to eat, but not before Arkturon had checked the room was sealed against any outside winds and dirt.

All except Lilith were exhausted and begrimed, her phantasmic nature was incorruptible and nothing could debase her pure form. When the meal was finished, Arkturon instructed the others that they, and he, must bathe thoroughly and then retire to bed and sleep or rest until about three hours before dawn. Then they would each bathe again and be able to re-enter the circle clean and fresh, ready for the ritual that would follow.

"There are some renovated ancient remains of Romannik baths beneath the house," said Mikael, "heated by thermal springs and perfectly usable. I suggest we use them – they are a bit more convenient than traipsing up to the cold pool out in the gardens."

"Perfect." said Arkturon. He sent Rebekah and the Corporal down to the thermal baths first, with four white cotton robes to wash. "We will wear these – and these only, tomorrow," He said. "No impurities must now enter the magik circle."

"I will show you where they are." said Mikael, leading them out of the kitchen.

After handing the Corporal a lantern, he guided the two women down some narrow stone stairs and into a dark cellar that appeared to hold even more junk than the observatory upstairs. They passed through the large room and on, further down, into a damp crypt like chamber that seemed to serve as a wine cellar, the further they went, the grubbier the ranks of bottles became.

"I have no idea what is in most of these older bottles." Mikael suddenly said conversationally, his voice echoing dankly. "A lot of the labels have long since rotted away."

A warm bath had initially sounded welcoming to Rebekah but now she wished she was bathing out in the clean open air. As they reached a small opening on the far side of the cellar Mikael spoke again.

"The previous occupants of this house obviously opened up these tunnels into the old baths and renovated parts of them. I think underground tunnels and chambers spread throughout the whole area of the house – and even out into the gardens. In fact they may even go further than that, it is just a question of finding them." He bowed his head and entered a narrow tunnel with the Corporal close behind and Rebekah following. They seemed to be rising at a slight angle now, and Rebekah was sure that the air, though still damp, was getting warmer. After about ten yards the tunnel came to an end, up a couple of rough and worn steps they passed into another room. It was plain and empty, the only feature being a raised section running along the wall to the left that seemed to serve as some sort of seating. There were two more doorways leading from this room, one straight ahead, the other to the right.

"Do you know any of the history of this house," Corporal Villovürt suddenly asked, "or its previous occupants?"

"Not much." He admitted. "From what I could gather in the library the place was deserted about a hundred years ago... the reasons for that are rather obscure but apparently it had something to do with the sorcery that was practised by the then occupants – the Karnells they were called I believe – the house had been in that family's possession for at least two hundred years. Whatever it was that they were up to – the locals didn't like it. They drove them out... or murdered them, I'm not sure.

"This is like an antechamber to the baths proper," said Mikael, changing the subject as he walked across the mortared floor, "a dressing room if you like." He went through the doorway to the right without waiting for the Corporal and the lamp, which she held high to discern the simple patterns on the mosaic covered walls. The formal designs were disrupted all about where the small pieces of colour had crumbled away leaving the bare mortar beneath.

When the Corporal and Rebekah joined Mikael in the next room he said "This is the tepidarium, the warm bath..." he pointed to another door opposite the one they had just come through, "and through there is the frigidarium, the cold bath."

Between them and the next doorway was a square pool about eight feet across, a soft warm mist rose from the clear waters there. Mikael went back to the changing room almost immediately though and said "Through here..." they followed him back, he was pointing to the second doorway that led from there."Through here is a much larger pool." Again he went through without waiting for Rebekah or the Corporal, or the light that she carried.

"This, I am afraid, is not usable though." He said as the two women entered the surprising and remarkable chamber. The flickering lamp could only light up one end of the large pool that was surrounded by ancient stonework, the dark stagnant waters lapping slowly against sides that had towering columns running along the length and breadth. Intricately mosiaced pavement and walls surrounded the whole thing with once colourful designs and now barely discernible pictures that reached to the ceiling five feet, or so, above their heads. The ceiling above the large pool was even higher and was lost in the darkness that loomed there. The atmosphere in that room was stale and oppressive. Corporal Villovürt, who had always been sensitive to the atmospheres of places – even from before her formal warlock training – knew straight off that she did not like it there. She sensed they were being watched from the blackness across the room, they were being observed by an unidentifiable... *something*.

"This is unbelievable!" said Rebekah "is all this really Romannik?"

"Whoever built the house reconstructed these baths, how much of it is original and how much was added later I do not know, but the house was literally built around it. We are in fact only about eight or nine feet below the present ground level so you can see that this room – or at least the part above the pool – actually rises up into the house somewhat." He could see a puzzled look on Rebekah's face so he added, "You must have noticed the ground floor constantly changing height; though very subtly – a few steps here, a few steps there – for the building covers such a wide spread area, but only the rooms near the kitchen are actually level with the ground."

Corporal Villovürt interjected, "The observatory, it must be directly above this room, if my sense of direction hasn't deserted me?"

"Yes, you are right." After a pause he pointed into the darkness, "On the other side of the pool is a steam bath, also not in use, and corridors that lead to what is left of other rooms belonging to a massive villa or temple complex that used to stand here... well over a thousand years ago."

After another moment of silence he added, "But I think we should go back through, I will go upstairs and let you both bathe in peace."

They went back to the dressing room and Mikael left them, finding his way with absolutely no illumination.

The two women started to undress in silence. Rebekah, feeling a little shy, was reticent about taking her clothes off in front of a stranger but the elf showed no such reservations. Corporal Villovürt was naked in no time at all, and Rebekah marvelled at her distractingly lithe and athletic naked form, which sported no body hair whatsoever. She felt an instant of irrational jealousy over the dark-elf's almost golden olive-toned skin, her shiny raven hair and unbelievably pert breasts... jealous even of her tapering ears and her beautiful almond shaped eyes – for a brief moment Rebekah felt herself a pink hairy grub in comparison, but it passed. As she finished undressing Rebekah said "I can't be calling you Corporal all the time, it doesn't seem right, I'm not a soldier. Can I call you by your first name?"

The Corporal looked at her a little startled, then actually smiled, the first time Rebekah had seen her do so – she had seemed so serious all the time that Rebekah was beginning to wonder if dark-elves ever smiled. "My name is Ellowiys-alqahalha Villovürt," she said, then – much to Rebekah's relief – she added, "But, seeing as I'm out of uniform, you may call me Elliy."

Elliy picked up the lamp and carried it through to the warm pool, putting it down by the steep steps that descended into the thermal waters that were infused with an almost emerald lustre. Rebekah followed her, noting that Elliy's buttocks were just as pert and proud as her breasts.

Following the elf she stepped down into the delightful warmth, it only came up to her chest when she reached the bottom but she could bend her knees and immerse her whole body easily. The silky smooth, almost creamy, water felt delightful on her skin as she rubbed the day's grime away – and revelled in the luxury of it.

Arkturon had returned to the library and was rereading the books of magic he found when a refreshed Corporal Villovürt interrupted him.

"Rebekah has gone to her bed to rest." She said.

"Good, good." said the old man, distracted. Marking his place in the book he was reading with his finger he suddenly looked up at her and said, "I've been thinking about our plan."

"Yes?" She said.

"I don't want you in the magik circle with us. I'm going to send you back to the Rangers in pursuit of our kidnappers. When we rescue Luwsiy I want you and the Rangers to continue on to Bäliyl's stronghold. We may have need to attack him on two fronts."

The Corporal nodded. He continued. "Before that though, we should send Lilith to check on Luwsiy and to try and reassure her that help is on the way. Also, it might be an idea for her to contact your compatriots as well, and let them know what we are planning... and that you will be joining them before dawn."

"If Bäliyl is who we think he is," the Corporal started, "are you sure we will be strong enough to defeat such an archaic and experienced adversary?"

Arkturon looked confidently into her large eyes. "If we keep our wits about us, yes – we will defeat him." He said.

She picked up one of the volumes of the 'Grimorium Verum Samielus' that he'd been perusing, and translated the Romannik title aloud "The true Grimoire of Samiyl." Her voice full of surprise "Is this really a translation of Samiyl's book of magik... I thought the existence of that ancient tome was a myth – and you found them here by chance?"

"Chance? I do not know if there is such a thing."

"Do you need these books to rescue Luwsiy?"

"No. They will help me hold onto her though, they provide me with knowledge of what Bäliyl could do to counter us, for they include black as well as white magik, so I should be able to oppose him much more competently... and, hopefully his actions will hold no surprises."

"But, is not such black magik dangerous to know?"

"All knowledge can be dangerous, if it is not treated with the care and respect it deserves."

He was about to return to his reading when the Corporal spoke again. "Have you been down to the old Romannik baths yet?" She asked.

"No. Not yet!" he replied a little tersely.

"There's something down there... the nature of which I'm not sure about."

"What do you mean?" he said. His interest piqued.

"There is a large pool that is a part of the old Romannik complex beneath the house; its position is directly below the magik circle in the observatory. There was a... presence there."

Arkturon looked into the dark-elf's eyes – he found they expressed much more than her words ever could. "Show me." He said. "But first, we should find Lilith and send her on our little errand."

The two left the library.

Lilith soared high over the forest, gradually increasing in speed and height; she had no definite form but was a simple amorphous globule of faintly glowing energy. Her mind was so intent on musing about Mikael that her shape had simply closed in on itself.

Mikael's love had filled her with an ecstatic abundance that was overwhelming, she felt complete and whole for the first time in her long existence.

There was a time, in the distant past when she was young, that the act of sex, with both men and women, was enough to satisfy her desires to the full – at least she had thought so then. Her first sexual experiences had been with her sisters, but they were given free rein with others, where as she was not – her father had forbidden it. He had plans for her... but he underestimated her greatly – *the fool!* He, of all people, should have realised her powers – her capabilities... the efforts he had gone to, to bring her into the world. Yes, he was powerful – he had to be to have fathered her on Lilit, the very demoness that she was named after. A demoness long forgotten by most mortals, but not him... he was one of her priests long, long ago... her greatest acolyte, back in the ancient Kingdom of Kanaan, in the land of Gnodd, to the East of Aeden, well over two thousand years ago... *but not anymore, he's high priest to only himself now, how dare he think that he could control me? I am my mother's daughter! I am a Night Spectre!*

As she seethed with anger the ball of phantasmic energy that represented her presence in the material world burned a deep, deep red.

She had slipped from her father's control with ease and wandered the forest a free thing... a blood thirsty thing. Preying on all that came before her. Using and destroying the men whose lust made them easy. Enslaving those women that caught her eye – making them her minions... her lilim, as her mother had done, so long ago. She became a thing of folklore in that time. Given a name by those that did not know who or what she was. Rose Blood they called her, a name to put fear in the hearts of men, women and children – a reason to stay out of the forest, to fear the night.

Then she met Mikael. He had been the first and only person that she could say that she had ever loved. She had intended to use him as she had all men before him. They had been victims of their own lustful urges. Mikael had lusted for her too, it was true, but he had more than just lust in his heart. He had love for her. He willingly gave himself over to her. It was the first love she had experienced and, to begin with, it had fascinated her greatly. Through time, as his love had grown, the joy and wonder of their couplings had grown with it. She fed off his love as she had fed off others blood. It was not until she had crossed over to the land of the dead that she fully realised how much she loved him back. She learned that their love for each other was a supreme, joyous ecstasy; all else that she had known had been mere blood lust and carnal pleasure... a poor shadow of what she now had with Mikael.

Lilith realised she was nearing to where Luwsiy should be, she slowed down and descended making herself totally invisible. Reaching the trail they had been following earlier she flew up its length until she found them sitting astride the trotting horse. The last time she had approached the kidnapper and his victim she had sensed the presence of a large black raven watching them, it was still there, hidden among the trees – hopping silently from one to the next, flying at intervals and keeping pace with them. The eyes of the raven were her father's eyes when he wished to see things from afar.

Luwsiy was dosing; she must be exhausted thought Lilith as she entered the girl's mind as a dream and told her that she would be rescued just before dawn. Though grateful for the news, Luwsiy was distressed at her fatigue, her captor being so obviously unbalanced and dangerous. This concerned Lilith greatly too, she had experienced this little man's madness at close quarters herself; the threat of her father had been the only thing that had saved her from his foul advances when she was a young girl. She had never told her father for she pitied him, but now she wished that she had.

Lilith induced sleep onto him after leaving Luwsiy's dream; she appeared before him, shrouded in mists and fog they faced each other in the featureless dreamscape of his barren mind.

"Mistress?" he said pathetically. "Is it you Mistress?"

"Yes Elbroag, it is me... I have come to warn you. My father is watching you, he is always watching – you must not molest or harm the girl."

"But the master trusts me, why would 'e watch me. You promised you would not tell 'im about me if I left you alone – you promised!"

"He trusts you Elbroag, I never told him. He never knew how you wanted me – but he fears for the girl, he does not want her taken from you by someone else – so he watches over you with his magic."

Elbroag looked about himself with frantic paranoia. "I couldn't 'elp it... she looks so much like you – and you know 'ow much I wanted you, 'ow I still want you..." He was close to tears.

"All right Elbroag, it is all right."

"If she didn't look so much like you – I would've left 'er alone."

"Well make sure that you do now, or my father will not be pleased."

"Yes - yes, I will..."

"Leave the girl alone, your life depends on it." Lilith said as she faded out of his dream.

She saw him wake suddenly and look rapidly around startled. The horse trotted on regardless.

Lilith flew invisible from that spot and followed the trail back toward where the Rangers, who were trailing the Dwarf and kidnapped girl, should be. She found them closer than she had anticipated but still a good hour behind their quarry. The Corporal had given her a phrase to say upon greeting them, so that they would know her as a friend. She descended to the forest floor, on the trail ahead of them, in human form so as not to alarm them unduly. She stepped out from behind a tree as they approached.

"The leaves of the tree turn yellow, brown then dead when the men of the Fifth take up their axes." She said in a clear loud voice.

The Rangers stopped and then the one upfront nudged his mount toward her. She was only slightly surprised to see that he was a black man. "I bring a message from Corporal Villovürt." She told him.

"I'm listening." He said with a suspicious look about. It was plain that he was wondering how she had got there.

Once she had informed him of the current location of his target, and of Arkturon's plan, she dissolved in front of his eyes and shot into the sky. She sped back to Mikael, wasting no energy on form or thought.

"Well," said the Sergeant as he returned to his men, "that's a turn of events and no mistake."

"What the hells was that, Sarge?" said Sinkhoal.

"That was one hell of a beautiful woman!" said Wellnap. "It's a pity she just disappeared like that."

"Shut it, both of you." said the Sergeant. "It seems we are very close to reaching our goal – we may be heroes yet!"

"Sarge!" whispered Gudrun urgently from the back. "There are horses coming up behind us."

"Please tell me that it's Corporal Lannik and his team." said the Sarge.

"It is." said Gudrun. "I think the Lieutenant is with him too, Sarge."

"Humph." uttered the Sergeant under his breath. "Of course he is, trust him to show, just as we're about to get to our prize."

Chapter Ten – Guardians of the Four Corners

Mikael was drowsing on his bed when Lilith returned; she entered the room through the large windows that were open to the warm night air. Amidst a shower of glistening, pinprick sized lights that sparked myriad colours, her fairy-like form glided into the room on wings as delicate as the finest silk.

Her graceful ethereal motion bewitched Mikael as she floated above his reclining body and slowly lowered herself until her lips met his. Lilith's milk white arms embraced him and her diaphanous wings lifted them both into the air between the bed and its canopy. As they hovered she freed him of the little clothing he still wore; when the last garment was cast aside Lilith dropped him back onto his resting place, with a playfully malicious laugh she darted in a blur of light down by the side of the bed and out of view. Mikael quickly looked over to where she fell but there was no sign of her, he then heard her giggling behind him and as he glanced back round she rose up on the other side of the large four-poster.

She crept onto the richly covered mattress beside him, on all fours and moving like a cat. Her wings had disappeared but as Mikael stared the naked girl sprouted a long feline tail from the base of her spine, black velvety fur covered the new appendage and spread up the centre of her back, thinning and fading away as it moved but widening on her shoulders to give them a very fine, downy covering. Once it reached her head the hair that grew there turned as dark as that at her tail.

Lilith purred and meowed provocatively as she arched her back and rhythmically swayed her hind quarters, "Rut me... from behind – quickly!" As her distorted voice called him Mikael saw large cat like ears unfold from her head and noticed that long claws grew at her finger tips.

Although aroused Mikael felt a little repulsed by this display and was at a loss as to how to proceed and act.

The creature then licentiously exclaimed. "Fuck me... quick – fuck me!" Her alien cat like voice yowled at him in a desperately wanton manner till he complied with her wishes, unable to resist, his lust drove away all revulsion. The cat woman's long rough tongue licked her lips and long canine teeth as he positioned himself kneeling behind her. As she pushed her bottom towards him Mikael had a clear view of her genitals, the more exposed lips had a light covering of fine dark fur that extended round to her now sable pubic hair.

Lilith's tail lifted right up and wrapped itself about him as he moved in close. The moment his erect penis pushed violently into her the feline claws dug into the soft material of the bedding and ripped it uncontrollably.

Their lovemaking was wild and urgent but they both thrilled in its primitive gratification.

As soon as Mikael's hot stream had ejaculated into her, Lilith disengaged herself and with legs apart she lay on her back before him. She slowly changed back to her more familiar human form as, breathing heavily, Mikael dispassionately watched his semen seep from her pouting vulva.

"I can be anything you wish Mikael," she said quietly, "from your darkest to your brightest fantasy... I can fulfil all your desires."

As Mikael stared at her sex he became aware of another change taking place, the soft curves of a rose petal changed to the elaborate curling of an exotic pink orchid while the pubic hair that fringed this delicate flower changed from a feathery dark auburn to a more wispy chestnut red.

He looked up at Lilith to see Rebekah lying there.

"You see," she said, "I can be anything, or anyone you want me to be," the girl looked down her body, "even down to the finest detail." She smiled mischievously, changing back to herself.

Mikael grabbed the teasing girl's ankles and pushed her knees back onto her chest, he then straddled her rump, pinning her down with his knees on either side of her and his hands holding her thighs down. "Wicked girls need to be taught a lesson." He said with a grin as her feet firmly planted themselves on his chest. She did not push nor struggle against him though as he pierced her again, Lilith accepted his renewed advances eagerly.

He repeatedly penetrated her heated little hole, *so tight and wet*; he slipped in and out of her as she bounced her thighs up and down, heightening their pleasure. The unusual and very submissive position did not allow her much movement, but her comparative helplessness and his almost absolute control increased her excitement rather than diminished it. Mikael's motion touched Lilith deeper and more explosively in this position than in any other she had experienced, her orgasm ejaculated screams of pleasure from her mouth and copious fluid outpourings from her quim as her trembling phantasmic body writhed beneath him.

With their desires totally satiated the lovers collapsed beside each other exhausted.

The night was still pitch black when Arkturon roused to find himself slumped over his precious books in the library. He was grateful for the rest despite it taking him by surprise, stretching his arms and body he felt highly confident that he could see the coming day through successfully.

Arkturon found the robes he had asked Rebekah and the Corporal to wash draped over some chairs arranged before a dying fire set in one of the hearths in the kitchen. They were thoroughly dried, in fact there had probably been no need to have lit a fire at all for the air was still incredibly warm despite it being the early hours.

Better to be safe than sorry though, he thought. *There would be nothing worse than having to wear damp robes while trying to perform a magik ceremony.*

He took one of the robes and a towel and went down to the thermal baths to clean himself. When Corporal Villovürt had taken him down there earlier he had realised that staying clean after their baths may be more of a problem than he had at first envisioned.

They would simply have to wear their boots and keep their coats on over the robes while traipsing through the dust infected house, until they enter the circle.

Before he undressed and bathed he looked in on the large black pool that the Corporal had been so concerned about. There WAS a presence there – but distant and weak, back in the unexplored depths of the tunnels beyond... he was sure that it held no threat. He certainly couldn't allow it to delay the magik workings he had planned.

After bathing Arkturon returned upstairs, he judged it to be about two and a half hours after the Low-Noon of midnight, he sought out a large gong he had seen the day before, outside what he supposed was a dining room. He struck it several times in quick succession with the soft headed drumstick that had hung beside it. The clamorous racket that ensued took even him by surprise.

Loud enough to wake even the dead, he mused dryly.

Rebekah listened to the fading rumbles of the tumultuous crash that had so suddenly woken her. She guessed its source and knew its purpose, but the knowledge that it heralded a day that would probably prove stranger than any she had yet lived through did not motivate her to get up. She just lay in the bed and wished everything could return to normal, that the coach had never overturned and that she had never met Mikael – *none of this would have happened... I would be home with Luwsiy... and father.*

Rebekah had dreamt of her sister again, she had been riding through a dense, dark forest with the same loathsome little man at her back, his wiry goblin like arms around her delicately slender waist. He was glancing about himself, turning at every slightest sound from the forest, he seemed to know he was being watched, but not from where. This had puzzled Rebekah... *Did he sense my presence?* She doubted it.

Thoughts of Luwsiy gave her the incentive to stir and get up for it was the day that they would rescue her young sister. She threw back the covers and dressed herself.

Mikael's footsteps could be heard passing her room and she knew that Lilith would be with him though her steps were silent. She waited until they had passed, giving them time to get down the stairs, before she opened her door and followed with a lamp grasped in her hand.

Rebekah's four strange companions were waiting in the kitchen. Arkturon was already wearing one of the robes, with his coat draped over and his boots peeking out from beneath, Rebekah would not have been able to stifle her laugh if it had not been for his deeply serious face.

"I suggest you eat what you can now," he said immediately. "We may be in the circle for some time and only simple foods like fresh fruit and water should pass its border.

But first you must bathe," he added handing her a robe and towel.

Rebekah undressed in the small changing room as before, but alone this time, then took her lamp through to the warm pool and put it down by the steps before descending them. The surface of the smooth water was nearly level with the floor so resting her head on the side and fanning her hair back to keep it dry she let her body float spread-eagled in the warm pool.

It was only then that Rebekah noticed the striking picture on the wall facing her, the other walls were decorated in a similar fashion to the changing room but now she found herself staring at a life-size depiction of a human figure. It was of a young man, naked with feet apart and arms outstretched, his flaming hair radiated out like a fiery halo. In his right hand was held a spear, in his left a lyre. His beautiful features appeared to stare down into the pool, at her.

Looking down at her own body she realised her position mirrored his exactly; it was as if she were his reflection in the water. The source of the warm water was beneath his feet, just under the water surface a carved face could be seen with its mouth open, she could just see the distortion the warm flow from there caused in the pool. She guessed that there would be an outlet somewhere below her head.

After finishing her bathing Rebekah peaked into the room holding the cold pool, she had no intention of getting into it but was curious to see if a similar picture would adorn the wall there as well. Again a naked figure with arms outstretched and legs apart was depicted, this time though it was of a young female and on a different wall, the male had been on the southern wall, she was on the northern. In her right hand was a silver cup, in her left an archer's bow, her long brunette hair cascaded over her shoulders.

Rebekah knew the names of these two Romannik figures, the male was Apollo, the female Diyana, his sister; the Saxanglish equivalents were the god Baldeag and the goddess Idunna.

What was it Arkturon had called her, she thought, *Sul, the maiden.* She wondered what the Britannik equivalent of the male was – *I must ask him when I get a chance.*

Rebekah went back through the tepidarium to the changing room; she dried herself then put on the white robe Arkturon had given her. She then put on her boots and cloak as he had instructed and, carrying her clothes, towel and lamp, she walked back to the kitchen.

While Rebekah was bathing in the house, Mikael went up to his cool dark pool and bathed amidst the cold stone myths that haunted his wild gardens. The faint star light that emanated from the summer night sky seemed to possess the dark grey statues with a strange kind of celestial life as he walked amongst them on his way back to the house, skirting the large overgrown maze he had vowed one day to explore and conquer. Robed in white he seemed a high priest, his bizarre congregation awed into silent stillness by his passage. Minotaurs and centaurs, fauns and dryads, nymphs and fairies, gods and demons, all were quiescent before him.

When he got back to the kitchen Rebekah was sat at the table, finishing a quick meal. As he entered she said "Arkturon is preparing the observatory for the ceremony, we are to join him as soon as we have eaten. Lilith and Elliy are already with him."

"If you are ready we can go now," said Mikael, "I have no need for food at the moment."

Rebekah nodded her agreement and after Mikael had draped his coat over himself they went. Avoiding the dustier routes he led her back up to the observatory, though her long red cloak still found enough dust to churn up fine clouds in her wake as it brushed the floor. When they arrived Arkturon and Lilith were already within the circle. Elliy was standing outside of the circle – fully clothed and armed with her Ranger weapons, guns, sword, dagger and a longbow with a quiver full of long black arrows. She looked very formidable indeed.

"Take off your boots and cloaks then join us," the old man said to them. They obeyed leaving them beside Arkturon's near the trap door, which Mikael closed. "And put your lamp over there," Arkturon pointed to a far corner of the room, "leave it lit." Rebekah did as he bid, there were three other lamps placed in different corners of the room.

Dressed only in their robes they then entered the circle; Lilith had been dressed in an ornate crimson gown but it transformed into a simple robe like theirs as they joined her. Mikael noted that Lilith made her garment much more translucent and closer fitting than their own, though covering her totally it in no way hid her voluptuous body.

Once all four were within the confines of the large mystic symbol Arkturon began to light the four thick candles that were set in the heavy brass sticks between the two circles on the floor, each was aligned with one of the four columns that surrounded the circumference. As he went from one to the other uttering words under his breath Mikael and Rebekah sat beside Lilith near the square altar.

When all the candles were lit, Arkturon then lit four braziers that were equidistant between the candles – each aligned with one of the four points of the compass. He sprinkled dust from another of his little tins into each as he went, all the while mumbling words of import that none of the others could make out. A wispy column of pungent smoke was emitted from each as he did so.

Once done, Arkturon stood at the hub of the magik circle, it was only then that Mikael realised that the square altar was slightly off centre allowing a person to stand at the true heart of the circle. Arkturon quickly snorted a little of the fine powder he had sprinkled into the braziers – it was laced with Yaggothiyan Fungi spores in order to heighten his wizardly power to manipulate phantasmic energies – and then picked up his staff from where it had rested against the large cube.

"You must all be totally quiet until I direct otherwise," he said grimly.

They silently nodded.

The old man then picked up a long ornate sword that had lain across the altar; he turned away from the stone. In his left hand he held the sword with its point resting on the floor, in his right hand was the staff, he raised its length and pointed the crown forward.

In a loud imposing voice that caught his companions completely by surprise he intoned "To the East I call!" He started to trace the shape of a pentacle in the air before him with the head of his staff, as his slow clear wording continued. "To the Kernunnos, the Divine Lord, who goes by the names of Matt, Frea, Freyr, Hermiyz and Merkyuriy I call. Your names are as many as the winds you rule. To thee I call, Lord of the beasts, Lord of the dawn, of spring and of the air. Aid us Lord, sharpen our wits and our tongues and teach us to see and speak only the truth."

As Arkturon spoke a strange fog billowed out of the smoky column that rose from the brazier before him, it stretched between the two pillars he was looking through. Mikael stared uneasily as a figure developed in the middle of the murky mists. Slowly the pale blanket dissolved to show a whole new, impossible scene between the columns. They all now looked into a clearing in a forest; it seemed lit by early morning twilight though it was still night all around them.

The forest was thick with animal life; birds, mammals and insects, all were still and silent around a naked man who sat cross-legged in their midst, his only ornament a silver torque about his neck. In his right hand was a shinning sword with its point in the dirt of the forest, his left hand rested on the rim of an enormous cauldron that held some kind of bubbling liquid though there was no fire beneath it. Across his shoulders and about his arms writhed a huge snake while just behind him stood a stag to his left and a large wolf to his right.

He was a mature man, of about thirty years, his hair and beard were a light, almost orangey brown and his sinewy body seemed to emanate an abundant virile strength. His phallus proudly stood erect between his legs.

The intelligent, dark brown eyes stared intently into those of Arkturon. The whole scene was constantly agitated by a strong breeze and as the god's tousled locks were ruffled Mikael became aware of two horns that rose from his head, matching the antlers of the stag behind.

"Hail to thee, Oh Lord" Arkturon proclaimed. "Praise and thanksgiving I convey to thee."

Mikael and Rebekah stared in amazement as the manifestation bowed his head in acknowledgement.

Arkturon then turned to his right and, putting the sword back on the altar, now picked up a rod of wood. "To the South I call!" Again he started to trace a pentagram with his staff. "To the Maponus... the Divine Youth, to thee, Luw I call... to Baldeag, Balder, Apellon and Apollo. Lord of day, of the sun, summer and of fire. Aid us Maponus, develop our skills and impart on us humility, may we never fall into the prison of pride."

Between the columns to the south a forest clearing again materialised but this time under the glare of a mid-day sun. A handsome youth of about seventeen years sat on a large flat stone in the middle of the summer glade. He too was naked but a golden shackle circled his left ankle, its broken chain lay in the grass. The god's lithe body was covered with a light golden brown tan and his bright fiery hair radiated out from his head like a halo. He held in his lap a lyre and resting against his shoulder and neck stood a long spear with a wooden shaft and a head of gold. Steaming water welled from the ground at the youth's feet; and fawns, kids and cubs of all sorts played and gambolled around him. In the trees birds sang and whistled joyfully. A large hawk was perched directly above the god; it surveyed its surroundings but seemed content not to pounce on any of the small creatures playing beneath its steely gaze.

The air was still and heat seemed to pour from the scene.

"Hail to thee, Divine Youth. Praise and thanksgiving I convey to thee."

The gods blue eyes flashed as he nodded to Arkturon's greeting.

These sudden and unthinkable appearances startled Mikael greatly, he looked to the two girls and saw that Rebekah was even more bewildered than he; the look of shock was evident on her wide eyed face. Lilith was the only one who did not seem to view these materialisations as incredible, she calmly watched as if nothing out of place was happening.

Arkturon had replaced the wooden rod and had now picked up a flat ceramic dish; it was muddy brown in colour with a dark pentagram marked in the glaze on its top surface. He faced another direction, this time the altar was before him. As Mikael turned to face the same way the noises and heat he had experienced while looking to the south faded away to nothing, glancing back they returned but only while he looked in that direction.

"To the West I call," Arkturon now said authoritatively. "To the Nemetona, the Divine Lady, to thee, Ariyanrhod I call... to Frouwa, Freyja, Affrodiyt and Veynus. To thee, Lady of the Sacred Groves I call, Lady of the dusk, of autumn, the earth and of love.

Aid us Lady, see us through the initiation of life and grant that we may all experience true love."

Between the two pillars to the west of the circle now reclined a voluptuous woman exuding erotic beauty. The early evening light in which she bathed imbued her auburn hair with the reds and golden browns of the autumnal trees behind her. The goddess' only adornment was a silver ring on the third finger of her left hand. Her cream coloured body lay sensually along the thick trunk of a fallen tree, all about her grew delightful flowers and lay baskets and dishes piled high with fruit, nuts, berries and vegetables; a harvest that testified to her fertility. She had no body hair and the soft curve of her bare pubic mound clearly showed the top most part of her sex.

The only animals that could be seen there were a single owl that sat in a branch above the goddesses head, a pair of hares that sat before her and a large black cat that sprawled lazily at her feet.

Mikael was ashamed to find himself aroused by the mere sight of this woman who, though appearing to be in her early twenties, must he thought be an ancient and immortal being whom he had absolutely no right to desire.

"Hail to thee, Lady." Arkturon's words interrupted Mikael's thoughts. "Praise and thanksgiving I convey to thee."

Mikael was sure that the woman's dark hazel eyes, so much like Lilith's, glanced in his direction as she bowed to the old man and he could swear that her lips formed an almost imperceptible loving smile... *but no... I must be mistaken.*

Finally Arkturon turned to the north, this time he held a silver cup in his left hand, formed like a chalice.

"To the North I now call! To the Koventiyna, the Divine Maiden; to thee, Sul I call... to Idunna, Idhunn, Artemis and Diyana. Maiden hear me, Mistress of the night; of winter, water and of healing.

Aid us Koventiyna, inspire us always and help us to be forever diligent in all that we do."

Again the four gazed on a god form in the semblance of a naked human figure, this time a young girl of about fifteen or sixteen. Her skin was so pale, almost alabaster white and her slim budding body crouched before them, alert and watchful like a wild animal. Her bright green eyes seemed to take them all in at a glance as they quickly flashed from one to the other. Cradled in her hands was a simple earthenware cup, full to the brim with what looked like milk. The beguiling girl's long brunette hair fell untamed from a plain silver band at her forehead and rested damp and dark against her pale, fine sculptured shoulders.

The bare winter forest around her shone with the light of a full moon, the trees dripped moisture and the sodden ground seemed full of potential life. Toadstools and mushrooms grew all about. A fast flowing stream gushed from a spring beneath her feet and teaming creatures tumbled in its cool clear waters.

Mikael's senses were convinced of a forest after a heavy rainstorm, the rich smell of damp soil and flora infused the moist ridden atmosphere that swept over him – so enlivening and invigorating it was.

Beside the girl, next to an archer's bow and quiver of arrows that lay on the ground, a giant wild boar rested, though its eyes, like hers, were constantly alert. On her other side a she goat, udders full with milk, and a white calf lay asleep. Diverse types of wildfowl rummaged in the undergrowth or settled in the clearing around her while in the background a white horse, with a single spiralled horn growing from its forehead, pranced nervously.

"Hail to thee, Divine Maiden," said Arkturon. "Praise and thanksgiving I convey to thee."

She nodded her acknowledgement to him.

Mikael, Lilith and Rebekah stood close behind Arkturon as they looked around themselves in wonder. It was as if they stood in an ancient stone temple in the middle of a clearing in a dense, primitive wood. But the wood was split into four different seasons at four different times of the day according to the direction one looked in. Elliy, outside of the circle, saw only the rising columns of smoke from the braziers.

Arkturon turned back to the east and, with head bowed, faced the horned god once more.

"Arkturon," the god said, as he rose to stand before them. His voice was strong but gentle and seemed to reverberate around them. "You have called us with the old names and visualised us as we were once seen. It is good that you have brought us in this way, your kind are now few.

We are your servants as well as your masters, what do you ask of us?"

"There are two souls in danger Lord, two innocents. One is here, by my side," he indicated Lilith, "the other is deep in the forest, a child; her innocence, her life and her soul are in deep peril. I ask that your servants, and the servants of your brother and sisters, aid her, rescue her and bring her here to those who love and cherish her."

A girl's sweet voice then sounded and they turned to see the Koventiyna stand. "I have been watching this woman-child" she said. "I see the rape of her body and the banishment of her soul if we do not act, but this horror does not amount to even half of what is planned. I sense great danger for this girl... and for all of us."

The Maponus then spoke, addressing the horned god. "My Lord, I see your dark brother plotting a foul intrusion into this material plane. His puppet has come too close to opening the door once already."

"Yes." It was the soft sensual voice of the goddess of love and they turned to face her now standing form. "It will not be so simple a remedy as two lovers this time," she glanced at both Mikael and Lilith. "We must act... my servants will aid these mortal's in the rescue of the woman-child but decisive action must be taken against this puppet Bäliyl - he must be destroyed!" Emotion filled her words.

"It is not for us to destroy a mortal life simply because it is being used by evil." It was the Divine Youth's voice that again filled the air about them. "He must be allowed a chance to see his folly and repent... he too has a soul worth fighting for."

They fell silent and focus was again placed on the Kernunnos. After a pause he said "My servants will aid you too Arkturon... use them wisely but I cannot sanction the destruction of Bäliyl."

"I thank you Lord Matt and you Lady Ariyanrhod for the aid I sought." Arkturon bowed to them both in turn.

Sul then spoke. "The spirits that serve me are creatures of water, I do not think they can aid you in this but if you have need of their help in your venture call them in my name. Be ever vigilant Arkturon and never ignore your intuition."

Arkturon bowed and thanked her then turned to the Maponus as he too began to speak.

"My minions are the spirits of fire, I too think that they cannot aid you now but if their aid is sought call them in my name. Always know your limitations Arkturon, never become arrogant."

The apparitions abruptly faded and dissolved into the familiar setting of the observatory as Arkturon stated his gratitude while bowing to the Divine Youth.

The darkened room suddenly seemed strangely empty and lifeless to the four within the circle.

Chapter Eleven - Elbroag on the Precipice

Elbroag stared into the forest, obsessively looking for eyes that might be watching him... that must be watching him – *beady little black eyes, evil eyes, watching me.*

He tried to remember all that he had said and done to the young girl... all that his master must have seen and heard.

The grotesque little man sat hunched and brooding by a small fire that he had lit in yet another clearing that they had come to. The girl was staring at him from the other side of the fire, her eyes glistening with hate.

Elbroag remembered telling her how he had wanted Lilith... *Master would know now!*

As he gazed at her young beauty he remembered ripping her clothes, touching her... *her soft white skin, so pure and untouched... so much like Lilith!*

He was rapidly coming to the conclusion that he had done enough already to anger his master – done enough to warrant torture... *and probably death!*

Bäliyl could kill mercilessly and without provocation and, in fact, Elbroag had often aided him. A servant's life was rarely very long in that cold dark castle for Bäliyl's temper had a very short fuse indeed. But Elbroag had always been very careful, in the hundreds of years that he had served his master he had never said a word nor put a foot wrong – at least, not within sight nor hearing of his master... *till now... all because of this girl – it was her fault... HER fault that I've angered the Master – HER fault that I must die!*

It was then, in his madness, that Elbroag realised he now had nothing to lose, no matter what he does, Bäliyl will kill him anyway.

So the girl is now mine, he thought, forcing his hysterical mind to a form of rationality. *I can use her as I wish. I could never have Lilith because of him... but I can have this sweet-meat – despite him!*

Slowly he stood up; he saw the concern on her face, the fear in her eyes. He was going to enjoy this, she will be the last girl he ever rapes but she will be the best... *the best ever.*

True – she's older than most o' the girls I've had; he thought, gleefully, remembering the many wretched peasant children he had forced himself on over the years. But then he shrugged – *no matter. Maybe it's fitting that I should end with a woman and not a child.*

He took delight in seeing her desperately clutch at the ripped bodice of her dress, trying to cover herself up before him.

I'll make sure his plans are now wrecked... she won't be a virgin for 'im, she'll be useless to 'im then!

That'll show 'im for not trusting me – for spying on me!

Bäliyl watched and cursed the betrayal of his most loyal servant. "The repugnant little shit will be ripped to pieces for this" he whispered acidly, "...very, very slowly!"

He knew Elbroag would not regain his senses; the malformed little dwarf could not be pulled back from the precipice of madness this time. He couldn't help but wonder if it was the unnaturally long life he had gifted the ungrateful creature with, which had contributed to his madness – some were simply not equipped to deal with an overly long existence in this world.

His concentration broken, Bäliyl had to stop using the eyes of his black-winged familiar. "DAMNATION!" He yelled impotently, "You conniving, putrid mound of steaming excrement!"

Bäliyl stood amidst a large magik circle on an open floor at the top of his castle's highest, most hideous tower – that impaled the clear night sky like the most vicious rape of purity possible. His increasingly angry, foul and blasphemous shouts and hollers ejaculated out of its phallic structure and called forth the foulest minions of the most heinous and malevolent demons that his dark powers could command. His eldritch words sped unnaturally swift and far through the dark ancient forest, all the way to the ragged ears of the barbarous band of savage wilding goblins that he'd had shadowing the miscreant dwarf for miles.

He ordered, begged and pleaded that his vile wishes be carried out with ruthless speed and wicked thoroughness; that their sinful depravity be only abated in dealing with the young girl and bringing her to him – with virginity intact and physical beauty unblemished. They were free to do with the snivelling little shit Elbroag as they saw fit... *and for as long as they wished.*

Luwsiy had been trying to build up the courage to ask him if she could attend to her toilette again, when the hideous little man had suddenly stood up after a very long period of brooding silence. She could see straight away that something was wrong... very wrong. Even by his standards the seething expression that now clouded his face was deranged beyond any slightest hope.

She tried to run, but he was on top of her in an instant, his weight dragging her to the ground. Luwsiy scraped and tore at the grass as she frantically tried to crawl from under him but his strength pulled her back easily. His bony hands gripped her hair and lifted her up, yanking her against a tree, handling her like a rag doll he sat her against its hard coarse trunk and then, menacingly, he stood over her.

Luwsiy gawped in horror as he fumbled excitedly with his belt and breeches.

"Oh little girl... you're gonna love this, you'll love it – you will, you'll love it..." He repeated the same words over and over again in a hideously rushed and breathless voice.

Luwsiy wanted to scream hysterically, to kick and thump wildly, but she was exhausted and knew in her heart that it was futile, he was too strong. She could only stare in silent shock, paralysed with fear and disgust as he got his penis out and held it in his hand, squeezing and pulling it, encouraging it to grow.

"- I'm gonna rut you little girl – RUT YOU HARD – like a crazed stallion – but you'll love it my Pretty... you'll love it!"

One of his hands tightly gripped the hair at the back of her head and neck while the other brought his foul fat tool up close to her face.

"Do you like it – do ya – do ya want it..."

Luwsiy instinctively closed her eyes and mouth as he began to smack her face with its thick swollen head.

"I'm gonna fuck your tight young cunt – then I'm gonna fuck the sweet little hole in that soft white arse of yours – get right up into you – yeah, right up... but first – first I'm gonna fuck your lovely... little... mouth..."

He pushed the hot, putrid smelling tip to her mouth but she kept her lips and teeth tightly shut.

"Open your mouth little girl... let me in..."

She prayed for unconsciousness as tears flowed down her screwed up face.

"OPEN YOUR MOUTH!" he suddenly screamed. "Open it or I'll break your NECK!" Painfully he yanked her head back by the hair. She screamed as her head whipped back and was cracked against the rough bark of the tree.

Elbroag cursed as the girl almost fainted away, he slapped her hard across the face and pulled her from the trunk by her legs.

As Luwsiy lay dazed, he tore at her already tattered clothes and ripped them violently from her. Luwsiy gaped as he then hurriedly undressed himself and revealed his malformed and scarred body, his huge phallus looking horribly out of proportion, it seemed at least ten inches long and the huge head was like a giant swollen plum. He urgently pumped its shaft with his hand and laughed loathsomely as he did so.

Elbroag knelt between her sprawled legs and began to paw roughly at her thighs and groin. Detachedly Luwsiy thought she heard the horse whinnying nervously and stamping its hooves as if sharing in her distress. Everything seemed to slow down and become painfully protracted as her head span and its thundering aching threatened to take her from reality. She wished and prayed that it would, as the grotesque man lifted her legs and rested her thighs on his.

Her confused eyes dizzyingly tried to focus on him but she could not, she was certain that figures were moving behind him, coming out of the trees, but the flickering firelight just served to confuse her vision even more.

He brought the tip of his penis to the tender lips between her thighs and she knew that if he entered her there it would surely mean her death. As his trembling heat touched her vulva she saw a terrifying vision, gargoyle like beings had appeared behind him, rearing up to grin and laugh cruelly at her – even in the midst of the unconsciousness that surely claimed her she would not escape from her suffering.

But they were not a nightmarish figment of her mind, they were real and they seized the dwarf, dragging him – startled and struggling – from her. His piercing screams seemed to clear all the fuzziness from her head as two wild creatures grabbed her too, lifting her up and holding her tightly to the tree that she had just been violently pulled from.

Luwsiy stared in disbelief, the frightening creatures were of a similar size to her kidnapper but stockier and their features were much more repugnant and unnatural. She watched petrified as the naked goblins, covered with strange and primitive tattoos, both male and female alike, molested the now pitiful man who had been so intent on molesting her. One of the male goblins, all of whom seemed permanently erect, brutally buggered him from behind while a female crammed his still erect phallus into her sharp toothed mouth and taunted his shaft and scrotum with long, jagged claws. Other goblins were slowly breaking the bones in his fingers and toes, then pulling out the nails and laughing as if it were a game.

The two that held Luwsiy sniggered and chuckled at their companions' disgusting activities and her terror grew as she thought of all the things that they could do to her. They were now using their long claws and sharpened teeth to rip and tear at his flesh, blood flowed freely all about his body and Luwsiy noticed too that blood welled from the female creature's mouth as she voraciously sucked on his penis. This hideous parody of the feminine then violently pulled back her head and – horror-stricken – Luwsiy realised that she had bitten the swollen head completely off, leaving only his shaft spouting dark blood that arched into the air and splattered onto the goblin woman's fearsome face.

The terrified girl retched but managed to keep from vomiting, her bladder though released and Luwsiy felt its hot contents cascading uncontrollably down between her legs. One of the creatures that held her, a female, saw its glistening fall and immediately interrupted the flow with her hand. She then brought it up to her mouth and eagerly supped and licked the urine from her fingers.

Luwsiy tried to turn away from the whole disgusting scene but they forced her to watch as the other goblins now began to bite bloody chunks from all parts of the little man's body. He could now, in his agony, only whimper. It was then that Luwsiy saw with horror that the goblin who had buggered him was now walking toward her, his odious phallus soiled with excrement and blood.

The numbing grip of those that held her suddenly forced Luwsiy to her knees – she screamed hysterically and begged them not to, as they brought her head to the level of the abhorrent erection that approached her – they then unexpectedly let her go.

Luwsiy looked around bemused, the two goblins had crumpled to the floor, a deadly arrow was embedded in the back of each, directly through the heart. She was sure that she would swoon as other creatures now swarmed into the clearing – carnage and confusion was all about her. The new creatures that entered the scene were tall and cloaked, and carrying sabres and bows. The goblins scattered in futile panic. The Rangers were swift, agile and deadly efficient, either shooting the goblins with their black, silent arrows or quickly putting them to the sword.

Their victims at least all died quickly, thought Luwsiy, and she was relieved to see that one Ranger – a black man – put her kidnapper out of his agonising misery with a single decisive thrust of his blade.

After a few brief but bloody seconds, Luwsiy was left kneeling and bewildered among a group of twelve desperate and rugged looking Rangers, cleaning their swords and retrieved arrows on their dark green wraps. She became extremely conscious of her nakedness, especially as she noticed a few of them were unable to hide their lecherous glances at her. One of their number came forward and crouched before her, Luwsiy was surprised to see the dainty face of a female, a dark-elf with overlarge hazel eyes and delicately pointed ears. The beautiful woman spoke with a strange though lilting accent in a voice full of gentleness.

"Luwsiy, we have been sent to help you," she said, "these Rangers have been trailing you for days and I have come directly from your sister." She stretched out and touched Luwsiy's hand, all the fear seemed to lift from the girl as she accepted the elfin hand, grasping it eagerly. As they both stood the elfin woman spoke again.

"You must depart from here straight away and get as far away as possible – quicker than we can achieve it. The elementals of the air that brought me here will now carry you to safety."

"Elementals?" asked a confused Luwsiy quietly.

"The sylphs... they are the servants of the Kernunnos – Lord of the Air."

The rest of the Rangers were stood in a half circle around the edge of the clearing as if waiting... soon Luwsiy knew what it was that they waited for. One second the air was still and empty, the next it was full of fleeting spirit like creatures that hummed around the clearing whipping up breezes as they passed.

At first Luwsiy backed off, but a reassuring elfin hand stayed her. The sylphs gradually settled before them and greeted Corporal Villovürt with a silent nod. They were human in appearance, with large diaphanous wings that reminded Luwsiy of a dragonfly's span, their naked bodies were slim, graceful and semitransparent; all had flowing long hair. Though white seemed mainly predominant none of them appeared to be of any one colour as all refracted the colours of the rainbow as they moved.

Without a word being spoken these life-size fairies took Luwsiy in their soft silken arms and lifted her into the air. She looked down to see the clearing recede below her and the Rangers diminish in size till they resembled nothing more than toy soldiers on a nursery floor. Soon all she could see was the dense and seemingly impassable forestation rush by as the sylphs flew her high above the twisted tree tops.

Bäliyl watched and mused darkly, his anger way beyond mere shouts and curses. His seething mind desperately grasped at solutions to solve this turn of events.

He held up his long ornately carved staff in one hand and began to slowly spin it round his head as, with words both foul and archaic, he summoned the infernal spirits of the air to follow and destroy their more heavenly cousins. Pale figures, cold and cruel, materialised around him, spinning round the magik circle – following the dragon carved crown of his staff. Faster and faster they span as more and more ghost like apparitions fell into the increasing spiral of phantasmic evil drawn from the very air itself.

Suddenly the staff stopped spinning and with a great wave Bäliyl pointed out over the forest. The wraiths streamed away from him as if fired from a canon to arch into the sky from his tower, wheeling and diving through the air toward the young girl he must possess.

Rebekah paced up and down within the confines of the magik circle, impatiently chewing on an apple she had picked up from a tray that lay on the round platform. She glanced at Arkturon for the umpteenth time but still he sat unmoving, cross legged with his back to the altar, head bowed and eyes closed in deep concentration. His only visible movement in fact was that every now and then he raised a long carrot to his mouth and took a bite, munching on it for what seemed an age before finally swallowing. Rebekah assumed from this that he must still be breathing though she could see no direct evidence to prove it.

Mikael and Lilith sat on the edge of the platform, saying and doing nothing; they simply held hands and waited patiently.

When the visions of the gods had disappeared, she and Mikael had subjected Arkturon to rapid and innumerable questions, only a few of which he tried to answer – briefly and hurriedly. They did not push for more answers for they knew that Luwsiy's life depended on Arkturon doing his work quickly; though neither of them had expected the majority of this work – after the summoning of the sylphs that had carried Elliy off over the forest – to take the form of immediately sitting down and closing his eyes. None would dare disturb him though.

Realising her walking up and down might disrupt his concentration Rebekah stopped and sat down guiltily, away from Mikael and Lilith. She looked again at Arkturon's map and tried to understand it, as he had said she should. He called it a map of the Otherworld and had said that the four god forms they had seen belonged to the four spheres of Avalon, a realm of moon and water and also known as the underworld. Maponus though, he had said, also belonged to Logrea – a realm of sun and fire. The Divine Youth balanced and bridged the Lunar and Solar worlds of Avalon and Logrea. His Avalon aspect was known as Bladud, a guardian god of thermal springs, while his Logrea aspect, Mabon, was a god of music and poetry. He was more usually seen as they had seen him, in his combined form of Luw, the god of skills and crafts both peaceful and warlike.

There was so much she did not understand, what he had told her was very confusing but she wanted to know more, much more. She had always felt that gods and places such as these existed, now she knew that they did but still she needed more proof – *more knowledge.*

Rebekah's thoughts were suddenly interrupted though, when Arkturon proclaimed "They come – the servants of the Kernunnos... with Luwsiy."

Mikael and the two girls immediately jumped up, discarding the map Rebekah rushed past Arkturon, who remained seated and concentrating, to the large telescope. She scanned the sky around the observatory, the old man had told her that the horned god's servants were creatures of the air and would carry Luwsiy on the wing, bringing her to them with the greatest of speed. Rebekah could see nothing but the pre-sunrise glow of the early morning though, she fell to the horizon and turned her eager gaze along its length... and there she saw them – rushing toward her.

Rebekah's eyes widened as she watched the palely glowing figures that carried her young sister to safety. Arkturon had called them sylphs, a more apt name she could not imagine and their streaming flight was like a pastel rainbow in the making.

Rebekah then became aware of two more pale ranks of figures that chased the first and then flanked them like a ceremonial guard. But these new figures were different, their paleness was cold – their features were cruel.

Arkturon suddenly stood and pointed to the fast approaching streams.

"Wraiths!" he shouted with alarm.

Rebekah sensed their evil and felt herself grow as cold and pale as they. Her heart pounded and seemed to leap into her throat as she watched the so obviously malevolent wraiths gain on the sylphs and over take them. They approached so fast that Rebekah, even without the telescope, could now see their features – both angelic and demonic – clearly, and there, in the middle, was the terrified face of the naked Luwsiy.

The dawning light from the east was growing rapidly as Arkturon shouted, "The glass! We must break the glass above us so Luwsiy can come through!"

Almost immediately Lilith leaped up into the air, changing into a fiery ball of pure phantasmic energy, and crashed through the glass – blasting splinters and shards outwards – before lightly coming back down again in her human form.

The wraiths were now ahead of the sylphs and were heading them off, coming between Luwsiy and the observatory and cutting her route to safety.

"While the sun is below the horizon the powers of evil are dominant," Arkturon exclaimed. "We must pray that I timed our rescue right and the sun rises soon – then the sylphs will be the stronger."

All four stood close together and watched the spectacular show in the sky with a mixture of awe, excitement and fear. They were now surrounded by howling wraiths that flew repeatedly around the observatory, leering and sniggering incessantly – some even passed within its glass walls.

"We have nothing to fear from them!" said Arkturon at Rebekah's concerned looks. "They cannot enter the circle."

"But how is Luwsiy to get past them?"

"The light grows stronger by the second – she will be safe."

The sylphs checked their head on flight without warning and suddenly swerved upwards, shooting straight up into the sky that now burned with red and orange.

"They rise to meet the sun!" Arkturon buoyantly proclaimed.

But the wraiths rose with them, always circling the magic circle for its influence projected up into the heavens like a cone focused on the centre of the earth.

Higher and more distant the strange creatures flew, trying to out-manoeuvre each other.

"The sun!" announced Arkturon. "The sun – it comes!"

The first hints of a shinning, golden red orb slowly began to appear over the horizon, its brightness gradually but continually increasing in intensity. Its searing light cleansing all before it, revealing all the deceptions that the darkness held as true.

Once in the light the sylphs grew visibly stronger and swifter, leaving the wraiths, dimmed and slower, way behind. Luwsiy was lifted high above the raging but helpless wraiths and crossed over into the protection of the circle where they quickly descended to the observatory. Howling with anger the wraiths could do nothing but follow the descent while circling their now unobtainable prey.

Through the hole in the glass roof that Lilith had cleared, the sylphs gently lowered Luwsiy to the stone platform where she immediately collapsed, both laughing and sobbing, into Rebekah's arms.

The sylphs rose back up and flew to the east, toward the rising sun. The furious wraiths dispersed and fled from the growing light.

A single black-eyed raven settled itself among the chimney pots of Rose Mansion.

Chapter Twelve – Merdhin, Arch Druid of the Isles

Atop his tower, Bäliyl emitted a satisfied and arrogant laugh. He'd gone from furious despair to outright delight in a matter of seconds. Furious that the girl had been snatched from his grasp, to delight at the sight of his wayward daughter – present in this material world once more. The path before him had just become that much easier, that much clearer.

True, they had been clever in their capture of the girl and in the hiding of Lilith within a magik circle – his own magik circle, in a house he had not known for centuries but still, one that he knew well indeed – *oh, but how they have made a fateful mistake in the bringing of the two together.* No impurities must enter the circle for it to remain an effective barrier, in their haste to save the girl they had let impurities in with her – she was soiled and unclean.

If that ragged trickster thinks he is a worthy adversary for me, thought Bäliyl, *he is grievously mistaken.*

The girl's contamination will work like a planted seed, all Bäliyl had to do now was to wait for that seed to take root and grow – *it will fester and cause doubt, breed dissent and bring disarray to the order carefully crafted by that impudent fool of a vagrant huckster.* Using his raven as his eyes, he will watch and wait for the fruit from that tiny unclean seed to ripen. Then, using his agents as his hands, he will strike and harvest that fruit two fold. *And, oh – what a bountiful harvest it will be.*

He now laughed heartily, so pleased at their foolishness, so confident in his own ability and powers.

Luwsiy hugged her sister tightly and wished she would never now need to let her go. Buried in Rebekah's warm arms it was sometime before she became aware of her strange surroundings and of the people around her, it was then that she remembered her nakedness. She pressed herself even more tightly to her elder sister but was lost for words to say, her mind still a confusing jumble of thoughts and images that not only disturbed but delighted her also – she never dreamed that such things as sylphs existed.

She heard Rebekah's soft voice ask for clothes to cover her and Luwsiy forced herself to mouth in a horse whisper "Bathe... I must bathe." She felt dirty and grimed and a bath would cleanse her of the little man's foul touches. The more she dwelt on what he had done to her – what he was going to do to her – the more urgent her need to bathe became.

The old traveller from the inn agreed that she must bathe and find clothes but he seemed reluctant to let her leave the strange circle marked on the floor. Luwsiy wondered what it had to do with him, and why Rebekah and the others seemed to be treating this vagabond with such uncalled for respect... *and why are they dressed in these strange white robes?* He finally decided to let her go – but only with Lilith by her side, not Rebekah. He instructed Rebekah to place her amulet of Woden on the Tree about Luwsiy's neck and then, mumbling apparent nonsense, he seemed to bless it and her – but in a way she had never seen done before, marking some unknown sigil in the air with his fore-fingers. Luwsiy was still so dazed from her past experiences though that she could find no words to question what was happening to her now.

Lilith, carrying a white robe like the ones the other three were wearing, led Luwsiy out of the circle and down through the strange house to the even stranger baths below it; on the way she found a coarse flannel for her to scrub her soiled body with and a soft towel with which to dry herself.

Luwsiy found she was unable to be surprised at the Romannik baths and simply entered the warm pool with great relief. She rubbed and wiped her skin vigorously with the flannel and filled her mouth with the warm, mineral-tasting water, swilling it around and then spitting it out. Slowly she began to feel herself purged of the sins committed against her as she immersed herself totally in the warming, soothing waters.

She combed through her tangled hair with spread fingers as it floated out from her head. When she came back up to the surface to breath she felt almost fully revived and asked Lilith for some drinking water that she may quench her thirst and complete her restoration.

Lilith appeared hesitant to leave her alone so Luwsiy assured her, "I have the All-Father to protect me." She lifted the amulet around her neck and showed it to Lilith, as if to emphasize her words, "I will be perfectly safe till you return." Lilith consented and promised to come back as soon as possible.

Luwsiy rose from the waters once Lilith had gone and she began to dry herself off with the towel, first her hair, then her arms, legs, stomach and chest. As she hurriedly rubbed it across her back and neck she forgot the amulet that she wore and the brisk strokes broke the clasp and sent the delicate chain and relatively heavy pendant swinging into the pool beside her. She watched it slowly sink to the bottom. It was way out of reach so she would have to submerge herself in the water again to retrieve it.

Luwsiy stamped her naked foot with a hollow slap and cursed, "Damn it to all the hells and back again!" She proclaimed aloud.

Lilith was returning with the drinking water when she sensed that something was wrong. She was in the total darkness of the wine cellar, having left the lamp with Luwsiy, though her spirit eyes required no light to see, she was aware of the darkness becoming thicker, danker and so much colder.

"Luwsiy?" she shouted. "Are you all right?"

There was no reply as Lilith speeded her already fast walk to a run.

Under the water Luwsiy's ears were filled with a dull but loud hum as her fingers blindly fumbled at the bottom of the pool trying to locate the delicate chain; she had never been able to keep her eyes open under water but the temptation to look was getting frustratingly unbearable.

A plan suddenly occurred to her, she simply had to stand up again, once her head was out of the water she would be able to see exactly where the amulet was – put her foot on it and then bend down to pick it up – *no need to feel around, no fumbling... it was obvious.*

As she lifted her head and shoulders from the warm waters she received a sudden and freezing shock – the air had become incredibly cold... and it roared around her like a furious tornado. Luwsiy quickly wiped the water from her eyes and opened them to a scene of total chaos that filled her with a now familiar horror.

The small room was crowded with whirling wraiths that immediately took hold of the girl, despite her attempt to dive back under the water, and lifted her up from the pool as she uttered a surprised and desperate yell.

Lilith rushed headlong into the room before she could stop herself, personal fear and concern for Luwsiy mixed in the appalled expression that appeared on her face at the sight of Luwsiy's plight. But she too was grabbed and lifted from the ground, then almost instantly pushed back – not back through the way she came – but into the deep dark of the bigger pool room through the tepidarium. The wraiths holding Luwsiy promptly followed those with Lilith and the whole, strangely silent horde rushed through the old Romannik baths and on into the black corridors beyond.

Unseen by the captives and unnoticed by the captors a pitchy, slick hand rose from the still waters of the large black pool as the ghostly procession raced past overhead. It grasped slowly and futilely at Lilith as she passed, then sank unfulfilled back into the mire when they were gone.

They hurtled deep underground through tunnels not explored in centuries, a cold clammy hand held Luwsiy's mouth closed as she stared in disbelief at Lilith's glowing and constantly changing form ahead of her. The woman twisted and writhed herself into various animals and creatures in an attempt to escape the clutching wraiths, the constant flow of metamorphosis were all to no avail though. They held onto her phantasmic force and form with that of their own - they were her equal and opposite in every way, but there were more of them.

Suddenly they speeded up and out of the tunnels and straight into the trees of the forest far from the mansion. Low to the ground they flew, amidst the cool shadows beneath the forest canopy, they dodged trees with breathtaking skill and at awesome speeds. Luwsiy felt sure that she would be dashed to a pulp at any second.

Lilith's transformations seemed to be reaching a climax, the mutations formed and passed so rapidly that they became an ever struggling blur – when suddenly they ceased. The futility had become too evident to deny, Lilith returned to her elegant human form and with the dignity that that provided she allowed herself to be led as a captive – but held herself as if a fairy princess leading her entourage... back into the Old Forest.

Rebekah was becoming impatient, Lilith and her sister had been gone far too long for a simple bath and Arkturon's only explanation, that it was well known that the female of the species takes much longer at her toilet than the male, was simply not good enough. She could see that he too was now getting worried but still he refused to let another of their number leave the magik circle. Mikael paced up and down while Rebekah simply sat, nervously biting her nails – a habit she thought she had lost years ago.

It was then that she heard Luwsiy's voice and relief welled up inside her, Rebekah looked to the trap door and waited for her young sister's familiar face to appear there. Some minutes passed and still she heard the distant voice but no visible sign of Luwsiy came. Rebekah concentrated on the faint words she was hearing... Luwsiy was calling to her and trying to tell her something... *but why would she call me from downstairs?*

Realisation suddenly dawned on her; the voice was not coming from below the trap door but was in her head... it was inside her mind. Rebekah closed her eyes and covered her ears, concentrating on the words... then everything came clear.

She saw Luwsiy and Lilith being carried through the woods, she saw the sallow hand over Luwsiy's mouth but still she heard her silent screams and pleas. She heard them as if they were yelled directly into her ear.

Rebekah jumped up in shock – both Mikael and Arkturon stared at her in surprise, "Luwsiy... and Lilith!" she blurted. "They have been taken... taken by the wraiths!"

"What do you mean?" shouted Arkturon, "How do you know?"

"I have seen it... Luwsiy was calling to me – I saw them... the wraiths were carrying them... carrying them away!"

Mikael immediately leapt from the circle and hurried down through the trap door.

"No!" Arkturon yelled after him. "We must stay in the circle – we must wait!" But his shouts were in vain and Mikael was gone. Arkturon seemed confused by the failure of his plans and Rebekah was torn between following Mikael and staying within the circle.

"What do we do now?" she said panicking. "What can be done – they were flying so fast... you must call on the sylphs to get them back... you must!"

"Silence!" ordered Arkturon. "A constant and potentially endless to and fro from wraith to sylph will not help us! I must think... there is always an answer but I need silence to think – Mikael should never have left the circle, he should be here – it was a mistake ever to have let anyone leave its protection! Your sister may have been naked and dirty but at least she was safe!"

Rebekah fell dumb at his fast and furious words, sitting herself down she meekly resorted to silent weeping... for Luwsiy and for Lilith... but also for herself – she had failed her sister.

Mikael tore through the house toward the baths, he prayed that Rebekah was mistaken but he knew that she was not; he knew Bäliyl would now soon have the two things he needed most. When he got to the anteroom of the baths he saw the white cotton robe carefully laid aside, moving to the tepidarium he saw a wet towel discarded carelessly. Looking into the pool Mikael saw the refracted image of the shiny amulet that shrank and grew as the gentle waves passed over it. Slowly the waves calmed and the image became still.

Bäliyl could hardly contain his glee as he watched the course of the wraiths with the eyes of his speeding raven. He pushed and pestered his sable feathered beast to greater haste as it struggled and strained to keep up with the pale phantoms, for he desired to watch his captured prizes at all times. He wanted to keep them in his leering view, to ogle them, while delighting in his possession of them and revelling in the triumph of his victory – that came sooner than even he could have guessed.

Fools indeed, he thought, *if they ever thought they could outwit me!*

Rebekah was surprised to see that Mikael's hair was damp when he returned; she immediately saw too that he held her little amulet of Woden on the Tree in his hand. He simply said "They have gone... both of them." with his head bowed dejectedly.

"Damn it!" yelled Arkturon as he thumped the altar. "I have been a fool from the foul, bloody beginning."

A stranger's gentle voice promptly calmed them all. "Cursing will not help you." it said, causing them to turn to its originator. A figure stood by the eastern wall of the room, till then unnoticed. They all stared at the interloper... then as one they recognised the Kernunnos, the horned god. Though this time he had no horns and was dressed in a simple loose fitting shift of orange, he still held a large sword in one hand but in the other was now a staff, the head of which was carved with two entwined snakes.

Seeing him like this, Rebekah could now find it easier to believe that he was a personification of the gods Merkyuriy or Hermiyz as Arkturon had told her.

"We all have been fools," continued the god, "the blame does not lie with you alone."

"My Lord Matt, you honour us greatly by coming when not called?" Arkturon bowed, surprise clear in his face and voice.

"Approach me, Arkturon." the Kernunnos ordered.

The demoralised and humbled man obeyed silently.

"It is essential that Bäliyl does not succeed in bringing my dark brother's plans to fruition, he must be stopped... at any cost. A god can not have a physical presence on this earth, the consequences would be catastrophic for the whole of creation – evil as well as good – so that presence must be forged from human stock and a god-man created. This is what my dark brother Hlewid plans, to recreate himself as a human, and Bäliyl is the intermediary that will make it possible, Hlewid will use Luwsiy's body, possessed of Lilith's soul, to sire a child and then he will possess that child from the moment of its conception, he will become that child and have a tangible presence in the physical world.

Of course Bäliyl thinks that it is he that is in control, like all black magicians he thinks that it is he that uses the very powers that use him.

So as Hlewid has appointed Bäliyl to be his representative I too must appoint a representative to combat and destroy Bäliyl. That task is yours Arkturon, I appoint you. Take this staff as a symbol of your office." The god held out the staff he carried to a stunned Arkturon. "It is a long time since the need for a Merdhin has been called for in this sovereign island enclosure of Britannika – not since the days of High King Arthur, when the Saxanglish had been nought but savage raiders – but she needs one now to guide her in another time of need... to save her as before." The Kernunnos proffered the staff again. "Take it!" He ordered.

Arkturon hesitantly gripped the staff and the room was suddenly filled with a blinding, awe inspiring light that emanated from its length.

The light dimmed as quickly as it came and Rebekah saw that only Arkturon was now left holding the staff. The god-form Matt had vanished. As Arkturon turned toward them, both Rebekah and Mikael gasped their surprise – the years had fallen from him, he was now a young man again, appearing about thirty years old, strong and powerful, with rich auburn hair and bright shining eyes.

"You are the Merdhin now, Arkturon..." intoned the disembodied voice of Matt. "Use your new powers wisely, Arch Druid of the Isles."

Chapter Thirteen - Niniyen and the Forest Saveadj

Luwsiy shivered from the cold touch of the phantom hands on her naked, damp flesh. Their icy caresses chilled her heart and froze her temples, possessing her and immersing her in an unbearable aching that numbed her entire body. Her struggles became weaker and fewer as she drifted slowly but relentlessly toward a frigid unconsciousness where the pain of cold was everything. It was like her body was becoming solid ice and she swore that even her shivering had come to a dead stillness. Her mind was entombed in a frosty slab and now even that, she felt, would slow within its chill, gnawing cavity.

"She is silent!" Rebekah shouted with concern. "I can hear her pleas no longer!"

But neither Arkturon nor Mikael replied, they simply continued with their urgent dressing.

Straight after Arkturon's transformation he had told them to change back into their clothes and prepare to leave immediately. Resting his new staff against the altar he had lifted his robe over his head and thrown it aside, without a hint of embarrassment he walked past them totally naked and, grabbing his staff, over-coat and boots, descended through the trap door to find the rest of his clothes that he had left in the kitchen. Rebekah and Mikael at first just looked at each other and then went to retrieve their own clothes.

Once they were all dressed Arkturon instructed Mikael to prepare horses while he and Rebekah would collect all they needed for the journey. Youth had straightened the old man's bones and Rebekah noticed that he now stood at what seemed the same height as her, muscle had tightened too so that, though he was still of a broad build, he was of a much leaner and fitter condition than before. His face though, despite its new found beauty of youth, still held the wisdom of age – the paradoxical mix lending his glance a mesmeric and beguiling quality.

"We will not need much" he told Rebekah, "for we will travel through the Otherworld, food and water will be found on the way." His voice too was lighter and somehow more expressive than before.

"But we must take weapons." He added, handing her a dagger sheathed in its scabbard. It was a good twelve or thirteen inches long, almost a short sword.

"When we arrive at Bäliyl's castle there will be a fight, it cannot be avoided and it must be done." He moved closer to her, looking into Rebekah's frightened eyes he continued "I tell you this now so that you may prepare yourself, you must be brave and face these dangers, your sister's life depends on it... your own life may depend on it."

Her stomach churned at the thought of having to use the knife on living human flesh. Pulling it from the scabbard, an impossibly sharp and shiny blade was uncovered – long, thin and lethal. She quickly pushed it back in to its enveloping sheath.

"I will protect you as much as I can, but there may come a time when you will have to use it."

Rebekah hung the weapon from her belt then tied the thong at the bottom of the scabbard around her thigh. "How will we possibly catch them though," she said, "how can we get there before Bäliyl does anything to Luwsiy and Lilith?"

"Time has no meaning in the Otherworld," explained Arkturon, "that is why we travel by its paths. It may seem to take days there when in fact only hours have passed here in the material plane. Equally, if the gods do not smile on you and you enter without their consent, a few days there can become years or even decades in this plane."

Mikael had returned quietly and he suddenly interjected "But I thought you could only enter the Otherworld in dreams – like we did to get Lilith."

"That is the usual way yes," replied Arkturon, "but you can also enter it physically... if you know the ways for they are few and shrouded in mystery."

"So there must be a way in and out at Bäliyl's castle," said Mikael, "to allow us to come back into this world and deal with him."

"Yes, or at least there will be when he opens a gateway for Hlewid, the evil aspect of the Kernunnos, to come through during the ritual."

"During the ritual!" exclaimed Mikael. "Is that not cutting it a little fine? What if Lilith's spirit has been forced into Luwsiy's body before then – we will be too late!"

"I am afraid that is a chance we will have to take for it is the only chance we have got! Bäliyl should have to open a gateway in the initial stages of the ritual though, so he is free to call Hlewid as soon as he has Lilith's spirit in place of Luwsiy's. This will give us time to act before the Demon is even called."

"I hope you are right Arkturon, if I lose Lilith again... I would have nothing left to live for."

"If we do not save them we will be dead anyway, there is no other option." Arkturon's simple answer silenced the exchange.

Rebekah could only watch the two men with anxious eyes, unable to voice her own fears and concerns.

Rejoicing, Bäliyl withdrew his vision from the raven that struggled to keep up with the stream of wraiths that carried his prizes to him. They would be visible from his lofty tower at any moment and, in his triumphant giddiness, he did not want to miss the sight of their approach. In his eagerness to see with his own eyes though, he missed something vital. A black arrow pierced the raven's heart only a beat after the beast's eyes became its own again. Spinning, it fell, dead, to the forest floor.

Lilith saw that immense dark clouds had gathered above the castle as she was rapidly carried toward it. They were low and heavy, threatening an awesome storm that could break at any moment, with ominous rumblings and flashes that emanated from within the murky depths. On entering the bleak woods surrounding her father's evil home the wraiths had left the cover of the trees and now flew above the tops, sheltered from the sun by the thick, benighted cloud cover overhead.

She felt again the seducing power of her father's madness, the sensuality of controlling pure evil... but she could not be fooled by that now, she knew the truth. She had experienced true power... that of love... sensual, joyful – all encompassing love... the love of Mikael, of herself, and of life – any life.

As the craggy castle loomed before her, Lilith saw three indistinct figures at a large, ornate Gothic balcony fronting a tall arched window halfway up the loftiest tower. They were female figures and as laughter drifted toward her she recognised her sisters; their shouts and catcalls, taunting and venomous, greeted her with nothing but disdain. Rising above her seductive though demonic siblings Lilith and Luwsiy were taken to the topmost height of the huge pillar of stone. They reached the most elevated floor of that structure, open to the elements bar a huge domed roof that sat atop six phallic columns like a black crown of despair, and were thrown down within the boundaries of a magik circle that Lilith knew to lie there.

They fell at Bäliyl's feet, Lilith cruelly awake and aware, Luwsiy in a frozen, open-eyed stupor.

"Why does she not move..." said Lilith moving to inspect the young girl. "What have you done to her?"

"Nothing," laughed her father coolly. "She is under an enchanted sleep, that is all."

Lilith stared at him, not believing, her eyes full of hate.

"Do not fret my daughter, I must keep it safe for that is the body that you are to have... virginal and pure. When my work is done you can join us as before, sharing my bed with your sisters again, sharing in our love... fully this time."

"You lie! I know your plans for me – to kill me when the demon child is born and then to barter my soul for power over it! You are a fool father – all our souls will be lost if you let him breed his unholy child on me!"

Bäliyl was obviously annoyed at the depth of her knowledge and his words rapidly became furious. "You are the fool – you have just been trying to put off the inevitable... so you know some of my plans – all the more reason you should know how futile it is to fight against me! Your fate has been sealed, in payment for you I get control of the demon's progeny – you see, my soul is safe. It will obey my commands. It will not threaten me... I've learned a lot since I begat you!"

Bäliyl lifted a trap door in the centre of the circled floor and began to descend down the steps below it. "You cannot leave this circle," he said, "so do not bother to try."

As he was closing the trap door above him Lilith shouted venomously, "Better to rot in hell than have to spend another night sharing your foul bed!"

The trap door halted a moment, but was slammed shut with a fierce reverberating thwack.

Lilith turned to Luwsiy again and tended her, trying to lift the unconsciousness that bewitched the girl.

One arrow lighter, Corporal Villovürt – scouting ahead for the rest of the troop – nimbly descended from her vantage point high in a tall tree. It had given her a view of the ruined castle and its blighted environs, and it had revealed the dire plight of Luwsiy and Lilith to her. It was now obvious that something had gone dreadfully wrong with Arkturon's plan.

She was sure the old wizard will not have given up, but she was now beginning to realize that the fate of the two captives might solely hinge on her and her fellow Rangers' abilities to get into that castle unnoticed. It was not going to be easy, although the once great fortress was considerably downfallen and rambling; she sensed that it housed numerous occupants that would be unquestionably hostile. She'd seen black robed acolytes going back and forth, a patrol of goblins on their black-shuk mounts, and even a pair of massive trolls standing guard at a fallen gate-house. All were under the spell of the ancient vampire Bäliyl.

The gods alone know what else might be lurking amongst the unfathomed shadows of that palace of evil. A whole malefic army could be hiding behind its broken walls and keeps.

The corporal mounted the horse that waited for her; it was Elbroag's horse, for she had sent her own back – carrying her report – to the Ranger Station's stables from Rose Mansion before the sylphs had transported her out here. She spurred Elbroag's horse back to where the rest of the Rangers waited; the beast was a swift mount indeed and she had known how to coax it into continuing on its way home – it had brought her straight to the sorcerer's castle by the end of the morning. The horse had bonded with her easily and gratefully, she surmised that the horrible little dwarf had not been the kindliest of masters.

Arkturon led them deep into the wilds of the forest, far away from all roads and following a simple narrow track that was close to disappearing. They rode single file, he took the lead and Mikael brought up the rear, with two or three yards between each horse. Rebekah was concerned that they were travelling too fast in the thick forestation, though her horse sped along as if under the control of someone else, someone who could judge the quick turns and undulation's of the track far better than she ever could. Her horse simply followed Arkturon and his horse, as if it had travelled this route all its life and knew it by heart. It needed no direction from her so she stopped trying to give it; she simply watched her surroundings go by and pondered on what the Otherworld would be like... and at how they could possibly enter it.

The cape fixed at the shoulders of Arkturon's long coat billowed impressively behind him as he rode and Rebekah wondered if her cloak and hair were swirling to such dramatic effect behind her also. She guessed, of course, that they were – but then rebuked herself for foolish vanity.

Rebekah soon became aware that the landscape around them was changing, the track had disappeared altogether but the forest was thinning, they were now weaving through the tall trees to find a way forward. The forest here was airy and beautiful, great oaks and mighty beach trees surrounded them as they travelled through dell and dale for what seemed hours. As the noon sun reached its zenith Arkturon unexpectedly pulled to a stop and signalled for silence as the others came level with him.

They sat atop their mounts and surveyed the locale, dappled gold and green by the brilliant sunlight filtering through the sighing waves of leaves above them.

"What are we looking for?" whispered Mikael.

"There." said Arkturon. Rebekah and Mikael followed his pointing finger into the blaze of shimmering sunlight. At first they saw only the glare and movement of sun kissed leaves but slowly they became aware of a young woman, dancing to the slow rhythm of the sighs and motion of the wood with a naked, innocent abandon.

Her mesmerising laughter softly lifted itself from the gentle noises of the wood as she came nearer to them. On seeing her audience she stopped her dance and stared, surprised but alert, her golden hair bounced about her shoulders as she started her merry tones of youth anew. Suddenly her slender, shapely body turned and danced away from them, her grace and elegance drawing them after her.

"We must not lose sight of her" breathed Arkturon, "she will show us the way!"

As the three followed the girl she constantly turned to them and with joyful giggles beckoned them forward, prancing and cavorting she swiftly moved through the summery woods ahead of them. In a blink of the eye the woodland child had come upon a brilliant white stallion and had vaulted onto its back, as the beast reared and turned its shinning red eyes fell on them. The otherworldly horse leapt and careered into the trees away from them, the young woman's laughter peeling into the distance.

"Quickly, after them!" shouted Arkturon urging his horse forward at a tremendous speed, the other two fell in behind him again, as they thundered through the forest in pursuit of the supernatural steed and rider.

Rebekah caught glimpses of the girl and her dazzling mount beyond Arkturon as their path turned and twisted, she felt herself filled with an overpowering need – a yearning – to follow the rider and catch her. Rebekah's horse had almost caught Arkturon's when – stretching out to peer round his bulk – she saw the white stallion leap high into the air over a wide stream, it and the girl on its back disappeared into nothing before touching the ground on the opposite bank. Rebekah gasped in disbelief at the sudden and baffling loss she felt, but was not given time to question anything as Arkturon immediately shouted "Do not think – just leap the stream, do not hesitate or..."

With that last word he too disappeared with his leaping horse. Unable to stop or even find time to close her eyes Rebekah's horse followed, she was jolted violently back by the jump and then plunged into blackness – or at least it seemed like blackness after the bright sun drenched forest they had left behind. Her horse landed hard and now jolted her forward as it slowed and trotted toward Arkturon. As her eyes began to grow accustomed to the low light level Mikael's startled horse landed behind her own and nervously trotted to her side.

All three sat atop their sweating horses, looking about themselves. Ahead stood the naked girl, watching them and humming a delightful, though barely audible, tune to herself. Her body gently swayed to its rhythm. Her white horse was now nowhere to be seen.

"We have crossed over and are on the path of the Forest Saveadj, connecting our world to that of Kear Sidiy, the dwelling place of the Nemetona. Our guide is none other than Niniyen... this forest is her home."

At Arkturon's hushed words Rebekah remembered that it was the path that corresponded to the Tarot card named 'The World'. A card that depicted a naked girl that danced within an oval wreath of dark green foliage, outside of which were four creatures, one in each corner of the card; a serpent, an eagle, a lion and a fish. The figure was depicted standing on the world while above her head had been a strange spiralling pattern. The figure, it seemed, was Niniyen - the girl standing before them. Rebekah wondered how much more of the imagery contained in the card would be explained in the coming journey.

Rebekah had no time to reflect further though for the girl had started her dance again and was moving away from them. They urged their mounts after her, into a strange and darkly unreal forest, its beauty too dreadful to contemplate. They were being led through maze like paths that formed in the dense lush growth around them, paths that slowly became tunnels as the alien trees linked branches above their heads and the weight of foliage, flowers and fruit grew so great as to bend the boughs and shoots down toward them. Varied fruit, so ripe and luscious, flowers so bright and colourful – compared to the dark green of leaf, stem and the lethally long, ever present thorns – that Rebekah became convinced that the dull hazy light surrounding them must emanate from them, for there seemed to be no other source and no single direction to the lustre all about.

The forest was full of noise, not just the singing laughter of the girl and the trample of their horses hooves, but the growl, roar, spit, hiss and caw of beast and bird unseen; the bustle and rustle of leaves and undergrowth in constant motion being the only visible evidence for the whereabouts of these raucous creatures.

Rebekah scrutinised the growth on either side of her, convinced that at any moment a huge, wild and ravenous animal would leap out from its cover and savage one of their number – dragging its prey back into the forest before anyone could act... but this never happened. The beasts remained largely invisible with only an odd sighting of the bright colours of weirdly beautiful birds flitting about the branches above their heads; or the shining eyes and glistening, snuffling snouts of small, curious mammals poking from the undergrowth.

The companion's route turned back and forth for hours before the threatening noises ceased and the light began to take on a definite direction. The forest opened up slightly and granted them a view down into a wonderful valley that filled all their hearts with awe. They were confronted with a truly preposterous scene. The valley was lit by a great shining ball of orange red flame that hung high above their heads and illuminated beyond it the craggy ceiling of an immense cave that stretched into the distance and curved down to meet the far reaches of the forest in which they stood. Rebekah could see no visible means of holding the ball there; it simply stayed – like the sun in the sky but with no sky – suspended in the centre of a huge cavern tens of miles across... *at least!*

Below them, in the valley, the forest changed character considerably and formed a huge circular maze, its twisting paths leading to a spectacular castle that spiralled up toward the subterranean sun with towers of pearl and ramparts of ivory that glowed like a magical sea shell turned inside out.

"Behold..." said Arkturon, "Kear Sidiy... the Spiral Castle, abode of Ariyanrhod the Nemetona - the Lady of the Sacred Groves."

They longed to stay and just stare at the wonderful sight before them, but Arkturon urged them on after the girl who was already descending along a path into the valley. It took them another hour to reach the valley floor, the forest growing less wild and more ordered the lower they ventured until it became the ornate garden of the huge maze with its manicured lawns, its shaped and trimmed hedges and regimental trees.

The pattern of the maze was not designed to be a puzzle; it had one wide route that circled backward and forward around the castle, leading them in a dance like procession after the girl. She gambolled and ran at impossible speeds, causing them to hurry their horses after her, their thunderous galloping never bringing them closer to her no matter how hard they pushed their mounts. The dancing girl led them close to the castle numerous times, only to lead them away again as they circled its splendid heights and it was not until they had almost returned to their point of entry that they veered directly for the castle again and gained the centre of the maze. Here they spiralled up a steep mound on which the castle perched, following a walled path that gradually merged with the structure of the beautifully pale battlements and towers until they reached a large high entrance that stood beckoningly open. The three riders pulled to a stop. The girl had disappeared inside.

With close proximity they saw that the sensual curves of the portal before them mirrored the curving pattern of the castle as a whole, not an angle or a straight line was in sight and the only points were probably those at the top of the winding towers. The sun above them bathed everything in a peach like pink, adding to the voluptuous feel of the place, and a warm but fresh – mild but insistent breeze flirted all around them carrying a subtly sweet, musky aroma.

"Enter slowly and with dignity." whispered Arkturon as he spurred his horse through. The others followed. Once all three had passed its threshold the portal walls closed in on themselves with a fluid, smooth motion like the lips of a mouth.

The nothingness was taking on a barely perceptible form.

Feeling and warmth could now be distinguished.

The cold numbness reduced as her aching mind gradually thawed and memories returned.

Luwsiy became self-aware once more as her skin seemed to be caressed and massaged by a continuous pressure and movement, soft and warm, all over her body at any one instant. A gentle coaxing voice urged her to consciousness, lifting the dullness from her head and shifting the dark layers of gauze that seemed to obscure her view.

As sight and light were restored Luwsiy's blurry vision perceived bright gossamer mists floating and eddying around the curves and hollows of her body and limbs – once her head and eyes cleared though she realised that the mists must simply have been the diaphanous material of Lilith's sleeve as it passed before her eyes on waking.

Luwsiy found herself laid with her head and shoulders on Lilith's lap, being caressed by her gentle hands and soothed by a mesmerising tune that she hummed, almost purring, to her.

Luwsiy saw her surroundings, the stone floor, the magik circle... she did not ask where she was, knowing the answer could only be bad... she simply let her tears flow and tightly clung to Lilith's hand, pushing herself closer to her warmth.

Chapter Fourteen - The Faery Court at the Spiral Castle

As the portal closed behind them, the forecourt in which they stood was rapidly crowded by a large number of fey elfin-looking people; happy gleaming faces with cascading hair all the shades of gold, brown and red, their lean graceful bodies were garbed in diaphanous colours of leaf and earth.

"These are the faery-folk of Ariyanrhod's court," explained Arkturon, "they are the elemental spirits of earth and vegetation." He laughed as the throng rushed forward, with sable eyes wide and slim arms welcoming, lifting the visitors gently from their mounts and carrying them to the open doors of the castle proper. The horses were led off to the side, to the stables Rebekah assumed; she was surprised by the nature of their welcome and found herself laughing aloud as these beautiful people transported her and the others inside.

Pearl-like walls seemed to glow from the sunlight outside and intricate carvings decorated the spectacular interior with enchanting sculptures, minute in their detail, awesome in their scale, towering above them. Giant sensual figures and huge, scaly snaggle-dragons supported the structure of the castle in place of columns and buttresses, the translucent membrane-like walls casting pale hues and tinted shadows all about them.

Rebekah stared, open mouthed, as they passed through various immense chambers before coming to what appeared to be a throne room. In place of a throne though – at the centre of a large silver-rimmed, wheel-like dais – was a curved and deeply cushioned chaise longue, ebony carved and scarlet draped. Regally reclining on this long low seat was Ariyanrhod, dressed in a slight white shift that covered only one breast and only barely managed to cover the top of her sensual thighs. Sitting at her feet was the golden haired girl that they had followed there.

The faery crowd set the three mortal's down before the goddess, then dispersed in all directions through the many ornate doorways leading from the room.

Arkturon bowed low to the image of love incarnate, when Mikael copied his action Rebekah attempted a curtsey, not sure if she too should have bowed.

"Come. Sit before me." Ariyanrhod's soft lilting voice beckoned them forward as she indicated the carpeted dais around her; it was amply covered with cushions, bolsters and pillows. "Please make yourselves comfortable... remove your mantles," she said, "it is very warm" – and warm it was, a musky warmth strengthened by a heady scent.

Without hesitation Arkturon divested himself of his long coat and then settled among the cushions till comfortable, Mikael and Rebekah too removed their over garments and reclined on the dais, but much more self-consciously, the disconcerting proximity of two nude – or partially nude – figures having an unsettling effect on them, especially in such a situation of apparent familiarity.

"I see your friends suffer from the usual mortal prudishness Merdhin," the Nemetona chuckled, "a pity, for two with such handsome features." Her infectious mirth made them both feel more at ease and Rebekah found herself wondering why she should consider the naked human form, a thing of beauty, to be shameful or in some way wicked. It is the mind or heart of the perceiver that is either wicked or shamed, she realised, not the thing that is being perceived.

"You will eat and rest while in my charge," the goddess continued as she clapped her slender hands together, "you will enjoy the pleasures of my palace and sleep, so you may leave its care heartened and refreshed... ready for the trials that lay ahead."

A number of faeries bustled into the room, laden with food and drink, and then joined them on the cushions, joyfully distributing their loads between the guests. Rebekah sampled the fare and was astonished by the delightfully lush fruits and the deliciously mild wine that seemed to heighten her senses and sharpen her mind rather than dull and intoxicate them. As she ate and drank a faery girl sat behind her and massaged her shoulders, neck and back while an equally attractive male removed her boots and gently kneaded her uncomplaining feet. As the three sapiens were cosseted and cherished no one talked – all enjoyed the food, warmth and friendship in companionable silence.

Ariyanrhod watched over their recreation with gladness of heart and when she saw that they had had their fill of her plentiful sustenance she instructed her minions to escort the mortal's to their individual apartments for solace and sleep. *Let them forget their troubles and take comfort in my citadel of love for one night – free from guilt, stigma, and the possible consequences of an earthly coupling. Let them experience the making of love for the sheer joy of sharing pleasure.*

Rebekah was led to her room by the two faeries who had massaged her during the meal, each extending a hand to take hold of her's. They were very similar, the male and female, both slender, both graceful and beauteous, though the male faery was broader with finely sculptured muscle and his partner softer and more sensuously curved. Both were sparsely dressed, appropriately so for the warmth of the castle, his hair was long and tousled, hers the same but with braids running through it – tiny ribbons tied at their ends.

Rebekah guessed that they were brother and sister and when asked they confirmed saying all the faeries serving the Nemetona were siblings and she their mother. A mother not through any act of birth though, she created them in her own image. The faery woman was named Juwniper, the man Rowan.

They finally led Rebekah through a doorway into a room that was furnished simply and comfortably, in fact it was furnished for nothing but comfort for its large round bed proved to be deep and soft and was bestowed with many pillows and bolsters. She was ushered toward it and laid upon the silken sheets – caressing, gentle hands undressed her until she was naked, unashamed and unperturbed before them. The faeries then undressed themselves revealing smooth silken skin that sported no body hair whatsoever, both the male and the female. They began carefully to massage her body, first into a restful stupor but then they revitalised her again with more ardent touches and kisses. They bathed her in lips and tongue, moist exploring that impassioned her greatly – dallying at her neck, breasts, stomach and even her groin... especially her groin – teasing licks and sups that sent her into rapturous oblivion – praying that they would never stop.

Juwniper left the male to busy himself between Rebekah's legs while she rose to her mouth, kissing her and seeking out her tongue in a gentle to and fro of slippery, succulent play. She squeezed and fondled Rebekah's breasts, laughing as she caressed them and then began to suckle the increasingly pronounced and inviting nipples.

The teasing movements of Rowan's tongue had stopped and Rebekah felt her rump being lifted up slightly to rest on his cushioning thighs. She felt the touch of something else between her legs, dipping into the moisture there. At first she thought it was his finger or thumb... *but no, it's too big to be either of them!*

She then gasped in wonder as the fat, hard and seemingly never-ending penis slid into her tight but wetted vagina – an instant of discomfort was rapidly replaced as the stretching and delightful rubbing friction it caused sent pure sensual ecstasy through her vitals. He repeatedly pushed in and out of her with a gentle roughness that made her sigh and moan. She pushed her hips to meet him in eager little convulsions and wrapped her legs about him – inviting him deeper as she yearned for the totally new sensations she was experiencing – sensations that became increasingly more intense the longer he worked – causing her to lose mastery of her cries – they came loud and straight from her soul in an uncontrollable flow – only abating when she felt her very life and being suddenly pour from her down between her legs – surrendering itself to the sweet death of trembling release. As the girl worked on her nipples and he on her sex she felt both amazement and fear as her groin was suddenly deluged with a copious explosion of wet – as she felt him spurt with a tremendous force into her writhing and ecstatic body.

After her climax Rebekah, her mouth gawping with the shock of it, lay flat out – unable to move. Juwniper cradled her while Rowan kissed and licked her tender and bloodied vulva.

The mortal girl dozed and drifted on their love, a soft delightful pillow that eased her through the night, never tiring and always gentle, loving, playful.

After hours that seemed like days of bliss, Ariyanrhod herself came to Rebekah and held her... spoke to her – told her that this beautiful dream would stay with her for the rest of her life, so she may never fear love, nor shy away from it... that she would never deny it. "Grab whatever chances at love there are and cherish them." The goddess then tempered this advice though, she warned against sinking into a hedonistic mire where the pursuit of sex was all. "Lust without love is nothing but debasing, a manipulation of others to satisfy oneself; it leads only to distrust, deceit, hate and hurt."

"Love," the Nemetona continued, "love anyone and everyone. That is the doctrine I and my children must exist by. We are Love. We are immortal and of the spirit. In your world love can mean many things; your physical, sexual love should only be given to a select few, you must choose them carefully and be totally sure.... trust is everything. Here though, in my realm, all is Love, Love is everything... so dream awhile longer."

Rebekah slept a deep long sleep and dreamed of love.

Ariyanrhod visited each of the mortal's that night, with comfort and encouragement for a perishable body and enduring psyche. Mikael's reverie was aided by a delightful faery girl and her soothing body pulled away as the Nemetona came and lay beside him. She dispelled the lingering guilt he was feeling over this dalliance with pleasure while Lilith was in peril, and assured him that he will be re-united with her, to love forever. "In fact" she insisted, "it is the reality of that overwhelming love that will ensure her return to you."

Arkturon had forsaken physical love long ago – grown out of it, as he would put it. But that is not to say that he had not enjoyed it when he was younger, for he had. After his last partner had died though, he lost the inclination... his heart had hardened under a protective shell that he himself had placed there. The loss of a love is a very hard thing to bear and it can make the idea of loving again quite inconceivable. His long age had meant that he had loved a number of times through his life, but watching a loved one grow old and die is hard enough when it is just the once, more than that and it becomes truly unbearable. When that last love died, he gave up the pretence of his own youth and allowed himself to grow old slowly and looked for love no more. Despite the fact that he now had the means to prolong another's life, in the vampirism that his last love had gifted him. They had lived together over a hundred years before her death, but that length of time had made the loosing of her all the more harder.

Now though... now that his body had unexpectedly found youth again, that his mind has been sharpened and focused anew... as he now finds himself abed with a vision of young beauty, and with the charms of the girl who had led them through the forest now astride him... he found his thoughts turning to love once more.

He knew this waking dream before him, Niniyen, was unobtainable, she was a creature of fancy, a demigoddess of worldly sensuality – she could soothe and entertain him awhile, but not forever. She had the dreams and fantasies of a world to serve; she could never belong to one... for she belonged to all.

When the goddess of Love joined them she knew of Arkturon's thoughts, of his re-awakening to his emotions, and she was pleased – she hated to see anyone turn their back on passionate desire, turn from Love.

"Now that you are young again Arkturon," she said, "seek the Love of youth, find a young woman to share your newly extended life – to share in your ardour, your wisdom and your understanding. Fate will always do its duty to Love, but it is up to you to seize the chances it puts there before you – it *has* put there before you... do not deny Fate again."

The next morning the three stood in the courtyard, waiting for their horses, wondering how the others had each spent their night. Rebekah was still astonished by the events that had taken place, her father had told her about sex some years before – at least about the basic mechanics anyway – in an embarrassed and somewhat embarrassing manner after her first monthly blood flow. He had simply spoken of it as the procedure of getting with child, he had never mentioned the feelings and sensations it could produce – the ecstasy it instigated. She realised this was probably to prevent him from becoming a very premature grandparent – *but still he could have hinted at it!*

But no, she thought, *knowing of such joy then would have only led me into trouble.*

She smiled at this thought as some faeries led their horses to them, the sapiens mounted the animals. Mute waves saw them off as they rode quietly out through the castle gate, a subdued air of sadly tinged happiness following them.

None of the three had breakfasted, none feeling hungry. In fact hunger had not bothered them since they had entered the Otherworld, nor thirst Rebekah realised, and she had not felt the need to pass water or defecate either. She wondered if their bodies were in some sort of stupor or stasis, not ageing or deteriorating while they were in these blessed lands. The food and wine they had consumed before retiring to bed had been light and had not over filled their stomachs. It seemed such meals were simply for the rousing of the taste buds and a stimulant for the mind. Providing no nutrition for none was needed – serving only to fortify the soul and spirit, not the body.

Leaving the Spiral Castle they saw the demigoddess Niniyen waiting for them, she danced and led them away from its walls, led them back through the maze to its edges then skirted round its outlying perimeter to a point far from where they had originally entered the realm the day before. There, a large stone archway stood in an immaculately manicured garden, at the end of a long winding lawn. Within the archway were two massive oaken doors that barred their way.

"This," said Niniyen, "is the Gate of Uffren – the Cold Place."

The doors opened silently inward, revealing a dark expanse that the light, from the cavern bound sun above and behind them, could not penetrate.

Arkturon nudged his horse forward into the darkness. Somewhat hesitantly, Rebekah and Mikael followed.

Lilith and Luwsiy were huddled together when Bäliyl returned, and he was not alone, his other daughters accompanied him. A trio of smarming spiteful witches that clutched and stroked at him and his ego.

Luwsiy shied away and trembled visibly as they came – floating rather than climbing – up through the trap door. She shrank from them as far back onto Lilith as she could. Bäliyl's strong physical presence was backed up terrifyingly by an invading psychological probe that entered her mind as soon as his callous, shadowed eyes fell on her. He was tall, broad and muscular. His femininely long black hair, greying at the temples, swept back from an angular, cruel face that sported a dark elegantly trimmed beard and moustache. He was dressed in nothing but a tight pair of black breeches, with a broad belt and high boots that came almost to his knees. His broad, tan chest was covered in a fine coating of dark hair peppered with grey and his bulging arms had strange archaic letters tattooed about them. Luwsiy saw also that his long sinewy fingers, that held an evil looking staff, had almost woman-like nails, long and manicured but each filed to a sharp point.

"I see your young friend has awoken." he said to Lilith with a cold laugh. His three evil daughters laughed with him, the sound was terrible and held not even a hint of mirth or joy. The three were strikingly similar and Luwsiy wondered if they could be triplets; all had long, coal black hair – even darker than Lilith's – and tall though voluptuous figures with sallow skin and pitchy eyes that seemed bottomless pits with distant fires burning and into which all light was drawn and lost forever. Their lips and nails were painted the deepest red and their long, body hugging gowns were made from the richest velvet brocade that trailed the ground; one was blood red, one black and the other was a deep dark mauve.

Their father spoke again. "Daughters – take this girl and prepare her, her virginity must be proven then she must be cleansed." On seeing Luwsiy desperately hold onto Lilith he laughed again, loud and with his mouth gaping. "She cannot help you, child – she is one of us!"

Luwsiy glimpsed two long and very sharp canine teeth as he guffawed at her and it was only then that she realised how truly desperate her predicament actually was – she had to go with these three witches quietly – it would only make things harder for them both if she did not. The only saving hold she now had to cling onto before falling into despair was that she must trust in what Lilith had told her – that Arkturon and his magik would save them from this sorcerous vampire – it dawned on her only then that the strange old man was their one and only hope.

"Take care of the pure little thing..." said Bäliyl in a condescending tone, as his offspring lifted Luwsiy from Lilith's arms, "but be thorough – there can be no mistakes this time."

Thoroughly cowed, the girl seemed resigned to her fate as she was led down through the trap door. Once she was gone Bäliyl turned to Lilith and said "Now, my youngest... my ghost child. Oh, I have long lusted for you – but could never fully possess you, not if my plans were to work. But now you have made things easy for me – not only have you led me to a virgin body suitable for the ritual, you have given me a chance to have you – to use you before putting you in that girl's sweet innocent shell." Having approached her during his arrogant diatribe he suddenly reached out and grabbed at her hand violently.

She changed instantly to insubstantial spirit and pulled from him, leaving nothing but air in his grip, and transformed into a huge black cat that threatened with teeth and claw as she growled menacingly into his unconcerned gaze.

Bäliyl simply laughed "You foolish child – I have spent the whole of my long life controlling spirits, elementals and even the foulest of demons. What makes you think that you are so different?"

He pointed his staff at her and a piercing pain erupted in her core, the illusion of the cat disappeared as she concentrated her energies on defending against the pain. She writhed unable to fight it – lifted by its power into the air.

Bäliyl pulled up his staff and she collapsed to the floor exhausted, her spirit reshaped into the mould imprinted on it by life, the shape requiring least effort and concentration, her shape... now human and naked.

Approaching her again he laid down his staff and released his growing penis from the tight crotch of his quickly unbuttoned breeches. He stood over her and with hands on hips he said "Come my daughter, bring those sweet lips to your creator... kiss the wand that begat you."

The cold fist of his penetrating mind tightened around her core and she obeyed, unable to resist the power of his will. Lightly she touched her lips to the tip of his phallus, as his erection increased his foreskin pulled back onto his shaft revealing the engorged glans.

"Yes," he said eagerly, "suckle on the wand of your making... suck it." His softly spoken words were replete with desire, but they did nothing to mask the underlying threat and hate that infused them. Lilith knew that it would be useless to resist, he did not need his staff to inflict pain – a mere wave of his hand, or even a glance of his evil eye, could burn her soul inside out if he so chose. She determined that she would do anything that he asks – he sought to degrade her, but she would show no emotion while doing it – she would not give him the satisfaction of showing disgust, or shame or fear. She would make her actions mechanical and cold.

She stared up into his face and, with both hands, opened wide the buttoned fly at his crotch, she teased free his scrotum and gently kneaded his balls while she took his penis full into her mouth and sucked him. Her tongue, lips and teeth played his cock till he began to groan and pant, till his energies were concentrated on his own gratification rather than her degradation. She stroked his shaft with finger tips till his domineering stance gave in and gently he held her head with a soft cry of, "Gods, yes!"

He moaned, "yes... yes," stroking her hair. As he rapidly approached his release he whimpered like a boy and closed his eyes. She stopped her working of him and his whole body trembled with anticipation.

"Please... please..." he pleaded as he was about come – and then looked down into her face... her eyes... so cold and full of hate... so emotionless and mocking of his lust, his weaknesses... and his defencelessness at that moment. She suddenly didn't care that he could inflict untold pain on her – for, in that moment, she could inflict pain on him – and she did.

Bäliyl felt her grip tighten painfully, her teeth pressing into his engorged shaft – fast, hard and sharp.

But, grasping her by the hair he invaded her mind instantly and burned her – searing her very being. "YOU FUCKING BITCH!!!" his afflictive vitriol exploded in her mind.

Lilith released him immediately – screaming, with her hands pulled to her head and heart. Her scream reverberated around the room and out around the open tower top.

She did not know how long it was before the pain stopped but when it did she was on all fours, shaking and weak. Bäliyl was behind her now and he pushed her head to the floor, pressing her face to its cold hard surface. He knelt behind her raised rump. "You are mine, you BITCH... your cunt is MINE – I own YOU!" He forced his penis into her phantasmic form again "I'll use you whenever I WANT TO!" With each thrust he screamed his words at her.

He knew this phantom could not feel the physical pain of his rape so he forced the pain on her psyche with each repeated shout of "You FUCKING BITCH!"

She did not scream again, she would not give him the satisfaction. She took all that he had to give silently, and allowed pure hate to fester within herself.

As he approached orgasm his screamed profanity was burned into her soul like a branding iron. "Damned CUNT!" he finally yelled hoarsely as his seed spurted into her.

After catching his breath he pulled his fat tool from her and, standing up straight, looked down upon his victim. She did not move. Smirking cruelly, he pushed her over with his booted foot. She sprawled but then curled herself up into a foetal ball, apparently defeated.

"A slave to my cock... that is all you are." He said as he left her.

Once the trap door was closed behind him, she stood up and, with legs apart, she manipulated her sex and expelled his semen – falling, it splattered onto the stone floor... Lilith prayed to her dark demonic mother that his life's blood would be spilt so easily.

Chapter Fifteen - The Priestess and the Cold Place

On passing through the portal they entered a pitch-black place both rocky and wet, their horses' hooves echoing dankly in the cool air. A breeze pushed into their faces and Arkturon led them into it, the twin-serpent crown of his staff suddenly flaring and lighting the tunnel around them and the way ahead with a continuous orange glow. They travelled in cautious single file on a winding path of smooth worn stone, flanked by rough hewn walls that were capped by an invisible and dripping ceiling that was lost in the darkness high above their heads.

Their course slowly began to incline downwards as the tunnel widened around them. Soon the well worn subterranean path they trod was surrounded by long, dripping stalagmites and stalactites, many of which had met and joined together creating bars that fenced them in on either side. The tunnel walls had receded into darkness on either side and they now travelled through a frigid stony woodland of sorts, that compacted around them as they slowly, but noisily trotted through. Some hours into this cold caged track-way they reached a fork in the worn stone path that they had been following. Arkturon paused there and seemed to ponder the two opposing routes. The constant icy breeze had increased in intensity; it carried their wispy breaths away and caused strange haunting howls to ululate through the calciferous forest all about. And now that their horses' hooves were silenced, they also heard the percussive accompaniment of the persistent drips and dabs from the ever-present falling drops of water from the invisible ceiling above. After a minute or so of deliberation the Merdhin came to a decision. He urged his horse down the right-hand path and Rebekah, with Mikael behind, followed him.

Eventually the stalagmites and stalactites fused into continuous limestone walls once more and the chill air began to rush at them. They became aware of a faint light ahead, a cool blue-white light that intensified as they approached. Arkturon darkened his staff as they entered a shinning grotto of sparkling crystal and stone, with winds that buffeted about and many tunnels leading from it. The light emanated from a face though, a beautiful serene face – that contemplated them with dark well-like eyes. The face belonged to the slender form of a young woman dressed in white and blue robes. She was sitting upon a large square stone and, behind her; she was flanked by two smooth columns, one dark – one light, with a peach coloured veil stretched between them. On her lap a large book lay open, her hands resting upon it, and above her a silver orb was supported by a horned head-dress that she wore upon her sable locks.

Scattered about the floor at her feet were narcissus stems and buds, as if they had just fallen there.

The three stilled their horses before her in the centre of the grotto where, like in the eye of a storm, no breeze could be felt, their breath and that of their horses was expelled in chill clouds of freezing vapour.

Arkturon bowed his head before the demigoddess and the others followed suit. "Greetings Priestess Kreruwiy," he intoned. "Oh bride of night, personification of the bright full moon in all its beauty and majesty, aid us on our journey to your mater's sister's realm. Give us guidance and save us from the attentions of your dread and terrible mother, Keridwen."

The pale young woman addressed them in an unnaturally strong and resonant voice that surprised them all. "The forces of good are with you Merdhin, and I am obliged to help you, so help you I will. My servant will lead you to the bright meadows of Kear Widiyr, keeping you from the dark domain of the Koventiyna Inversus. The forces of evil know nothing of your presence here yet, as long as that remains so, you have a chance." She raised her right hand, upturned it and indicated the direction that they had just come from.

They looked to where she pointed and slowly became aware of the approaching sound of a single horse's hooves.

Rebekah gasped as the unicorn entered the grotto, it trotted to Kreruwiy and rested its large head on the book at her lap. The demigoddess stroked its neck once then it reared from her and moved behind the veil between the two columns. Violently it pierced the silken material with its horn and ripped it asunder – causing a single, piercing scream to escape from Kreruwiy's lips. A scream of joy and pain entwined.

Their horses moved skittishly as the unicorn then suddenly pranced for the far side of the grotto and galloped away from them down one of the far dark tunnels. Arkturon called his companions on after it, with a wave of his staff that flared orange again he rode out of the grotto in pursuit.

They followed the unicorn through miles of stony tunnel till the walls eventually lost their cold solidity and transformed first to the brittleness of disintegrated rock and earth, then to the moist softness of damp clay and soil. Dirt and decomposed organic matter started to fall in clumps about them as they urgently rushed through the narrowing and increasingly claustrophobic tunnel; water dripped and cascaded down the walls, roots, both pale and delicate and dark and mighty, pushed through at them from the ceiling, sides and floor. They struggled through desperately, Rebekah and Mikael cutting at the clinging tendrils with knife and sword, Arkturon burning them with his staff, the worm like shoots shrinking away from its incinerating light.

The unicorn seemed unaffected by the obstacles that slowed them down and it suddenly became obscured ahead of them. Arkturon forced his mount after the beast, crouching to its back as the passage way became smaller around him and he was plunged into darkness. The light from his staff was now totally blocked by the amount of falling debris and water that covered him, urging his panicking horse through the tightening burrow he was suddenly enveloped in mud and slime. Closing his eyes and holding his breath he kicked his horse on to one last effort that achieved his sudden release to open air and out of the tunnel. Wiping his eyes free of dirt the brightness glared him; looking back he saw the head of Rebekah's horse slowly pushing through a wall of sliding mud, so he quickly pulled up his horse and turned it. Grabbing the reins of the horse following he helped it through, giving the blinded animal a direction to push in. Once it too tasted the fresh clean air though it needed no more impetus and was through in seconds, Rebekah clinging desperately to its back – choking and gasping at every breath as the mouth of the tunnel collapsed behind her.

"Mikael!" Rebekah managed to scream at the hollow that had suddenly appeared in the wall of sliding mud. She was shivering uncontrollably as the cold air froze her sodden and clinging clothes and tears ran down her muddied face. Arkturon dismounted and charged into the disappearing tunnel mouth, driving his way back through the mud slide with brute force alone.

Petrified, Rebekah stared at the place at which he had disappeared, not daring to take her watering eyes away in case she missed any sign of the two men struggling to come back through. She carefully dismounted. The hollow that the cave-in had made was slowly disappearing as the constant flow of mud wore all trace of its existence away. She longed to look at her surroundings to see where she was and assess her situation but she dare not lose the place Arkturon had run into. She was standing in a huge and growing pool of mud and water that was getting deeper as the slipping sides of the steep hill ran down at her. The flow was beginning to slow though, but still she wondered where all the water had come from, the sky was relatively clear and the air dry, she could only assume that a massive and sudden downpour had just preceded their emergence from the tunnel, and had then ceased as quickly as it had started. The flow before her had almost stopped now and the pool that had collected in the ditch where she stood stopped rising, having reached up to her knees. The ditch seemed to totally surround a large hill... the hill she had just come from – Rebekah cursed herself with frustration – she had looked away from the spot of her exit and now she was unsure of its exact location among the uniformity of slick mud. Common sense told her that she had not moved so it was still directly in front of her but she could not stop the irrational fear that she had somehow lost it... and therefore had lost both Arkturon and Mikael.

The so recently still wall of mud moved suddenly – or at least a part of it did. Something pushed from it with a sucking squelch... *just a clump of dirt falling away... No! A hand punching through... a hand!*

Slipping and stumbling Rebekah ran to it and grabbed at its smeared warmth, its reassurance. She pulled – desperately tugging at it, her very life depending on it. If she were left alone... alone here... she would truly die. An arm encased in clay emerged... followed by a shoulder and head, Arkturon's features were grimed almost beyond recognition – weakly he drew in a gasp of air as Rebekah put her arms about him and pulled him to her. He seemed half dead and so heavy as she desperately shouted at him to keep moving forward – their motion was causing another landslide about them and her grip slipped from his neck – she fell at his feet as he tumbled over her with Mikael on his shoulder. She feared she would drown or be buried alive – the awful realisation that she was in danger of both, forced her to her knees and she crawled on all fours away from the falling hill face. She then scrambled back over to Mikael and pulled him from Arkturon's back – Arkturon was face down in the quagmire that had collected and she pulled at his clothes to turn him over – then to sit him up and get his face out of the water. Slowly she achieved it and she collapsed exhausted on top of him, shouting his name with the little strength she had left. He stirred and lifted her "Get Mikael out of the water..." he said "quickly..." He raised himself to help her and, stumbling and slipping, they slowly lifted the unconscious Mikael onto the back of her horse.

Rebekah was shocked that she had not even given a thought to Mikael but had simply been concerned for Arkturon... this puzzled her and filled her with a guilty turmoil.

"We must get away from here!" said Arkturon, urgently looking back at the muddy hill face – there was fear in his stern expression. Rebekah glanced back to where he looked and was horrified to see a number of malformed and hideous hands and arms reaching from the liquefied clay and grabbing blindly into the air. She could only have been inches away from their grasp when she had rushed to aid Arkturon... and when she had fallen!

Arkturon led the two horses left to them quickly away, the beasts needed no encouragement to distance themselves from that place and neither did Rebekah, as she saw more of one of the strange creatures that pushed out from the watery mud. It was like a weird fish-man, pushing on the surface of the sodden hillside but seemingly unable to enter the air. She saw the back of its bald human-like head, with tattered and pointed ears, followed by a bony neck, a finned back and a giant fish like tail as it arched out of, and then back into, the slippery and muddy bank.

"What are they?" Rebekah shouted with disgust. "...mermen?"

With an emphatic shake of his head all Arkturon could say was "No!"

They circled the hill, looking for a place that they could rise out of the ditch that surrounded it. About half a circuit round from the tunnel entrance and its strange creatures, the ditch floor rose up at a slight incline and they clambered out. Once on the outside rim they paused to catch their breath and rest. Arkturon tried to revive Mikael, while Rebekah tried to take in their new surroundings. The hill they had just escaped from now showed itself to be a large barrow type mound; its conical symmetry could only be man-made. It was one of many that were scattered along a bitter windswept shore where crashing waves drove in and out over an expansive stone and pebble beach. Thick dark clouds were rushing away toward the horizon across the troubled ocean.

On emerging from underground, Rebekah had thought it was day, due to the blinding light that had startled her, but she now saw that it was in fact night and the source of the now not so bright light was a huge, full and sepia coloured moon that hung low in the sky, the shore leading a curving path toward it.

It seemed that Arkturon was not able to bring Mikael round. "Is he all right... what is wrong with him?" She asked, suddenly concerned and fearful. She came to his side and looked into Mikael's ashen face, he was barely breathing.

"I do not know... he is still alive – but in some sort of stupor. It may simply be the effects of being caught in the mud slide or it could have something to do with the kelpies... those creatures," he pointed back to the mound, "if they managed to get a bite at him he will be poisoned. There is nothing we can do here though, whatever the cause, we must get him to Sul as soon as possible... we're on the boarders of Kear Widiyr now – once we reach Sul, she will be able to heal him."

"The kelpies... what are they – where did they come from?"

"They are the creations of Keridwen... they were trying to drag Mikael into her realm – the reverse of Kear Widiyr as she is the reverse of Sul. I think they caught him merely by chance, Keridwen cannot know of our purpose – she is always out to ensnare heedless travellers... the paths in the Otherworld can be very dangerous places for the unwary." Arkturon spoke as he secured Mikael's helpless body over her horse. He tied its reins to the saddle of his own and then instructed Rebekah to mount up. When she had – he joined her.

"But I thought the Otherworld was supposed to be a paradise, a heaven!"

"It is... but also a hell – I told you that each of the gods and goddesses have an evil aspect. Each realm that the paths link have both a blessed side and an infernal... the paths join them all – so are influenced by both the good and evil realms – for they, and the demigods that rule them, are neither."

Arkturon turned their horses to the moon and, bringing them to a gallop, he followed the beach toward it. The noise of the horses' hooves on the pebbles and shale silenced any further conversation between them. Pushed through the cold air at speed Rebekah's sopping clothes froze to her anew, shivering she was glad that Arkturon was so close, with his powerful arms flanking her and the warmth of his broad chest at her back. She knew that his garments were as sodden as hers yet she did not even feel him tremble once. She felt safe and secure... *and exhausted* – and despite all her efforts she began to fall asleep, slowly and fitfully her head fell back onto his shoulder.

The shallow slumber that overcame her was not strong enough to survive the cold and constant jolting of the horse ride though and she was startled awake and upright. Rebekah was annoyed to hear the Merdhin laugh at this... but also a little thrilled, it was the first time she had heard him laugh. She turned to look at his face, to make sure she had actually heard it right – above all the other noises. His wide grin confirmed it, a big white smile in a bearded face darkened with mud and dirt.

They rode for what seemed an age when the shore line formed a huge bay before them, curving out to sea and away from the moon, forcing the wizard to steer inland – to keep the now silvery orb in their sights. Rebekah was beginning to ache all over and her shivering was becoming uncontrollable. She prayed that they would reach Sul's home soon, and that it would be warm... *very warm!*

In the half light an uneven landscape stretched before them. They traversed the monotonous moor land wearily, the coarse grasses and bracken slowing down the horses' plodding hooves. As the coast-line receded behind them the more unpleasant flora was replaced by ever spreading clumps of heather, just as encumbering but much easier on the eyes and spirit. In the more low lying areas of the moor the heather gave way to mossy marsh but Arkturon doggedly struggled through these too, not varying from the course set by the moon. This course led them into a valley, shallow at first, which deepened and narrowed into a gully, with a fast flowing stream that bubbled along with them at their feet.

Rebekah wrapped her cloak tightly about herself in an attempt to fight off some of the cold, hugging herself vigorously. Arkturon sensed her discomfort and held her more tightly to him, wrapping his opened coat about her and his arms around her slim frame. Pushing her head back onto his shoulder, he leaned forward and pressed his cheek to hers. He was incredibly warm and she sank onto him gratefully, giving in to his care.

They followed the gully floor for some time before its high walls claimed their view of the moon, the sides were too steep to climb out of so they could do nothing but follow the stream's sunken path.

The gully's sudden ending could not have been more different from its subtle beginning, the steep sides simply ceased to be and the stream tumbled out down a sloping hillside into a lake about four furlongs ahead of them and two below. The lake was huge and covered what seemed to be the bottom of a large crater, the other side of which was paled by mist behind a mound like island in the centre of the lake. Atop of this island stood a tall, many faceted tower; a glass tower... *or was it ice?* It almost seemed so to Rebekah. The full moon hung almost directly above it.

"Kear Widiyr?" She asked falteringly, not sure of the pronunciation.

"Yes." said the wizard simply.

"How do we get across?" she quizzed further.

"There will be a way." He said, easing himself off the horse, he then helped Rebekah do the same. He handed her the reins then untied those of the horse that had the unconscious Mikael on its back.

"We have to get down to the shore first though." He added, and carefully began to lead the horse, with Mikael on it, down the slope. Rebekah cautiously followed with their other mount.

Slowly and steadily twelve Rangers made their way through the ancient shadowed woods that dominated the approach to the battered gatehouse that marked their chosen entrance into the baleful stronghold. Gusting winds whipped the tree tops as a rainless storm raged above their heads. Of course, the fallen gates themselves would prove no obstacle to these determined soldiers, but the two troll guards posted there would be another matter entirely. They were big Jotnar trolls from across the Nordik Sea; each was about nine feet tall and a good five feet wide. One carried a massive war-hammer and the other a huge flanged mace – a single blow from either of which would kill even the biggest man of the other races outright if he were caught dawdling within striking distance. These trolls were a formidable obstacle indeed.

The Rangers approached them cautiously and unseen, taking up positions, well within arrow range but still a fair distance away, in a semi-circle around where the trolls were stationed. A goblin patrol had passed a few minutes earlier, skirting the overgrown and now drained moat that surrounded the ruined complex – and it would be at least fifteen minutes more before another band of the barbarous wildings would pass that way again.

Lieutenant Styuwert Lethbridj walked out from the cover of the trees and stood, alone and silent, on the track way that led up to the guarded gatehouse. The two trolls didn't even notice when the cloaked figure came into view. They were both leaning against the inside walls of the large arched gateway, one on either side. One seemed to be dozing, while the other was intent on picking his massive wide-nostrilled nose.

The Lieutenant coughed, loud enough for the two big trolls to hear it over the tempestuous atmospherics, but quiet enough for the sound to not travel much further than they.

The troll picking his nose stopped his picking immediately and quickly looked round – his finger still firmly planted up his nasal cavity.

The dozing troll continued his dozing, till his partner slapped him across the chest with his mace and pointed – with the finger that he finally pulled from his cavernous nose – to the mysterious windswept and hooded figure that stood twenty or so yards from them. "Who's 'at?" He said to the other.

"Dunno..." said his startled companion. "Is 'e one o' the Master's men?"

"Dunno."

The two waddled forward to confront him. "Ere, oo goes there?" The troll carrying the mace gruffly shouted as they came out from the dark shadows of the gateway. In earlier times there had probably been some sort of drawbridge across the moat at this location, not any more, that part of the moat had been filled in with dirt long ago so that the path ran right up to the gates.

Once they were both in the open and had reached the point where the top of the drawbridge would have reached when down, the Rangers loosed five or six long, black arrows into each, and the Lieutenant immediately started to run at them. The troll with the huge flanged mace was dead instantly – three of the arrows had embedded deep in his heart – and he fell back, straight and rigid, hitting the ground with a hard slam. The other was mortally wounded but managed to remain standing, stunned and confused by the appearance of a cluster of long arrows in his barrel-like chest. Before he knew what was going on or could react in anyway, the Lieutenant was before him – the Ranger's sabre sliced through the troll's throat in a quick fluid motion and then he quickly stepped aside. The troll dropped his massive war-hammer and fell, dead, to the floor – face first.

All the Rangers then broke their cover and, struggling and straining, they dragged the troll cadavers back to the gatehouse. They removed their arrows and propped the bodies up as if they had fallen asleep – then, arrows re-notched and ready, they silently and sneakily slipped into the outer bailey of the forbidding fortifications.

Chapter Sixteen – Three Witches, Four Queens

Silently Luwsiy let herself be carried down the long twisting stairs of the tower by the three giggling sisters, their touch was very warm, unnaturally so – *almost hot!* – but also incredibly dry, not a trace of sweat or moisture. Plunging into the dark depths of the stone tower they brought her to their own chamber, halfway down, a chamber made for luxurious slumber and languorous revelry, richly and ornately furnished, draped with dark soft pelts and furs. A large fire roared in the carved stone hearth set opposite a tall open balcony that billowed silken white weaves on a warm, heady and powerful breeze.

The vampire sisters set her feet down on the floor of fine carpet but did not leave her side, they remained close and touching, always touching.

"Bathe her... Bathe her..." the one behind whispered with soft eagerness as her hot, wet tongue traced up Luwsiy's spine from her bottom to the base of her neck.

"Yes – Yes..." breathed the one in mauve to her left as she licked the girl's breast.

"No, her innocence... her purity – we must test her purity..." said the one in black as she knelt before Luwsiy, stroking the inside of her thighs and parting them. The hot caressing fingers rose up to her sex and gently brushed over her. "Oh... she is wet – so wet." said the vampire dreamily.

Behind her, the one dressed in red kissed her on the right hand side of her neck and said, breathing hotly into her ear, "she knows what is coming... a delving, a delving into her sex," the woman's voice was excited, "I think her fingers have been up there often... playing..." the vampire woman's tongue then suddenly dipped into her ear, then out again with a giggle.

"Yes... she probably probes herself... every... lonely... night..." said the one at her breast as she kissed and supped at the nipple there.

"Well... let us see," said she that knelt before her, "let us see..." an abnormally long and pointed tongue then suddenly reached from the creature's smiling mouth. It whipped back in as she moved up close to Luwsiy's belly, kissing her there – and then, as she crouched down, at her pubic mound and below. Luwsiy felt the long tongue glide across her labia, then push between and into her with strokes of sheer pleasure. She found herself panting and moaning as the tongue suddenly quit her little hole.

"Oh – she is so tight... so deliciously tight... but the hymen is pierced..." said the woman in black, looking reproachfully up at Luwsiy. "I think you could be right Aggareth... she has been fingering herself, or maybe someone has been doing it for her..."

"Let us check her mind and see... see what sweet memories she holds on to." said Maqlath still teasing at her left breast. "What say you Aggareth?"

The woman kissing Luwsiy's neck then replied, "Yes... we must make sure no man has been inside her..." and she then kissed and nibbled at her ear again, delicately and playfully sucking her lobe while her hand massaged Luwsiy's right breast.

Though Luwsiy feared these three women she now desperately wanted their touches and kisses, she needed to be the object of their desires, the merest glance from one of them she craved. She tried to convince herself that she was simply prey to their bewitching glamour... but the pleasure they gave – and the promise of what they could give – was so real... so very real... it overwhelmed her.

The one kneeling at her groin licked her once more and then rose up, trailing the heated tongue up Luwsiy's body, over her navel, between her breasts then up her throat and across her chin causing Luwsiy to lift back her head. "I will enter her mind," she breathed at Luwsiy's mouth, their lips almost touching, "I will test her..." she then suddenly kissed Luwsiy full on the mouth – pushing her long tongue into her there.

Briefly Luwsiy tasted and smelt her own sex as Maqlath softly whispered in her ear, "Iit will not hurt, Igymeth is so careful... so gentle."

Igymeth ended her kiss and pulled back slightly, staring hypnotically into Luwsiy's eyes, the intrusion into her mind filled the girl with a wondrous uneasiness similar to that she had felt when the woman's tongue had entered her vulva... unnerving – *but so arousing*. Luwsiy could not help putting her arms around Igymeth, as if to hold the woman's gaze on her.

The woman closed her eyes to break the spell with a laugh, "Oh she is so naughty this little girl... so salacious" opening them again she lifted Luwsiy by the waist. "She longs so much for love, for pleasure... for sex." Igymeth carried her over to a large, low, rounded bed that almost filled one end of the room and laid her on it. "She has spent every night of her young adolescent life touching and teasing herself, desperate for a tall, handsome man to love her... or a girl... so eager for her sister's touches also." The woman lay beside Luwsiy and then added, "Come sisters... let us give this little virgin some pleasure... an appetiser to prepare her for what is to come... gods how she will love that!"

As she lay there Maqlath and Aggareth moved over to a large mirrored table against one of the walls, Igymeth held her hand. "Now we must cleanse you," she said, then with her free hand she gently tugged at Luwsiy's pubic hair "and get rid of all this... not that you have much, but still, it must go," she then lifted Luwsiy's arm, "and here," She said, quickly licking her there also.

Maqlath returned, carrying two small silver boxes, which she put to one side, and a phial made from glass and silver that was half full of some clear liquid. Aggareth carried a slim pair of shining scissors, a shallow bowl – in which a very thin bladed knife rested in some steaming water – and a thick towel.

"You will have to spread your legs again." said Maqlath as she and Aggareth sat at her feet. Luwsiy did so immediately, feeling the excitement at exposing her sex build in her loins. Igymeth placed a number of pillows beneath the girl's lower back for support. Aggareth put down her bowl and the towel then leaned over Luwsiy's crotch, with one hand she gently took hold of a tuft of hair and with the other she snipped it close to the skin. Moving round Luwsiy's vulva she did the same with all the hair that was there, a gentle but electric tug followed by a sudden release by a snip of the scissors. Lifting Luwsiy's legs she trimmed the slight hair at her bottom also, then Aggareth carefully collected all the short hairs she had cut and placed them in one of the small silver boxes.

Maqlath stood up and unhooked the front of her dark red dress, opening its bodice and letting the garment fall to the floor, revealing her naked body. She then climbed onto the bed and knelt between Luwsiy's open legs, Maqlath poured a small amount of the liquid in her phial onto her hand, Luwsiy could see that it was thick and slow moving – *an oil* – and its rich sweet scent filled her nostrils immediately. Maqlath then began to rub the cool, soft and delightfully smooth oil onto Luwsiy's groin, the girl gasped as the kneading hand slipped over and around her, softening the short bristly hairs that the scissors had left behind.

Aggareth and Igymeth then took hold of Luwsiy's ankles and they parted her legs as far as possible, lifting the girl's backside high onto Maqlath's lap. Maqlath then poured over half the contents of her phial over Luwsiy's gaping groin, the oil cascading down her stomach – to collect in her navel then flow onto the bed – and down her bottom onto Maqlath's own belly and sex. Maqlath rubbed Luwsiy again, rubbed the oil between her legs, along the length of her thighs and her calf's, into her skin from her stomach to her feet. Then Maqlath put down the phial and took the thin knife handed to her by Igymeth. She then shaved Luwsiy, scraping the cold sharp blade across the girl's skin, every inch that sported hair, no matter how fine or downy – it was carefully shaved. When she had finished the lower part of Luwsiy's body they made the girl kneel and they started on the upper, snipping the hair under her arms and then oiling her, covering her chest, back and arms, and they shaved her, leaving only the hair on her head.

When she was fully shaved Luwsiy could not resist putting her fingers on her now bald sex, she fingered her delightful smoothness and used the trace of oil that was still there to lubricate the passage of her digits deep into herself. "Please... lick me again," she said to the vampires, her voice droning and laconic but full of lust and desperation, "please, I want your tongues... your fingers."

As she spoke Aggareth and Igymeth undressed as Maqlath had.

"You will get better than tongues and fingers soon." said Igymeth. "Our father has arranged something truly wondrous for you to put there." She pointed to where the girl's fingers played.

The three approached Luwsiy as Maqlath whispered "Now we bathe you..." like giving a proclamation of a dream once promised. They lifted the girl again as she frigged herself with one hand and pulled at her nipples with the other, panting sensual moans and groans continuously. They took her to the other side of the room where they parted a gossamer like drape to reveal the section of the room it partitioned off, Luwsiy saw that it hid a huge sunken bath, made from dark green marble, and steaming water bubbled into it from a spouting gargoyle-like head on the far wall. They stepped down into the water carrying Luwsiy with them.

Rebekah skidded down the last part of the slope to join Arkturon at the bottom. Now that she was by the lake side she could get a better impression of the island at its centre, it was much bigger than she had at first perceived and seemed to be covered in trees... *apple trees,* she thought, *in blossom... paradoxically considering the weather and terrain they had just travelled through... and that the Koventiyna is supposed to be a goddess of winter.* She asked Arkturon about this.

"I think my saying that Sul was the goddess of the north, of winter and of the night – during the ritual – has misled you somewhat" he spoke while beckoning her along the shore. "In essence it is true, but it is not quite as cut and dry as all that. You see... they are merely pointers or labels that help focus the mind... they are symbols or metaphors that make the visualisation of the deities easier. Do you understand?"

"No." She replied honestly, after a slight pause.

"Although man is at heart an emotional creature he also suffers from an illness called logic." explained the wizard. "He has an irresistible urge to categorise everything, even that which defies categorisation. He must associate one thing with another to make it more understandable... in this case he equates the gods and goddesses with points of the compass, the seasons of the year and the times of the day. It is an attempt to make the unreal seem real. They are associations made by man rather than by the gods themselves and are simply used as an aid to the act of ritual and belief.

Do you understand now?"

"I think so..." she said, still unsure – but she determined to think it over in her head till she did.

"Ah... here we are; our crossing point." Arkturon said, indicating a short jetty extending away from the shore.

"But there is no boat!" said Rebekah.

"There will be... we just need to wait awhile. Patience is all that is needed." Leaving his mare and Mikael, Arkturon strolled to the end of the wharf and casually sat down. "Patience." he said again.

"Should we not get Mikael down," she said, glancing over his unconscious body, "ready for when a boat arrives?"

"No. The horses will be coming over with us so we might as well keep him as he is; he is as comfortable as he can be for now."

Rebekah looked Mikael over again, doubting that last statement but leaving him where he was anyway she joined Arkturon at the edge of the jetty.

The mist on the lake seemed to be thickening as it drifted across the still surface, banks and eddies constantly dissolving and reforming in a slow eerie dance.

"Our ferry will be here soon!" said Arkturon.

Rebekah looked around quickly but could see nothing. "Are you sure? I see only mist."

"Exactly... and it's getting thicker – especially in front of us."

"Oh, I see... it's just going to appear – isn't it!"

"Yes," said Arkturon with a laugh. "I think it is. You are beginning to understand how the Otherworld works now... you just have to keep your eyes open and be ready for the subtle signs. Of course, it will not always be as straightforward as it is in this case."

No, Rebekah thought, *things never are when you explain them.* She was, nevertheless, greatly satisfied when a vessel began to take shape from the shifting mists about a hundred or so yards from where they sat. The foggy haze hugging the water surface slowly evaporated as the ship became more solid, and quite a ship it was too, for to Rebekah's eyes it was a ship straight from Arthurian legend. It was large, dark and – or so it seemed to Rebekah – brooding. A single mast supported a huge black sail that hung, with no breeze to fill it, straight to the deck like a veil. In front of this cloth stood three women, three queens splendid in their glory... and intimidating in their aspect.

Rebekah recognised one of them, to the left stood Ariyanrhod, though looking more solemn and less animated than she remembered her. Then she realised that the queen to the right was almost identical to that on the left, but her beauty was less natural – more glamorous and contrived. Between them stood a young girl of about fifteen, her face seemed weighted by the knowledge and resignation of someone much older. Rebekah felt sure that she should recognise this queen too but it was not until she noticed a fourth figure sat in a throne below and before those standing that she realised why. The queen that occupied the throne was Sul; she was identical to the girl that stood behind her except that her face was still light with the joy and innocence of youth.

The young goddess of the night was the only one that was not downcast with solemnity. They were all dressed entirely in black, except for their crowns and jewellery and all four faces shone with a strange unnatural lustre.

The ship drifted toward the jetty with no visible means of propulsion.

"Who are those women behind Sul?" asked Rebekah perplexed.

"They are all images only," Arkturon replied standing. "The one in the middle is Keridwen – Sul's dark sister. The one on the left is a projection of Ariyanrhod and the one on the right is of her evil aspect, Andreast."

Rebekah stood too, watching the boat approach. Arkturon then went to fetch the horses and Mikael, ready for embarking. Rebekah stared at the nearing ship until, as Arkturon returned, it glided smoothly alongside them, tight to the jetty's end. Before Sul's throne was a large flat deck and it was onto this that Arkturon led the horses. Rebekah followed hesitantly. She sat with Arkturon at the prow of the boat with the horses standing quiet and calm behind them as the vessel eased away and turned toward the island.

Half an hour's slow and silent journey later they docked at the island and disembarked. The air was perceptively warmer, like an island of early spring amidst the winter. Once they were all ashore the boat and its mute occupants dissolved into mist and dispersed.

There were no buildings at the wooden dock, just groves of apple trees as far as the eye could see; some in blossom, some in full fruit, and others winter bare. Arkturon headed toward the centre of the island and the tower, leading them up the slope and through the pan-seasonal wood. There were birds aplenty in the apple tree forest, for their song was deafening, though the moonlight shadows cast by the trees hid them from view. Rebekah trudged wearily alongside Arkturon, up the steady incline through thick verdant grasses that flourished on every scrap of land.

The bird song was suddenly silenced by a thunderous squeal-like roar that echoed through the hushed forest. Rebekah halted, grasping at Arkturon's shoulder, eyes round with fear. The noise had struck a primeval memory in her subconscious and her automatic reaction was to freeze on the spot.

"It is safe." Arkturon offered immediately. "That is the guardian of Sul's temple – we have nothing to fear. It will be our escort to her threshold." Taking her hand from his shoulder he held it. "There is nothing to fear."

As he spoke something large moved ahead of them. Slowly a giant boar dissociated itself from the optical confusion of the trees and shadow. Amidst its huge twisted tusks two wide nostrils flared and sent gushes of steam exploding from them with an unearthly snort. Glancing at them only for an instant it turned and leisurely waddled away from them.

"Come," said Arkturon quietly. "We must follow."

They trailed the beast a good half mile before reaching the island's crown; close up, Kear Widiyr – the Glass Tower – proved to be just that, a fairy tale palace of strangely shaped, cut and moulded glass shot through with a myriad moonbeams coloured turquoise and pink. The apple trees immediately around it were all in spring blossom and the air was cool and sweet after their trek up the hill. Between the trees and the outer walls of the tower stood huge monolithic stones in a regimental circle like a palace guard surrounding their charge.

The wild boar did not cross that boundary of stones, roaring one last time; it then ran and crashed back into the forest, disappearing from view even quicker than it had appeared.

A paved road leading to the tower gates surfaced from the grass inside the line of trees, the monoliths that directly flanked it were larger than the rest and were carved with images that depicted a procession that spiralled up the height of each stone. With closer inspection the participants in these two twisting relief's proved to be entirely female and all were carrying assorted offerings – dishes and cups full to the brim, swords and spears... it was then that Rebekah realised it was the same four figures with the same four gifts being repeated over and over again.

They entered the stone circle and approached the tower. Its gates were closed and its walls were silent.

"We have among us one who needs healing." Arkturon shouted to the cold, glassy parapets. "We crave entrance for his sake and the sake of others who depend on our journey as their only hope." He paused then bellowed "Moon Maiden Sul – please aid us!"

The gates opened silently. They led the horses through to be greeted by three female creatures – almost human but undeniably touched by the piscine. Their hair was a dark sea green and hung in limp tangles about their head and shoulders while their skin held a pale incandescence, glowing with a submarine like lustre. At their legs, just below the knee, the skin changed though, it became green and scaly and covered the skin down to their malformed feet that seemed far too long and clumsy. The naked creatures were very slim, long and fine boned limbs and fingers stretched out in greeting to the visitors, tissue thin membrane linked each pearly nailed digit to its neighbour and also their upper arms to their streamlined bodies.

"Undines" Arkturon explained in a whisper.

Rebekah stared at one of the creatures faces as a soft hand closed around hers, translucent eyelids slowly blinked over wide beautiful eyes and pale thin lips formed a reassuring smile below a small, slightly turned up nose.

As Arkturon began to lift Mikael from the horse one of the strange women spoke, her voice struggled between alternate bouts of high pitched screeches and hoarse, husky croaks. "No weapons of destruction can enter further into the palace, they must stay with the land creatures," she indicated the horses. "Only weapons used for the hunting of food are allowed – blades, spears, bows and arrows... those death-spitting mechanical's are not allowed!"

Arkturon put Mikael down and took the flintlocks from the unconscious man's belt and put them in the saddle bag of one of the horses. One of the undines led the horses away while the one that held Rebekah's hand took the hand of Arkturon in her other. The third, the one who had spoken, lifted Mikael and then led them toward the tower proper with slow, awkward steps. The large, open doorway that they approached shimmered as they neared, at first Rebekah thought it caused by some sort of heat haze, but she soon realised that it was water – like the surface of a pool except that it stood unnaturally vertical before them, held in place by some hidden force.

The undine leading them suddenly put Mikael down and said "You should remove your clothes; they are not necessary and are an encumbrance." She began to undress Mikael. Arkturon undressed himself without an apparent thought or care and, though Rebekah was surprised by the request she found herself undressing too, something she would never have done in such strange company – *or any company for that matter* – only days before. Once all were naked the undine picked up Mikael again and entered through the doorway, breaking the surface caused ripples to radiate out from her point of entry and then echo back from the sides. Rebekah tried to convince herself that it was not water as they too were led through into the watery realm, but she failed miserably. Once the initial panic had passed, she found that she could still breath and – much to her relief – that she was not going to drown after all.

Chapter Seventeen – Healing Waters at the Well of Tears

Being bathed by the three vampire sisters kept Luwsiy in a constant state of heightened sensual diversion. Her only thoughts were those of physical pleasure and gratification, and she could feel the need for something more, more than what they could give, build up within her to intolerable levels. All she could think of was the little man who had abducted her and of all that he said he would do to her... for that is what she wanted now – *to be fucked!* His evil intent and unbearable ugliness mattered not a jot compared to the simple fact of the sexual pleasure he could have given. She could not believe the fear and naivety that had consumed her when she had seen his huge penis... now she would give anything for such a tool to work herself on.

The sisters could read her desires and they laughed at her craving, she would be satiated soon they told her, their father will see to it that she is served as she wishes, she will wish nothing more once he has provided what she needs.

They lifted her out of the water and began to dry her, and each other, with the softest of towels. Maqlath then retrieved the scissors that they had cut Luwsiy's hair with and began to trim the girl's nails at her hands and feet. Once done the clippings were collected and placed in the second silver box, as her pubic hair had been in the first.

"Now you are ready for our father," said Igymeth, then added with a giggle, "in every way." They lifted her once more and then carried her from the room.

The sisters and their charge then continued down the rest of the stairs in the tower, right down to its base where the structure widened and delved into the earth. They entered a spacious chamber where Bäliyl waited for them, he stood naked within a large magik circle, identical to the one that crowned the tower but much bigger. His muscular and swarthy body was splendid in its nudity and Luwsiy could not pull her voracious eyes from him. Beyond the magik circle a ring of black-robed acolytes surrounded them, their faces hidden within the dark shadows of their voluminous hoods. The ceremonial candles and braziers of the magik circle filled the room with a thick, heady scent and smoke.

"She is ready father." said Igymeth. His half smile set Luwsiy's sex ablaze as he indicated a massive stone altar with a nod of his head. They ushered her to it. Maqlath handed over the two small, silver boxes to her father while Igymeth and Aggareth lifted Luwsiy onto the altar. The cloth that covered the top of the large stone gave way as her weight settled on to it – the stone was moulded into the shape of a body, hollows were filled by Luwsiy's buttocks, back, shoulders and head. Her arms were raised and pulled behind her to be tied with silk to a large brass ring at the head of the altar. Luwsiy's bottom was at the edge of the other end of the stone and her legs were spread to full stretch, lengths of silk tying each ankle to two more hefty rings that were fixed to the stone floor.

Luwsiy knew that this would enable Bäliyl to enter her sex while standing before her powerless body – between her helpless thighs – and the mere thought had her vagina's juices dripping down the side of her stone bed. Her unbearable hunger for him voiced continually in her moaning groans of "Fuck me... fuck me... please... fuck me..."

She did not know, of course, that it would not be Bäliyl that entered her... but it would not have mattered – the enchantment that she was under filled her with an all consuming and desperate lust that had to be satisfied at all cost.

Seeing the flow that seeped from Luwsiy's vulva, as she tied one of the girl's ankles, Igymeth could not resist a quick flickering lick before she parted from her duties. She savoured Luwsiy's taste as her father dismissed his three daughters from the room.

Now that the undines were in their natural element Rebekah could appreciate their true grace and beauty, clumsy feet fanned out unexpectedly to form delicate long fins and slim limbs moved with an elegant and deliberate slowness, their limp hair filled with sudden body and untangled itself as it floated about the lazily blinking faces.

Rebekah and Arkturon clumsily floated with the graceful undines as they were led down a long corridor of shimmering, diffused light. The floor beneath them angled down quite severely and the strong beats of the undine's fins pulled them down with it. Their passage was surprisingly swift, though the sensation of weightlessness and motion remained pleasant and invigorating.

As they ventured deeper their surroundings changed, the cool crystal shapes of translucent glass became cracked and broken, gradually becoming opaque and stony, sand covered the widening floor and structures of multicoloured and differing coral began to crop up about them, becoming larger and more numerous as they went.

The corridor suddenly opened out in to a huge, almost limitless, chamber that was lit by a large moon like orb that hung suspended high above a columned Hellenik temple in the centre of a sandy plain. High up, on the distant walls and ceiling, blue and turquoise patterns played like the reflections of light off undulating water. The pale temple was bathed in a soft sepia tone from the light source above but in its shade traces of a cool aqua-blue could be seen.

The undines carried and led the humans to the rectangular building which seemed to take on awesome proportions the nearer it loomed, the chamber was much more expansive and the building much bigger than Rebekah had at first assumed. They gradually floated down to the temple threshold and settled on the steps that led up to it on all sides. Once her feet had lightly touched the white stone they climbed up to the row of columns that made up the four walls of the sublime structure. Passing through into cool shade they saw a simple, backless throne on a dais at the other end, between them and it was what seemed to be a large well set in the middle of the floor. On the throne sat a young dark haired girl, her casual nudity was innocent and in no way sexual, her green eyes stared at them with an alert and unashamed curiosity, it was the sort of intense stare that only children can hold without feeling self-conscious, it was Sul – the Moon Maiden.

The undine carrying Mikael then spoke. "My Lady... we have brought the sapiens that have petitioned your aid." Her voice was very soft and musical, not the coarse tones she had made in the air outside of the tower.

"Bring them to the water of healing." The goddess said quietly as she stood and walked to the stone well before them.

Rebekah and Arkturon were led forward and Mikael was carefully laid by its side. Rebekah was surprised to see the rippled surface of what appeared to be water within the wide, pool-like well... *surely we are in water all ready... but then* – if it were water as she knew it in the real world she would not now be able to breathe... *I would be dead,* she thought dryly.

Sul knelt beside Mikael and lifted his head onto her lap; she stroked his unconscious face then cupped her hands and scooped some of the water from the well. She let it drip onto his face slowly, onto his forehead, his eyes, nose and mouth. The strange water was thick, slow moving and alien, it seemed to have a life of its own as it flowed over Mikael's face in a green-blue globule, each drop that fell from Sul's hands added to the large one that massaged the prone man's face. Once her hands were empty the globule began to disappear, when it was almost gone the routes of its exit bccamc apparent – Mikael's eyes, nose, mouth and ears.

Sul lent down and kissed Mikael lightly on the lips, she giggled – like the little girl that she was – as the man resting on her lap suddenly spluttered and choked, he sat up with eyes open wide, his face expressing shock between his many but decreasing coughs. He then saw his nakedness, and that of the young girl on whose lap he had languored, puzzled and embarrassed he awkwardly stood and backed away from her, his hands covering his manhood.

The girl stopped her giggles and then, feigning seriousness and letting a furrow crease her young and perfect brow, she said "Modesty is not necessary... not here." and she indicated his surroundings with a slow and leisurely motion of her right arm. Mikael's eyes followed its graceful arch, he saw Rebekah and Arkturon, then the undines – all as naked as he – he saw the temple that surrounded him and the pool by his side, then his gaze again fell on the child that was almost a woman. Recognition crossed his face and, as he met her eyes, more understanding than mere sight could have registered became apparent in his visage.

"Forgive me... My Lady... I..." He was going to try and explain his initial confusion, make excuses for it, but to his relief, for he could not find the words, she interrupted.

"Forgiveness is not necessary, be at ease... that is all you should be." Her smile was natural and came with the ease of innocence.

Mikael relaxed his posture and found himself wondering what it was about his nakedness that had so concerned him. He looked to his two smiling friends and joined them, hugging them both freely; his last memory was of overwhelming water and mud, of not being able to breath, of fear and of terror... of grasping hands and biting teeth. But that had gone now, he did not know why, or where... and he did not care.

The young goddess stood too, she moved to the small but deep pool and stared into it. Her stillness as she stared was complete. As the three mortal's in turn stared at her, she suddenly sobbed a sound of heart wrenching sadness and she leant over the water. Sul's tears flowed freely and fell, slow and dark, into the well. Concerned, Mikael moved toward her but was held back by Arkturon. The older man just shook his head at Mikael's questioning glance. As the goddess cried so too did Rebekah, Arkturon's eyes filled with tears and Mikael could also feel himself begin to weep in sympathy with Sul. Her face was so sad... so deeply hurt... she seemed to be suffering from a truly devastating loss.

Slowly the sobs ceased and she looked back up to her visitors, her smile now tainted... older somehow. "The sorrows of the world..." she said indicating the water, "its hurt, its fears... its grief... all taken on and shared... eased by my tears... my healing waters."

Sul, the Koventiyna, then turned from them and slowly returned to her throne. When she sat down and faced them, once more her smile had returned, her first smile that is – young, cheerful... innocent. Her sorrows and those of the world's many peoples were now hidden – seemingly forgotten. With her hands tucked beneath her thighs and her legs swinging over the edge of her seat the goddess then said to them, "Please... take a drink, it will refresh you and prepare you for the rest of your journey... do not fear, drink."

The three companions obeyed; cupping their hands they each took a drink. It was salty but sweet, creamy but bitter, it was sorrow and it was joy, security and fear... it was everything and it was nothing... it was life and it was death... it was the Elixir.

When Rebekah woke she was laid face down with her arm draped over Arkturon's large hair covered chest and her leg was crossed with one of his, her face rested on his broad shoulder and his arm held her. She was naked and so was he, thankfully he was still asleep and she could pull herself away before he came round to see their apparently intimate proximity. She wondered how on earth she had got this close to him, or he to her. As she moved slowly away from him she felt something behind her, turning she saw Mikael, he too was asleep... and naked. *What the hells?* She asked herself, sitting up quickly – and then, seeing her surroundings, she realised and remembered. *Of course, the drink... it must have knocked us out – sent us to sleep.* The sexual tension dissipated as she remembered they were in Sul's realm.

The drink... Rebekah remembered and she found herself weeping... a melancholic happiness overwhelmed her. Her soft, tearful sobs of laughter woke the two men beside her; they greeted her with loving hugs, tears and smiles, they all had experienced true sorrow and true joy, it now bonded them as never before.

An undine hovered at a discrete distance beside the well and waited for the friends to stand. As they did, she spoke to them, "The Koventiyna hopes that you are rested and wishes that you follow me." The creature then led them back out of the temple, Sul was nowhere to be seen but two more undines waited at the threshold. An undine took each of the mortal's by the hand and swam up away from the temple, pulling them back the way they had come. Up to the glass faced corridors of the tower and on to its threshold. Before passing through the water's surface at the doorway the undines set the humans down onto the floor to let them walk across into the air, the creatures did not seem inclined to come through with them so it was Arkturon that led his friends out of the watery realm.

The air seemed cool and fresh when it greeted them and although it made their bodies seem heavy again it allowed the movement of their limbs to be as free and as fast as it should be. The slow motion forced onto them in water, though relaxing and luxurious, would always be alien. Mikael seemed confused by the doorway; he walked back to it and dipped a finger into the vertical wall of still water – ripples expanded out from where he touched it.

Their clothes were still piled where they had left them and their two remaining horses waited over beside the open gates, they clothed themselves then crossed the courtyard silently to join their mounts. Patting the animals, Arkturon took hold of the reins and led the beasts out into the open, once past the circle of standing stones he paused and handed Mikael back his flintlocks. "Now we must find the path that leads us to Kear Pedrivan." He said quietly. They were the first words any of them had voiced since drinking from the well of Sul's healing tears.

They passed back through the apple groves and came to the shore where the large black-sailed ship waited to take them onboard.

The outer bailey of Bäliyl's castle, and its various associated buildings, were in ruins and clearly not in use, the encroaching woods and undergrowth of the Old Forest had reclaimed it long ago. A path to the inner bailey gatehouse was the only part of it cleared. The Rangers avoided that path and used the cover of the rampant vegetation on either side to approach this next, much larger and certainly better maintained, portal. The still standing gates were closed, but no guards were to be seen. The gatehouse itself was a formidable structure, topped by castellated battlements and with a black stoned face that was peppered with defensive slits like the grim, stout round-towers that flanked it. It was impossible to tell what eyes may be watching from those lethal loopholes, or what stood guard – if anything – behind the sturdy looking doors of the inner gatehouse. The walls on either side of these structures were largely standing, but not entirely so, ruination had breached their defences in a number of places.

Communicating with hushed tones and hand signs the Rangers, already split into two groups by the cleared path, decided that each group should go to the nearest breach on either side of the gatehouse and try to gain entry to the inner bailey on their respective sides. The Sergeant and his three man team, accompanied by Corporal Villovürt and another, a stalwart and stony faced man named Rigormort, would go left of the gates. The Lieutenant, Corporal Lannik and the remaining four Rangers would go to the right.

The Sergeant led his five companions toward their allotted breach, a pile of rubble that spilled out from the gaping wall where it had been brought down in some long forgotten siege, about seventy five yards from the gatehouse. He instructed the others to wait at the bottom of this hill of broken stone while he slowly and carefully climbed the jagged mound to see what lay beyond. A big V shape had been blasted from the solid wall; this triangular gap came to meet the summit of the mound about half way up the defence's original height. Laying low at the top, the Sergeant peeked over into the inner bailey. The large courtyard beyond was, unlike the outer court, free of undergrowth and trees... *free of any cover what-so-ever*. Across it was the massive square keep, with round towers at each corner and one, the tallest tower of all, at its back. Watch towers and various old ancillary buildings were butted up against the inside face of the inner bailey wall. There were no visible signs of occupation - except for the faint glow of fire light in a balconied window halfway up the tallest tower. He signalled his group of Rangers to cautiously come forward and join him.

Once they were all together he whispered, "We're going in slow and to the left, single file, hugging the walls and buildings round the courtyard – the light is pretty poor so there should be enough shadow to give us cover from glancing eyes – then it's up the stairs to the doors of the keep. Hopefully the Lieutenant will do the same from the right, and we'll meet him there. Any questions?"

"Yes Sarge," said Sinkhoal, "what if the doors are locked? How do we get in?"

"Don't worry about that, son – that's what our Warlock's for." replied the Sergeant. "Corporal Villovürt will get us in." He looked to the dark-elf for confirmation.

She simply nodded. She was trained in the making and breaking of wards and seals; and had yet to encounter one that she could not master.

"Right," said the Sergeant, "stay close to me and the wall. Let's go."

Staying low he passed through the gap. The others followed, one at a time. Down the slope of rubble inside, that mirrored the mound on the outside, then along the wall they continued, skirting the open courtyard. Slow, steady and silent, keeping their eyes and ears alert. About halfway to the keep, the Sergeant halted suddenly and signed for those behind him to stop too. They did so immediately. He could see the dark cloaked figures of the Lieutenant and his group starting to skirt the far side – they had come through a giant fissure in the inner bailey wall close to the far corner of the courtyard. He waited for them to be level with his group and then they all continued on.

Just as they reached the near edge of the keep, and had started heading inward towards the stairs on either side of its entrance, the heavy wooden doors were flung open and a black cowled figure stepped out onto the stone balustraded platform at the top of the steps.

All the Rangers stopped advancing as one. The Sergeant readied an arrow and aimed it at the figure. Although he could not see it, he knew that the Lieutenant, leading his group on the other side, will have done the same.

The black robed acolyte walked to the balustrade that edged the front facing edge of the platform, as the doors closed behind him he hacked up a gob of phlegm and spat it out and over the stone barrier. He then turned to his right and headed for the stairs down to the courtyard – he may have glimpsed the Sergeant looking up at him before the Ranger's arrow embedded itself in his heart – but the Sergeant doubted it. The acolyte stumbled back a step, but didn't drop – this worried the Sergeant as he, with the rest of his group behind him, ran up the stairs. Unsheathing his sabre as he rapidly approached, he sliced the acolyte's head clean off with one powerful swipe. He did not know if this creature of Bäliyl's was a vampire or not, but he had it on good authority – Corporal Villovürt's – that it was the surest way of killing such a thing and he wasn't going to take any chances. The acolyte's hooded head went sailing over the side in much the same way as the creature's gob of phlegm had, and the body collapsed to the cold stone floor of the platform – it was, the Sergeant figured confidently, now most definitely dead.

The Lieutenant's group started rushing up the stairs to meet the Sergeant's, just as a raucous horn sounded above the storm from the outer bailey's gatehouse. It was a goblin horn. The Rangers realised that the dead troll guards must have been discovered. Another goblin horn sounded in reply, and then another – it was the three goblin bands that patrolled the outer perimeter of the castle.

"Sergeant, take your group into the keep." ordered the Lieutenant. "We'll hold this doorway till you return."

A few stray goblins rushed into the courtyard from the various buildings around the perimeter, surprised and startled by the horns and seemingly not sure what was going on. The Lieutenant's Rangers picked them off with their deadly arrows as the Sergeant quickly led his group through the doors and into the keep.

Chapter Eighteen – The Cave of Afagddu

Lilith waited impatiently – not that she was at all eager, for what was about to happen, for she was not. The inevitably of it though weighed heavily on her mind and filled her with an awful dread – so she rather it happened sooner than later. Having to wait for something bad to happen was much worse by far, she decided, than being forced to wait for something good. She just wanted the torment of waiting to be over.

She paced back and forth inside her imprisoning circle and, despite her impatience at the intolerable waiting, she desperately tried to think of ways to slow her father and his ritual down. *To stop him even* – though she thought this unlikely – *if not impossible now...* unless she had help, which was why she must disrupt the order of his work as much as possible – *to give them time! That is all I can do... but how!* The thoughts vexed her for she had no answer.

Suddenly the floor rushed up toward her with giddying speed, her limbs flayed helplessly as she collapsed to the stone surface and smacked into it, not onto it – she noticed as the instant of terror slapped her daydreaming thoughts away – but into it. She was being sucked through the solid floor below her. He had summoned her.

Thrusting all the solidity her phantasmic form could muster into her hands and arms she pushed herself desperately upward against the stone around her, her legs had already been pulled through and the stone floor was now up to her waist. She heaved against her father's summoning but no matter how hard she tried to deny it she was of the spirit, not material, world and she was governed by its laws and nature. But still she tried. She clawed at every hand and finger hold she could find in the stone, she held at each till only her finger nails clung on, finger nails that she changed to claws stronger and more powerful than any beast's.

The cold pressure of the heavy stone work had enveloped her breasts now and had risen to her arm pits, she spread her arms as wide as possible but the inexorable downward pull could not be stayed for long, the encasing floor claimed her neck and head with ease as she scrambled for a hold but her arms were forced up as she was swallowed, her last chance to cling to anything came as all but her fingers had disappeared below – so cling she did, briefly digging claws into rock. But, inevitably, even that last pretension to solidity and the material could not hold, her fingers dissolved into spirit and slipped through the stone as had the rest of her body.

Exhausted by her efforts Lilith still struggled as she was drawn through the structure of the tower, large facing stones and the smaller rock and rubble of in-fill all provided her with nooks and crannies to fill and hold to, but the more she held the weaker she got and, in the long run, the faster her descent became.

Without warning Lilith found herself falling through air, not stone, the shock of the sudden speed startled her, she was in the spiralling stairwell that ran down the side of the tower, plummeting uncontrollably. Coming to her senses she lashed out to grab at anything around her, the walls, the stairs – but it was no use, she had no energy left to grip or to even render any part of herself substantial enough to try.

Gaining her balance though she was able to right herself then concentrate all her will into reversing her descent. She strained with the effort but the force that pulled her was like an icy grip on the soul at her heart, a fist that squeezed her very being and dragged her down with it.

Her father's voice, using the archaic language of ancient Kanaan from the land of Gnodd – the land of his birth many thousands of years earlier – repeated his summoning in her mind, *Lilith Samiyl, by the powers I control I call you unto me, I command your presence by the arts of Ketev, Pahhad, Maqlat and Lilit. I command it by their power granted unto me, Bäliyl Samiyl, your father and master.* His cold and cruel whispers grew louder the nearer she came to him. *The bonds that hold you to my servitude can never be broken and I demand that you honour me. You will obey me always, unable to question and beyond doubt.*

His words dispelled Lilith's weak and last remaining drops of free will; they seeped mournfully from her in the form of glistening, pearly drops at her eyes. Now that all resistance was gone, Bäliyl pulled her down to him, straight through the stone of the castle and down to the chamber in which he stood.

"Still the wilful bitch, I see." he said to her once she stood before him. "Well, no longer." he then gloated triumphantly.

Lilith stared out at him, unable to move or to speak without direction from her father. Her mind though – that last spark of identity, knowledge and memory that was Lilith Samiyl – was free, not even he could command that, but it despaired in the cage of control that was now built around it.

Arkturon brought his two companions to a cave entrance, a very dark and unpleasant looking cave that had a most unsavoury stench drifting out of it.

"We are not going in there." Rebekah stated adamantly, turning on the saddle to look at the man who sat behind her.

"I am afraid we must," said Arkturon. "We do not have the time to find another route."

"But it smells foul!" she said with disgust. "The gods alone know what's in there." Rebekah refused to imagine what might be found within such a cave and she was hoping she would never find out – even when Arkturon replied, "Oh, I know what's in there."

The smell was of stale sweat and rotting food, with a faint trace of urine and faeces. Despite herself, she found herself asking "What?"

"Well, it is more a question of whom," said the wizard, "he is a demigod called Afagddu. His path is represented by the card 'The Devil' in the tarot pack, but by no means is he one – not as you would understand it anyway. His Saxanglish name is Oeddi, but you may also know him as Pan. I believe that the Kanaaniyts called him Azazel."

Pan, she thought, *makes sense looking at the surroundings.*

After leaving Sul's island they had continued on and set out through an expanse of increasingly pine dominated woodland toward some distant mountains they could see. A day's hard ride brought them to the foot hills and lower regions of the range. Almost the only life they had seen were the goats that clambered about the rocky slopes and some even perched atop the stunted trees around them now. The light was fading as the moon disappeared behind the towering peaks ahead of the travellers.

"We must go this way; we can waste no more time."

Rebekah nodded to Arkturon's words, her curiosity had been baited now.

They dismounted and led the two horses into the large mouth of the cave, Arkturon's staff flaring to light the way. They were hardly ten yards in when a loud bellow halted them.

"I am not too sure about this either." said Mikael as the deep call echoed about them, he rested his right hand on the butt of one of the flintlocks at his belt. "I'm getting a really bad feeling about this cave."

"There will be no need for them." said Arkturon, and as if to illustrate his words a soothing music suddenly started up, a resonant melody made with some sort of reed-pipes filled the cavern.

Apart from the small circle of light that they stood in the whole cave was in darkness, they could see squat shadows within the gloom but no detail could be made out clearly. Then one of the shadows stood up. The silhouette of an extremely well built man about seven or eight feet tall moved to stand before them, his footfalls echoing strangely – it was a man with the horns and back legs of a goat, and he was playing a set of panpean pipes.

Arkturon lifted his staff and moved closer to the demigod, casting a revealing light over him. From cloven hooves to waist the creature was covered in dark shaggy fur, all except its large penis which hung pale against the thick hairy growth at his groin. The fur thinned at Afagddu's muscular stomach and his broad chest and massive arms were almost bare, but his chin and head had that same curly and matted fur as hair and beard. Two large and heavy looking horns twisted out from the fur an inch or so back from each temple. He lowered the pipes from his lips and smiled a strangely playful grin that showed long yellowing teeth, underneath a large forehead and protruding brows shined mirthful eyes that seemed to properly belong to a mischievous child and not this ugly half-man, half-beast.

Arkturon spoke as the giant looked his visitors over. "Lord Afagddu, we ask that we may pass through your home, we have an urgent errand blessed by the gods."

In reply Afagddu simply made an exaggerated show of sniffing the air, "Ah... yes" he said loudly, "I smell a female... a young female. Bring her to me, is she pretty? Show me." He spoke in that false child like manner that all condescending adults use when addressing a small child. He lent down and peered at Rebekah as she hesitantly moved closer to the light in Arkturon's hand, "Oh," the demigod said, "a pretty little thing... for a sapien."

He extended a huge hand toward her, pushing out a long finger and tickling her under the chin with an over-grown, filthy, broken and frayed finger nail. "Hello, pretty girl." He said.

Rebekah tried not to show her revulsion and stood her ground, but as he leaned nearer to her and grinned, she realised that it was probably his breath alone that caused the awful smell in that cave.

Afagddu then quickly took hold of Rebekah's hand as he straightened back up to his full height. "So sweet and pretty... follow me, my friends, I will show you through my caves, but your beasts must stay here till you return, they will only slow you down now. I help you because you're my friends... you *are* my friends – are you not?" He said, addressing the last bit to Rebckah only and holding her hand to his chest.

Rebekah hesitated only slightly before adopting her best demure pose. Smiling as sweetly as she could she said, "Yes, of course we are your friends."

"Good – good... come, follow me then." The demigod then led Rebekah into the cave, tightly clinging on to her hand with his own. The others followed close behind, leaving their perfectly content looking horses behind.

The skin of Afagddu's hand was very rough and becoming increasingly sweaty as he took her through a confusing maze of tunnels and caves, her uneasiness at the proximity of this huge, powerful and incredibly ugly beast-man also grew as they walked. Though she tried desperately to avoid it, her gaze kept getting drawn to his long and lolling penis as it swayed in time with his strides. It was the one thing in the world she would least like to see or get closer to, the very thought literally filling her with horror and revulsion, but still she could not stop herself from looking, it was a kind of fatalistic fascination that was simply beyond her control.

Due to her gaze being continually distracted she was ultimately taken by surprise when he suddenly stopped and said, "Here we are, this is the border of Kear Pedrivan."

They stood in another large cave; the walls were of natural rock as had been all the tunnels and caves they had so far passed through, but the opening which they now looked out from was an arch of worked stone like the portal of a castle, at its threshold an immense stone stairway descended before them. They looked out over a huge labyrinth, at the centre of which was a tall and many turreted citadel looming from the mist at its base, in many ways the scene mirrored the lands of Kear Sidiy, but where that had been fashioned from nature this realm seemed cut and built from stone, it was the product of intellect and artifice rather than nurturing and emotion. Above the castle was suspended a light source of orange and yellow, its radiance cooler and sharper than that of Kear Sidiy, a sun rising in early spring rather than that setting in mid autumn.

Afagddu, still gripping Rebekah's hand, led them down the dizzying height of the stairway, its steep descent twisting back and forth on the cliff wall that spread almost limitlessly on either side and above them. The wall showed a slight curve inward at its furthest, barely visible, reaches so

Rebekah guessed that it in fact formed a huge cavern, as had Sul's realm, the ceiling and distant walls too far and shadowed to be seen.

As they neared the labyrinth below they saw that it was not just a construction of stone, it included gardens and stretches of water amidst its stony paths and courtyards. Fountain's and statues of such artistry and beauty competed with ingenious mechanisms powered by fast flowing streams and waterfalls for their attention and admiration. It was a wonderland of technical achievement designed to amuse, puzzle and astound those who attempted to find a way through it.

"I can guide you through the maze," said Afagddu as they reached the bottom of the stairs, "but only as far as the lake on which the castle stands. Once there you must find your own way across."

"We understand... and are grateful." Arkturon said to him, giving Rebekah a nudge and inclining his head almost imperceptibly to the demigod in reply to her sudden glance.

"Oh... yes – very grateful." She smiled to the tall beast-man still holding her hand. He slowly bowed and lifted her hand to his lips, the kiss was soft and barely touched her – but still sent a cold shiver up the centre of her back.

The labyrinth had many levels, accessed by stairs and slopes, the paths were sometimes flanked by high walls – sometimes by shear drops – but were always crossed by arches, portals and doors of infinite variety and style. Each doorway led to a new wonder, a new marvel, but not just of inventiveness, for the labyrinth was by no means deserted, it was also peopled, though sparsely, by the strangest of inhabitants. They did not seem to live there, for there were no houses or buildings as such, they simply wandered leisurely, conversed, laughed and played among the pools, squares, gardens, bridges and passage ways. They too, it seemed, were seeking a way through the maze, but with no sense of urgency or import, it all seemed just a game to them. There was food aplenty, fruit and berries grew everywhere, fresh water was all around and if sleep should be needed, then lie down and sleep, the sun was warm and the air still.

Some of the races represented there they recognised; faeries, undines, sylphs, and even some of the mortal races were present; but there were also many they did not recognise – at least Rebekah and Mikael certainly did not! Similar to the faeries that they knew as Ariyanrhod's children, there were what Arkturon called poukas, these had pale yellow, straw-like hair and incredibly pale blue eyes that contrasted sharply with their dark bronzed skin, they were dressed – both male and female – in simple white loincloths only and were the children, he said, of Rhiyannon – the Great Queen and mistress of Kear Rigor.

Arkturon then pointed out the zephyrs, these inhabited the air as did the sylphs, and occasionally flew over their heads, they seemed less human in appearance and much larger than the sylphs but were just as insubstantial. They reminded Rebekah of a knight in full armour astride a horse – a horse with two legs and wings though – with cloak and colours billowing, but where the knight ended and the horse began she could not tell, they seemed moulded as one.

"They are vassals of Arrawn, the Great King." said Arkturon.

They certainly look noble, Rebekah thought, *and imposing... they could be terrifying I'm sure* – but, in that moment at least, they lacked any air of menace.

The next corner they turned brought them face to face with a creature of water, not as an undine is of water but literally made from water, the shape was of a bald human-like woman but the substance was clear, bright and glistening from the light above. She smiled at them and passed, the refracted image of the wall beyond could be seen through her pure body, there were no internal organs or bones to render her opaque and hold her up, no skin to hold her in, she was held by a greater force.

"A sprite." said Arkturon as she passed them, his eyes full of wonder.

But most striking of all were the creatures of fire that they came across. First were the salamander's, servants of the Maponus, they were dark skinned and their hair was flame, that flickered slowly about their heads, their eyes too seemed to burn but with a cool fire of ochre. They were naked, but their lithe glistening bodies seemed to show no trace of gender, no breasts and no visible genitals, their pubic region was bald and simply tapered smoothly between the legs. The second creatures of fire that they saw Arkturon called corposants and they were composed entirely of a blue flame that writhed and sparked violently within the shape of a human figure. They were capable of flying at incredible speeds, for one shot past them – startlingly – as they crossed a narrow bridge close to the castle.

From that tall bridge the path they were led down descended sharply and passed below the plane of the labyrinth, the high walled alley they then walked through had increasing numbers of arches and bridges that passed over head until it almost seemed a tunnel. The walls narrowed toward them while the spans above became more distant, it was dark and cool in the gently curving alleyway and just when the darkness was becoming a hindrance the curve they were following ceased and their path straightened to show a tall, slim slither of light ahead of them. As they neared this exit they could see an expanse of water beyond and a mist that seemed to hang above it, level with the bridges and arches above them.

Leaving the labyrinth they found themselves by the shore of the lake or moat that surrounded Kear Pedrivan, and what little they could see of the castle's outer walls, between the water and the mist, defied explanation. The square castle did not rest in the water, or on an island, but seemed to be floating about a yard or so above the lake surface – and the walls were slowly revolving.

Afagddu turned to them and said "I must leave you now, it is up to you to find a way into Kear Pedrivan, it is a test you can only do alone... just believe and have faith that there is a safe way across." He bowed to them and again kissed Rebekah's hand, then without another word he returned into the labyrinth.

Rebekah and Mikael looked to Arkturon. "Well," he said, "let's walk round the lake and find the bridge."

"It is as easy as that?" said Mikael sceptically as they began to walk.

"Er... well no – not quite." answered Arkturon. "But I will explain when we get there."

The labyrinth skirted the round lake side as a very tall and smooth wall made from huge blocks of stone that fitted together almost seamlessly, it would be impossible to scale it in either direction and the only entrance seemed to be the one they had come through. The bottom of the castle revolved anti-clockwise and they were circling it in a clockwise direction, making the movement of the spinning walls seem that much faster and more perilous.

When they finally came to the bridge, Mikael looked at Arkturon incredulously, "We cannot possibly cross that!" he said. "Our feet would get cut to shreds or we'd be slice in two."

The bridge was in fact a blade, as sharp as any Mikael had seen, like a very long sword laid edge on, that stretched from the shore to stop just short of the revolving corners of the castle walls. At each of the four corners there was the base of a round tower – the heights of which were lost in the mist above. The blade was suspended – somehow – about a yard above the waters of the lake.

"Not at all," said Arkturon, "it is an illusion – it is perfectly safe as long as you believe that it is safe, once you doubt, it will indeed be as the blade you see."

"What is that supposed to mean... is it a blade or not?" asked Mikael perturbed.

"No... it just looks like it is. It is a deception... look." Arkturon stepped out onto the bridge, not even taking care to place his feet centrally over the blade, as he did so the water bubbled around him. The heel of one foot and the toe of the other were the only parts that touched the razor like edge, if the bridge were true it would be impossible for him to be that balanced; he would topple... and loose half his toes at least. He stepped off again, "See."

They had seen it, but Mikael at least seemed not completely convinced, he crouched down to the floor and peered at the sword bridge side on – he then gingerly tested it with his hand and discovered that the bridge was in fact just less than a foot wide. *Still very narrow*, he thought, *but much better than walking on a sword edge.*

""Now try standing on it," instructed Arkturon.

Mikael stood and stepped onto the bridge, then quickly stepped off again, "An illusion." He confirmed, smiling.

Rebekah never doubted it and stepped straight on to the bridge without a word, waiting to look at the bubbling water that broke out beneath her before moving back to the land. As soon as Arkturon had said it was safe she had believed him.

"Right." said Arkturon. "We will cross single file, but together. Me first, then Rebekah and then you Mikael, but keep close and stay centred over the blade – the bridge is still very narrow. Do not look down into the water – its motion will play havoc with your sense of balance, just look straight ahead to the person in front. When we reach the other side we will have to wait for the steps to go by and jump on as they do." He pointed to one of the round tower corners of the castle – it had some steps, which jutted out to meet the end of the sword-bridge and led up to a large door. "There will not be time for us all to get straight on in one go, so we will have to do it in turn as the steps come round again.

Well, let us go then." He stepped onto the bridge and began to walk across with the others following behind. The water immediately thrashed and churned around them and Arkturon again told them to stare straight ahead and to give the water below no heed at all. They slowly spanned the perilous bridge and came to a halt at its end; the castle seemed to be revolving a lot faster now that they were close up. Looking up they could see glimpses of golden light, with a blue sky and trees so green, through the narrow slits and windows between the imposing stone buttresses as they rushed by.

Arkturon turned his head to Rebekah and said, "Once I am on the steps wait for me to come round again and hold your arms up, I will grab you as I go past."

She nodded and they waited briefly before the few stairs approached them from the left, Arkturon leapt just before they aligned with him and he landed deftly on the lower two. He was disappearing round the other side before any of them could say anything. Without Arkturon's steady bulk before her, Rebekah found the fast moving stone walls extremely disconcerting, so rather than keep looking ahead she looked to her left and waited for him to re-appear. She found it very off putting as each massive rounded corner rapidly approached her, then passed with a swoosh that threatened to blow her off her precarious perch, but she ignored it. It was surprisingly soon when the fourth corner came again, with the stairs and the waiting arms of Arkturon. Lifting her hands above her head she jumped into his embrace as he deftly lowered himself to catch her.

Mikael was sure the castle's speed was building up, but despite this, it seemed – to him at least – to take even longer for the stairs, now with Arkturon and Rebekah on them, to come round again. He too found the motion of the solid wall ahead of him disconcerting – but he looked down away from it, the water was swirling and bubbling at his feet, and becoming more violent, it was then that his eyes fixed on the impossibly thin blade – the blade on which he stood. He looked immediately to his left – *for the stairs* – and tried to dispel his sudden panic, he was beginning to shake and he knew his balance would soon fail him; he summoned all his willpower as each corner swished by – so close... *it is not a razor thin blade – it's an illusion!* The stairs finally came round into view, *it's an illusion...* coming very fast, *an illusion...* he jumped...

Mikael tumbled onto the steps as they sped past, pulling his feet from under him, but Arkturon grabbed at his waist and stopped him falling into the now churning water below. They quickly mounted the steps to the top one where Rebekah waited.

Before them stood a tall, dark and heavy looking wooden door, bound by thick brass strips and rivets with elongated triangular hinge brackets crudely cutting across the uniformly vertical grain of the wood. In the centre of this door, at eye level, was fixed a large brass face, its mouth was open and out of either side twisted a leafy branch that split and circled the face at top and bottom like hair and a beard, its tongue rolled out to rest on its chin and its eyes stared wildly out from beneath two bushy eyebrows. Despite the aged metallic bronze and green colouring, it looked remarkably life like. Arkturon briskly grabbed the tongue and lifted it with a squeak of a hinge before bringing it back down sharply three times.

The knocks it produced seemed to be out of all proportion to the size of the knocker itself and when the echoing inside faded a voice suddenly sounded around them, a man's voice, strong and powerful.

"Name that which is always right and never wrong." The voice intoned. "Name what can heal the most intolerable grief or hurt but can cut deeper than the sharpest sword. It can be the most soothing balm or it can be the bitterest pill of all. Name it and enter."

Arkturon turned to Mikael and Rebekah, "Any ideas?" he whispered with a worried look on his face.

"Do you not know?" said a concerned Mikael and Rebekah together.

"Oh yes... I just wanted to see if either of you knew the answer?" He waited.

"I have absolutely no idea." confessed an exasperated Mikael with an emphatic shrug of his shoulders.

"Is it honesty?" asked Rebekah softly, after giving it some thought.

"Very good... almost right, I'm impressed. It is *truth*." The wizard turned to the door and shouted his answer.

The door opened outward, causing them to move to one side and out of its way. They passed through an arched passage that took them through the base of the round tower and, as the door closed behind them, they entered a large square garden of lush grass and tall trees. At its centre was a monumental spiral staircase hewn from stone, which rose into the mist above their heads, a diffuse golden light bathed everything but neither sun nor other source could be seen. The garden was very peaceful and they could not tell if the grounds that they stood on, and the high walls around them, were still revolving or not. All seemed so still and quiet.

Rebekah was tempted to rush up a narrow set of steps on the inside of the wall to the left of the doorway – they led up to a balustraded gangway that provided access to the windows and arrow loops in the wall – so that she could look out over the lake and labyrinth beyond, and see if the castle was still in motion.

"Come on then," said Arkturon though, "let us get up these stairs." referring to the ones at the centre of the garden, "Up and onward." he added with a laugh as he strode toward the ivy covered construction of battered stonework that looked as if it had stood for an age and more. Mikael and Rebekah traced his steps and followed him to the spiral staircase.

Chapter Nineteen – Through the Black Mirror

Lilith could see that Luwsiy had been bewitched into a sexual frenzy by the three sisters; the spell cast upon her by them would ensure her weakened state and diminish her will to resist Bäliyl's wicked plan as it comes to its awful fruition. Lilith despaired at the thought that she would be the instrument – and the reason – for the girl's murder, no blood would be spilt, neither skin nor bones broken, but murder it would still be, a murder of the darkest, foulest kind.

Bäliyl was standing by a small hexagonal table made from a carved hard wood, a silky cloth of black and gold was spread between its surface and the various oddments scattered upon it. His naked body was covered in sweat, produced by the intense concentration required for such evil work, and he glistened in the flickering light of the many pungent black candles and smoking braziers around him. He was erect but Lilith knew that it was not the naked young girl bound and begging obscenities of him that had him aroused, it was the ritual – and the power – that he lusted after.

He picked up a small silver box off the table and opened it, picking out some short, curly blonde hair with his finger tips he then sprinkled it onto a copper tray that was suspended on a small ornate tripod beside a thick, grubby looking candle at the centre of the table. Then from a second silver box he picked some nail parings and did the same, once he had closed that box he added various powders, herbs and extracts to form a small pile of matter in the tray before him, all the while he mumbled incantations to himself as if in a trance.

Lilith guessed that the hair and nail parings belonged to Luwsiy, and that a similar operation would have been performed only moments ago with her own hair and clippings – gained surreptitiously, probably years before – in the calling and binding of her own spirit.

Bäliyl then lit a taper on the thick candle, made from the fat of a hanged though innocent man, and, with his murmurings becoming frantic and excited, he lit the material in the copper tray. It flared dramatically at first then died to a steady flame that sent a pale stream of smoke to the blackened ceiling above. Luwsiy's ranting and raving ceased almost immediately and – following a slight struggle and a lingering tremble that travelled up and down her body and limbs – her shimmering, perspiration covered form became suddenly motionless.

Luwsiy's body still housed her spirit and soul, but now her mind was entranced –spellbound and bonded to his whim and his will.

Bäliyl lifted an ebony handled knife from the table and approached the prone girl with a bowl shaped vessel of slither thin sardonyx; crouching between her legs he carefully scraped the knife over and round her groin, collecting her sweat and vaginal juices in the almost translucent red bowl. He then nicked her inner thigh and added a few drops of her blood to the mix. Putting the bowl and knife down he then began to rub himself against the now entirely unresponsive girl, pushing his engorged penis over her labia, clitoris and pubic mound; being very careful not to enter her. As he approached his climax he lifted himself onto the girl and ejaculated onto her stomach, his semen collecting in the hollow of her navel. With his knife he lifted some of his seed and deposited it in the bowl with the girl's fluids, then added his own sweat, spittle and blood to the potion; he began to mix it all together with the point of his knife.

Still muttering his ritual recitations he returned to the table, put the bowl down and lifted a small phial, opened it and dropped some of the contents into the mixture. Lilith guessed that they were her own bodily fluids. She then guessed that it was her own hair and nail clippings that he added to the fire on the copper tray for once he had done so she began to be drawn toward Luwsiy's spread-eagled body. She resisted as best she could, but she knew that it was purely a token gesture, for she could do nothing to stop it. Her phantasmic form was melting and flowed toward the girl – like an image in a distorted mirror, bending and shifting out of shape – the substance of her fetch was being drawn into the orifices of the living, breathing prison before her. Fear for Luwsiy dispersed before her own sudden fear of living again; life meant pain, despair, loneliness and grief. That brief time of true freedom of spirit she had experienced was everything to her – that and Mikael – and she was about to lose both. Lilith screamed within her mind, a scream of total despair and desperation, a scream of desperate love and passion – of a spell that truly bound her long before any contrivance of her father's on her spirit, she was bound – spirit, soul and mind – to Mikael and to his love for her, and her's for him. Her scream shattered Bäliyl's spells of binding but left her shocked and dazed as her phantasmic essence was forcibly entered into the soft, moist, warm and terrified flesh of Luwsiy.

Rebekah was beginning to feel the dizzying effects of vertigo, she was already out of breath and her thigh muscles were burning from the long travail up the countless, twisting steps. The mist around them prevented her from seeing any great distance up or down, but the simple fact that they had been climbing the spiralling stone staircase for so long now – meant that they must be at an impossible height for such an old and battered looking structure. She desperately tried not to think about how it could possibly remain standing.

"I think we are nearly there," said Arkturon, puffing from the exertion. "I can see something coming down out of the mist."

Rebekah looked up and squinted into the distance above, she could see nothing at first, but then something did begin to loom toward them, something huge and extremely disconcerting. A seemingly limitless revolving ceiling of stone crept toward them as they climbed; straight ahead was a circular hole through which the staircase ascended. Around the large hole there were channels cut into the stone and radiating out were many slits and smaller holes, all were defensive and seemed to be for various forms of pouring, shooting and throwing through, though none looked as if they had ever been used. The surrounds of all these features were very ornate and elaborately decorated and formed a huge flower like pattern on the underside of the spinning ceiling. Rebekah's dizziness heightened as she realised that it was the stairs that were in fact turning, not the ceiling. She remembered that the castle proper was not revolving when she had seen it from a distance earlier in the labyrinth – only the lower section was turning and these stairs were attached to that.

As they followed the thread of the spiral staircase up into the hole, they left the mist and light behind. Though not complete, the darkness closed in rapidly and Arkturon was forced to blaze a light at the crown of his staff so that they could keep their tired footing sure. The glowing tip of his staff quickly became unnecessary though, for a diffuse and many coloured illumination was soon meandering down the round stairwell to greet them, it seemed to be carried on a fresh and gentle breeze, along with a very fine, almost imperceptible, cooling spray that acted like a refreshing sea-fret. With no prompting at all, their steps quickened into it.

The stairs began to widen and the curve of the spiral became larger as they neared the top; old, battered and cracked stones had been replaced by newly hewn, that were smooth and polished – and a soft sound drifted down to them, it sounded like wind passing over hollow reeds and through deep and resonant sea caves – but still so soft, so distant.

The three companions ascended into the peripheral antechamber of an enormous hall; floor, walls, columns and arches were all made from the smoothest, shiniest marble of differing shades and pattern. Cascading stairs circled the hall leading to numerous balustraded levels and landings that rose high above their heads to be lost in the brilliant shafts of light that were refracted down to the centre of the floor through hundreds of coloured windows and open balconies. The finest scented mist descended down on them, twisting and turning in eddies and currents created by the ever present breeze.

The place seemed aglow and there, in the incandescent centre of the hall's circular floor, sat the god Matt on a shining throne atop a multi levelled dais that was occupied by representatives of each of the various non-human races they had seen outside. "Ah, you are here." said the divine Guardian of the East loudly, after turning from a conversation with a male sylph at his right hand. "You do not have much time I am afraid, so I must send you on your way almost immediately... but not without help. Come, approach me."

Arkturon and the others did as he bid. Once they had reached the dais, the god – with earnest solemnity and an intense, bright eyed urgency – said to them, "From here you will be delivered to the reverse of my realm, the realm of my dark brother Hlewid, once there you must be swift and find the gate to your own world as it opens – and pass through without hesitation. To aid you and to divert the forces of my brother, I and my kin have nominated some of the best of our children to enter the evil realm with you. They will gladly sacrifice their lives for you and our cause." Matt indicated those that stood on his left side, "First, to act as your guide, is this daughter of the Nemetona." A cloaked and hooded faery came forward, she carried a long bow and quiver at her shoulder and a long but thinly sharp sword at her waist, Rebekah flushed immediately as she recognised the lithe and beautiful girl that came and stood beside her. The god added, "Juwniper will desert you only in death."

"As a diversion a group of others will also enter with you," he continued, "but will separate and draw attention away from you for as long as you are in danger of discovery within that evil realm." This other group was comprised of four; a sylph and a zephyr, with a pouka and a salamander. Only the pouka seemed to be carrying any weapons – a sword and bow like those belonging to Juwniper.

Matt then spoke briefly and silently to the sylph at his right who nodded when the god had finished and descended the dais toward them.

"Akanthis will show you to the point where mine and my evil brother's domains conjoin," said Matt, "there is such a point of reversal in every god's realm, though, as you would expect, they are little used."

"Follow me." requested Akanthis of the two groups. His voice, face and manner reminded Rebekah of Bodkin when in one of his more officious moods.

Arkturon bowed low to the god – a reverential action quickly imitated by Mikael and Rebekah – and then thanked him for his help. They were led past the dais to the far side of the huge hall and on through a tall doorway into a small ante-chamber, to the left was another doorway which led on into a long passage way, at the bottom of this stood a huge black mirror – covering the entire wall and framed with baroque silver and gold.

"This is the portal you must traverse," said Akanthis. "I wish you all luck and blessings." He then stood aside with little ceremony.

"I think we should enter first," said the zephyr of his group, "if we should be unlucky enough to encounter any of Hlewid's wraiths or were-beasts straight off we can draw them away before you enter. So hold a couple of minutes before following us." His laconic voice was quiet but authoritative and only hinted at the power that his formidable appearance all but screamed of. It was hard to tell where the creature's and his mount's – if it were a mount at all – muscle, horn, bone or hair began and where its apparel, robes and armour ended – and Rebekah felt too uncomfortable staring at him too obviously, so she remained unsure. One enigma was suddenly answered though as the zephyr dismounted, and – having heard no opposition to his plan – cautiously led his graceful winged-horse like creature into the mirror which flexed and distorted soundlessly as they passed through. The sylph, pouka and salamander briefly looked to the others before following him.

"Good luck." Rebekah found herself saying. She was trembling and only then realised how frightened she had suddenly become. An otherworld full of sylphs and faeries had been one thing – exciting and comparatively easy to take – *but demons and wraiths and other such monsters...* she desperately vexed, *that's a different matter entirely!* Things were suddenly developing very quickly, the hour of reckoning was upon them, and she did not like it one bit.

"Mikael," said Arkturon, "save your flintlocks for Bäliyl when we meet him, in the realm of Hlewid use your blade – that goes for you too Rebekah, unsheathe them now – and be ready. Make all strokes swift and sure, go for the heart or head. Wraiths can be killed too."

They stood in a row in front of the large mirror, their dark reflections staring back out at them. Rebekah saw cool determination in each of their faces, Juwniper's, Arkturon's and Mikael's, in all except her own – where she just saw fear... and a girl who did not belong. Arkturon caught her eye in the mirror as he too unsheathed his sword, he smiled and his look said more than any amount of words. Her fear and insecurity was met by a grim determination.

"Let us go then." He said, and stepped into his reflection. Rebekah looked into her own eyes and moved toward them.

Beyond the mirror it was dark and ominously silent; there was no sign of the four who had preceded them; a cold, clinging mist pervaded and soon soaked them to their skins.

"Stay close to me." The faery said as she primed her long bow with an arrow and, half crouching, started down the black marbled hallway alert and seemingly ready for anything, skirting the pools of water that had collected at intervals along it.

Rebekah quickly glanced back to see a mirror identical to the one they had entered through, their four receding reflections rapidly getting lost in the darkness of its glass. She gripped her long knife tightly and looked down at its cold and bright blade as she followed the others, its image flashed in the shiny floor as she turned and twisted it, focusing beyond she again saw the diffuse pale oval of her own frightened face looking back.

"Against the wall!" Juwniper suddenly whispered sharply as she pushed herself against the right-hand side of the passage, the mortal's copied her action immediately. There were sounds of a skirmish coming from somewhere in front of them; it seemed to be getting nearer and more furious – at an unnervingly rapid rate. The faery edged toward an intersection ahead and stopped as she reached the corner. The sounds of battle were almost upon them.

She peeked quickly round the corner and pulled her face straight back. "Over there – now!" the faery shouted, pointing to the corner opposite from where she stood. Arkturon rushed across the passageway to the left-hand intersection that led to another dark passage way, Mikael pushed Rebekah ahead of him and she ran to Arkturon – glancing into the right intersection she saw the mounted zephyr battling with a swarm of screaming wraiths that set upon him mercilessly, he was being pushed back toward them.

"Run!" shouted Juwniper as she moved to join Mikael as he too crossed the passage. The wraiths were being cut to shreds by the zephyr who seemed to have produced claws as big as knives as he span and thrashed at his assailants, but their numbers were increasing and unstoppable. A stray and lone wraith saw Juwniper run and immediately flew at her back, a warning shout from Arkturon though, turned her toward it and she loosed her arrow straight to its coldly luminous heart. The arrow struck true and was suspended momentarily before the shaft burst into flame, the creature too was halted and it dissolved with a piercing scream as its death's head seemingly shattered into tiny shards. A wisp of smoke curled to oblivion as the metal arrowhead tumbled to the floor.

"Quickly – get away from here before any more of them see us!" said the faery girl as she swiftly ran past them– putting her long-bow over her shoulder and drawing her sword. Not much further they came to a broadly sweeping stair case that descended down into the depths

At the bottom of the long winding stairs a sunken waterlogged passage led to a massive hall full of columns and drapes. They dodged between the rows of broad pillars and the black draperies that were spread, like very fine netting, intermittently between them. Rapidly they left the sounds of the vicious fight and the hideous screams of dying wraiths behind, the group slowed and cautiously halted for breath and to assess their situation. The columns and increasingly moth-eaten drapes conspired to form a kind of maze that prevented any overview of where they – and their way out – might be.

"Where do we go now... which way?" said Rebekah, frantic.

"I think we should just pick a direction and cut our way out." answered Mikael simply, slicing one of the filmy drapes.

"Good idea – but which direction..." commented Juwniper as she flicked her now dripping hair from her face, "the door to your world could appear anywhere within this cursed citadel."

"It will be somewhere close to the centre – close to Hlewid's throne room," said Arkturon "...but not too close, probably in one of the antechamber's around it."

"Right, then this way I think." said Juwniper as she cut her blade through the damp and clinging material opposite the one that Mikael had divided.

As they moved deeper into the antithetical Kear Pedrivan the fine mist became a spray that fell from the invisible heights of the castle above them, soon large drops were descending on them like a black rain from the darkness. Rebekah shivered from the cold and damp, and from the fear – there was a heavy presence within this castle that was made even more oppressive by its great contrast to the light airiness she had experienced in Matt's abode. Sharply but briefly it seemed to become more manifest, making her stomach set on edge then roll in on itself, she was sure she would throw-up at any second.

The sudden increase in tension had not gone unnoticed by her companions either. "The door to our world – it has opened!" hissed Arkturon. "We must find it now – or we will be too late!"

The deathly cold had increased too, unbearably so. Down another waterlogged sunken hallway leading from the drape and column maze, Juwniper dropped to one knee as she reached a large arched doorway that led to a steep and upward curving stairway. "The Dark Lord..." she whispered hoarsely, "he is close... so very close!" Her wide eyed face looking desperately at Arkturon.

He paused only briefly. "We just keep moving – stop for nothing and no-one... come on!" Splashing noisily he passed her, mounting the stairs and running up them as they swept to the right and out of sight. The others followed quickly with only a fleeting hesitation.

Once the heavy oaken doors of the keep had closed behind them, the Sergeant and his Rangers found themselves in a wide, torch-lit passage. There were defensive holes in the ceiling above and arrow slits in the walls on either side, thankful that they seemed unmanned the troop quickly and quietly ventured further into the keep. About twenty feet in, the band of elite soldiers came to a cross section. "Which way, Corporal?" asked the Sergeant softly.

Corporal Villovürt at first listened carefully and then seemed to sniff the air from each direction in turn; first to the left, then straight ahead and then to the right. She tried to sense a trace of Luwsiy or Lilith. The dark-elf took a small soft pellet of Ariyanan hashish from a pouch in one of her pockets, popped it into her mouth and started to chew – it was a concoction of her own making, she had lightly infused the purified resin of the Green Dragon plant with Yaggothiyan fungal spores and ground Ffrijiyan-Cap shrooms. Her mouth soon filled with bitter-sweet saliva, which she swallowed. Once the rush hit and opened her mind, Villovürt mentally probed the structure around her; cautiously she sent an invisible fragment of her phantasmic fetch ahead – seeking the two captives... and the sorcerer Bäliyl. Seeing the psychic landscape through that of the material with her astral projection, his presence soon became apparent, it was like a yawning black pit, drawing on the energy of about eighteen thralls he had in his power... they stood in a wide circle about him – still and silent, freely offering their phantasmic life-force in service to him and his evil magiks. The streams of sapped psychic vigour were converging beneath the keep like a whirlpool of dark, foul waters – drawing shadowed phantasmic energies from throughout the area of the ancient castle and the surrounding environs of the malignant Old Forest. And there, close to the centre of that evil and malevolent maelstrom, were Luwsiy and Lilith. Villovürt indicated that the Rangers should go straight ahead.

With arrows still nocked and ready, they cautiously advanced past the two side passages and continued farther, with the Corporal taking the lead and the Sergeant at her side. The next juncture, another twenty feet or so further in, was a T-junction. The Corporal again sounded and sniffed out the two possibilities, then led the group into the left-hand passageway. Just as all the soldiers entered this slightly narrower stone bound corridor a door opened down its right-hand equivalent and a deep gruff yell of "Hey!" was sounded behind them – then a shout of "Intruders!"

The two Rangers at the back, Rigormort and Gudrun, immediately span round to face the man who called out and they instantly had their arrows trained at his broad, studded leather clad chest some four or five yards away. Simultaneously, both projectiles were loosed at the bearded, axe-wielding and wild-looking woodsman that had blundered into the corridor. Before the brute could react, both lungs were pierced right through by the long black arrows. Bewildered, he looked down at the black feather fletching and the few inches of slim lacquered shafts left visible at his front, he staggered back emitting a frothy and desperate last couple of gasps, then collapsed dead to the floor.

Upping their pace, the Rangers continued on – but another door opened just as they were passing it. Again, it was a wild-eyed woodsman, but this one had been waiting for them to pass – clearly warned by the shouts of the first. He pounced out of the doorway and swept his axe down at Wellnap's skull – which would surely have been cleaved in two had not the alert and spritely Ranger side stepped out of the way with just a hair's breadth to spare. Wellnap dropped his longbow and unsheathed his dagger in one fluid motion as he stepped aside, and then stuck the sturdy, double edged blade into the attacker's heart, through the left side of his rib cage under his arm, and twisted it around to the front, scraping along the thin rib-bone there. Quickly removing the blade the Ranger then pushed the already dead woodsman back into the doorway he'd just come through.

Corporal Villovürt led the Rangers toward the rear of the keep then down a flight of stairs. Along another torch lit corridor and then to another flight of stairs which would lead them deeper into the structure and close to the place where Bäliyl worked his sorceries. But, it was at the head of this second stairway that they met with the largest golem that any of them had ever seen before. And, to top it all, it was a golem carved from a huge chunk of black stone, cut and polished like a multifaceted gemstone of jet or opal – golems carved from rock and other solid substances, as every Ranger there knew, are the hardest to deal with. Arrows, guns and swords could be next to useless against this rock hard elemental adversary.

"Only those with the Mark of Bäliyl can pass." It stated with loud, strangely resonating and cracking tones as the group cautiously approached. The heavy set creature, which was stood to attention when they first saw it, now changed its stance to a more offensive position, as if it was ready to wrestle or even charge them. The Rangers stopped their advance in unison – the stone sentinel just stood there... ready.

"Any suggestions?" whispered the Sergeant to his men in general, but to Corporal Villovürt in particular. He was praying to any and all the gods that might be listening, that she, their occult specialist, would know how to deal with such a formidable magikal creature as this.

"What's this *Mark of Bäliyl*?" interrupted Rigormort quietly from the back. "Maybe we can bluff our way past this thing?"

"The mark could be a sign or sigil that his followers have on them – branded or tattooed." said the Corporal. "It might even be on a piece of paper or parchment that they carry... or maybe its Bäliyl's blood, so only vampires infected by him can get passed his sentry?"

"Rigormort and Gudrun," said the Sergeant, "go back and quickly check the body of that last kill. Check every inch of his body and then every stitch of his clothes. See if you can find an obvious sign or sigil on him."

The two Rangers retraced their steps, back up the stairs toward the woodsman that Wellnap had so ably killed.

Sergeant Rinawn then asked of the Corporal, "If we can't bluff a way passed it – how do we put it down, there must be a way?"

"I know of three ways that would effectively nullify such a creature, Sarge. But none of them would be easy. The first would be with a massive hard impact, a sudden blunt or sharp strike, made with enough force to crack the stone and potentially break it into pieces. The second, is to somehow obliterate or destroy the three magical glyphs of vitalisation that will be marked or carved somewhere on its body. The third would be to destroy the parchment that has the spell of binding written on it, it's what makes the golem obedient to only its master's words, and is probably hidden in the creature's mouth."

"All right then," said the Sergeant, "well at least that gives us some options to work with." He seemed to think a moment and then added, "What do the glyphs of vitalisation look like?"

"They resemble the letters G, L and M – it's where the name *golem* comes from – and will be marked in a row, and in that order. They're usually carved or somehow written on the creature's forehead... but not always." Villovürt studied what she could see of the black shining golem in the poor light provided by the few flickering torches suspended about the walls. "I can't see them in this light, but they could be quite small... and hard to spot. I don't think it'll actually attack unless we try to pass it, so it might be safe to approach the thing and get closer for a better look."

The Sergeant sent a quizzical look at her. "Are you sure?" he asked.

"Not entirely," she said honestly, "but it's worth a try."

The dark-elf took a step forward. The golem did nothing.

She took another step forward. The golem adjusted its stance to centre its gaze on her, but did not attack. She was now within about four steps of the towering stone figure.

As she took the next step forward, the creature raised its huge fisted arm as if to strike her. She immediately stepped back, and the golem froze again, its arm still raised and its gaze still centred on her. "Seems this is as close as I'm going to get." said Villovürt under her breath. She studied the shinning multifaceted surfaces visible to her, looking for a trace of the magikal vitalising glyphs. Then, suddenly she saw them. The three glyphs were quite large, but cut subtly shallow, they covered the flat expanse of the stone-golem's broad and protruding forehead. "Found them." She said quietly as she stepped back to the others. "A good and heavy pickaxe would be useful – smashing a chunk off its forehead will break the vitalisation spell... or break its mouth and jaw open to break the binding spell. Either would do... if we could get close enough to deliver the blow."

"Damn it to all the hells!" whispered the exasperated Sergeant. "The only pickaxes we have are with the rest of the gear back with the horses."

Then Wellnap spoke out, "Sarge, I think I know where there might be some pickaxes."

"Well don't keep it to yourself man... where?"

"Back in that room that the last Wildman came out of, it looked like some sort of store room – I'm sure it had all kinds of tools, weapons and other stuff in there."

"Get back there then," said the Sergeant with urgency, "have a look and, with Gudrun and Rigormort, bring back any heavy tools you can find – pickaxes, sledgehammers... anything that might crack open this giant black jewel of a beast."

"Yes, Sarge." the Ranger said as he sprinted off.

Wellnap bounded up the stairs and ran down the corridor then turned left round a corner to see the two other Rangers searching the woodsman's body and clothes. "Find anything?" he asked as he approached them.

"Nothing." said a dejected Gudrun.

"Don't matter, lad" replied Wellnap. Reaching them he pointed to the store room beyond, "We need to get some pickaxes and hammers or something... anything heavy – we're going to smash that moving statue to smithereens."

There were all kinds of weapons and tools scattered about the room amongst the many crates, boxes and chests piled high. As the sounds of a volley of gunfire echoed down the corridor from the entranceway the three quickly scrambled about and retrieved three heavy pickaxes, a couple of mighty war-hammers and a massive two-handed mace. "Sounds like they're having fun at the door." offhanded Wellnap, "Let's have some fun of our own." Laden down with their finds, the Rangers started back to the rest of their companions.

Wellnap took the lead with the ever stern Rigormort behind him and young Gudrun bringing up the rear. Just as they were about to reach the first corner, Gudrun was grabbed from behind and dragged violently backward. His yell of alarm turned rapidly into a blood-curdling scream as a ravening sharp tooth maw tore at his throat and ripped a gushing and spurting chunk of bloody, sinewy flesh from his neck.

The two leading Rangers span round to see the younger trooper's blood spraying from the mauled remnants of his neck and froth, gurgling, from his bitten windpipe. He sat there, twitching, as the life left him – a look of absolute horror on his ashen face – and behind him the figure of a semi-clad woman rose like a primeval predator, her fanged and bloodied mouth hissing at them, her eyes burning with pure hate and full of insatiable blood-lust. The two experienced soldiers stood there, frozen with a primal fear instilled by the appalling act and the invading mind and chilling presence of a vampire sorceress no less dangerous than her powerful primogenitor – Bäliyl himself.

Wellnap stood gawping, enthralled by the hideous beauty before him. The sounds of a second volley of gunshot resounded from the front doorway of the keep as Rigormort forced himself to act with a herculean exertion of will, that broke the witch's enchantment – he dropped the heavy weapons held in each hand then unsheathed the dagger at his belt, throwing it straight and sure at the woman's heart.

Aggareth, with cat-like reflexes and gracility, immediately bent her body backwards to avoid the blade which skimmed over and past her – leaving a long and bloodied nick in her left breast. She continued her motion backwards, cart-wheeling onto her hands then back again onto her two feet. She glared at Rigormort – who was now unsheathing his sabre and advancing on her. With unnatural agility and speed, Aggareth almost flew from the Rangers, back down the corridor and out of sight.

Rigormort was about to give chase when Wellnap, now released from the witch's spell, put a firm hand on his shoulder, saying, "Don't be a fool – she wants you to follow – we need to get back with the others!"

"Damn!" fumed Sergeant Rinawn on hearing of Gudrun's demise. "After we've dealt with Bäliyl, I'm personally going to hunt down each of those three bitch daughter's of his and gut them... slowly!" He could barely contain his anger. "Give me that pickaxe!" He stared at Wellnap like a man who would kill absolutely anyone that defied him or got in his way.

Wellnap handed him the pickaxe. "Sinkhoal, you take that big, fucking mace." That left Wellnap with a war-hammer and Rigormort with another pickaxe.

The Sergeant heft his pickaxe in both hands and faced the black statue that blocked their way. "The glyphs are on the golem's forehead – so, by the gods and all that's holy, we're gonna smash its head to pieces. First me, then Sinkhoal, then Rigormort and then Wellnap..." He glanced back, "Got that?"

They all nodded.

With lightning speed the Sergeant charged with the pickaxe raised behind him – within feet of the golem he swung the heavy pointed tool down on to its head, it skittered off to the side and hit the golem's shoulder, sending shards and fragments of black stone in all directions. The golem's fist swung at the Ranger but the Sergeant dodged it easily before backing up. The golem stubbornly stayed put at the top of the stairs that they so desperately needed access to – only able to step aside for those that bore the mark of Bäliyl.

Sinkhoal charged the thing with his massive mace swinging, it smashed into the side of the golem's head with a thundering smack – causing the animated effigy to sway to one side but remain standing as its other fist side-swiped the big Ranger who went reeling to the wall, winded and clutching his chest – sure that every rib he possessed was broken. Almost immediately Rigormort's perfectly aimed pickaxe landed just above the golem's forehead – cracking it open and causing the whole ugly face, glyphs and all, to shear off and clacker to the floor. The animated statue stopped dead, but remained standing... till Wellnap smacked it square in the chest with the mighty war-hammer that sent it toppling backwards down the stone stairs behind it, causing a deafening clamour of clattering and shattering stone to irrupt from below among billowing clouds of dust and thrown shards of black stone detritus.

Chapter Twenty – The Sorcerer's Gambit

Lieutenant Lethbridj and his group of Rangers took what shelter they could behind the ornate stone balustrade of the stairs and platform that fronted the doorway into the keep. He was determined to keep the exit clear for when the Sergeant and his group came back out, hopefully with the kidnapped girl safely in his charge. Random confused goblins and the occasional robed acolyte had run into the inner-bailey courtyard from the buildings on either side as the alarm had spread. They had been picked off relatively easily by the Rangers and their longbows, but now arrows from the various watchtowers that dotted the inner-bailey's defensive walls were starting to sail in at them too. And, suddenly, the gates of the inner gatehouse burst open and two troll guards rushed into the courtyard – followed rapidly by a troop of about six wilding goblins mounted on their large and vicious looking black-shuk hell hounds.

"Take out the mounts first!" ordered the Lieutenant hoarsely. "Then the trolls and then the goblins!"

The barking and howling goblin mounts bounded past the relatively slow moving trolls and broke across the courtyard toward the invaders, straight into volley after volley of the Ranger's deadly black arrows. The mounts at the front were cut down immediately, squealing and yelping, and throwing their goblin riders to the hard stone flooring. Those behind leapt over their fallen comrades – baying for blood – but again were cut down mercilessly by the concentrated salvos of black arrows.

Most of the goblin riders – dazed, battered and bruised – were up and advancing on foot pretty quickly though, and the two big Jotnar trolls were making ground on them too. The Lieutenant knew that he and his men would be running out of arrows pretty rapidly but he was confident that each man was a sure shot when it came to targeting and they would use each last arrow to full effect. "Now take out the trolls!" He shouted, and his men did just that.

But, as the massive, hulking monsters crashed to the ground the five goblins still standing were almost upon them and the three Rangers who still had arrows were now reaching for their last. The others unsheathed their sabres just as one of their number – a young Ranger on the Lieutenant's left – was hit by one of the scrappy goblin arrows that came flying in from the watchtowers, he stumbled back with a gasp, then sat down heavily onto the cold platform floor, grasping the arrow at its point of entry high in his chest, just in from his right shoulder. The Ranger's loosed their last arrows, taking down three for three, and then the others finished off the last two with their swords at the base of the steps.

The Lieutenant knelt beside the young wounded Ranger – a raw recruit, Pendal was his name, but he'd already earned the nickname Panhandle among the tight-knit unit. He was alive, but shock and pain were evident in the expression on his face. "Don't worry son," the officer endeavoured to reassure him as he pulled him up against the balustrade, "you'll live."

The Rangers hunkered down again, all back behind the balustrades, as stray goblin arrows were continuing to rain in, clattering on the stones about them. Lethbridge was considering sending a couple of his men out to retrieve some of their own arrows, when twelve more mounted goblins came through the gatehouse opposite their position – it was the other two patrols that they'd seen circling the castle's outer walls.

"Load up your Dragons, men." said the Lieutenant coolly as he prepared his pair of short barrelled blunderbusses for firing. "But wait for my command before firing." He then quickly and proficiently loaded the young wounded soldier's guns too. Handing them to him, he said. "Hold yours till they're right on ya, son." Panhandle gave a grim nod in reply.

The charging mounted goblins were already most of the way across the bloodied and body-littered courtyard – divided into two groups they rapidly approached the bottoms of the split stairs leading to the keep's doorway.

Lethbridj ordered his men to the top of the stairs; they opened out the big wooden doors of the keep to provide some additional cover, and waited for the first goblins to attempt the climb up either set of stone steps. Three Rangers covered each approach with two blunderbusses each. "Anything tries to mount the stairs," the Lieutenant ordered – shouting over the baying of the big hell-hounds, "shoot its legs from under it!"

The leading goblins, on their black-shuk mounts, bounded up the steps on either side almost simultaneously – and were met by a fusillade of hot metal shot that ripped into them, splattering gore and splintering bone as it tore through the muscled ranks of fast moving black-shuk limbs. The bulky and shaggy furred beasts uttered terrified screams as they tumbled onto the lower steps – their legs blasted from beneath them and throwing their goblin riders face first into the punishing square-cut corners of the solid stone stairs.

At the bottom of both sets of stairs an instant barrier of two or three lamed, yowling, bulky and biting beasts, driven mad by shock and pain, was formed – blocking the goblins behind and giving the Rangers time to reload, ready for the next volley of deadly shot to be unleashed. Those thrown goblin riders still conscious, dazed and bloodied, with fractured sculls and broken bones aplenty, were more concerned with avoiding the deranged and slobbering maws of their own mounts than attempting to continue the assault on the Rangers. A couple of them managed to painfully and desperately scramble over the balustrade, leaving the fray, but the others fell victim to the crazed mauling of their own crippled mounts.

The now dismounted goblins at the back were forced to kill the maimed black-shuks that blocked their way before attempting to climb over the bloody mess of corpses, and continue their faltering attacks. As they clambered over, they were met by the second volley of lethal shot that put a shattering end to any thought of advance from those lucky enough to have survived those first two salvos. The few remaining goblins left alive fearfully sheltered behind the barricade of dead flesh, while their surviving mounts, demoralised and whimpering, shied away from the killing ground completely and sought a surer safety by putting as much distance between themselves and the thunderous guns as possible.

A trickle of arrows continued to arc in at the Rangers, mostly inaccurate except for those from a particular watch-tower – the occupant of which was proving to have better aim than the rest. They were increasingly falling closer to the huddled Rangers around the open doorway and another one eventually succeeded in finding a mark, painfully piercing the grimacing Lieutenant in his upper right thigh. "Damn it!" He spat through gritted teeth. "Inside, every one... or they'll pick us off one by one."

The Rangers moved into the shadowed shelter of the entranceway, keeping the doors half open they could spy the stairs on either side through the gaps between the hinges – should any goblin be foolish enough to try another assault, their dragons were loaded and ready. Panhandle was helped in and propped against the wall opposite the Lieutenant who instructed, "We'll cover the corridor – Pendal, anyone or anything comes down that passage that isn't a Ranger or the white haired girl, fucking shoot them – the rest of you, make sure nothing gets up those stairs or in that doorway."

"We'll make damn sure, Sir." said Corporal Lannik in earnest.

Luwsiy's psyche had retreated into shock – curled and shivering it hid, like a small child in fear of a drunken, belt wielding father; frightened and huddled in a darkened corner of a lonely room.

The child, Lilith realised, would soon be fleeing that room, and the house around it, altogether... *into death*. Lilith strove to prevent this as best she could, to prevent the departure of the very mind, soul and spirit that she herself was displacing – she clung and held onto the girl's inner being. She tried to comfort Luwsiy but she knew that the girl's fear was justified – she felt it herself – and that hindered her efforts. Her spirit was now free of Bäliyl's control, but Lilith knew that once she should dare to show that freedom, he would assert his will once more, he was still too powerful for her to take on alone. She would have to wait until he was at his most distracted, when summoning the demon, before she could show herself and strike, it would not leave her much time but it was all the time she could hope for. *If only help could come, but no* – she was alone, and will remain so, so she must fight him alone. But till then she could not allow Luwsiy's life to go – she must hold onto it... desperately. But the girl's body was the only hiding place she had, if it came to the choice of letting Luwsiy go or revealing herself to Bäliyl before she was ready... she would have to let the girl go. *Death,* she now knew, *was not such a terrible thing.*

Bäliyl extinguished the binding flame inside the copper dish with the mixture of fluids that he had concocted within the small bowl. The first stage of his ritual was complete, the next – the opening of the door, he began straight after.

For this he held the staff in his right hand and a sword in his left, he drew a pentacle in the air to the east with the head of his staff while loudly intoning archaic words of power. He called on the dark deities of the otherworld to empower his staff as the key that would open their domain to this realm, the mortal realm. The crown of his infernal rod then flared a glowing ochre light that he traced from the ground at a point east by north east on the magic circle, up to the highest his reach would take it, then across till it pointed east by south east and down again till it reached the circle on the floor once more. In its wake the crown had left a burning trail, a portal to the infernal otherworld.

The outline of this doorway throbbed a dull red after the intense light of its creation had slowly weakened, a low pulse of energy charging the room with each fading beat. Within the borders of the glowing portal all went dark as if a black mist had fallen.

Bäliyl then stood still, unexpectedly waiting, his gaze directed at a high corner of the room. Curious, Lilith lifted the head of the girl to look through her eyes, trying to see what held his attention so intently. There was nothing to see, she assumed he must be looking beyond the confines of this chamber and his castle – *probably waiting for some alignment of the stars or the correct tide of night... or both.* She rested the girl's head back down,

Suddenly, he stirred and his actions seemed to take on a greater urgency. He silently nominated two of the mute and motionless robed acolytes that stood to attention in a wide circle around the room and pointed them toward an exit over to her right – she knew that it led to stairs that went up into the keep. The two acolytes bowed their heads and obediently headed into the shadows behind them. Lilith could hear the echoing sounds of steel striking stone coming from the stairs – but she couldn't comprehend what it could mean. Then she heard the screams of the two acolytes as an almighty crash of falling stone exploded from the stairway. Regardless – if not oblivious – with staff and sword in hands outstretched, Bäliyl called upon the Kernunnos Inversus, the lord of deceit himself but by his Kanaaniyt name, Pahhad - the Terror.

As the loud shouts of Bäliyl's arcane words were bellowed into the darkened doorway, Lilith knew that her time to act had come. She lifted her invisible self from Luwsiy's spread-eagled form with trepidation, and was about to rush for the ritual knife he had left on the square silk covered altar stone behind him – when his excited words were abruptly stopped in mid flow.

Lilith stared in disbelief; there – in the magikally summoned doorway – was Mikael and Arkturon. They split to either side of the portal as Arkturon shouted "Shoot him... do it – now!" Mikael knelt on one knee and raised one of his flintlocks, aiming at her father's heart. Two other figures then entered at a run, both were cloaked – one was Rebekah, the other an elfin Fay with an arrow trained on her father. Mikael fired.

Bäliyl immediately crouched and span with dizzying speed, dropping his staff and sword – the pellet from Mikael's gun slammed into the back of the sorcerer's right shoulder, exploding straight through – shattering his shoulder blade and spraying blood as it exited. The faery's arrow was loosed at his face as he turned, but with supernatural skill the sorcerer intercepted its flight and deflected it with his left arm, the arrow-head gouging a long and bloody furrow in his forearm. Laughing Bäliyl then stood and as Mikael aimed his second pistol and Juwniper primed her next arrow he raised his arms as if nothing had hit him and sent two bolts of piercing blue energy through his finger tips, which were held like claws, toward the two adversaries. The blasts hit them head on and threw them back, sprawling helplessly. Mikael was propelled out of the magic circle to slam against a wall – Juwniper being pushed straight back through the portal.

"No!" shouted Arkturon as he raised his staff and pointed it at Bäliyl, the pulse of yellow energy from its tip glowed strongly then flung itself toward Bäliyl who span to face him – crouching again he crossed his forearms in front of himself in a defensive action that, at first, seemed almost futile. The energy pulse hit – but was deflected by what proved an invisible shield inches in front of the sorcerer – Arkturon immediately followed the pulse with a continuous blast of bright yellow energy – it pushed Bäliyl back slightly as he skidded on the floor but his conjured phantasmic barrier held.

Arkturon pulled up his staff and Bäliyl stood swiftly to face him. Smirking, the sorcerer jumped to a one knee kneeling stance and he thrust a punch out in the direction of Arkturon with a strenuous, angry yell. As his arm stretched to the limit of its reach another pulse of energy crossed the room, flying from his taught fist. This time it was Arkturon who adopted a defensive stance, standing straight he gripped his staff with both hands, one above the other, with forearms perpendicular to the vertical rod he thumped its base squarely to the floor and repulsed the bolt – deflecting it straight into one of the mute and still acolytes off to the side. As the robed figure reeled and then collapsed dead to the floor, Arkturon detected a brief and very slight grimace infect Bäliyl's otherwise overly confident face.

Bäliyl laughed again, "Very good... I am going to enjoy killing you, wizard." His words were full of sarcasm and he infected the last one with as much distaste as he possibly could. The naked sorcerer then pointed at Arkturon's staff, "Your paraphernalia serves you well." he said, smirking again.

Arkturon cast aside his staff, followed by his bag, coat and belted sword. "They mean nothing..." he said simply.

"No, it is you that are nothing." Bäliyl stood side on, crossed his bloodied left arm over his right, which was pointed at Arkturon, and with legs apart he formed a fist and fired such a powerful bolt that it caused his elbow and shoulder to recoil violently. As if deflecting a physical blow, Arkturon quickly moved to one side and pushed the strike away with crossed forearms, deflecting it aside and past to harmlessly hit the wall behind him. The wall cracked with the impact and dust spilled from above.

Arkturon immediately faced Bäliyl again, he swiftly cut a line down on his forehead with the thumb nail of his left hand and then dabbed the tips of the index and first middle fingers of his right in the blood that appeared there. Holding the two outer digits in with his thumb he then pointed the two bloodied tips toward the sorcerer. Seeing Arkturon's actions Bäliyl had quickly copied them, finishing just in time to meet the small ball of intense red energy that shot from the tips of Arkturon's fingers with one of his own making. The two glowing phantasmic globes vied with each other in mid air, each a symbol of its master's power and each controlled by thought and will alone.

Wizard and sorcerer stood opposite each other, motionless and with concentration etched into each of their faces. Rebekah stirred as if out of a daze, the confrontation between Arkturon and Bäliyl had stopped her in her tracks and had momentarily held her transfixed. She skirted the magik circle to move round them and get to Luwsiy – for Lilith, who seemed to have appeared out of nowhere, was trying to release the prone girl's bonds. As Rebekah passed Mikael, who lay unconscious – but still breathing – on the floor, she became aware of the black robed figures that surrounded the large Magik circle. Their silent, but still, presence took her completely by surprise and she brandished her long, sharp dagger at the nearest instinctively, but mercifully they all remained mysteriously passive and did not move. Suddenly, a black arrow flew across the expansive chamber of sorcery and passed right before her eyes – it pierced the heart of one the dark static acolytes, felling him instantly. Startled she looked for the source and saw four green-hooded Rangers emerge from the black shadows across the room from her – behind more of the static black robed acolytes – and there, looking right at her, was Corporal Villovürt, gesturing for her to get down. Rebekah did just that, as the Rangers picked off each and every motionless acolyte one by one with skilful precision and speed.

Lilith released the silken ties at Luwsiy's ankles and wrists then headed for her father's knife once more. Rebekah rushed to her sister and, hugging her, helped her off the large altar stone, the sobbing young girl was weak and trembling uncontrollably.

Lilith lifted the small blade and approached her father's broad back. As she plunged it deep toward his heart agony loosened her grip before it fully reached its target. Bäliyl laughed aloud as his blood flowed from this newly inflicted wound, the ball of power under his control was giving ground, but still it held. The sorcerer's blood defied all natural laws as it flowed; it twisted and arched up toward Lilith instead of falling and splattering over the ground. His blood pushed into Lilith's chest and washed over her heart – her soul – building up and forming a sloshing sphere round her shinning core. Her mouth opened wide and her head pulled back but the scream was silent as her form began to fade, being replaced by a growing spinning globule made from her father's dark and glistening blood.

"Do something!" shouted Luwsiy to her sister and the Rangers, but Rebekah only stared in horror at the gruesome sight and the soldiers seemed awestruck by the magikal display... all except the dark-elf, who aimed her next arrow at the sorcerer and loosed it. The arrow buried itself deep into Bäliyl's chest but barely seemed to affect him – he casually turned his head to meet the Corporal's gaze and inflicted a burst of pain on her that brought her to her knees. Luwsiy looked to Arkturon but his face was as stone and his eyes fixed as he controlled his symbol of power in its fight with Bäliyl's. Finally she looked at the sorcerer, his face was a grinning demon, shinning from the profuse sweat that poured from him, his muscles flexing in sympathy with every vying movement of his power ball. Unbelievably the bastard's member was still erect.

Luwsiy took the long knife from Rebekah's hand – *I know your weakness you fucking bastard!* She ran at him, dived and tumbled to arrive at his feet, kneeling and knife ready – she took hold of his phallus and scrotum in one hand and with the other she sliced the razor sharp blade down at the member's root – severing the man's genitals in one sudden stroke. The pain that his mind forced on her heart was mercifully brief but still it threw her back. Bäliyl's face became an expression of total shock as the horrific realisation of instant terror overwhelmed him. His concentration dissipated, along with his phantasmic ball of glowing energy and, unopposed, Arkturon's radiant pellet of burning energy hit him square in the face – it lingered for a split second as it burned its way into his skull. Bäliyl's forehead suddenly bulged and without warning his cranium exploded with a splintering crack, splattering its contents all around.

The blood around Lilith's phantasmic heart sloshed to the ground and with a grave gasp her instantaneously reconstituted image fell back onto the stone floor.

Luwsiy was amazed at how long Bäliyl's headless body stood there, before dropping to the floor – though probably only seconds, it seemed an age before it did so. Then, before their eyes, the corpse shrank and shrivelled and its copious spilled blood and gore dried and turned to dust, his sorceries no longer defying the age of countless centuries.

Standing, Luwsiy looked down at her own body, her beautifully pale and soft skin was liberally caked in the ancient desiccated remains of blood and brains – even at her groin, "Ugh..." she exclaimed horrified with arms held out, and fingers splayed as if to show everyone. His shrunken, dried and shrivelled cock and ball-sack rolled from her fingers and fell to the floor where they hit and crumpled to dust like the rest of him. There was a cut on her left arm that bled freely, she touched it lightly and felt a splinter of bone, pulling it out she realised it must be a piece of Bäliyl's skull, "Oh my gods!" She threw it to the floor – though it was already dust by the time it reached it – with a second expressive "Ugh!!!" and an exaggerated shake of her hand. "Someone get this filth OFF ME!!" she suddenly screamed, frantically trying to brush the offending material off herself.

Rebekah fought back the urge to throw up and took off her cloak while moving to her naked younger sister, she went to wrap it around the girl's shoulders but she shrugged it away shouting "No... get this foul stuff off me first!" stamping her foot hard to the ground.

"Let me..." said Arkturon quietly – he seemed exhausted but picked up his staff and pointed its crown at Luwsiy. A soft hazy light spouted from it and collected around her, the foul matter dissolved as the cleansing light rushed around her body like a current of air and then dispersed taking all the dust of death with it. Her cut had congealed to form a small scab. Luwsiy then gladly took Rebekah's cloak and wrapped it about herself.

Lilith had recovered quickly and, after picking herself up off the ground, she tended to Mikael as soon as she saw him, "It is over, Mikael," she whispered to him, "it's over – we are free!" Her tears fell to his face. He was coming round to consciousness but was still dazed from the bolt of energy that had hit him – as was Juwniper when she staggered back into the room from the otherworld darkness of the doorway. She was pointing back the way she had come and was obviously alarmed by something that followed, putting as much distance between herself and the portal as quickly as possible, "The Dark Lord..." she said, breathless with fear, "he comes..."

All faces looked to Arkturon, "Out of the circle" he said, "quickly! The demon will not be able to leave the confines of the circle."

Rebekah, Luwsiy and Juwniper moved with him to join the Rangers, Mikael and Lilith were already against one of the walls. The temperature of the room was dropping dramatically and the atmosphere becoming heavy and leaden, oppressing them all. They were all now looking expectantly at the otherworld doorway and could see the darkness within it bulge out into the magik circle, as if probing and testing it. The darkness slowly intruded three times before it broke and a huge cloven hoof stepped into their world, dragging in with it a foul dark wake, Hlewid – the Kernunnos Inversus, was a warped and disarranged mutation of vile man and noble beast. Each step that the demon took was a deafening, thumping, mistimed heart beat resounding within their stomachs, chests and up into their throats. His drooling stag's head, with huge and unnaturally curved and vicious antlers, looked down at the remains of Bäliyl briefly before turning to the cowed and dumb-struck group of souls that he so effectively dwarfed and dominated.

As he faced them his large and hideous bright red eyes scrutinised each of their faces, giving them all enough time to ponder fearfully on every unnatural aspect of his loathsome presence. With each trembling breath Rebekah's eyes rose up the twelve foot devil, from the large hooves and the sable coloured, shiny smooth pelt of his muscularly cervine legs – the tops of which were as wide as her hips – to the shaggy, white flecked fur at his groin and the huge, bulbously angled head at the end of the long, ridged shaft of his dark hanging penis. Her gaze rose up the sharply defined musculature of his human-like abdomen, broad chest and strongly veined arms to the large, black and evil-looking stag-head set on his shoulders, behind all this, from the centre of his back, were raised two huge and folded bat-like wings.

His malignant voice entered their minds like a savage rape. I HAVE COME FOR WHAT WAS PROMISED UNTO ME!

Arkturon bravely spoke up, "You do not belong here Lord... the person who promised such things is dead."

A deep throaty laugh was expelled from Hlewid's jaws, DEAD – BUT NOT DEPARTED... chuckling now, HIS DISEMBODIED FETCH

NOW WAITS BY MY THRONE FOR ME TO RETURN, DEEP WITHIN MY CASTLE... AND THE FETCH OF HIS DAUGHTER BELONGS TO ME ALSO!   LET US CONSIDER HER MY CONSOLATION – A PAYMENT FOR HIS UNTIMELY REMOVAL FROM THIS PHYSICAL PLANE? SHE WILL CONSOLE ME IN MY LONELY NIGHTS. He laughed again but the laughter, like the words, was purely malicious.

"No!" shouted Mikael, standing shakily and drawing his sword – an action that only caused another hideous laugh to issue from the beast's slobbering mouth.

MY EXCREMENT HAS MORE BRAINS... he noted distractedly. AND MORE CHANCE OF EARNING HER LOVE THAN YOU... SHE HAS BEEN USING YOU EVER SINCE KILLING YOUR PARENTS – AND THAT DARLING LITTLE SISTER OF YOURS! He paused briefly as his eyes glared at Mikael. THE ONLY REASON THE BITCH STAYED WITH YOU WAS BECAUSE SHE NEEDED A GOOD FUCK EVERY TEN MINUTES... AND YOU WERE THE BEST SHE COULD DO. LOVE DID NOT COME INTO IT – YOU WERE HER PET COCK... THAT WAS ALL – SOMETHING TO TWAT HERSELF WITH IN HER IDLE MOMENTS!

"You lie..." screamed Mikael with tears in his eyes. Despite himself he could see a vague truth in the foul words.

DID YOUR BELOVED TELL YOU HOW SHE KILLED YOUNG EMMA... SHE SUCKED HER DRY, SUCKED ALL HER BLOOD THROUGH THE LITTLE GIRL'S CUNT – AND SHE LOVED IT, YOUR SISTER, SHE LOVED EVERY SECOND OF IT...

"You fucking bastard..." shouted Mikael moving toward the demon with his sword raised and ready.

"No Mikael... he lies..." cried Lilith as Arkturon went to intercept Mikael and try to hold him back.

SHE PROBABLY DID NOT TELL YOU BECAUSE SHE KNEW YOU WOULD BE JEALOUS... FOR YOU WANTED YOUR SISTER'S LUSCIOUS LITTLE QUIM FOR YOURSELF, DID YOU NOT. YOU WANTED TO FUCK HER, MIKAEL – YOUR OWN SWEET AND INNOCENT SISTER... YOU HAD DREAMED OF FUCKING HER EVER SINCE SHE WAS TWELVE...

Mikael pushed Arkturon aside violently and lunged at Hlewid.

"No..." shouted Arkturon "that is what he wants... you must not re-enter the circle..." but Mikael was already in, slashing at the beast. The demon laughed aloud as he swatted the blade from Mikael's grip with his left hand and then took hold of the mortal's neck with the right. He lifted Mikael up till his head was level with his own.

YOU WORTHLESS MAGGOT, I OUGHT TO KILL YOU RIGHT NOW... AND I WILL – UNLESS LILITH COMES HERE THIS INSTANT! His burning red eyes singled out Lilith. Mikael struggled pathetically, choking in the painful grip of the beast's massive hand.

COME HERE NOW... he ordered Lilith sharply, pointing to the ground beside him, then added with an ugly and distorted grin – MY SWEET AND WICKED BRIDE TO BE! Hlewid then held his left, clawed hand out to her.

Of the four Rangers witness to this scene only Corporal Villovürt was immune to the demon's awful majesty and not subject to the grim despair that inflicted the others with muted inaction. She aimed an arrow at the demon's heart, drawing the bowstring to the limits of its elasticity – and her own strength – before loosing the deadly projectile. The slim black arrow slipped past Mikael's dangling form and hit the great beast's chest right on target – but bounced off as if it had hit steel plating.

The demon cast a baleful glance at the dark-elf and laughed menacingly, YOUR WEAPONS CANNOT HARM ME! He exulted, I AM AS A GOD, YOU MISERABLE WORMS – YOU ARE NOTHING, ALL OF YOU! He proffered his hand to Lilith one more time and with dark insistence ordered her to COME HERE!

Resigned to the fact that she had no choice, Lilith crossed into the circle and silently put her hand in his. He closed his all encompassing fist around hers, holding her as if in a vice. His other hand then suddenly tightened too as his appalling laughter thundered out, his sharp nailed fingers crushed Mikael's throat as if it were nothing. The man's piteous, gurgling screams soon came to nothing too, and Hlewid then threw Mikael away like a piece of garbage, sending his lifeless body tumbling back out of the circle and back up against the wall.

"NO!!!" writhed Lilith furiously but her hand was held fast. She had no way of fighting the demon – no way of escape – all she wanted was to run to Mikael – to hold him and to give her love... but she could not.

Mikael was gone, destroyed by the towering demon that now led her unremittingly by the hand back into the otherworld - the spirit world...

where all pain and degradation committed against her would be real, for she is of that world and belongs to it. She prayed – to any gods that might listen – that she may escape the fate forced on her by her father... that her love may deliver her to the blessed realms of Anuuwn and not the cursed...

But Mikael is not gone! She suddenly calmed herself, *He is of the spirit world too now...* he can find her again, there – *but what chance Mikael against this demon?!*

Chapter Twenty One – Consort to a Demon

The atmosphere in the subterranean room beneath the castle keep immediately became less chilling and leaden as the sinister demon returned to his own diabolic domain. But the overpowering feeling of existential dread and shock that the demonic visitation had brought upon the awestricken mortals present, would take a lot longer to dissipate and, in truth, a part of it would inflict them for the rest of their lives. For a brief moment they all stood in stunned silence.

Rebekah rushed over to Mikael's corpse and knelt there, she couldn't believe that he was dead. Tears filled her eyes.

Luwsiy knew her sister had loved him, though in a mostly latent and unexpressed form – and she felt that she too should weep, the potential for love had been with her also... but she could not – she had simply been through too much. Arkturon, now mysteriously young to Luwsiy's eyes, comforted Rebekah with a tender – *almost a lover's* – arm at her shoulder. Luwsiy realised that things had changed so much now – they themselves had changed so much – there was no going back to normality now... for her, or Rebekah.

It was Sergeant Rinawn who was next to stir, "We need to leave this place!" He said urgently – looking, with trepidation, at the mysterious dark portal. He didn't want to be around should anything else come back through it.

"I'm going after that abomination," said Arkturon grimly, retrieving his coat, bag and sword from where he had cast them aside. "I cannot desert Lilith and leave her to her fate... it was I that put her at risk in the first place – I cannot forsake her now."

"I will come with you," said Juwniper, "but we must enter quickly – before Hlewid closes the doorway."

Rebekah was incredulous, "You can't seriously mean it..." she addressed Arkturon, "what chance would even you have against that thing? It seemed indestructible!"

"In this world, yes," said Arkturon, "but in Anuuwn, he is not much more powerful than a mortal king or lord would be here."

"But we can't just leave Mikael like this!" she cried.

"That broken body is but an empty shell – Mikael has already passed on to the otherworld and, if I've learnt anything about that young man, it's that he will be once again seeking to join Lilith... his love will draw him to her and I'm going to do whatever I can to aid him."

"Then I'm coming with you!" said Rebekah stubbornly as she resolutely stood to face him.

"I cannot ask you to put yourself through more danger," said the wizard, though he was clearly torn. "Your father has been avenged and you helped rescue your sister, you've done your part - the Rangers can see you both home now." Her attitude remained full of steely persistence however, and the wizard found himself unable to say no to her... this intrigued him. He withdrew his objection with a simple nod.

"What do you mean; *your father has been avenged*?" Interjected Luwsiy, then to her sister, "What happened to our father?"

Rebekah turned to her younger sibling, tears filling her eyes anew. "I... I'm so sorry, Luwsiy – father is dead, he was killed the night you were abducted."

"No... no!" was all that Luwsiy could say at first. Deep down she had known it, but now it was confirmed. She felt that she should cry, or at least shed a tear, but not a single one came. She stepped back and turned away as Rebekah approached her with a comforting hand held out and an expression of conflicted emotions on her face. Luwsiy realised that her elder sister was leaving her again to go with Arkturon and help Lilith and Mikael. Something inside made her reject the tender gesture... reject the duplicitous compassion of her sister. "Go," she said, "I just want to go home – I'll be fine with the Rangers." Then, to them all, she said, "The three sisters will be returning soon, to see the results of their master's handy work – I do not want to be here when they do." Despite the fact that their spell over her had been broken, she still found her genitals flush at the thought of the voluptuous siblings and a deep and distant part of her mind regretted and wondered at her own words. She tried to dispel such thoughts and calm her stirring loins.

"We'll deal with those witches if they show, Miss." said Sergeant Rinawn, a grim determination set his jaw. Then, to the rest, he said, "No time for goodbyes – so, if you're goin' through that blighted portal then I say good luck to ya and I hope you know what you're doin' - if ya not goin' through that portal, I suggest ya come with us now cause we are leaving... Rangers – we're goin' back the way we came, so be ready for a fight!"

Corporal Villovürt put a protecting arm over Luwsiy's shoulders and bundled her into the small group of Rangers as they shadowed their Sergeant back toward the rubble strewn stairway.

Hesitantly at first, with a single look back at Luwsiy, Rebekah joined Arkturon and Juwniper on the threshold of the otherworld doorway and then they passed back through.

Luwsiy did not look back.

The darkness was briefly overwhelming, no breath could be drawn, no sight, smell nor sound could be sensed... then suddenly everything was chaos – every sense aroused.

"Where are we!" shouted Rebekah above the roaring wind that whipped at their clothes and hair, "- this is not Hlewid's castle!"

They stood on unkempt grasses surrounded by high and thorny, overgrown hedges; the smell and taste of earth, bark and sap filled the whirling air... and carried on its winds were the sounds of beast and bird, their call and cry a beckoning to a wild and unrestrained feast or rut. "Where are we?" she repeated as they all looked around, bewildered – the overpowering carnal tension was almost tangible.

"Hlewid has shifted the doorway... we were too late – too slow!" said Arkturon, "we could be anywhere within the realms of the blessed or of the unblessed!"

"I know this place," said Juwniper as realization slowly dawned on her face. "This is the reversal of mine own blessed home Kear Sidiy... we have been sent to the realm of the Nemetona Inversus, the Lady of the Pyre herself, Andreast! We are hostage to the goddess of lust, cunning and retribution. This is her enclave in the Forest Saveadj, though close to the Wasteland this labyrinth is like a spider's web, and our only way out is through that unholy spider at its centre."

Rebekah was not quite sure what the Faery girl meant by *our only way out is through that unholy spider*. It didn't sound pleasant, whatever it might mean, but Arkturon seemed to know.

"In that case," he said, facing them with resignation, "we need to get to the centre of this web as quickly as possible." The wizard pointed up over their heads, making them turn to look, over the hedges; in the distance was a large towered castle that loomed like the black upturned carcass of an enormous insect, its many fat and jagged legs, contorted and rigid in death, curled up round a single massive impaling pin – an incredibly tall central obelisk-like tower.

At first the strange castle seemed – to Rebekah at least – to be built on a steep slope, jutting out perpendicular from it at an impossible angle for such a grandiloquent building. It took only a second for her realise that her orientation was all wrong – the castle was at the horizontal bottom of a huge bowl like crater and it was they that were up on the slope, just inside the outer edge, it was they that were stood at an angle... she suddenly suffered a mercifully brief but disorienting spell of vertigo that made her stagger a step down slope before she regained her balance. There were fires burning at various points around the castle, big ones, from which black and acrid smoke rose in columns into an already dark and overcast sky. Streams of speck-like black birds started issuing from the lofty central tower and then ranks of – less speck-like – spiders started emerging from the castle gates at its base.

"Her minions are coming to claim us." said Juwniper ominously.

Mikael had been here before, he realised, so was not as surprised or panicked as he might have been to find himself in this state of nothingness. It was neither cold nor warm, neither light nor dark; there was no up nor down, no left or right – just forward. It was no trance or sleep like state that had brought him here though; he had passed over to the other side for real this time. He laughed, not knowing why... nor even caring. He just waited for the wilderness of the path of the Moon to appear. When it did not he was startled... and at first, confused.

What did materialize was a ragged and rocky shore, with an insurmountable cliff before him that stretched to the distance on either side and far, far above him. Mikael stood at the windswept and sea sprayed end of a large slab of stone that stretched out from the shore like some sort of jetty and led, as a path ordained, to a black cave mouth at the base of the huge cliff face. His only route from the shore was into that cave, so he set forth toward its dark and yawning mouth.

Eventually, after traversing through the shadowed cave to a long twisting tunnel and on then into other caves and caverns, with more rambling, rocky passageways between them, he came to another, larger, cavern which finally seemed to be the end of his meandering subterranean sojourn. Between himself and the roughly circular cave mouth he saw three draped and hooded women sitting near a small but blazing fire; one sat at a spinning wheel, another at a table and the last at a loom. The cave was dark and shadowed but the outside beyond afforded a glimpse of the bright and lively world of Kear Pedrivan, its labyrinth, and at the centre, its castle. Mikael vaguely remembered Arkturon's map and that there was a third path leading from the mortal world, one that led straight to Kear Pedrivan. It had been marked, if he remembered rightly, 'Fortune' and in brackets, 'The Norns'.

The aspects of each of the women's faces were as the phases of the moon. The first, working the spinning wheel on his left, was as a crescent moon, overcome with the shy innocence of youth, only part of her pale beautiful face peeking from the darkness of her hood. The second woman, mature and sure of her beauty and experience, faced him as a full moon, hiding none of her face. She seemed to be apportioning lengths of thread and cutting them with scissors. The third, to his right, was hidden in total shadow with her head and back hunched over a loom in which she wove the lengths of thread. He guessed that she was an old woman, shamed at her ugly age and hiding her decrepitude. She was as the dark and, paradoxically, new moon, and she was the first to speak.

"And so sisters, this thread in the tapestry of his existence is fast being woven to an end, shall we tell him of the outcome?" Her voice screeched and grated like rusted metal on stone as she wove the thread repeatedly in and out.

"You know that is forbidden sister." said the young girl in timid pubescent tones as she peddled the wheel and spun more thread.

"Yes sister... you know you only say such things to tease our visitors, they are usually bewildered enough." The voice of the middle woman was strong and sure, as a mother's should be. "Not that young Mikael here will be bewildered; he has passed into the otherworld before. Have you not Mikael?" She snipped another length of thread.

"Yes... sister?" he said, a little confused.

"You will find Lilith again though... we can tell you that," the middle woman said, "but no more."

"Will the demon harm her... use her?" Mikael asked vehemently as despair filled his heart.

"I am sorry, we can tell you no more." she said. "Her fate, and yours, has been set... knowing will not change it."

"You should leave now," said the young girl sheepishly.

The old woman added, "- and go to the revolving Castle of the Four Corners, Lord Frea has a gift for you." Her disconcerting cackle lingered as he moved past them. Mikael knew that Frea was the Saxanglish name for Matt, but what gift, he wondered, could Matt possibly have for him?

The great dark towers of Kear Pedrivan Reversus were a case hardened shell that housed and glorified the evil works of their master Hlewid, the current incarnation of the Kernunnos Inversus. At the heart of the supremely twisted gothic structure there was a throne room, a large chamber that pumped its black malevolence out into the castle and its surrounding deadly labyrinth like an overflowing powerhouse. The evil work that was charging the room at this moment was the pitiless defilement of Lilith Samiyl.

He manipulated her body, limbs and head like a cruel and insane puppeteer as he copulated with her, using her more as a tool for masturbation rather than a partner – whether willing or not – in sexual intercourse.

He had brought her straight to this room on re-entering his domain from the mortal world, eagerly leading his prize by the hand like an excited groom with his virgin bride after a long and chastity enforced courtship, as if leading her straight to the wedding bed. Lilith would have seen this behaviour as comical in such a beast, if it had not been for the fact that the so-called bride was so unwilling... and that it was her.

In the huge throne room was a very long table set with a feast for hundreds, all the foodstuffs that filled the table were of animal origin and all the place settings had simply a plate and a bowl before each very ornate and carved chair, there were no knives or forks nor other utensils. On entering, Hlewid dragged Lilith round to the top of the table where his throne presided and sat her on the table where his plate should have been. To the right of the throne was sitting Bäliyl Samiyl, her father. Delighting in her predicament, his eyes were full of barely concealed hate.

I EAT OFF YOU TONIGHT. Said the demon with a lecherous laugh and clapped his hands once as he imperially sat before her. A great number of the demon's minions then filed into the room, first came a procession of sepulchral wraiths that paraded in and surrounded the table like a guard of honour. Then there came many loathsome satyr or faun-like creatures – grotesque hybrids of man with goat, deer, horse, pig and wolf, among others. They solemnly entered the chamber and only stopped coming when all the places at the huge table were filled. Hlewid clapped once more and the throng at the table all simultaneously attacked the foods before them, biting and ripping the meat and fat from bone and guzzling greedily from the pots of grease, stock and blood. Whole animals were being reduced to gnawed bone and spat-out gristle in seconds but there was no sign of the flesh running out... more was continuously being brought to the feast by attendant wraiths. It was then that the demon began to control Lilith's limbs, making her stand on the immense table and forcing her to parade her nakedness up and down its length for his feasting uncouth court that spat and threw food at her, poured grease and blood over her, and then, when she was returned to Hlewid, he made her lay before him and, slobbering, he licked her every curve and crevice, nipping her painfully with his long misshapen teeth whenever he came to her more tender parts.

As the guffawing and belching of the dinner guests became riotous, Hlewid put her on all fours like a beast, her knees on the hard edge of the table in front of him; he stood behind her and began to rub the hard dark head of his now enormously erect cock on her sex and backside. Suddenly and repeatedly he began to ram it into her vagina, the huge head stretching and filling her painfully. In and out it went, getting deeper with each agonising thrust, unbelievably deeper for she was sure she could feel the hot member delving up into her abdomen and even her chest. The ribbed and gnarled length of his shaft scraped her labia, clitoris and vaginal walls as it speedily travelled in and out of her, her screams of pain just spurred him on and were mocked and echoed by the slobbering creatures around her.

When the demon finally came his seed deluged her, inside and out, it poured from her vagina and down her legs like a burning torrent, the eruption within her turned her stomach violently and she retched as if to throw up, then – impossibly – the burning seed, like steaming bile, cascaded up her throat and projected out of her crying mouth and running nose – spraying the table, food and guests alike. The creatures seemed as eager to consume their master's fluid as they had the food and drink that he provided.

With his lust spent Hlewid withdrew himself from her and pushed her away with a hard and severe force that sent her skidding helplessly on her stomach down the greasy, drool and now semen covered table.

Shocked and degraded she lay still against a large, half eaten spit-roast pig and whimpered and choked as the demon and his horde laughed and jeered at her. This was hell, she realised – a hell she deserved and had earned with the sins and evil actions of a long and wicked life. Countless souls suffered within the borders of this realm – or their own personal versions of it – and she was but one of them, but she was different... no mere mortal, she was a daughter of the Koventiyna Inversus and a demoness in her own right. She would not be toyed with. Her father had tried to use her and now this demon would do the same. *He can try*, she thought acidly, *but like my father before him he will fail!* With sudden and vicious contempt Lilith looked up at the hideous faces nearest to her and they were silenced in an instant for her grim countenance was terrible to behold. She slowly and purposefully got to her feet, casting aside all shame and degradation, all care and concern. She would be victim no more. Her skin turned the colour of the moon – searing away the grime of demonic seed and the juices of countless butchered animals – and her hair, eyes and now claw like nails turned raven black. She grew in stature and levitated from the table as great, black leathery wings sprouted from between her shoulder blades.

"I am Lilith, daughter of Lilit, consort of Hlewid!" she proclaimed angrily, revealing long sharp fangs as she spoke. Then, in each of their minds she voiced the threat, CROSS ME... AND I *WILL* CONSUME YOU!"

The whole table was silenced.

The demon stood to face her. All of his cohort's eyes turned to him expectantly and waited. He seemed to deliberate then finally spoke. MY CONSORT HAS SPOKEN – CROSS HER AND YOU CROSS ME!

Lilith was gratified to see that her father was seething.

Sinkhoal, still sitting against the wall where he had been left after the encounter with the golem, nervously gripped his locked and loaded dragons – protecting the rear for the rest of the Rangers who had continued on down the stairs. He was feeling isolated and was in a tremendous amount of pain, his chest burned and his broken ribs scraped his lungs with every rapid, shallow breath he took. Sounds from below drifted up to him. First, as his companions left him, he'd heard a low pitched voice, droning in some foreign tongue, which increased in intensity and apparent import but stopped quite suddenly. Then came the muffled sounds of conflict with the occasional loud shot, shout, scream or manic laughter rising from the din... then all was quiet, but only briefly. The voice he now heard disturbed him greatly, its heart-stopping and echoing tones reverberated up the stairs and deep into his head, filling him with fear and instilling a terrifying feeling of absolute dread throughout his now cold and clammy body. He shivered at the thought of what could be emitting such a sound and was glad that he could not see it... but felt despair at what it might mean for the Rangers that had gone on without him

When the hideous and oppressive voice finally stopped he felt pure, unadulterated relief. Whatever it had been, he prayed that his friends would soon be joining him again for he could bear being alone in this dank, forbidding place no longer. Then there was a footfall from the steps leading back up into the keep, then another – barely audible but definitely heard. Sinkhoal pointed one of his two short blunderbusses in the direction of the sounds, waiting to see who – or what – was coming down the stairs. There was another footfall, soft and still hardly perceptible, and then there was another one – just at the bottom of the stairs it seemed. Then another – within the wide corridor where he was sitting – but he could still see nothing. The next footstep was closer, louder by only a smidgen, something invisible was coming toward him – he'd swear to it. He could see nothing... at least not directly, for there – suddenly – he made out the shadow of a prowling woman, cast by the flickering flames of the torch mounted nearby. The wounded Ranger fired one of his guns at where the source of the strange shadow should be.

The deafeningly loud retort of the fire-arm bounced off the stone walls but still it did not obscure the harsh sound of a woman's angry gasp of pain. Before his eyes the shapely figure of a woman was revealed, naked – but for a long gauzy loin cloth – and her left arm and shoulder was bloodied and peppered with at least some of the shot he had fired. He took aim with his second gun, right at her face. Igymeth's eyes were seething with anger and her fanged mouth opened wide as she hissed pure, poisonous hate at him like a cobra spitting venom. Sinkhoal fired again. The vampire ducked into a crouched stance with what seemed supernatural speed, tucking her head low she dodged the deadly shot completely, then slowly and purposefully her viscously beautiful face lifted up to look at him eye to eye – predator to prey - Igymeth was preparing to launch herself right at him.

Sinkhoal desperately went for his dagger as she started at him but Sergeant Rinawn had, at that instant, charged into the corridor from the steps leading down, his sword drawn and swinging. The long curved blade whistled horizontally through the air – missing Sinkhoal by a matter of inches – it cut deep into Igymeth's throat and sliced through more than half of her neck. The vampire woman's head lolled and her blood sprayed as she reeled from the stroke that almost decapitated her. Igymeth collapsed to the floor, writhing uncontrollably till the Sergeant put his booted foot on her head and finished the decapitation with another stroke of his sword.

Sinkhoal gawped as the vampire's voluptuous body shrivelled into the desiccated semblance of a withered, eon-old crone. The Sergeant wiped his sword on his cloak and sheathed it before proffering a helping hand to the sitting Ranger, saying "On your feet soldier, we're leaving this gods-forsaken hell hole."

The big man took hold of his Sergeant's wrist, as he held his, and the two eased him up between them. Sinkhoal grimaced as he shakily got to his feet, the pain of multiple shattered ribs was almost unbearable but his desire to get out of this place overrode his hurting discomfort. He took a couple of faltering steps.

"Are you walkin' out, Sinkhoal?" asked the Sergeant. "Or am I goin' to have to carry ya?"

"I think I can walk, Sarge." He said, staggering a little.

"Good," said the Sergeant, not entirely convinced. "Wellnap, put Sinkhoal's arm over ya shoulder and help 'im."

Wellnap replied, "Yes Sarge" and immediately did what he was told. Sinkhoal accepted the support gratefully as the Sergeant led his team, with Luwsiy in their charge, up the stairs and back into the keep proper. When they got to young Gudrun's body the Sergeant paused, he instructed Rigormort to put him over his shoulder. "We're not leaving him here." he said.

Chapter Twenty Two – Pixies and the Witch's Kiss

Arkturon led the two women from the tightly packed and tangled hedge rows to the nearest of the wide, spoke-like avenues that led straight down to the centre of the huge maze surrounding Andreast's brooding fortress. Hundreds of ravens circled above them and a throng of giant, thick-legged and hairy spiders were fast approaching – many of which had strange goblin-like creatures riding them, standing on the flat carapace backs of the their respective mount's massive fore-sections and they steered the things with heavy leathery reins that attached to the arachnid's pedipalps.

"Pixies!" exclaimed Juwniper. She despised these minions of Andreast with a passion; they were her hated enemy – the antithesis of all that she was – of all that her people and their mistress stood for. If faeries were for the giving of pleasure, pixies were for the taking of it... and they took pleasure from all kinds of dark and distasteful deeds. They were base and ugly, with their sallow skin and black, baleful eyes – not dissimilar to the many hungry eyes of their eight legged mounts. Juwniper spat on the ground before them as the terrifying riders and mounts drew near and surrounded the three interlopers.

"Use your staff!" said Rebekah urgently to Arkturon, "kill them with your magik!"

"I could not kill them all – and even if I did, escaping from this realm would be very difficult indeed!" he said. "We would be hunted down by their kin in hordes... and then, if we lived, we would have to answer to the wrath of Andreast – and, believe me, that you do not want. As things stand now, she may let us pass out of her domain unhindered and, hopefully, unharmed."

He then turned his attention to the tall, thin and skeletal pixie that seemed to be the leader of his mounted brethren – he was also the one with the widest and most disgusting grin. He was standing on the biggest spider by far and dressed, like the others, in black plate armour made from what appeared to be segments of exoskeleton from some massive and strangely horned beetle – though his was more ornate and elaborately decorated. He held the reins in one hand and a long vicious looking spear in the other.

"We crave to go before the most beauteous and wise Lady Nemetona Inversus," said Arkturon to this pixie, "to offer our supplication that she may grant our humble plea in her magnificent presence."

"To offer your supplication?" the pixie leader laughed sarcastically – but Arkturon knew that the creature was now honour bound not to harm them, he had to deliver the three companions to Andreast – for no plea for an audience with a deity, begged for on the threshold of that deity's realm, can be denied – not even if that deity is nothing more than a debauched and vengeful demon. "Very well." he said, not even trying to mask his thorough disappointment. "Follow me; I will lead you to an audience with our queen." Waving his spear behind him, the throng of spiders parted to form a path down which he led the three.

With the leader out in front the rest of the band of mounted male and female pixies shadowed them down the long avenue, they passed all sorts of statues and ornaments that stood within the wild grassed pathways and small overgrown gardens leading from the wide thoroughfare. All of the figurative ones were obscene, many depicting various forms of intercourse and self abuse, and the constructions which were of a more abstract nature seemed to be aids and platforms for the performance of copulation and masturbation whether on, in, beside or under them. Even the more mundane garden objects like benches and drinking fountain's seemed to have been twisted to a double and more debased meaning or use.

Rebekah stared wide eyed at each pale, stone and marble work that they passed, some were all too obvious in their intent, some stretched her imagination, some excited it, some she even found amusing – but some were quite simply beyond her. Rebekah found herself thinking that – if it wasn't for all the pixies and giant spiders swarming everywhere – she would quite like to explore this strange place!

The pixies urged them on by means of prodding with sword and spear point, Juwniper getting the worst and roughest treatment by far; simply it seemed – for being a faery. Rebekah was hardly touched, in fact her wide eyed curiosity seemed to amuse the pixies no end. She could not help, however, but feel uneasy about some of the leering glances she was attracting – much more than the others seemed to attract. She held her hand fast to the hilt of her sheathed short-sword and kept glancing about and behind – eyeing the grotesque throng suspiciously.

The many towered castle loomed high above the tall hedges of the savage maze, like a huge dark galleon on a tumultuous sea of thorny green. Brooding above the dark and ominous structure a giant orb burned a dull red amid rising columns of acrid smoke, it hung heavily over them as if waiting to drop and crash to the earth. As they neared the abode of

Andreast the maze became increasingly populated by more and more pixies, those that did not come to ogle at the sapiens and faery were, much to Rebekah's disgust, simply using the grounds as somewhere to urinate and defecate, somewhere to eat the slop that they seemed to consider food, and to use it – and the various sculptures and furnishings – for fornication, sodomy and, seemingly, any form of depravity imaginable... or unimaginable!

Fights and petty squabbling broke out everywhere and easily. It seemed that scrapping, eating and orgiastic sex were the main ingredients of a pixie's day.

One from the ogling crowd came close and tried to grab at Rebekah's hair, she shied away, unnecessarily so for one of their guards quickly jumped from his spider mount and violently shoved the miscreant away – unceremoniously decapitating the female creature with a swift hack of his curved and jagged sword. The rest of the crowd simply laughed at this as if it were an entertainment for their benefit, a pair of undaunted and eager pixies then collected the body and its severed head and the ensuing experimentation in necrophilia acted out on both parts served to distract the attention of the crowd even further away from the three shocked companions. The horrible laughter and catcalls were, thankfully, soon left behind.

In the immediate vicinity of the castle there were many closely packed elder trees that formed a large but low, dense wood around it. A narrow path led through the wood, only wide enough for the giant spiders to pass in single file, and brought them to the gates of Kear Sidiy Reversus, a much more overtly vulval opening than the entrance of its blessed counterpart. They passed between the soft curves of the inner labia and through the narrow oval that they formed.

The moist warm air inside was strongly accented with the heavy scent of sex. Crossing an outer courtyard they were led straight into the vitals of the castle by their now dismounted pixie guard; up a long, elliptical and smoothly ribbed passage to the large vaulted chamber where Andreast waited for them. The heat, smell and the arousing tension heightened as they approached.

The Nemetona Inversus was recumbent on a large, almost bed like, seat; she was facing them, her full, deep red lips and her dark shinning eyes were smiling provocatively – daring them to look at her and not be aroused. She lay on her side with tousled, unkempt hair falling about her finely shaped neck and shoulders and full, hard nippled breasts. One of her curvaceous legs was flat against her recliner, its knee pointing directly at them, the knee of the other was lifted straight up, at the right angle of these pale and creamy limbs rested the dark V of her pubic thatch, it split and thinned between her legs to reveal the pink slit of her sex which was repeatedly being hidden by the bobbing motion of a small female pixie's head as she kissed and licked her Mistress's genitals from behind and between her legs.

When Arkturon, Rebekah and Juwniper were stood before her she lifted her foot and kicked away the cunnilingus performing pixie girl – who went sprawling but recovered rapidly and backed away from the demon, bowing repeatedly until she came to one of the many exits around the chamber wall and disappeared into it. The guards that had brought them also backed away and withdrew from sight. They were left alone with the Lady of sex, lust and emotion run riot. The Nemetona Inversus shifted her body to sit facing them – her legs still apart.

"So..." said Andreast lazily with her deep, lascivious voice, "you have a petition for me... an entreaty?" The tip of her tongue repeatedly brushed her playfully pouting lips and while one hand constantly fingered a nipple the other absently stroked between her legs, she rocked slowly backward and forward in time with her delving. Her breathing was slow and her eyes heavy.

"We wish to pass through your domain unhindered," said Arkturon, trying to keep his mind on the task ahead, "we have an important errand and need to be swift. Please aid us oh beauteous Lady Andreast, our task is elsewhere but can only be carried out with your blessing and the wise intervention of your help." An increasingly uncomfortable erection was starting to bulge in his tight breeches; he tried not to think about it but was powerless to prevent it.

Andreast laughed slowly as her fingers still worked. "Oh... such a wise and yet duplicitous gentleman, with his carefully crafted words that say everything but mean nothing" she said with a knowing smile and sighing with pleasure. "I will let you pass – despite bringing such pretentious and holier than thou scum with you!" Her words had become angry as she looked sharply at Juwniper, but was distracted as she interrupted herself, unconsciously whispering "Oh yes..." as she gently pulled her clitoris with finger and thumb. "I must ask a payment of each of you..." she said, pausing to quietly moan with pleasure, "before you can leave." She lifted her feet onto the seat and parted her legs wide; she now fingered herself with both hands and was moaning more loudly. "A kiss... is all I require... on the lips..." she laughed as she parted her slick labia with her fingers, "a proper kiss mind..." pushing her fingers inside herself, "I don't want just a peck... I want to feel your tongues inside me..." her fingers started to work faster, pushing her on to a climax as her speech developed a very excited edge, "especially from you, Merdhin... you... you must pay homage to me – to my cunt... you must... humble yourself... before me..." she suddenly expelled a loud and triumphant groan of pleasure as her fingers were deluged under her orgasm. Then she burst into hysterical laughter.

Arkturon had suspected that such a condition would be applied and he knew that it could have been a much more degrading act that she could have demanded of them... a true witch's kiss – showing total submission in their supplication... an anal kiss. He was grateful that this particular demon was so preoccupied with sensual gratification, for that would be the one thing he was not sure he could bring himself to do. Still he suspected he would have a hard enough time convincing his friends to accept the situation and do as requested, but there was no other way. He turned to his companions and said "We have no choice – it is our only way out." He saw the hesitant surprise on Rebekah's face and the look of indignant disgust on Juwniper's. "It is a loss of face – yes, but an unavoidable one. If we wish to help Mikael and Lilith, we must do it!

"Girls first." said Andreast laying back, her sex still exposed in the same shameless way, with knees pointing straight up. "Come... kneel and pay homage to me... to my quim!"

"The longer we wait," said Arkturon, "the more humiliating the act will prove to be!"

Andreast giggled expectantly.

Juwniper was the first to make up her mind and accept the inevitable, approaching the demoness she knelt before Andreast and touched her lips to the soft wet labia, quickly she flicked her tongue between them – but not so quick as to be ineffectual. The faery stood and retreated, a furious scowl on her face as she wiped her lips with the back of her hand.

At first Rebekah was going to refuse but then she too approached and knelt – hardly believing that she was doing it – and then hesitated a fraction of an inch away from the kiss, she found herself breathing the scent, savouring the close heat and letting her eyes feast on the moist, curving flesh. She had often fantasised about being kissed between the legs but had never really thought of kissing another there – she was curious though, she had to admit. *Kindred spirit!* The Nemetona Inversus chuckle in her mind. Rebekah kissed the genitalia slowly and deliberately, pushing her tongue between the *ever-so-moist* lips, concentrating on the taste and feel of it – but not too obviously she hoped. She pulled herself up and drew away – only a little ashamed and feeling her cheeks flush as she turned and her eyes briefly met with those of Arkturon.

Andreast sat up again and looked to the man. "Well Arkturon... it's your turn now." Her smile was wickedly wanton. "Do you have the courage to humble yourself before me... you – the great and good Merdhin... to kiss my wet and pouting pussy..." She laughed salaciously, "on his knees like a common slave... a pixie girl."

He knew the ridicule would go on so he approached Andreast and knelt before her, she was still sat up and she stared triumphantly at him as he kissed her. Just as he was about to pull away she laid back completely and lifted her legs up onto herself, exposing her bottom, then whispered with a threatening, insidious tone, "Now kiss my sweet and puckering little arse hole, Merdhin. Show that you truly submit to my will."

She could see his shoulders tense and his jaw clench. She hissed gleefully then said "Do it! A kiss... and then a lick of your verbose though clever tongue."

Arkturon bent down once more without a word and kissed the small brown circle of her sphincter and brushed his tongue against her – *so soft and smooth, like nothing else* – he felt a shiver of pleasure run through Andreast as his tongue passed over her anus. Arkturon stood and stared down at her, stony faced but also secretly shamed at the pleasure he too had felt, before turning away.

The demoness giggled like a spoilt little girl who had just got her way. "Get them out of here!" she suddenly shouted, then added venomously. "Get them out – away from my realm!" as the guards hurriedly returned.

Mikael found that negotiating the labyrinth of Kear Pedrivan without a guide was not half as difficult as he had suspected it would be. He had simply tried to keep the castle ahead of him or to his right, always following the paths that circled clockwise – as Afagddu seemed to have done – and that radiated into the centre. He had been forced to retrace his steps a couple of times after reaching dead ends but on the whole he felt he was doing remarkably well and the castle was now looming up high above him, he was very close, he just had to find that narrow, high sided lane that led to the lake above which the castle floated.

He reckoned he must have been walking a solid five hours but he felt no fatigue what so ever, and though never feeling hungry he could not stop himself from partaking of the delicious fruit that grew all around in the many ornamental plaza's and courtyards – he had eaten many of them while on the move. Though the labyrinth had been populated before, it was now literally over run with people, there was still about the same amount of otherworld visitors but adding to the numbers were so many more human peoples, they were all about him and of all kinds; men, women and children, of all creeds and all races. He felt sure that in fact they had been there all the time but that before he had been blind to them – or at least most of them for he did remember seeing a few. It must simply be that now he is dead, as they are, and he sees with his soul – not his physical self – and it is their souls that he sees.

He circled the immediate environs of Kear Pedrivan, searching for the way in, but it was only when he had almost completed the circuit that he remembered the bridge that they had crossed before descending to the lane and the lake. So he moved back out, away from the castle, and started another circuit, but this time looking for the bridge. When he finally found it another two or three hours had gone by since first reaching the centre. He crossed the bridge, descended into the dark, tunnel like lane and finally came to the lake.

The sword edge bridge held no fear or doubt for him now and he leapt to the fast moving steps of the spinning castle walls with certain and sure feet. He climbed and knocked with the curled brass tongue that protruded from the life like face on the door, he knocked steadily – three times.

And a voice bellowed, and it said... "What do you seek beyond this door, what truth lies there for you? Name what it is that you seek... and enter."

This took Mikael by surprise, somewhat naively he had thought the question would have been the same as before, he hadn't expected this and had almost blurted out that what he sought was the truth, before reconsidering and taking time to think about his answer. He realised quite quickly that because this was the realm of truth – that is exactly what he must tell, the truth. He had only one chance at an answer, it had to be right and, searching deep down, he knew the only thing he wanted, his only single and true desire...

"I seek the only person I have ever really loved... Lilith..." he said falteringly. "I seek a way to join her... to save her." He felt his throat constrict and tears well in his eyes as that basic truth of this statement fully dawned on him and the true importance of her to him was revealed, he fought the tears back as the door slowly opened.

He entered the high walled garden and climbed the worn spiral stair case up into the blue tinted mist. Mikael kept climbing till he came to the top and was, once again, before Matt... but a different Matt; older, blonder and more regal, though unmistakably still Matt – his aspect, no longer coloured by the Britannik expectations of Arkturon, was purely that of the Saxanglish god Frea. The now blue cloaked god, with a gold and bejewelled cross-like brooch clasped at his sternum, greeted him and beckoned him forward with a truly sorrowful face and sympathetic manner. "You have a hard and desperate ordeal ahead of you Mikael." Frea-Matt said, adding, "Mikael – you were named wisely, it is a good name for one who is to battle with a demon – for it is derived from a name by which the Divine Youth, Baldeag-Luw, was once known in the distant land of Gnodd – as I was Rafayel he was Miykayel. I feel you will not dishonour it." The god paused, searching Mikael's face, looking deep into his heart.

He then continued "We will not send you against this demon unprotected though, nor unarmed."

Frea-Matt stood up from his throne and accepted a long-sword from his servant Akanthis, who laid the shinning blade horizontally on the gods outstretched hands. It was the same sword that Mikael had seen the god carry when he appeared to them back in the magik circle at Rose Mansion. Frea-Matt then approached Mikael and offered him this sword. "Take it," he said, "without it you have no weapon against Hlewid but your love." The sword was light and excellently balanced, it was a thing of precision and extreme beauty, and it was lethally sharp. "Its name is Sumbrandr and it possesses a will to fight all its own. If wise be he who wields it, nothing and no-one can stand against them."

The god then repeated the process with an ornately decorated and embroidered belt and scabbard. Mikael sheathed the blade and buckled it to his waste after discarding his own, old belt and sword, for his spirit was clad as his body had been on death.

"You must now go to the realm of Kear Sidiy," said Frea-Matt, "there, my sister Frouwa-Ariyanrhod will provide you with armour fit for the warrior who carries such a weapon as Sumbrandr."

Mikael thanked the god profusely and swore that he would neither dishonour the name, or the sword.

The Kernunnos then instructed Akanthis to show Mikael to the path of the Lovers, "the long, rambling road that leads to Kear Sidiy."

Lieutenant Lethbridj was losing blood and sweating heavily, his mouth parched and lips dry, he longed for a long, cool drink of ale. He seemed to be getting weaker and his tiredness grew as each long moment passed. Slumped he sat and blearily he peered, barely able to keep his eyes open and his wits vigilant. The pain in his leg was excruciating and with the arrow embedded deep in his muscle each and every slightest movement seemed to scrape the metal arrowhead agonisingly against his thigh bone. He embraced that exquisite pain as the only thing that could keep him conscious – keep him watching the dark corridor, guarding against attack from within.

A strange shade came over him, though there was nothing to cast such a shadow. He figured it was a symptom of his flagging alertness, but quickly glanced over to the wounded trooper opposite to see if he had noticed anything unusual. Pendal seemed awake and watchful – though clearly suffering from his own wound, he was scanning the corridor with dragon up and pointed – and had patently detected nothing amiss.

However, the Lieutenant could not dismiss the niggling doubt that someone or something unseen had passed them by. He looked back toward the double doors that exited the keep where Corporal Lannik and the three others were sheltering from the light but constant drizzle of arrows from the inner bailey watchtowers. The heavy clouds outside had obviously thinned considerably for a diffuse moonlight now lit the doorway and cast disperse shadows, of the doors themselves and of the men, onto the corridor's stone floor and walls. *Had it simply been one of those shadows crossing over me*, he wondered.

The moonlight shadows suddenly crystallised into sharp focus as the thinning cloud cover broke completely and a bright shaft of silvery light was cast through the foot-wide gap of the doors – fanning out and down the centre of the corridor floor. It cast a shadow that should not be there. The Lieutenant blinked his apparently untrustworthy eyes. The mysterious shade remained and was moving – he tried to work out if it was of something coming down from the ceiling or of something approaching the doorway along the floor... *either way*, he thought – *there's nothing there to cast it... or is there?*

He squinted, trying to discern what it was that was not there, and then he saw it. There was a distortion in the light, a figure, standing between him and the gap in the doorway – barely perceptible, but definitely there. Just as he was about to shout a warning, the figure lunged at the nearest Ranger, pushing him back up against the wall with phenomenal speed and uncanny strength. The soldier screamed hideously as a gaping hole was ripped into his throat and as his startled comrades at the door all span round to see what was happening. They stared, shock etched into each of their faces, as a barely clad woman of bewitching beauty and inhuman cruelty materialised among them and let go the bitten soldier, gushing blood as he slouched and crumpled lifeless to the floor.

With a bloody, viscous scowl Aggareth turned and slashed her taloned fingers at the Corporal as he tried to bring his gun to bear. The sharp, long nails of her left hand clawed into his forearm and pushed his arm and weapon away and up – so it fired its shot into the ceiling and then ricocheted about them – and with her right hand she swiped at his head, knocking him back and leaving deep gashes across his cheek. Before the rest of the soldiers could react, the vampire witch – inhumanly agile and preternaturally deft – leapt away from them to the wall like a cat, and then from the wall to the ceiling, clinging like a spider on all fours she swiftly and eerily manoeuvred upside down back along the length of the corridor.

The Lieutenant desperately fired his two blunderbusses at the witch as she rapidly spider-walked above him, but she was quicker by far than even he could aim and shoot. She was gone... and he was a Ranger down.

"Hold your fire!" a shout came from down the corridor, "Rangers coming!"

It was the Sergeant's unmistakable voice. "Well thank the gods for that." said the Lieutenant to himself as Sergeant Rinawn came round a corner with his Rangers and the girl in tow – but the officer noticed that he too had one dead... and another wounded. *Damn*, he thought, *but this is turning into a costly affair!*

Chapter Twenty Three – A Conversation with Keridwen

Arkturon, Juwniper and Rebekah were led briskly to the borders of Kear Sidiy Reversus by the same pixie guards who had brought them before Andreast. They were led to a darkened and shadow infested dead-end corner of the iniquitous maze that surrounded the carcass-like castle of the demoness, and for an instant Rebekah suspected some form of foul treachery and deceit – that their shame had been for nothing but a cruel, duplicitous death. But they were led safely to a gateway as promised. There was no pause for ceremony or leave-taking though, as the pixies all but forced their guests out of the Nemetona Inversus' lands, through the crumbling and moss covered stone of an isolated archway and into the black portal it framed.

Arkturon flared the twinned serpent crown of his staff, to shed some light on their new surroundings. It was cold and it was damp, a dripping stone passage that all three of them recognised. It was the path of the Priestess, that led either to the warm embrace of the child like huntress Sul, or to the cold and clinging arms of her dark sister Keridwen. In silence Arkturon led them on.

He had no control over where the strangely shifting passages would lead, destiny and fate would decide for him, his only power was his ability to act on and, if possible, take advantage of any situation that presented itself. He had a bad feeling about his present steps into uncharted darkness though, once already he had only just escaped the clutches of Keridwen and her servants, when dragging Mikael from the mud. It had been as if they were hunting him, calling him almost... and he felt that now... Keridwen was calling him to her... dragging him down to the dark depths of her watery realm. It seemed that no matter which direction or turning he took he was leading his friends down into even danker tunnels and through ever more chill chambers, far from where he had hoped to meet Kreruwiy, the Priestess again. It seemed he was fated to meet her dark mother instead.

But he voiced none of his concerns; the girls seemed enough on edge as it was. His mind raced though, trying to remember the old legends and folklore of Keridwen, the witch's goddess, holder of inspiration and the secret of the cauldron of knowledge, as Sul is... but corrupted by it... all purity and innocence long gone.

Arkturon suddenly stopped, skidding slightly as he checked his long and fast strides. The others came to a halt behind him for the passage that they currently negotiated was too narrow to walk any more than single file. They had come to the end of the tunnel and an apparently huge black chamber opened up before them, for the scale of the emptiness ahead weighed them down to insignificance even though they could see no further than a few yards. The lost, lonely and distant echoes of drops dripping into water drubbed and dabbed through the cold cavernous void toward them.

Holding onto the bottom of his staff, Arkturon thrust out the lighted crown to the extent of his reach in an attempt to reveal the expanse of the chamber. A narrow mossy ledge could be discerned spreading out on either side of the entrance in which they stood, ahead – just below the lip of the ledge – was a glassy sheet of still, stale looking water, its blackness giving no hint of its depth and even the wizard's bright light could not reveal the limits of its surface. Arkturon realised he had been holding a deep breath within his lungs as he held out the staff, he let it out as he brought the staff back and a frosty cloud was expelled into the darkness. He bent and picked up a large pebble, weighed it in his hand and then threw it out into the chamber. It's long, slow arch came down well out of sight but the deep ka-plop it created as it entered the water rolled back to them on a tide of echoes. Slow ripples radiated out to them from the blackness, visible only as narrow lines of reflected light from the tip of the wizard's staff.

"Unless we have a volunteer to test the depth," said Arkturon quietly, "I suggest we try circling it on this ledge." He looked to them for any comment.

The two women looked at each other, not sure if he was being serious about testing the water.

"Couldn't we just go back," said Rebekah "and try another tunnel?" The cold damp that pervaded the air had penetrated her clothes and left them feeling icy and wet against her skin.

"No..." he replied, "it would be futile – we would just end up back here... the paths of the otherworld sometimes have an annoying tendency to take you where-ever destiny demands rather than where-ever it is that you would like them to take you. I'm afraid this is one of those times." When they stayed silent he began to edge his way out onto the eight inch ledge. Somewhat hesitantly the girls followed; first Rebekah, then Juwniper carefully sidled out onto the barely lit ledge.

With her back up against the slimy stone of the wall Rebekah side stepped along the narrow shelf after Arkturon. It too was getting increasingly slimy and she had almost skidded twice, her back and legs were tensed and aching with the effort of trying not to slip, her heart was pounding and her throat and lungs were becoming sore from the chill air that was being frantically drawn through her open mouth. She stared out at the stretch of inky blackness before her, filled with the uncertain fear caused only by facing the unknown. She'd felt it before, a similar kind of stale oppressiveness, at the black pool back in the Romanik baths below Rose Mansion.

Her breathing suddenly stopped as she held the freezing air within her lungs, she had seen something – she was sure of it, a flash of reflected light on a shimmering wet body that arched out of the black waters of the lake, but it was in the distance and disappeared almost immediately. She could not be sure if it had been there at all, the darkness before her paled as she let out her cloud like breath and continued moving after Arkturon.

Then she saw it again, crossing the other way and nearer to them. A human torso with a large piscine tail and tattered fin below, it arched out of the water and in again.

"There's something in the water!" she whispered. Rebekah found herself shaking – and not from the cold – she tried to convince herself that maybe it was an undine, but she just knew, deep down that it was not, it was a kelpie... she was almost positive.

"Just keep moving!" Arkturon's sharp words confirmed and heightened Rebekah's fears. Then she saw two of them arch out quickly and dive back down, she saw their bald ugly heads and their ragged and pointed ears. They were kelpies, she now had no doubt, and they approached at a terrifying speed.

Arkturon quickened his steps but the ledge that they followed was becoming increasingly uneven and seemed to be slowly sinking into the impenetrable depths. Franticly trying to keep up with him Rebekah slipped, letting out a desperate yell as her foot flew from under her, her arms flailing she grabbed for anything that might steady her. Juwniper took hold of her arm and pulled her toppling form back toward the cold and solid security of the wall behind them. Standing still they held onto each other. Rebekah's heart was beating a deafening rhythm.

Arkturon halted and turned his eyes from watching his feet toward them, "Keep moving," he repeated, "we must not -" his words were cut short though as, in an instant, the pale and hideous head, shoulders and torso of a kelpie reared up out of the water directly in front of him. Bony, clawed hands gripped his calf muscles and pulled him down to the water. Arkturon disappeared into the black lake; falling vertically he went straight under with almost no disturbance to the still surface. The two women stared into the now complete darkness; it was as if Arkturon and the light that he commanded had never existed.

The terror of vulnerable blindness overwhelmed them; they could not have been more exposed and helpless as they were in that brief but everlasting moment as they stood in total and silent confusion and panic. Desperately waiting for a sign or sound of Arkturon or even of a struggle, but no sound was granted to them – except the constant drip dripping – and no light came as proof of his safety.

The two hunched together on the precarious ledge, subconsciously seeking security in the closeness of the other.

"We must keep walking," said Juwniper, finally breaking the hateful silence, "find a way off this ledge and get away from the water, we can't help Arkturon by standing here and shivering."

"Help him!" said Rebekah's tearful and shaky voice, "How could we help him... he's dead! Drowned!" she was verging on hysteria. "And soon we will be... they'll come back – and drag us in... we'll drown!"

"No!" hissed Juwniper. "No – he is alive... he's been taken to Keridwen. Like when you were submersed in the waters of Sul's realm – he is safe for now... but we can't stay here waiting forever. We must keep going."

Rebekah calmed herself, "Yes... yes I understand... I'm sorry; it's just that I thought... I'm sorry."

So they started along the ledge again, in total darkness and very slowly this time, keeping extremely close to one another and clasping hands tightly. They sidled along like this for what seemed hours and the stone ledge was now becoming perilously uneven and broken – and, or so it seemed to Rebekah, was at least six inches below the water surface. She could not be sure if it was the result of the ledge getting lower, or of the water getting higher.

Their blind and trembling sideways advance did eventually bring them to an exit from the seemingly limitless expanse of cold dark water. With her back pressed to the wall Rebekah almost fell head over heels when it's stony support gave way behind her to open out on another passageway, she stumbled over the step rising from the water at its threshold. Quickly followed by Juwniper, they huddled tightly together for warmth and for the practicality of not losing one another in the blackness. Following the right hand wall of the passage they kept moving, afraid to stop or even pause their progress, afraid to contemplate how long they might be wandering blindly before finding a way out, afraid to even think of not finding a way out.

Speaking in short, hushed bursts they decided to ignore all turnings and intersections and to just keep going forward, where possible, and right, where not, for as long as they were able, trusting their wellbeing to fate. After what seemed numerous miles of fumbling – though the passing of time and the passage of distance was impossible to accurately gauge – the two allowed themselves a touch of growing optimism as they became aware that the cold and damp of the air was slowly abating. The severity of the conditions was perceptibly decreasing and either their eyes were becoming accustomed to the dark or a faint light was slowly beginning to defuse from somewhere. It seemed likely to be the latter of the two for no length of time could encourage eyes to see in complete blackness.

By the time the temperature had crept its way up to being no longer cold they could see each other quite clearly, all tinted by a warm red glow that came down the passage ahead of them. With the warmth also came a smell, though once Rebekah had found it extremely unpleasant she now welcomed that smell as the scent of life and of nature; it was a friendly and familiar smell and she actually found herself smiling.

"I think we've found Afagddu." said Juwniper, with a smile all her own.

"You know him too?"

"Oh, indeed I do." was all the faery said.

Rebekah would swear that Juwniper blushed somewhat, though in that light it was impossible to tell.

The light and heat seemed to be coming from at least one, but maybe a number of fires within the chamber ahead for they could hear the sputtering and cracking of the flames, but no other sound could be heard above that. The promise of warming their bodies and drying out their damp clothes spurred them on to quickly reach the end of the tunnel and the two rushed into the large cave that opened out there. It was heavily lined with soft and thick furs from all kinds of animal and two huge fires roared away at each end of its length. There was no sign of any occupants, though there was a number of dark passage ways leading from it.

Without a care Juwniper stripped naked and put her clothes by one of the fires to dry, but Rebekah kept on her under vest and the short bloomers that she wore beneath her breeches, uncomfortable with the thought that Afagddu could come in on them at any time – and she for one did not want to be naked when he did.

They huddled to each other before the blazing flames and Rebekah asked "What are we to do... how are we going to find Arkturon." She was very anxious for him and it was slowly dawning on her that she loved him; she could not bear to be parted from him now. This scared her a little for how could a man like that – powerful, strong and wise – love her, young and foolish... still a girl. Her heart truly ached at the thought.

They stared into the flames for some time, as if mesmerised, each with their own thoughts.

"I think only Afagddu can help us with that." said Juwniper finally.

"When we are thoroughly warm and dried we should search this great warren of caves he calls home, find him and ask his assistance."

"I would always give you my assistance," a deep voice gently boomed behind them, "my little fay." Afagddu had entered silently and crept up behind them as they stared into the fire. He stood there as they turned with surprise. Juwniper leapt right up and jumped into his arms, hugging him with a laugh. The beast man laughed too, and said "Oh, it has been so long since your travels have brought you here... my adventurous faery friend, always on some errand or other." Rebekah was surprised to see Juwniper give the ugly demigod a full open mouthed kiss as part of her greeting. After hugging her, Afagddu gripped the sprightly faery in his large hands and lifted her up at arm's length – taking a good, long and smiling look at her naked form before putting her down. Her pale, slim body looked so small next to his, and Rebekah could plainly see that Afagddu's member was engorging slightly to become semi-erect.

Rebekah suddenly remembered she was dressed in only her underwear and lunged for her still damp tunic to cover herself. She could feel the hot flush of her face turning red. She did not blush through modesty though; it was at the thought – which had come unbidden into her mind – of Afagddu and Juwniper coupling.

"Rebekah." he then greeted the sapien, bowing to her, his eyes and face beaming.

Rebekah smiled, nodding her head to the giant and trying not to look at his fat member.

"I sense distress and concern in you both," he said, "so if one of you can tell me of your problem I can decide how best I can help." He sat cross legged on the floor near the fire. Juwniper, seemingly in no rush to get dressed, sat before him in a similar fashion, and Rebekah sat close by. Juwniper steadily told him of all that had befallen them since she had first taken part directly in the events, from joining Rebekah and Arkturon in Matt's castle, right up to their present situation. He seemed grim when his fay friend had finished the tale.

"Then, I'm afraid I must leave you both." He said sombrely. "Arkturon has undoubtedly been taken to the Koventiyna Inversus. You must wait here for my return, but be assured; I will be back as soon as I can. Hopefully with Arkturon... but, my mother can be difficult."

Afagddu left them, heading into one of the many dark tunnels leading out from the warm chamber.

Once Arkturon was immersed in the freezing water he realised the futility of struggling, he was held fast by two of the loathsome kelpies and they pulled him down at a merciless rate – he barely held onto his staff, the light from which had been completely extinguished, leaving him in total blackness. As with the waters inside Sul's castle, he could breath – but not as easily, it was more viscous and heavy, and was icy cold – it took some time for him to will his initial shock and panic away. The numbing cold was pervasive though and, as he was continually dragged down, his extremities began to lose all feeling and he could no longer be sure that he held his staff. The wizard tried to picture his hand gripping tightly in the hope that this effort would somehow translate through his growing numbness and he would retain his hold on it.

A hazy, blue tinged light was slowly beginning to diffuse out of the darkness below; huge crystalline shapes loomed up at him and his captors. It was an ice castle, not unlike like that of Sul's but more rugged, and this one under water. As the light grew Arkturon saw that his tightly gripped hand held nothing, cursing himself as a ham-fisted dunderhead he despaired at the thought that he'd lost Matt's staff. The kelpies swam him down to the black-sand bed of the lake and approached a tunnel that ran into the massive shard that was the central tower of Keridwen's ghostly-pale castle. Around the tower were lesser shards, standing in a huge circle; and beyond them, Arkturon could just make out the dark, undulating shapes of an immense seaweed forest where darker shapes dwelt – shapes that suggested tentacles and pincers and strange elongated limbs belonging to horrors he did not care to ponder on.

They entered the tunnel and soon came to a shimmering barrier – Arkturon surmised that it was the vertical surface of a huge pocket of air, the opposite of the similar portal that marked the entrance to Sul's towering home. As the two kelpies brought him close, the wizard noticed with great relief that a third – which was following close behind – was carrying his staff. Whether he had dropped it himself or the kelpie had taken it from him, he did not know – either way he was glad, the prospect of having to search for it in the eldritch forest that covered the bottom of this lake was not a pleasant one.

The kelpies deposited Arkturon at the threshold of the portal, they handed him the staff and then bodily pushed him through. The shock of entering the air was nowhere near that of entering the water but a shock it still was. His lungs desperately coughed up the thick, viscous liquid he'd been breathing and urgently he tried to accustom himself to the air once more. On his hands and knees he coughed and spluttered till his breathing became regular and his heart rate eased. To his right the tunnel continued, gently inclining down and gradually bending into the structure. From this tunnel, pale naked figures approached, corpse-like but beautiful beyond compare, male and female, alluring yet dreadful to behold. As Arkturon stood, dozens of the creatures thronged around him. Incubi and succubi they were, the children of Keridwen – the night terrors. Taking him by the hands they led him into the tunnel. Their chill touch was horrifying, but perversely arousing too, and though a part of the wizard wanted to pull his hands away, another part did not want them to ever let go.

Descending through that winding tunnel seemed to take an age before Arkturon, after countless and ever increasing circumferences of the castle, was finally brought to the true heart of Kear Widiyr Reversus. It was a huge chamber, with a black sand floor and icy walls that rose up into the distance at a slight taper. In the centre of the mile wide floor stood a temple, of archaic design – there was an outer circle of monolithic standing stones, topped uniformly by cap-stones broad and flat; and within was another circle but of taller and more massive stones, capped in pairs. High above hung a shinning orb of the coldest and palest blue. Only when he'd been brought right up to the outer circle of stones were his hands finally let go – to his relief and dismay – and the undead throng lifted from the dark sandy floor, dissolving and morphing into strange and terrifying amalgams of moth, bat and owl. They flitted and flighted up and away, fluttering and screeching they circled the temple and then the great orb high above, till they were lost from sight.

Arkturon entered the temple, walking between the massive columns of stone, and there within the inner circle, sitting by a great cauldron suspended over a roaring fire, huddled a heavily cowled figure, seemingly bent and weak with age. She greeted him with contempt and in a haggard and ancient voice. "Merdhin," she said with a cackle, "it's been a long time since a Merdhin dare approach me."

"My Lady Keridwen?" said Arkturon puzzled and fearful – though grateful for the warmth that radiated from the fire, "I am honoured to be brought here before you, but I beg your leave to depart, I have an urgent and vital errand..."

The cloaked figure then swiftly stood, allowing her wrap to fall at her feet and revealing the young girl that Arkturon had been expecting, physically she looked the double of Sul, but she was a girl far from innocent and full of love. "Just like all the others," she spat at him, "you wizards, always on urgent and vital errands – always with important business that takes precedence over everything and everyone else... but the first of your kind was a deceitful thief, he stole his wizard powers..." she then shouted with disgust, "and passed it on to his mortal bloodline! A gift he had NO RIGHT to give – it was meant for our FIRST-BORN-SON!"

"But, my Lady," Arkturon tried to appease her, "I cannot be held responsible for the actions of another long before I was born!"

"WIZARD!" she screamed. "You of all people should know that time is irrelevant – you are a consequence of that thief stealing our Afagddu's birth right! You are *Wuodhen*'s heir. You are he, in our eyes – the same duplicitous neophyte we entrusted to monitor and stir our sacred cauldron for a year and a day!"

Of course, Arkturon knew the legend of how the first of his kind came about, but he had always thought that it was just that – a legend. It seemed to him more likely that the powers of wizardry had been simply an accident of birth, a one in a trillion mutation that was subsequently passed down the line of descent. The ancient tradition among his forebears was that it coincided with the coming of the rogue Black Planet, Yaggoth, before the Age of Ice – an eclipse of the sun and three days of red rain it brought, that seeded this world with the Yaggothiyan Fungi and thus all Magiks were born. But he also knew that the otherworld, and its denizens, were malleable – they were phantasmic products of the collective unconscious fashioned by the current worldviews, beliefs and superstitions of all the mortal peoples – the construct of a universal gestalt mind where myth, legend and folklore held sway and were made real.

"Please, my Lady," he said, "it was not by deception but by accident that Woden denied Afagddu his birth right – on the hundred-and-first day the first three efficacious drops of the boiling potion splashed his hand, he instinctively brought it to his mouth to ease the pain. It was an accident."

"An accident?!" she glowered at him, "A very beneficent accident for him, and fortuitously timed! But not for our son!" The demonic young girl suddenly turned maudlin, "We just wanted to help our son, grant him a gift to make up for the fact that he took after his foul father while his twin sister took after us. She, Kreruwiy, got beauty and wisdom, while he got nothing but ugliness and base instinct – through no fault of his own. We just wanted to help him."

Keridwen started to sob and Arkturon was almost tempted to put his arm round the young girl, but he did not – *that could be a very dangerous thing to do when dealing with a demoness such as her*, he reminded himself. "I understand your anger at Woden," he said softly, "but, could you not have made another potion?" He regretted the question immediately.

Ire flashed in her eyes briefly. "Do you not think that if we could have done so, we would have? For a Merdhin, you ask some surprisingly stupid questions... for that alone, we're tempted to hang you from a tree for nine years – just like we did with *Wuodhen*, when we finally caught up with him."

"There is no doubt that you and your son were wronged." He said, suddenly seeing a way to draw her thoughts away from again punishing Woden by punishing him. "Perhaps you will allow me to make up for that wrong by helping another of your children, a daughter of yours I believe... by the sorcerer Bäliyl Samiyl?"

"Do not mention that foul Kanaaniyt's name!" She said ominously, her black eyes stared terrifyingly at him. "His betrayal is more raw and greater than even *Wuodhen*'s... he was our high-priest once – we should have killed him for what he did. Foolishly, because he was his father's son, we took pity on him and only had him banished. He paid us back by piling sin upon sin against us... the greatest of which was investing an aspect of us – now forever fractured from us – into a viscid golem of pitch with which he copulated and, it seems, inseminated. If we ever get our hands on him..."

"He's dead now," said Arkturon, "I killed him myself."

"You impress us, wizard. He was a mighty sorcerer indeed. We see that there's more to you than meets the eye. Did he suffer – we hope he did?"

"Oh he did, my Lady," he assured her, "and even now I'm sure he languishes in the dungeons of his new infernal master – the Kernunnos Inversus."

She laughed sardonically at that. "Do not underestimate him, wizard. He is a clever and crafty opponent – more than capable of outwitting the Kernunnos Inversus. He used us – he could easily manipulate our brother, Hlewid, to his own ends. The sorcerer could be more dangerous in this plane than he ever was in yours... but what of this daughter?"

"Lilith," said the wizard, "Bäl... that is, the sorcerer – bargained her phantasmic soul to Hlewid, as his consort." He saw a rage flash in her eyes once more.

"He will pay for this," she seethed, "yet another sin against us... to take her name from our Kanaanite cult – and then do this to her... he is taunting us – he worshiped us as *Lilit* once; long, long ago – and now he does this! He mocks us yet again!" She was now pacing back and forth, her wrath building.

"My Lady, I seek to deliver Lilith from this fate – allow me leave, and I will see it done."

Keridwen stopped her pacing and looked at him hard. "Why would you wish to do that, wizard?" She asked stonily.

He almost told her that he felt responsible, but decided that that would probably not be a good idea. "She is my friend," he said instead, "she helped me when I needed it, so now I will help her."

"Then we shall help you, wizard. We shall help you." She approached him and linked her cold arm with his, holding it tight she brought him closer to the fire. "Shall we take a look in our cauldron of knowledge?" she said, conspiratorially. "Many things can be seen there; past, present and future." Then, coldly "But do not cross us, wizard! For we never forget those who cross us. No matter how long it takes, vengeance *will* be sought and the punishment *surely* meted!"

Chapter Twenty Four – The Path of the Lovers

Frea-Matt had warned Mikael before leaving for the Path of the Lovers that it was a road of decisions, of questions to be answered and choices to be made. "It represents the ultimate dilemma in the form of the taking of a lover," he had said. "It could be the choice between vice and virtue, good and evil, love and lust; or a choice between chastity, fidelity and promiscuity. It is a path that all must travel whether in life or beyond for it is a choice that all must make, sooner or later."

Mikael had made his choice before setting foot on this path, and he determined to stay true to it, never wavering from his love for Lilith despite all that was offered to him on that winding and lengthy road. All manner of pleasures were offered, tempting him from the path, every woman he had ever lusted after, naked and wanton, all beckoned him, provocatively exposed. They were there to delay, waylay and divert him from his purpose. He scorned them all. He had chosen fidelity - fidelity to Lilith.

The final temptation, however, struck at his heart, filling him with grief, shame and – he could not deny it – desire. It was Emma, as she was at fifteen, just blossoming into womanhood. She lay there before him, her smooth soft body open to his gaze, ready for his touch. He knelt before her with tears of confusion in his eyes. He remembered that this was how she had been that night so long ago, they had lain naked together, touched and explored, playfully kissing and squeezing one another. A part of him had longed to pierce her with his eager manhood, but she had shied from it and he dared not insist. He knew that they had been right not to continue. They had loved each other, yes – but they could never have been lovers.

The Emma before him now though, she fingered and opened the soft, fleshy, down covered lips of her sex and invited him in, begged and pleaded with language lewd and abandoned. She swore at him and insisted that he prove his manhood to her – insisted that he take her now as he should have done then.

Mikael stood, this was not Emma. Emma was loving but chaste, she had only a child like love, playful, but full of innocence. This was not her. He walked on.

The last temptation overcome, the path led him through the foothills of a great mountain range, slowly rising till he eventually came to a large tunnel mouth that led deep into the bowels of a particularly large and precipitous peak. He entered with a great sense of accomplishment and relief. The encounter with his pseudo sister had in fact cauterized a great deal of guilt and shame from his subconscious. Mikael had now come to terms with his love for Emma, no longer suppressing his feelings for her with misplaced chagrin and reproach. They had done what they did out of innocence and love, there was no wrong in that. He could never have done anything to hurt or offend her. His love had given some joy to her short but precious life, he could only be thankful for that.

The tunnel led him into the sphere of Kear Sidiy and back into the throng of a multitude of dead souls. He was expected, and the two faery girls that had comforted him on his last visit greeted him as he came out onto the border of the huge gardens, they guided his steps to an audience with Frouwa-Ariyanrhod within her spiral castle.

"Your soul – so much older and wiser Mikael," she said to him, "and now perhaps a little sadder too... though beneficial – experience has its penalties." She reclined on her lounging throne, dressed in a short and very slight shift of ivory satin, her warm smile accentuating the sadness she felt with him. "But they are not over yet, there is still a large share of sadness ahead for you yet, and a great deal of joy too. They go hand in hand until the final goal can be attained.

"You faced a lot on the Path of the Lovers and you deserve your reward for passing them as you did. Your sister was lucky to have you for the time she did, many go through life with no kind of love at all, coming here when they die is a pure revelation." Mirth and pleasure now all but shone from her eyes. "Emma has longed for your soul to come here, to come and see her. When you bodily came to my castle before, her little heart broke that you could not see her, could not greet her."

Mikael's heart ached at the words the goddess spoke, they filled him with unbearable sorrow and unbridled hope.

"Mikael." said the girl's voice from behind him, gentle, quite and almost afraid. Unable to prevent a heartfelt sob escaping his lips he turned and saw her. Young and radiant, filling the long satin shift she wore with a womanly voluptuousness that so contrasted with his memories of her wasting form before she died. He rushed to stand before her, unable to find suitable words to say. They hugged and kissed... and cried.

After the brief reunion, the goddess Frouwa-Ariyanrhod and the maiden Emma Feraiyn adorned Mikael in a finely wrought, segmented and interlocking set of plate silvered adamantine armour, expertly fashioned by the faeries of the Sacred Groves. Its silvery sheen, which gave off a strange eerie glow, was exquisitely emblazoned with the images and symbols of the Nemetona herself in a delicate combination of forest-green lacquer-work and intricate engraving. The perfect form of a naked woman with arms outstretched was depicted on his chest plate and that of a mighty tree was on his back – around these two images were engraved the mystic signs and sigils of the goddess. Finally, a velvet lined barbute style helmet was placed over his head. It was forged from a single plate of the same eerie metal with a low ridged crest running from front to back over its crown. Except for the Y-shaped opening for his eyes and mouth – which resembled a young sapling with two offshoots, each sprouting a single oval leaf – it covered his head and neck completely.

The suit of armour was surprisingly light and, despite being closely moulded to his body, it did not hinder Mikael's movements by so much as an inch or degree. All the while she dressed him in this magical shell, Frouwa-Ariyanrhod whispered incantations – stroking and signing across its surface with the gentle caresses of a loving and enchanting spell. Thus she completed the covering of his being with a blessed and charmed protection. To finish his raiment Emma belted the sword Sumbrandr at his waist.

Mikael, now ready, was escorted from Kear Sidiy toward the path of the Priestess which would lead him on to Kear Widiyr and Sul, from whom he would receive his last gifts to aid him in the confrontation with Hlewid, to protect him in his contest for the soul of Lilith.

"There he is," said Corporal Lannik, pointing out the persistently accurate goblin archer through the gap in the doors, "every time he gets ready to shoot, his bow comes out over the parapet of the watchtower – giving away his position. A well timed shot should take him out."

He was talking to Corporal Villovürt, she being the best marksman from the whole squadron at the Meadengiat Ranger Station. "I see him." she said as his arrow whistled in at them and stuck itself into the thick wooden door right beside her – she hadn't even flinched, the dark-elf could tell, from the moment it was loosed, that it wasn't going to hit her.

The goblin's bow disappeared into the darkness that existed between the watchtower's parapet and its overhanging conical wooden roof. She took aim with her own arrow, right at the spot where the goblin's bow had disappeared, and waited. Half a minute later she spied the bow, and a goblin arm, emerge from the shadows, she immediately loosed her own arrow right at him. It sailed across the open space between them and zipped into the blackness beneath the watchtower's cone-like cap. The goblin's bow fell, clattering down the length of the tower to the ground – his arm flailed and disappeared back into the shadows.

"Got him." she said, confidently.

"Great shot, Corporal." said the Lieutenant, who was standing behind her. "Now that he's out of the way, we're going to make a break for it." Although his leg was inflicting him with great spasms of pain every time he put any weight on it, he ignored the acute agony it caused him and was confident he could get himself back to their horses unaided. "We're going left, down the stairs and round the perimeter of the courtyard, then out through the gap in the inner bailey wall." He pointed to the great fissure that he and his team had entered by less than a couple of hours – though it seemed an age – earlier. "Is everybody ready?" He asked of them all. They all nodded – glad to be leaving the cursed castle grounds.

"Sergeant, you take the lead." the Lieutenant continued. "Corporal Lannik, you bring up the rear. Villovürt, you guard the girl with your life. The rest of you, just keep moving... and kill anyone who gets in our way!"

The Rangers and their charge streamed out of the doorway behind the Sergeant who, with sabre in one hand and dragon in the other, jogged down the steps toward the pile of black shuk and goblin bodies at the bottom. He bounded onto the crest of the bloody pile, behind which two skulking goblins – both very much still alive – lay in wait. One immediately fled in panic as the other leapt up to block the big Ranger's sudden advance – only to be sliced by the Sergeant's cold steel blade as it flashed before him and opened up his throat. As the first goblin's body and blood spilled to the floor the Sergeant then shot the other in the back with a barrel load of hot, heavy metal as he ran away. That fleeing goblin stumbled then fell hard to the stone paving – his face and chest skidding a foot or two along the dusty dirt of the floor before coming to a rest.

Luwsiy and the rest of the cloaked troop scrambled over the bulky and slippery cadaverous obstacle at the bottom of the stairs, giving helping hands to the three wounded and the two carrying their dead as needed. They continued on around the wide perimeter without further interruption, except for the few inaccurate arrows that flew in wildly from the watchtowers opposite. One by one they clambered through the cracked fissure in the great stone wall and on into the overgrown expanse of the outer bailey.

As they approached the broken down outer gatehouse a lone, barely clad, female figure stepped out of the umbrageous gateway to confront them. "That girl is ours!" Maqlath hissed brazenly, and pointed a long taloned finger at Luwsiy. "She is one of us now – she does not belong with the likes of you."

Luwsiy shuddered at the vile vampire woman's words, and wondered at them fearfully.

Corporal Villovürt moved to stand protectively in front of the girl while Sergeant Rinawn sidled to the right of the vampire, and the lean Ranger behind him, named Lickety, sidled to the left. The Lieutenant limped forward between them to face the woman.

"You've lost two of your number already," said Maqlath indignantly at the Lieutenant, "do you really want to lose more – all for the sake of a foolish, wanton child?"

The grim faced Lieutenant said nothing.

As the three lead Ranger's cautiously advanced, the vampire slowly backed up – step by step – toward the enveloping and obscuring shade of the shattered gatehouse from which she came.

Maqlath bared her fangs defiantly, just as she stepped back into the blackness. The Lieutenant could see right through the arched gateway and, for a brief second, could clearly see her seductive silhouette standing there. The womanly form suddenly crouched as if ready to pounce right at him, he braced himself in anticipation of her deathly leap and raised his sword in defence, but the form continued down beyond what her bodily mass could feasibly allow – and seemingly dispersed into the black of the shadowed floor.

"She disappeared!" exclaimed the Lieutenant.

"It must have been a fetch." said Villovürt. "A phantasmic projection – she wasn't really there."

"Damn these vampires!" Said the vexed Sergeant angrily as he rushed into the darkness of the large archway and slashed his sabre into the shadows to the left and right, then above and below – *just to be sure*.

"Let's just keep moving," said Lieutenant Lethbridj urgently, "the sooner we get to the horses, the sooner we can get away from this place."

The Rangers moved quickly through the gatehouse, past the still slumped bodies of the two massive troll guards, and on over the dirt infill of the old moat. As the last of them crossed the moat, a fell voice reached them from the highest tower of the castle.

Luwsiy recognised the dread vocalisations as that of Aggareth, the language she did not recognise, but it was clear to her that the words were full of heart-felt hate and they bristled with malignant power. The strange archaic phrases, as if carried on an ill wind, drifted past them and on into the dark forest ahead.

A vengeful Aggareth stood on the balcony from which she had spat the necromantic spell; she furiously cast aside the long pipe in which she had smoked hashish laced with the fire-impervious spores of the Yaggothiyan-Nekromansiya Fungi. Her black heart, full of impatience, waited for the tiny, lighter than air spores to be carried on the wind and take effect – they were charged by fire and were resonating with the words of power voiced as she so vehemently exhaled the potent smoke to the wind. The method of her magik and the sorcerous incantations she had used were memorised from an ancient musty copy of Abdul Alhazra's Kitab al-Azif, the Servant of the Prohibited's Book of Weird Song. She had found the infamous tome hidden in her father's old library long ago, feverishly and secretly she had learned its forbidden contents by heart.

Sure enough, the dead, bloodied and battered men, goblins, trolls and shuks scattered about the inner bailey below soon started to stir and stumble to their feet – she allowed herself a smirk of dark satisfaction. The undead husks, with shattered skulls, broken necks, torn flesh and busted bones tripped, limped and shambled toward the gates. Some came close to the swiftness that they possessed in life, while others could only crawl with painful slowness, but still they all went forth with the grim inevitability of death itself. Compelled by the black-magik of the vampire witch, the re-animated corpses' only imperatives were to kill the Rangers and bring the girl still living back to their mistress.

Aggareth consoled and calmed herself with the knowledge that her arcane and eldritch spell would be carried out into the forest... calling every corpse or carcass that lay in its windblown path into undeath, however long they may have lain there – and it would bind them, each and every one, to her will and purpose.

Lilith screamed as her orgasm convulsed her body, surprised – and a little ashamed – that the bestial demon could have caused it within her... with his heavy handed, laboured and clumsy copulating. She was laid out for him on a huge bed of black silk and he had been working his hideous fat tool on her and in her since before she could remember. His fingers and his tongue had been all over her countless times; she was covered with – *mercifully temporary* – scratches from his jagged nails and soused in his spittle and burning seed. She longed for him to finish so she could will her phantasmic body clean and whole again, removing all trace of his foul defilement.

He reminded her of a big, ugly and blundering pup, earnestly trying to please his mistress with dogged determinedness. A small part of her found this enthusiasm amusing – a larger, and for now hidden, part of her found it contemptible. Though she was grateful that Hlewid was so easily manipulated, she saw this weakness as just another reason to hate and detest him. Lilith kept her contempt suppressed, *for now* – concealing it with loyal devotion, for he would be extremely dangerous if angered or alienated before she was good and ready to make her play. The time will come soon enough to scorn him – *but not yet*, she thought. *Not yet.*

As the demon laboured on with his coitus, Lilith then considered the complication of her father and how, in time, she would deal with him. She was confident she could turn the demon against him; after all, what need Hlewid of a right-hand-man when he had her by his side. Beyond that, all that she was certain of was that when the time comes, her retribution must be absolute and completely final.

Rebekah and Juwniper, dressed in their now fire-warmed and dried clothes, both paced back and forward impatiently. It seemed like hours since Afagddu had left them there, though Rebekah had no way of telling how much time had actually passed. She remembered that Arkturon had told her that time passed differently in the otherworld, sometimes slower than the real world, sometimes faster. She hoped that time was passing much faster than it seemed to her.

But, if time is passing faster than it seems... does that mean it's actually taking longer... more time will have passed? So should I be wishing that time passed much slower than it seems? The confused thought strong-armed its way into her racing mind. *Which of them would mean that Afagddu, hopefully with Arkturon, would return all the sooner?* She had no idea – and was entirely unable to concentrate her thoughts into a coherent answer. *I just want Arkturon back!* She silently demanded of the universe at large, unable to bare the idea that he might not return – that she *might not see him again!* Wilfully Rebekah suppressed that thought, as she did the tears that welled in her eyes.

It was with those blurry eyes that moments later Rebekah glanced across the nearest fire to see two figures enter the large cave. It was Afagddu and Arkturon, the latter was sopping wet and, evidently, freezing cold.

Arkturon wasted no time and made no apologies for immediately taking his sodden clothes off in front of the girls, he simply strode to the nearest fire to warm and dry himself and his garments.

Rebekah could not contain her joy at seeing him again; she rushed to him without hesitation and hugged the naked man, unable to stop her tears as she did so. Arkturon laughed, slightly taken aback, but hugged her wholeheartedly in return, kissing her on the cheek as he did. He seemed reticent to let her go and she did not mind in the least.

"Ah, but it's so good to be warm again," he said, and added in a whisper that only she could hear, "and to be back with you."

"Where have you been," blurted Rebekah emotionally as they broke their embrace, "what happened? I thought we'd lost you – I couldn't bare it!"

"I was summoned to an audience with Keridwen, the Koventiyna Inversus herself – apparently she takes umbrage at random wizards passing through, or even close by, her domain."

Afagddu chuckled loudly at that. "I don't know what he did or said to her," the demigod stated, "but when I got there, they were as thick as thieves – and there was I, expecting to have to cut him down from a tree – or some such."

"Let's just say that our current mission is of personal interest to her," said the wizard. "She wants what we want... and will help us achieve it."

"A demoness will help us against another demon?" said Juwniper with surprise.

"Oh, do not assume that all demonic beings are allied or in cahoots," explained Arkturon, "quite the contrary, they often hate each other more than they hate the so-called gods. Both demons and gods can be capricious beings – both are just as liable to help or hinder. Believe me, Keridwen has many reasons to plot against Hlewid, and to detest Bäliyl who now, it seems, stands by his side." The wizard was suddenly bothered by a troublesome thought, he was beginning to wonder if perhaps Bäliyl had intended for their encounter to end the way it did. *But if he had planned it that way all along... what would his endgame be?*

"And how has this demoness chosen to help us?" asked Rebekah, trying to hide the concern in her voice.

"As we speak, Keridwen is seeking out a way for us to go forward... a way to get us into the heart of Hlewid's realm just as Mikael makes his play. She has shown me many things and it is clear that Mikael, with the gods on his side, will stop at nothing to be reunited with Lilith. When the time is right, Keridwen will come for us."

"So we must wait?" Rebekah said, having had enough of waiting, "For how long?"

"Long enough to rest and warm ourselves by our gracious host's fire." said Arkturon holding his hands up to the flames, "In the mean time I suggest we make ourselves comfortable. Sleep if you can, conserve your energy... you'll need it more than you know."

What the hells am I doing here? Rebekah suddenly found herself wondering – not for the first time. *What was I thinking, meddling in the affairs of demons and demonesses? I could have gone with the Rangers and Luwsiy... and be on my way home right now.* But, deep down, she knew why she had chosen this path over the other. It was *to be with Arkturon* – and that scared her the most. He had been an old man when she first met him, *the gods alone knew how old*, though now he seemed in his prime, so full of the strength and vitality of a man bordering on thirty years. His broad and muscular body shone vigorously in the firelight. His eyes, still inculcated with the wisdom of age and the surety of experience, blazed within his chiselled features. His gaze fascinated and excited her, but filled her with trepidation – she knew that she loved him... but could he love her? *Surely, in his eyes*, she thought, *I'm nothing but a fool – too young and untested for a wizard to bother with. How could he ever love me, an inn-keepers daughter who'd seen very little of the world?*

"Are you all right?" Arkturon asked her.

Rebekah realised that she was staring at him, and had no idea how long she had been doing so. "Why did you let me come with you here?" She blurted. "How can I possibly be of help to you? What use am I to this otherworldly cause?"

His smile almost made her heart break. Rebekah longed to feel his lips upon her – as the niggling memory of faery lips between her legs tortured her loins and senses.

"You undervalue yourself." He said, putting his hands on her shoulders. "You're quick witted, sharp, intelligent and brave. When fate puts a more than capable companion before me – I'd be a fool to turn them away. And anyway, I like having you around."

"You do?"

"Of course." He said the two words as if they were clearly self evident.

Arkturon detected the doubt within her... as well as the love for him that she feared would not be reciprocated. He longed to tell her that he loved her in return but, for the first time in many a year, the wizard found himself at a loss for words.

Rebekah suddenly was not, as an idea furiously formulated among her racing and fevered thoughts. "Then make me a vampire," she said, "make me like you and Mikael – it'll make me stronger, better able to help you."

"Rebekah," exclaimed a surprised Arkturon, "do you know what you ask? I told you how vampires are made... and that they should be lovers."

"I remember perfectly well." She stated, looking round to see where Juwniper and Afagddu were, they had apparently wandered off somewhere. "A true vampire takes the blood of his chosen mate," continued the girl, moving close to the wizard once more, "and she of him. They feed off each other's blood till eventually they can feed off each other's love. I remember."

She placed a warm hand softly on his chest. He could not find it within himself to resist her advance or refute her request and he gently caressed her cheek as she looked up into his eyes, pleading.

He took her in his arms and pressed her to him, kissing her firmly on the lips. Rebekah's arms circled his heated body as she opened her mouth to his. Arkturon picked the young woman up, cradling her in his strong arms to carry her over to a bed of fur and pelts beside the warming fire and gently lay her down upon it. He lay beside her prone curves and touched them with soft eagerness as she unbuttoned her top and adjusted her vest. Caressing her smooth skin with fingers and lips; her face and neck, shoulders and breasts; he kissed and stroked her with a reverence she could hardly believe.

He teased her nipples with his oral play while his fingers began to stroke and rub her stomach and thighs through the material of her breeches.

Arkturon ran his fingers up and down the seam at her crotch, tickling and pressing the soft warm channel that it followed. Her breathing intensified, causing quiet little drawn out moans to escape her lips in time with his kneading. While his free hand and mouth tweaked and squeezed her nipples the other hand worked at her crotch, his fingers pushing at her sex while his thumb rubbed and stroked her pubic mound and clitoris with a circular, rhythmic motion.

Excited trembles travelled through her legs and body as he played her with all the dedicated skill of a master at his art. Rebekah, feeling his phallus press hard against her thigh, reached out an eager hand and grabbed it. She gently squeezed and manipulated him as he lifted himself from his tasks and sat astride her thighs. He began tugging at her breeches and bloomers, pulling them down over her hips, she lifted her rump up off the bed to aid his progress as he slowly revealed the wispy pubes and fleshy cleft that had lain hidden. Rebekah was forced to let go of his heated phallus as he pulled away and drew her breeches down to her boots, first he removed them and then continued with her breeches to render her lower body totally naked. With no pause at all Arkturon fell to kissing her legs, slowly rising to her sex, licking the insides of her thighs and savouring the taste of her skin.

She could feel his breath rousingly caress the lips of her vulva, she longed for his lips and tongue to follow - her labia seemed to burn with the electrifying promise of his touch; her hands gripped the thick pelts on which she lay, her teeth clenched and her legs tensed... and then his tongue lightly flicked against her - and then again, pushing into her. He lifted and opened her legs wide.

Delightfully Arkturon's mouth closed over her vagina as his tongue slickly probed and slipped over and into her melting flesh. He began sucking on the little fleshy folds of her inner labia and then on her clitoris, he was driving her wild - her moans getting louder and more frenzied as his lips and teeth began pressing with more force. Rebekah threw her head back, her sex was beginning to feel raw and abused but she was loving it, she wished it could go on forever, or at least until her orgasm.

"Rebekah?" she heard him say breathlessly. She looked up at his head between her legs; he stared at her with his mouth open.

"Don't stop!" she blurted between panting breaths as she returned his gaze, at first puzzled she then saw his teeth – the top canines were growing fast. He was a vampire myth made true and he was asking her if she would join him.

Rebekah was on the verge of an overwhelming orgasm, any further delay would spoil it, she laid back with eyes closed and gave her gasping consent with a plea whispered desperately "please don't stop... do it!"

Arkturon immediately went down on her and she gave a little cry as the two needle sharp teeth entered the soft fatty flesh of her pubic mound just above her clitoris. He sucked and lapped at the sudden well of blood that poured over her genitals and she screamed at the exquisite agony of his touch. Losing all control she came, a massive flush of fluid emitted from her quim and with it, she was sure, her bladder had released as well. Arkturon made no reaction other than to continue lapping and sucking at her, forcing her to be lost and floundering in a delirium of multiple orgasms.

Arkturon bathed the two little wounds amidst Rebekah's pubic hair with his spittle, licking them as they healed over almost immediately. She lay flat, exhausted. He moved up her body and then whispered in her ear, "You must now drink mine... my blood."

Arkturon bit into his forearm to provide her with two puncture holes to suck from before his teeth transformed back to their normal shape. He put the fresh wounds to her mouth and she supped on them eagerly, sucking his blood with growing vitality and strength. The girl pushed him over onto his back and she straddled him, holding his arm to her lips and gulping his life's juices down as he laughed.

"Not too much - not straight away!" He said with a grin as he pulled his arm away from her bloodied mouth. Licking her lips she grinned back, running her hands over his chest she began to kiss him there. She edged down to his stomach, passionately stroking and kissing him, then on to his still stiff rod – massaging and kissing still. Rebekah pushed its swollen head into her mouth – determined to consume his love's juices, as he had her's, she lapped and suckled and squeezed incessantly. When Arkturon came the hot liquid filled her mouth with a sudden spouting, pouring from her lips and down her throat causing her to gulp frantically and lift from his swollen tool to catch her breath and recover. Spluttering she giggled as if intoxicated with his seed.

This time it was Arkturon's turn to topple Rebekah onto her back; She drew her legs around him as he mounted her and their copiously slickened genitalia coupled with a soft slippery squelch that sent them both into hushed fits of giggling laughter.

Chapter Twenty Five – Labyrinth of Despair

For the second time Mikael traversed the path of the Priestess, this time without incident, and he exited its tunnels with only the memory of smothering mud and clinging kelpies to hinder him. His passage now seemed somehow charmed. He emerged from the dark subterranean path into bright sunlight, having expected moonlight, and was now right by the shores of the huge lake surrounding the Koventiyna's apple island and her shard like tower.

The underground path had opened out into a large stepped grotto of stone that led down to the lake side. A bubbling thermal spring emerged on his left; its steaming waters cascading down a small channel to an enclosed rocky pool before being channelled on again out toward the lake edge, where it poured – mist shrouded and babbling – into the larger expanse of water beside a wooden dock. There, the goddess Idunna-Sul herself stood unattended at the prow of a large swan-like ship and wordlessly invited him aboard, tendrils of steam ghosted about her as the ship slowly bobbed beside the long jetty of the dock. He boarded and the vessel glided out into the lake with not even the slightest breeze to bother its huge white sail.

Once he was beside her, the divine young girl gracefully crouched and lifted a large, heavy looking shield to him, its silvery sheen flashing in the sunlight. Adorned on its face was a hunting scene in black relief, seemingly of ancient Hellenik design; a young maiden stood with only a short shift at her waist and flowing hair to cover her nubile body, she was drawing a bow with arrow ready to fire at some unseen prey. A fawn and young dog stood waiting at her heels and another young maiden waited behind her with a quiver of arrows ready for use. This whole woodland scene was circled within an intricate and interlocking geometric pattern.

Mikael accepted the shield without a word, fearing to break the silence between them – for, as he knew, that was her right alone.

The goddess then spoke to him, "I have another gift for you Mikael." she said as she helped him strap the shield over his back, "A mantle for you to wear – a special mantle." Idunna-Sul removed the dark robe from her shoulders revealing pale, pure skin and a shimmering silken dress that softly hugged her childlike form. She handed the robe to him; it was of the blackest black he had ever seen. "Wear it as a cloak but when you need to be hidden wrap it fully about yourself, pulling the hood down over your face. None will see you while you will see all."

The ship slowly circumnavigated the island of Kear Widiyr and carried him and the goddess over to the other side of the lake. It continued on toward the beach on which he had landed the last time he had left her realm, but then turned and made for the mouth of a large cave that lay hidden among treacherous rocks and cliffs away to the starboard of the vessel.

"This route will lead you directly into the dark realm of Kear Pedrivan Reversus." said the Koventiyna.

They passed through a gauntlet of jagged rocks that closed in on either side, and the ship entered into a dark and forbidding caved passage, the uneven rocky roof was just clear of the mast as the ship rose and fell on the swell of the lake's waters. Soon a cavern opened up around them and there, on the far side, was a small harbour and jetty cut from rock, and a path which led through an arched tunnel of carved stone. Burning torches were set at intervals into the walls around the harbour and they lit the ship as it quietly slipped into dock.

Mikael threw the goddess's cloak over his shoulders and the shield at his back as he prepared to disembark. Although it had not looked overly large on her small frame the black mantle now covered him easily and reached to the floor when he had expected it to be at his knees. Idunna-Sul grabbed at his armour covered hand and held him. "Remove your helm." she instructed. He lifted his helmet and held it by his side. The goddess moved before him and stood on her toe tips as her green eyes shone into his. Mikael bowed and the girl kissed him twice, a brief glance against each cheek as her arm quickly circled his neck.

"The gods are with you Mikael." she said as she let him go, "Have strength in that. And in Lilith's love."

Mikael cautiously crept down the darkly lit tunnel as quietly as he possibly could; his way lit intermittently by the animated red and orange glow of sparsely burning torches. With cloak wrapped tightly around him he hoped his endeavours would remain unnoticed by all that were ahead of him. An atmosphere of oppression and filth was steadily increasing the deeper he journeyed down the slowly turning passageway, filling him with the unshakable feeling that he was descending into a huge and festering pit.

It seemed that he had spent hours on this path before he came across any intersections and openings of other tunnels, when he finally did they were countless and all seemed full of foul and distant whisperings and sounds. He continued to follow the same tunnel though, hoping that it was the right one, trusting fate and destiny to bring him to his goal. The temptation to draw his sword and continue with it ready for any chance encounters pestered his mind, but he kept it sheathed for the weapon would be a betraying beacon of light in such a dark place. Mikael rested a hand on its pommel while keeping himself covered by the goddess' mantle, its hood was up but not pulled forward so his face looked out from the cloak's blackness like a ghostly willow-wisp sentinel guiding the souls of the damned to their doom.

The appearance of a wraith up ahead took Mikael by surprise; it had come out of one of the intersecting tunnels and was now turning to face him. Without thinking Mikael pulled the hood down over his face to mask any hint of the pale and dimly glowing helmet, and dodged into a tunnel opening on his left. He stood waiting and quietly held his breath, confident that the creature had not seen him, he would have to wait a couple of minutes before raising the hood and risking a look to see if the baleful creature had gone.

The pale luminescence of the wraith's ghostly form stabbed at Mikael's unprepared eyes within the total blackness of his enshrouding hood as it passed the opening of the tunnel in which he hid. The wraith was startled by his shocked intake of breath and stopped at the mouth of the passage. It peered into the darkness at him but seemed to be blind to his presence. Mikael stared back at it; even with the mantle's hood over his eyes he could see the wraith with a startling clarity. As his eyes adjusted to the darkness he realised that he could also see the dark floor and walls around it and the words of the Koventiyna came back to him – *None will see you while you will see all.*

The wraith slowly approached, looking at him, beside him, above and beyond him. He was entirely invisible to it, but he backed off, his hand tightly gripping his sword, ready to act if forced to. The wraith stopped its advance, obviously not trusting the evidence of its eyes; it knew something was there, somewhere. The creature floated upwards a foot or so and spread its clawing bony hands to span the narrow tunnel easily, the skull like face was grinning horribly as it started to advance again.

Mikael cursed the little involuntary sound that had given him away; he drew his sword and thrust his cloak and hood back. The creature cowered at the sudden glowing appearance of such a heavily armoured adversary, Mikael raised his sword ready to strike but the wraith flew at his arm, gripping his forearm with unbelievable strength and making as if to bite him. Mikael punched the creature violently with his other arm, his gauntleted fist smacking into the skull with a loud crack. Its grip loosened and Mikael shook his sword arm free of its clinging hold, sending it sprawling against the wall and to the floor. He grabbed at the wispy white hair that sparsely flowed about the thing's head and yanked the creature up. The wraith emitted a terrible scream as his sword sliced through the air in a whistling arch and on through its neck. The wraith's body crumpled to dust but its ugly head remained, still emitting it's piercing screech through grinning yellowed teeth. Mikael swung it by the hair and dashed the skull against the stone wall. The screaming stopped as the skull shattered from the impact.

Mikael had been surprised by the creature's solidity, the wraith seemed so ethereal and phantom like, but its appearance belied the physical presence it held in this otherworld. He now knew that they could be dealt with, they could affectively be killed, and that engendered less fear in him. He continued on his journey with a greater optimism and feeling strangely buoyant and invigorated. He now kept the goddess's cloak wrapped tightly about himself and the hood resolutely pulled down over his face as he weaved his invisible way through the tunnels leading to Kear Pedrivan Reversus. Careful not to make the slightest sound he passed many wraiths patrolling the pathways, some alone, some in groups, they all seemed to be searching for an intruder.

And that intruder is I, thought Mikael darkly, *that scream must have summoned them from miles around.* He allowed himself a smug smile as two more wraiths glided by while he stood aside and watched their blind ignorance.

Moving on he eventually found a wide tunnel mouth that looked out over the abyss like basin that held Hlewid's demonic fortress. An assembly of about ten wraiths collected there, presumably as a guard against him getting beyond the tunnels. He approached them silently.

The first that these lich-like sentries knew of Mikael's presence among them was his blade cleaving through one of their number's splintering skull, he dodged and parried its comrades attacks and whorled around slicing and shattering as many of them as he could. His cloak billowed out as he fought, offering the wraiths blinding glimpses of his shining armour. These sudden and brief appearances of a fully armoured warrior in flowing black cape as they were hacked to pieces only served to confuse and affright them even more. The remainder of the group that had gathered to guard the tunnel exit fled in terror. Mikael allowed himself a malevolent laugh as he made sure the cloak fully covered him again before passing through the huge portal.

The demon's castle was an ominous sight. It was surrounded by a dizzyingly complicated labyrinth that stretched into the dark mists of the far distance. The black fortress conjured a picture in Mikael's mind, as he stared down upon it, of two disgustingly mutated beetles fighting or mating over a steaming mound of filth. Their primitive action frozen in time, with huge horns and claws pushed up into the air, twisted and locked, and with their foul armoured bodies thrust together and joined as one.

As Mikael looked down over the labyrinth he saw no resemblance to the one that had surrounded Matt's castle; there were no gardens to be seen, no bright courtyards, he saw only dark shadows, burning fires and the smoke and steam of some unknown but vile smelling industry. The distant screams of tortured souls rose up to greet him.

He ventured down the steep and winding steps toward the malefic maze and prayed that soon he would be out of it and done with its denizens and their odoriferous works.

Mikael secretly moved through the labyrinth with increasing determination, ignoring everything around him, he met those that unknowingly blocked his way with the swift impartiality of Death itself, silently dispatching any creature that came between him and his goal. All his concentration was kept on his single minded progress down the maze of paths leading him to Lilith. He tried to see none of the dreadful place through which he traversed, none of the instruments of torture, none of the arenas for violence and slaughter. He paid no heed to the perpetual mutilation and abuse inflicted on the pitiful souls of the deceitful dead, when it confronted him he cut straight through it all, his sword spreading a deadly panic as it appeared in mid air to part and destroy whatever it was that hindered his passage.

The panic soon advanced before him like an ally, rumour and fear permeated out into the labyrinth, wraiths and other creatures of darkness listened and futilely looked out for this avenging and invisible angel of death that would silently come amongst them and then cruelly butcher with its mighty and blazing sword. It seemed that the greater their belief in his invincibility grew the more potent and feared Mikael's power became.

The gateway into the festering pile at the centre of the sprawling labyrinthine torture garden was high up in the bleak walls of the forbidding structure. It could only be attained by crossing a broad and burning abyss-like moat and the only bridge across was a slim and deadly looking blade accessed at the apex of a tall, jagged and thoroughly soot covered tower. Mikael approached the tower cautiously for a large body of strange, hybrid goblin-like creatures – though some appeared to have been human once – loitered by the arched stone gateway through the high jutting defensive wall that separated that access tower from the rest of the labyrinth. The heads of these horrible were-creatures were those of wolves, pigs, toads and other hideous beasts that Mikael did not immediately recognise but, he suspected, were that of gross overgrown insects the like of which caused his stomach to turn. They were all heavily armed and armoured but Mikael's confidence was soaring and his determination steely. Rapped in his cloak he carefully moved into the midst of them while his hand, repeatedly grasping at the pommel of his sword, itched to obliterate the abominations about him.

A momentary calm stillness descended on him before he erupted into a sudden whirling storm of billowing cloak, shining armour and a rapidly circling sword named Sumbrandr that effortlessly sliced through the blackened armour and flesh of all around him. Blood of darkest red spurted and mingled with that of putrid yellow as the singing bright blade cut its swathe through the group of grotesques; malformed limbs flew, monstrous heads rolled and bloated abdomens split and yawned before him. Two full circles he span before slipping the shield from his back to his arm. These beasts were not the cowering and fleeing kind though and Mikael was forced to battle them to the last; blocking and parrying, thrusting and swiping – on and on, till none were left standing.

Mikael felt battered and bruised but otherwise uninjured, his armour was intact and his shield still whole. The sword was as bright and sharp as the day it was forged, the blood and gore just slipped from its pristine surfaces like water from a drake's hind and it seemed to seek his opponent's weaknesses and openings with a will of its own. With every kill Mikael felt invigorated – it was like the sword sapped its victim's strength and gave it to the wielder. He turned to the heavy, elaborately brutalist, ornate iron gate of the tower's defensive wall, he pushed and pulled as it rattled in its rusted frame, then kicked it as hard as he could. The fixings pinged and skittered across the small courtyard inside before the gate fell straight in, loudly clanging twice on the stone floor.

Opposite was a sturdy looking iron bound wooden door – to the tower itself – flanked by two large, dragon-like gargoyle guards carved from stone. Sword in hand and shield ready, Mikael strode forward and kicked the door too. It buckled; the rusty and degraded hinges and bars bending in. He kicked again near the large key-holed lock, the frame there gave way and the door splintered open. He strode on into the tower.

Level by level Mikael ascended the tower, killing every foul grotesque he came upon. Each kill filled him with renewed vigour and determination and when he finally got to the upper most level, that accessed the knife edge bridge, he felt damn near unstoppable. From his smoky vantage point he could see three troll sized bull-men guarding the huge fortress door on the opposite side of the flaming abyssal moat.

Mikael's purpose was clear to him and he crossed with eyes straight ahead, confidence and faith sured his footing while Sul's mantle hid his advance. The three hulking creatures, which combined the bulging bodies of – *what could only be* – Jotnar trolls with the heads, legs and aggressions of massive snorting bulls; each held a giant spiked bludgeon in one hand and a long scimitar blade in the other. They were standing to attention, or as close to it as such malformed monstrosities with grossly oversized heads and horns could be said to be. If it wasn't for the snotting and steaming of their wide bull nostrils and the heaving of their broad troll chests straining and wheezing, Mikael would have guessed that they were statues. Initially he had thought just that, but as he got nearer across the bridge he soon realised how wrong he was, and how big they actually were. It dawned on him that the task might not be as easy as he at first anticipated; a single swipe from any one of them could send him over the edge, from the all too narrow platform that fronted the doorway and then down into the fiery abyss below it.

Mikael stepped onto the jutting stone threshold and appraised his – luckily still oblivious – opponents. There was not much room to manoeuvre; the platform was about two yards deep and seven yards wide. There was a creature at both ends and one in the middle, directly in front of whom Mikael now stood. There was about a yards space behind this middle bull-troll and Mikael quietly occupied it. The blackened entrance to the castle was a single and extremely heavy looking wooden door – reinforced with massive iron brackets and bars – that had a rather prosaic, though huge, brass ring knocker or handle positioned centrally, just within Mikael's reach. He could not let himself worry about how to get past the door though till he had thought of how he was going to deal with its big, ugly trio of guards. He mentally allowed himself a droll laugh as an idea came to mind.

Stepping right up to the back of the middle, and largest, of the troll were-bulls, he then said, in as loud and base a voice as he could muster, "Gods, but you two ugly munts are as thick as steaming shit!" then stepped back as close up against the door as he could.

The two, now somewhat perturbed, bull-trolls at the sides looked at each other and the one on the left said, "Wot did you just call us?" to the one in the middle who was now turning.

"I didn't say nought!" he stated angrily. "But you call me a munt again and I'll kill ya!"

"'e didn't call ya a munt – you called us munts 'n' don't try t' deny it!" said the one on the right as he prodded the big bull-troll in his massive chest with the end of his bludgeon – which infuriated the simmering central guard even more.

"Do that again 'n' I'll splice ya!" he said raising his scimitar to the one on the right.

Who did it again – only harder.

The middle bull-troll swept the bludgeon of the one on the right violently aside and it went sailing out of his hand and down into the burning pit below them. The two then set upon each other with nothing less than murder in mind.

The third bull-troll on the left watched his compatriots in amazement, wondering if he should intervene – when a disembodied, shining armoured arm with a long blazing sword gripped in its gauntleted hand suddenly appeared before him. Before he could even react to this, the blade had run him through and his phantasmic essence had passed into Mikael, who immediately enveloped himself in his cloak of invisibility once more.

The two fighting trolls were too intent on furiously wrestling each other to notice what had happened to the third member of their guard. After a mighty struggle the bigger of the two, who had been the one in the middle, took advantage of his greater weight and size and bodily threw the other from the platform. Huffing and heaving from the exertion the big guard turned to the one that was left, ready to start on him too, then stopped short when he saw that the oaf was already dead.

He stepped forward saying, "Wot the fu-" when Mikael, with hands suddenly gripping the huge door-knocker – his back braced against its solid door – kicked out with both legs and planted both feet squarely into the bull-troll's chest, pushing out with all the strength that Sumbrandr's slaying had invested him with. The big troll fell back, with astonishment in his big bulging bull eyes, and his bulk hit the edge of the stone platform hard – the weight of his massive head and upper body was well beyond the unguarded lip and it carried him over, snorting in rage and panic, tumbling down into the pit.

As Mikael had hung from the knocker or handle – he still wasn't sure which it was or if it even mattered – and then kicked, the heavy door had swung silently inward about a foot or so. *Well, that's that problem solved*, he thought – then it occurred to him that, *if it had been unlocked this whole time, I probably could have just snuck right through.*

He made sure he was covered by the cloak and then, with a shrug, he silently entered the castle.

Chapter Twenty Six – An Undead Horde

Just as the Rangers reached the first sparse few trees from the gate house, the sound of two low-pitched, throaty and gurgling moans of agony could be heard behind them. Corporal Lannik, the furthest behind, turned and saw in a glance that the two trolls they had left for dead, propped against the gate posts, were getting clumsily to their feet. He shouted ahead, "Those trolls we killed... they're not dead!"

"Of course they are!" shouted the Lieutenant back at him without turning. "I made damn sure of it!"

Luwsiy and Corporal Villovürt looked back, as did a number of the others; the two trolls were starting to stagger toward them, their throats gaping and heads lolling. "No... they're not dead," the dark-elf Ranger exclaimed, "they're undead!"

The Lieutenant stopped in his hobbled tracks – the pain in his leg was getting more tortured with every step – and turned to look. His face drained ashen.

"That fell voice we heard," Corporal Villovürt continued, "it must have been necromancy – a re-animating spell... calling the dead to the speaker's will."

Elliy's words chilled Luwsiy to the bone and a fearful sob escaped her as the rest of the group came to a stop.

"We keep going," said the Lieutenant, starting a quick limping march onward, "we get to the horses... cut down any corpse that gets in our way – we just keep moving!"

"But, Sir..." said Elliy, "we're carrying two corpses with us!"

The Lieutenant's shoulders visibly slumped, he turned again, anguish etched in his face. "Drop them!" he ordered the two Rangers carrying their dead comrades. "We can't bring them with us."

"But, Sir!" said Rigormort, who was carrying young Gudrun's body over his shoulder.

"No!" Wellnap cried out, stepping toward the officer. "We can't just leave 'em, not here!"

"Step back, Wellnap!" warned Sergeant Rinawn, placing the flat of his sabre across the subordinate Ranger's chest. He looked back at their pursuers then told his men in no uncertain tones, "You two drop them bodies. Now!" He could see the two lumbering undead trolls slowly gaining ground, "We don't have time for this!"

The first Ranger let his grim burden drop to the floor, but Rigormort hesitated just as the two corpses started to stir and the dead Gudrun suddenly grabbed onto Rigormort's tunic and a rattling, evil-smelling caw was emitted from his shredded throat. The big Ranger immediately flipped the dead body of his comrade over and off himself, but Gudrun's deathly grip on his tunic was vice like and Rigormort was brought to his knees by the dead-weight of the clinging corpse as it hit the ground.

The Sergeant's sword sliced through Gudrun's arms and Rigormort fell back, a look of absolute horror on his face. The disembodied arms still gripped him as he scrambled to his feet and desperately started prying the cold, grasping undead fingers from his tunic. He threw the jerking and twitching severed arms away from himself with utter disgust.

"Get moving, all of you!" the Sergeant shouted. "I'll be right behind you!" He added as they moved off, and then quickly chopped the remaining limbs from his two undead companions – preventing any pursuit by them at least. Breathing heavily and with dolorous eyes and a bloodied sword he looked up as he finished the dreadful work. The trolls were perilously close, two re-animated goblin corpses were coming through the gate and an undead black shuk came hitching close behind on shattered, mangled stumps and with a flopping, black-drooling maw.

Sergeant Rinawn briefly thought about making a stand, buying his fellow soldiers and the girl some time ... *only a little time though,* he quickly realised ... *too little!* He turned and ran.

The Sergeant soon caught up with the stragglers of his unit, it was the Lieutenant and Panhandle Pendal. Both the men were seriously wounded and would not be able to keep going, even at the pace they had, for long – especially Panhandle, he was flagging badly, so the Sergeant propped him up and helped him along as best he could. The forest terrain was tough underfoot and only getting tougher as they fled headlong, deeper into the brush and wild growth, back towards where they had left the horses. For the first time in years Sergeant D'Geai Rinawn found himself praying to the old gods of distant Namib, the homeland that had orphaned him at ten and from which he had been sold into slavery by his own uncle at twelve. It was a harsh and unforgiving land, as were the gods that ruled it – but he prayed anyway, that the horses would still be there. Then chastised himself for doing so, the gods had never helped him as a child when he prayed, why would they do so now.

The troop of Rangers were spreading thin as they ran, the fit and fast getting further ahead as they neared to where the horses should be – *but they'll have time to ready the mounts for the slowest,* thought the Sergeant. *If we can just get there before the undead horde catches us, we can all make it out of here.* He allowed himself another glance back. The massive trolls were slowed, crashing and thrashing through the trees and undergrowth, but the lamed and tattered shells of the dead goblins and shuks were a little swifter and had caught, and were overtaking, their big blundering brothers in death. *It's going to be close,* he thought, but then despair set in as terrible sounds reached them from ahead.

Damn the gods to all the hells! It was the blood-curdling screams, shrieks and squealing of their terrified and panicked horses being slaughtered.

The Rangers' fleeing foot falls were suddenly sped by a burst of desperation as the awful cries of their horses in mortal peril echoed through the forest. Luwsiy tumbled to the uneven root-strewn ground, letting out a shocked, shrill scream of her own. Her naked feet were already red raw and suffering when she caught her shin on an upraised loop of thick sinewy root, awkwardly she sprawled, grazing hands and knees as she hit the unforgiving forest floor hard. Her smacked shin smarted something awful and tears welled in her eyes as Elliy bodily lifted her with a surprising surplus of strength and ease. The dark-elf carried the girl up a rise that some of the Rangers had already topped.

There, over the rise, in the wooded dell where they had left their horses was the barely clad Maqlath, covered in blood, a frenzied bloodlust evident in her bulging, evil eyes and manic, slobbering grin. Half a dozen horses were felled – their throats ripped out – the others, stricken with fear and emitting dreadful screeches as they stomped and pulled at the bough-tied reins that bound them to the blood splattered spot. The air was thick with the coppery smell of fresh spilt blood. The first few Rangers balked and despaired at the hideous sight, momentarily frozen in shock at the lip of the dell. Maqlath saw them immediately and launched herself in a crazed, headlong trajectory of interception at the lead soldier of the troop, Lickety, nicknamed so for he was the fastest runner in the squad.

He also had the fastest reactions, Lickety snapped out of his trance-like terror as the instinct to survive overrode his fear; he unsheathed his sabre and swashed it through the air at the oncoming vampire who ducked under it easily, changed direction and jumped at his nearby companion. She slammed into the unprepared soldier's chest, legs either side and with hands gripping his shoulders, bowling him to the floor and snapping viciously like a wild dog at his neck and throat, tearing through the sinewy flesh and revelling in the fresh spurting of blood pumped vigorously by a truly terrified heart that sensed its time was up. Lickety swiped his blade at her again, but again her unnatural swiftness saved her, she leapt back without even a look in his direction – it was almost like she had heard the deadly blade coming.

Maqlath reared and faced him with haughty defiance, then spat his friend's blood at him. A black arrowhead suddenly burst through the vampire witch's chest, just below her right breast – it had come from Corporal Villovürt's longbow, from only yards behind.

Lickety seized his chance and lunged his sabre at the vile woman; she turned and tried to dodge his blade a third time, almost succeeding, but the razor sharp blade sliced across her abdomen as the determined soldier slid it forth and back with a relished forceful flourish. She stumbled back and seemed to slump a little as the other soldiers began to close in around her. At first, Lickety thought she was collapsing, but Maqlath simply crouched and then leapt straight up into the branches above their heads and propelled herself with ape-like efficiency through the tree tops back toward the castle.

Corporal Villovürt managed to loose one more arrow at the fleeing witch, it hit her square in the back and she tumbled and crashed from the trees at a distance from the gathering Rangers. They all watched where she fell, right at the feet of the steadily approaching undead.

"Never mind her," said the pale faced Lieutenant as he painfully limped to the crest of the rise, "let's just get to the horses and get out of here!"

Just behind him Sergeant Rinawn, now carrying Panhandle's limp form, grimly mounted the hill and took in the horrors of the dell. "Just six horses standing," he stated hollowly, "most of us'll have to double up – lose everything we don't need to carry."

"Villovürt," ordered the Lieutenant, "get yourself the fastest horse, take the girl and ride out as fast as you can."

"Rigormort," he continued, "pick a horse, to carry you and young Pendal, and go with them. Wellnap and Sinkhoal, ready the rest of the horses. The rest of ya, get your dragons primed – we're going to slow down these undead abominations even more."

The Rangers went to their tasks immediately

By the time the Lieutenant, Sergeant Rinawn, Corporal Lannik and Lickety each had two dragons, locked and loaded, the fleeter of the undead goblins and shuks were almost upon them. Luckily the trolls were having a much tougher time barging through the forest and up the slope.

"Legs then arms!" shouted Lieutenant Lethbridj from the high ground at the top of the ridge, "Fire!"

The still struggling undead were advancing slowly but inexorably toward the height of the wooded slope when the eight gun volley of lead shot erupted down into them – splintering bark, shattering bones and splattering globs of flesh and congealing blood, it exploded down the incline.

Corporal Villovürt was mounted with Luwsiy in front of her but she waited while Wellnap quickly helped Rigormort get Pendal mounted in front of him. Once he was ready the four of them rode into the forest – *on the two fastest horses*, thought Wellnap, wistfully pensive, as he helped ready the four remaining mounts, ditching any unnecessary equipment they had been carrying. As far as he was concerned the sooner he was on a horse and riding away from this place the better. Those witches scared him, the one that had killed Gudrun most of all – *she had me in her thrall, if Rigormort hadn't snapped me out of it...* although there had been fear and hatred in him when she bewitched him, they had been outweighed by lust and adoration – and that scared him most of all. *Her enchantment worked on me, I'd have been her willing victim... or her slave – and she knew it.*

A shiver ran down Wellnap's back. "Someone just walked over my grave." he said absently. It was something his mother had told him often, about unexplained shivers and 'funny feelings' down your back, but Wellnap was never sure whether it meant that somehow someone in the future was walking over your grave or that someone in the present was walking over the site of your future grave.

Sinkhoal, the pain from his multiple broken ribs etched into his face, looked at Wellnap and replied rather sardonically, "I feel like a heard of bulls just stampeded over mine." He then shouted up the short distance to the ridge, "Lieutenant, the horses are ready!"

The four Rangers at the ridge were hacking the remains of limbs from the more agile of the undead attackers with their sabres when

Lethbridj heard Sinkhoal's shout and ordered the others to the horses. "Wellnap and Sinkhoal," he shouted, "take one horse and go. Lannik and Lickety take one each and go. Me and the Sarge will take the last one and be right behind you all."

The Rangers scrambled for their horses. Wellnap and Sinkhoal were mounted in a second and turned their horse to the forest – Corporal Lannik and Lickety were just getting to their stirrups – when the rotten cadaver of a large, undead brown bear rampaged into the dell from the forest off to the left. The foul decayed creature swiped its big-clawed right paw at the head of Wellnap and Sinkhoal's horse and it connected devastatingly – ripping the animal's skull from its spine and hefting the decapitated horse's head right across the dell. The poor horse's body crumpled under the two appalled riders, who sprawled left and right to get away from the oncoming bear – which stopped mid stride and turned, as if sniffing out its prey, and then bound disjointedly away in the direction that Villovürt had taken Luwsiy.

Lethbridj and Sergeant Rinawn scrambled for their own skittish horse, Lannik picked up Wellnap on his and Lickety picked up Sinkhoal. "We've got to take down that bear and destroy it!" said the Lieutenant. "It mustn't get to Villovürt or the girl!"

The six Rangers rode out on the three remaining horses as the last few remotely ambulatory undead from the castle stumbled, crawled and leveraged themselves over the ridge and into the dell behind them. Relentlessly the broken husks, as best they could on bullet blasted and sword hacked stumps, continued to blindly follow the quarry; still these undead remnants of once living things strived to carry out their necromancer's will.

Two black robed undead acolytes immerged from the castle gate afresh, they did not join the pursuit, but they instead carefully retrieved the prone body of Maqlath and reverentially carried her back to the keep.

Luwsiy, still wrapped in Rebekah's red riding cloak and hood, was sitting dazed in front of Villovürt as their horse thundered through the thick of the Old Forest. She barely registered what had just happened let alone what was happening now, her thoughts were lost in the words of Maqlath – *That girl is ours! She is one of us now!*

She kept getting visions of the vampire woman, covered in the blood of both horse and sapien – *so much blood* – and the words kept repeating – *That girl is ours! She is one of us now!* Luwsiy absently scratched at the small though mostly healed scar where a piece of Bäliyl's skull had embedded into her. The words repeated again in her mind – *but what did they mean? Am I one of them now, a vampire? Can it be true?* She scratched the wound a little harder.

Corporal Villovürt's senses were supremely alert as she deftly weaved the horse through the trees, heading for the track that had brought them here in the first place. She found it without incident but she was acutely aware that the forest around them was potentially full of dead things that would have been reanimated by the necromantic spell. There was no way of telling how large the area of magikal influence would be, even the subtlest of winds have an uncanny and unpredictable way of carrying such incantations a surprising distance. When Villovürt had heard the spell she was pretty sure the wind had been blowing to the south-west and the track they were about to take was going south-east. *Not ideal*, she thought, *but it'll have to do.* She was confident that if the message she'd sent back to the stables with her horse had been read, then reinforcements would surely be coming up that track. She prayed that they would come sooner rather than later.

On their horse, Rigormort and Pendal burst onto the track behind her. She glanced at Rigormort, Pendal was unconscious in front of him, and said "We're just gonna ride as fast as we can back down this track – we've gotta get as far from the spell zone as quickly as we can – keep your sword ready in case we meet any undeads."

Unsheathing his sabre, Rigormort gave her an uncharacteristically emphatic nod of absolute agreement, and they rode on, as fast as their already terrified horses would carry them.

All of Lieutenant Lethbridj's concentration was occupied with steering the sprinting horse through the trees while bringing them close to the surprisingly swift undead bear; while Sergeant Rinawn, seated uncomfortably behind him, leaned out with sword in hand and readied himself to hack at the beast's mouldering haunches. Lickety and Sinkhole were doing likewise on the other side of the creature while Lannik and Wellnap were coming in close on its fetid heals. They all frantically weaved their way through the heavily wooded forestry, ducking under low boughs, jumping fallen timbers, dodging thorny thickets, evading sprawling twisted roots and desperately trying to get close enough to bring the foul thing down.

Corporal Lannik's vision suddenly went black as the horribly cold carcass of a rather large undead crow seemingly came from nowhere and smacked him in the face. It fluttered dustily, clawing and pecking at his eyes and cheeks, before Lannik grabbed it with both hands; he twisted its decomposing maggoty body hard and snapped its wings then threw it aside, spitting dry black feathers and blinking cloying dust from his eyes. His horse veered to the right unexpectedly to avoid a huge tree in their path then violently stopped its headlong rush as if to protest the Corporal's sudden neglect of its reins. Both Lannik and Wellnap, who was sitting behind him, were thrown from their mount. The two men crashed to the ground, Wellnap tumbled into a particularly wild patch of undergrowth, but the Corporal was dropped head first into a small hollow below a thick anchoring root of a large oak – over which his body was flipped by its own momentum and causing his neck to snap like a twig.

Dazed and thorn scratched, Wellnap staggered to his feet. "Corporal," he said, "you alright?" but he could tell from the impossible angle of Lannik's head that he was not. "Ah, damn it." He said sullenly.

Their horse had trotted a few yards away and now stood rather skittishly, looking at him with wild, wide eyes.

"Easy, girl." whispered Wellnap encouragingly as he approached the animal slowly. The Rangers on the other two horses had continued on in pursuit of the bear, Wellnap doubted they had even noticed what had happened to him and Lannik so couldn't risk losing his mount. As he neared the horse it moved away from him and started heading back the way they had come.

"Whoa, whoa." he said, trying to keep his voice soft and soothing. It seemed to placate the nervous beast briefly and the horse stopped – but again, as Wellnap approached, the flighty animal suddenly started as if in surprise and ran off a little way further.

"Oh come on, girl." He was starting to get exasperated but tried to keep it out of his voice. He clucked at her a couple of times as he approached again, holding his hands out as if to show he had nothing to hide. Its ears were back, flat against its head – which wasn't a good sign – and sure enough, when Wellnap got close, the horse snorted and ran from him again. *Gods damn-it*, he cursed to himself and stood there a moment, debating whether to continue pursuing the horse or to just take off on foot.

I'll give it another go but if that stupid mare runs just one more time I'm turning my back on her and riding shanks' pony out of here.

He cautiously approached the troublesome animal a fourth time. "Good girl." he said as he got near to her, then, saying "Come to papa." he reached for the reins. He saw a flash of the whites of her eyes and he knew he was in trouble – she reared up, emitting a deafening roar-like whiney, and then started to turn, bucking and kicking as if a demon were on her back. The animal gave a last high kick with its back hooves, one of which connected a powerful, though glancing, blow to Wellnap's temple and sent him reeling, before she galloped furiously away into the thick of the forest.

The concussed Ranger fell to the floor of the now spinning forest, his vision blurred then blacked out – before returning, though still blurred and accompanied by a throbbing, aching head that was reverberating like a hammer struck bell. Though feeling weak he tried to sit up, but it made the spinning and aching of his head even worse and threatened to bring on the blackness again so he laid himself back down immediately. He then felt like he was going to throw-up, so tentatively he tried laying on his side, the last thing he wanted was to pass out on his back and choke on his own vomit. *Gods*, he thought, *how did it come to this? Should've just started walking!*

And so he lay there on his side, he knew not how long, waiting for the spinning and the aching and the nausea to subside.

A light scuffling sound came from behind him. *Probably just some little critter*, he thought, but then he remembered the undead things, and so he forced himself to turn over. Sure enough he could see a small furry animal rummaging through the undergrowth and leafy detritus of the forest floor. It was heading in his direction so he spat the word "Scat!" at it, thinking it would run away. It didn't. It stopped and lifted itself up on its hind legs and peered at him with one beady little eye – the other was missing, just a gaping hole. It was a mangy thing, a rat, a big one, putrid and undead.

Wellnap scrambled for his dagger as the rat raced straight at his head. As it got close and seemed to prepare for a leap at his face he pinned the thing to the ground with ten inches of steel, *just in time*. "Ha, got-ya – ya little fucker!" he said, forcing himself, shakily, to his feet as the world span around him. He put his boot on the small undead creature, withdrew his dagger, then stomped on it hard till every little bone in its body was crushed – *you're not goin' nowhere*, he thought as the aching in his splitting skull ascended to new heights of absolute agony.

He only managed a few steps before the blood rushed from the trembling Ranger's dizzy head and he collapsed to all fours and then threw up. He managed to crawl a little further before giving up – *for now*. He lay himself down, semi-prone, with his head and shoulders propped against a tree so he could see any other critters that might come his way.

What he saw was not a critter though. Two of the robed Acolytes they had killed, with the Ranger arrows still embedded in their chests, were walking lifelessly, like grim automatons, toward him. Behind the walking and horrible hooded cadavers came the vampire woman that had killed Gudrun – she was staring right at him, a cruel smile of recognition smirked on to her cold beautiful face.

Wellnap did not have the strength to fight – and once his eyes were caught by the vampire's gaze, he no longer had the will.

Sergeant Rinawn severed the undead bear's meaty front left limb with a hefty hacking swing of his sabre. The bear crashed to a very messy halt, tumbling on to its back. The Rangers pulled their two sweating horses to a sudden stop, the Sergeant and Sinkhoal dismounted quickly from the backs of their respective mounts and started hacking at the furious, biting and slashing beast till it was entirely limbless and effectively an immovable torso with an angry snapping head attached to it. Rinawn halved its head with a mighty sideways swipe through the creatures gaping, breathless mouth.

"Quickly, mount up the both of you." said Lieutenant Lethbridj, keen to get moving again and onto the track that would lead them away from this place. "Anyone see what happened to Lannik and Wellnap?"

The Rangers looked around and back but there was no sign of the other two. None of them had seen what had happened to them.

"Well, we can't hang around waiting for them here – let's get moving." ordered the Lieutenant.

Sergeant Rinawn inwardly fumed at the idea of leaving without finding what had happened to Wellnap and Lannik – but he followed his orders without a word. Both he and Sinkhoal remounted the horses, sitting behind the Lieutenant and Lickety once more, and the Rangers moved out at a slower rate than they had arrived – letting the horses cool off and catch their breath after the exhausting chase.

Peter Guy Blacklock

Chapter Twenty Seven – The Demon of Deceit

Arkturon, Rebekah and Juwniper followed the small cowled figure of Keridwen down into the deep depths of the cave and tunnel systems well below Afagddu's lair. She was taking them by a darkly secret path that, the demoness had told them, leads to the very bowels of the castle at the heart of Kear Pedrivan Reversus, a path that avoids its labyrinthine environs and one that cuts under its deep fiery moat. The air was hot, heavy and humid. They'd been walking for hours, it seemed, and Rebekah's heart was thumping a deafening beat within her chest as her lungs inhaled and exhaled hard to get as much as they could from each sparse and stifling breath.

They were lightly equipped; Arkturon carried his sword and staff – which was giving off a slight glow to light their way – Juwniper carried her sword, bow and arrows, while Rebekah carried her short sword and a small, round, buckler-sized shield that Keridwen had given her. Its convex front, around the central metallic boss, was like a black mirror of obsidian, which was rimmed by a further metal band, slim and sharpened at its outside edge. Its adamantine boss and rim will glow red, the demonic girl had told her, whenever the bearer is in the proximity of one who intends harm against them or their party – a very useful thing indeed, she had said, especially when dealing with the Demon of Deceit and his kind. Its maker named it Aedjis, which means thunderstorm, she added, and it is both shield and blade in one.

Rebekah gripped the padded handle behind the boss in a sweaty and nervous fist. She was uneasy in accepting a gift from a demon and while they walked through the heated tunnels she sidled up to Arkturon asking, "Why has she given me this shield – I mean, why give it to me?"

"Keridwen has access to the future, or at least to possible futures," replied the wizard, "she obviously saw a potential need for it... and maybe for you specifically to have it. It's best not to question Otherworldly gifts – it certainly doesn't pay to refuse them, even though accepting one will have a price all its own."

His answer did not put Rebekah's mind at ease.

Keridwen suddenly stopped ahead of them and they approached her. They were standing in a featureless tunnel of hewn rock that continued both beyond and behind them into utter darkness.

"We are directly under the great citadel of Hlewid," said the demon girl. "Through this doorway," she pointed to the featureless tunnel wall at their right, "is a staircase that will bring you to another hidden door that leads into the mines and lower dungeons below the castle. I cannot enter there; Hlewid will sense my presence like a thorn in his side. You must go on alone." She waved her hand at the wall and a large rectangle of otherwise indistinguishable rock silently opened outward toward them.

Arkturon led the way through the doorway after thanking Keridwen profusely for her aid – for the wizard always figured it served well to give extravagant thanks or praise when dealing with the fickle whims of god and demon alike.

As the door closed behind them, just as silently as it had opened, they found themselves closely confined within a constricting stairwell and confronted with tightly twisting stone stairs that spiralled up into the sulphureous heat. In single file they steadily climbed into the thick oppressive blackness above.

They climbed and they climbed till Rebekah was beginning to think that the stairs were never-ending. Higher and higher the slow ascent took them, step after turning step till finally they reached the enclosed top. Arkturon waved his hand as Keridwen had when they were down below. Nothing happened. They shuffled uneasily in the small space at the top of the stairs. The wizard turned slightly to the left and waved his hand once more. A door opened silently outward and a blast of even hotter air came rushing in.

Arkturon signalled for Rebekah and Juwniper to stay while he stepped cautiously through the opening. He looked about then waved them on. When all three were through, the door closed and disappeared into the wall once more. The interlopers were at one end of a huge, long and blackened vaulted hall lined with the biggest boilers – or at least what she supposed were boilers – that Rebekah had ever seen. The heat was almost unbearable. Arkturon led them between the two ranks of squat and roaring metal chambers that nested among countless pipes of vary thickness leading into, between and from each one. Some of the largest of these pipes burrowed into the ground below them, while others snaked the walls and climbed into and beyond the high vaulted ceilings.

They passed through the deafening hall and came to the large arched entrance way at its far end; it proved to be one of many, no doubt leading to countless similar halls that filed one after another round a truly massive hollowed out cave-like chamber which plunged before them and rose high above. Despite countless monolithic columns of supporting vaulted stone the expansive ceiling seemed to sag under the incalculable weight of the castle above. The air within the gigantic expanse was thick with coal dust and it dawned on Rebecca that the chamber was a huge mine, she could see people, thousands of them, slaves working under the threat of whips wielded by strange and grotesque were-creatures. They were digging down below, digging ever deeper in a pit at the centre of the cavern floor. Coal was being brought up continuously on a massive scale and transported out to the edges on large tracked trolley ways where it was fed into giant furnaces through glowing archways identical to the one in which they stood.

The archways snaked in a coil round the cavern, each one fed by the same broad road that rose up the sides from the bottom to the top. Arkturon led them resolutely up that road from the approximate mid point at which they had emerged. Over two full circumferences they walked round the mine, past innumerable archways leading to unfathomable workings powering or facilitating unknowable ends, before reaching the formidable portal leading up into the castle proper.

A number of times the three had to duck into the nearest archway as fresh slaves of all the human races – souls of sapien, elf, dwarf, goblin, hobb and troll, males and females, young and old – all were marched down into the pit by malformed beast-men guards and overseers.

When they finally reached the top, wide stairs took them up into the eerily silent and shockingly cool fortress; their sweat covered bodies suddenly chilled by the drastic change in temperature, though the atmosphere remained oppressive and was weighted with a sickening dread.

They wandered down corridors and climbed up stairs as they came to them, the higher they got the more they sensed a turmoil that raged throughout the citadel. Alarming sounds of commotion and screams that froze the mind and frightened the heart to a maddening pace seemed to haunt the dark passageways and halls. They all instinctively held their weapons ready, for the sounds of distress were often startlingly close.

After Arkturon led them through a large chamber of columns and dripping, tangled drapes, they came to a freezing, waterlogged hallway and the diabolical inhabitants of the place finally interrupted their so-far secret intrusion. Briefly total confusion ruled. Wraiths hurtled in at them suddenly from a sweeping staircase at the end of the passageway. Many of the creatures were panic-stricken and hysterical, more affrighted – it seemed – than any of the three intruders. The two sapiens and the faery lashed out immediately as their pent up fear and tension was suddenly released into desperate violence. The adamantine boss and rim of the shield Aedjis smouldered red as the three crashed into the startled foe and the staff of Arkturon exploded in a blazing radiance that blinded the wraiths' dark accustomed eyes.

The trespassers battled up the stairs and burst into a giant shadowed hall among a clamouring torrent of shrieks and hollers – the clank and sickening crunch of the skirmish echoing up into the huge vaults of darkness above. They fought furiously through the oncoming ranks.

Rebekah thrust her blade into a wraith as it rushed her, the cold metal flashing as it struck – the wraith screaming at her before collapsing to dust and brittle bone. With no time to think or even panic, again another one hurtled at her, they were all around and above, blinded and hysterical from Arkturon's magic, but also it seemed terrified by another power from which they were fleeing. With short desperate glimpses she could see beyond the raging melee, the wraiths were being hastened into the hall like frightened but dangerous sheep from a far entrance. They were fleeing from something terrible, straight into their path.

One of the frenzied creatures knocked Rebekah off her feet, ripping into her arm with its jagged claws and causing her sword to loose from her hand as she toppled. In that initial desperate moment of panic as the evil spirit descended she lashed out with her shield to defend against its attack, yelling into its face. As the adamantine boss crashed into the side of the evil spirit's skull like head, it blazed a fierce and burning orange and caused the wraith to explode – as if shattering the very fabric of its existence. Rebekah lay stunned for a fraction of a second before scrambling to her feet and using the shield as a new and more powerful weapon to force a way through the storm of wraiths. The pain of the lacerations in her sword arm was almost unbearable, it numbed her whole limb as if it were paralyzed, but with her other arm she swung Aedjis wildly – the adamantine rim and boss blazing like molten metal whenever they made contact with an evil foe.

Arkturon thrust his staff forward and a shield of energy emanated from its crown, flashing and sparking as the wraiths and now were-beasts too were pushed aside by its phantasmic force. There were so many of them, constantly pouring into the immense chamber, filling its darkened expanse with hysteria and alarm. Arkturon slowly led them through the gathering throng into the centre of the hall, Rebekah and Juwniper stayed close to Arkturon's back and attacked any diabolical creatures that came foolishly close. Past towering columns and over wide stepped daises they pushed their way toward an intense darkness that glowered oppressively – toward the light sapping hub of the citadel and of the labyrinth around it. Their desperate struggle was taking them toward the source of all its evil.

They pressed onward, nearing the centre of the great chamber, just managing to keep together as a group, when a blazing figure entered the fray from the distant doorway that their foes had been streaming through. It was a knight in glowing armour and a billowing black cloak, cleaving his way toward them with shining sword and shield as if on an unrelenting quest of utter annihilation.

The evil darkness was all about them when suddenly it became concentrated; it seeped from all the confusion around and collected at a huge throne on the highest dais in the centre of the hall. It was like a storm gathering – a raging angry storm. The baleful figure of Hlewid, the Kernunnos Inversus, materialized ominously before the throng upon a charnel-house throne constructed from what appeared to be the burned bones and ivory of some great mythical beast.

Mikael fought his way toward the enthroned demon, his eyes suddenly catching sight of the slight motionless figure standing by Hlewid's left hand that had only become apparent as the demon appeared.

Arkturon saw her too. He led the others toward the apparently spellbound Lilith, directly across the path of the demon lord's burning hateful eyes. Hlewid stood up, towering above them all.

Mikael was almost level with his comrades, swiftly cutting through the wraiths and assorted were-beasts like a sharpened broadsword through boneless flesh.

"THIS INTRUSION IS SACRILEGE!" screamed the demon Hlewid suddenly as he stepped forward threateningly and unfurled his wings in a display of power, his minions instinctively cowered and backed away – leaving the intruders exposed before the great dark lord. "YOU FOOLS," his voice reverberated, "LILITH BELONGS TO ME – HEART AND SOUL – SHE IS MY WILLING CONSORT!" He held out his left hand to her.

Lilith looked to the demon and moved away from him. "No," she said simply and confidently, "I will never belong to you or to anyone – my destiny is mine."

The demon fumed with anger and confusion, Lilith even detected that he actually seemed hurt by the betrayal – she revelled in his anguish, however slight, and savoured the delight that filled her because of it.

"Ha!" said Arkturon, unable to contain his mirth, as he fired the biggest ball of energy he could muster from the end of his staff right at the demon.

Hlewid raised his right hand and stopped the sparking phantasmic energy ball in mid flight.

Juwniper came from behind the wizard and loosed an arrow straight at the demon's head but Hlewid caught it with his left hand barely inches from his right eye.

Simultaneously, and without thinking, Mikael threw his sword Sumbrandr at the diabolical lord. The magikal blade curved through the air as if it had a mind of its own and pierced Hlewid's chest, skewering his foul heart through.

The demon staggered back and looked like he was about to fall when he suddenly paused, with a wave of his right hand he cast Arkturon's phantasmic bolt to the floor and with his left he threw Juwniper's arrow aside. He stood up straight and flexed his wings. "YOUR MUNDANE AND MORTALWEAPONS CANNOT HARM ME!" he triumphed. Turning to his left he called contemptuously, "WORM! COME HERE... AND REMOVE THIS TROUBLESOME NEEDLE!"

From the veiled shadows behind the charnel throne came the submissive fetch of the fallen sorcerer Bäliyl Samiyl, cowed and diminished he urgently rushed to carry out his master's command. The fetch of Bäliyl grasped the hilt of the magikal sword Sumbrandr, as if to pull it out of Hlewid's chest, and immediately the phantasmic essence of the great demon Hlewid started to sweep into Bäliyl – diminishing the first and massively empowering the second.

Mikael realized what was happening immediately and cursed himself for throwing Sumbrandr away. He ran to Lilith and shouted her name.

"We've got to leave!" she replied urgently, as she too ran to him.

Then Arkturon figured out what was happening and shouted "We must find the Black Mirror and get out before Bäliyl becomes the new

Demon of Deceit!" Niggling in the back of Arkturon's mind was the notion that Bäliyl had somehow planned this all along.

"The portal to Matt's realm is this way!" shouted Juwniper, pointing back to the entrance that she, Arkturon and Rebekah had just fought their way through.

"Lead the way." said the wizard franticly to the faery girl.

It was at that moment that the sword fully exited from the demon's chest and there was a violent and thunderous, phantasma-splitting reverberation that seemingly shook the very foundations of the immense Underworld fortress.

Hlewid and Bäliyl were suddenly nowhere to be seen, the wraiths were swept away by the first and strongest of the few strange but rapid shock waves that rippled out from the site of the demonic transmigration – the more bestial minions were left behind, demoralised by the disappearance of their lord though, they fled in confusion from the hall. Lilith staggered forward and stumbled from the high dais as Mikael rushed up toward her. Their embrace was brief – but triumphant none the less.

"We cannot trust that the demon is gone... we must leave!" insisted the wizard loudly.

Mikael started to run for one of the doorways. "No!" shouted Arkturon after him. "This way!" he ran toward the passage that Juwniper had pointed out and to which he was already running. "The portal to Kear Pedrivan is through here!"

They all ran from the hall, weapons at the ready where they had them, and they splashed into the large waterlogged hallway beyond. Juwniper led them down the passage followed by Mikael and Lilith and with Arkturon and Rebekah close behind. Both Mikael and Lilith suddenly slipped and fell with startled yells cut short as they disappeared beneath the cold black surface of the otherwise shallow waters. The others stood stock still, afraid that they too might step into a hidden hole beneath the obscuring water line

"Mikael?" shouted Arkturon alarmed, "Lilith!" He probed the waters with his staff but it seemed, paradoxically, that the depth where the two had disappeared was no more than about a foot and a half.

The waters were calm but for the swirling movements caused by Arkturon's sweeping and searching staff.

"DID YOU REALLY THINK IT WOULD BE SO EASY?" Bäliyl's now demonic voice echoed within the long chamber and pierced into their minds. "WELL DID YOU?!" he screamed, his evil intonation chilling them all.

A sudden disturbance in the water's surface drew their eyes with a dreadful certainty. Something was rising from the dark pool amidst them.

Mikael rose grimed and dirty and with Lilith in his arms, coughing and retching he looked ready to collapse! "We must stop... must rest." he exhaled between desperate breaths.

"But what happened?" exclaimed Arkturon with a visible relief shared by them all.

"That does not matter now!" shouted Juwniper forcefully. "Let's just get away!" She urged them on with an emphatic wave of her hand – toward the way out, "There is no time to rest!"

Rebekah waded hurriedly to Mikael's side, to aid his flagging strength.

"Rebekah – watch out!" It was Arkturon's voice that shouted the warning but Rebekah did not need it, for she saw the cause of his concern immediately, her adamantine buckler was glowing red and comprehension dawned as she approached, it was Mikael or Lilith that caused it, *one... or the both of them* meant her harm!

Mikael, suddenly strong and grimacing, threw Lilith bodily at Arkturon – he knew he had been detected as an imposter and lunged for Rebekah, grabbing hold of her with his jagged claws suddenly growing and ripping from his gauntleted fingertips, and lifted her from the floor. Both he and Lilith transformed into large, winged and beast like wraiths – Lilith while in mid air – bigger than any that the three had seen before, their huge and dreadful wings distended raggedly, beating a frozen but fetid air over the company.

Rebekah wasted no time trying to free herself, she simply twisted in the Mikael-wraith's grasp and slammed her shield's magikally hardened boss right into his now skeletal face as forcibly as she could. The shock of the impact shattered the transformed creature's skull and forced it to loosen its grip, allowing Rebekah the freedom to quickly shift and force the orange burning rim of Aedjis down in to its huge ribcage. Its fractured skull screamed into her face as its hideous leathery wings desperately fanned and momentarily lifted them both higher into the air, black water dripping from them into the black pool below. Then it collapsed back to the water from whence it came – releasing Rebekah as she kicked spitefully at the crumpling creature as it disintegrated to dust. "Bastard!" she whispered vehemently between frightened and exhausted breaths. It dissolved, bubbling in the water.

The one that had been Lilith clawed at Arkturon, grasping for his staff, its hideous teeth snapping at his face and hands. Frantically trying to fend it off Arkturon waved and whipped his staff at the giant bat like creature – unable to bring its crown to bear. He managed to dodge past it though and put some distance between himself and the thing as it turned to face him.

Juwniper swiftly moved to the back of Arkturon, drawing back an arrow in her bow she waited for a clear shot at the beast beyond the man. The wraith reared up and Arkturon braced to receive its quickly advancing attack. Juwniper shot the arrow straight for the beast's sharp toothed maw; hitting the target dead on, the force of the arrow pushed the creature back giving Arkturon space to wield his staff. He pointed and unleashed a fiery phantasmic pulse of energy, with a piercing cry, the wraith burst into a cloud of dust and rags that descended slowly to the disturbed water's surface.

"But, where's Mikael... and Lilith?" Rebekah breathlessly questioned in the moment of silence that followed.

Mikael burst from the water, feeling an urgent demand for air that seared pain into his lungs. He coughed and spluttered agonisingly, his eyes tightly closed against the stinging water. Lifting himself from his knees he stood shakily; straining against the freezing air he realized that Lilith had gone, they all had gone – he was alone.

"Lilith!" he shouted, then "Arkturon?" He desperately looked round for a sign of them, perplexed. Then turned and whispered "What's going on?" to no one in particular.

He felt alone and unprotected, wishing he still had his sword he tightly held onto his shield. The ink-like waters before him suddenly burst upwards causing a torrential downpour. A giant serpent, feet thick and who knows how many long, reared amongst the spray, towering above Mikael – its fanged mouth gaping, a blackened and forked tongue jutting from the hissing and spitting throat, it danced back and forth, side to side, in an evil jig of hypnotic intensity. The creature's guttural sibilation was deafening as it lunged for him.

Mikael fell backwards with his shield held high as the serpent hit his defence sharply, stumbling and struggling to keep above the water

Mikael backed away. The impact had shaken every bone and strained every muscle within his weakening body but the snake had been burned by the blessed shield of Sul, which had flared bright at the touch of the serpent's concentrated evil.

Without warning the serpent's powerful tail whipped round at Mikael.

The scaly appendage cut through the water at an incredible pace and slammed into Mikael's side, his shield was deflected away from him but Mikael just managed to cling on to its strap by finger tips as he crumpled in an explosion of water onto his side. Desperately he scrambled to the side of the wide passageway, till he felt the solid security of a wall at his back, stumbling he crouched beside it. With heavy and laboured breaths he looked around, disbelieving his own vision, the waters were deathly dark and still. There was no serpent to be seen.

Lilith stared at the still water around her. She was confused and alone but her fear had completely dried up. She looked about herself like one who could no longer be affrighted or scared. Lilith had been through the worst he could throw at her, what could possibly harm her more than what she had already been put through. Mikael had found her once, he would find her again. She moved forward toward the passageway leading from the cold sunken pool that numbed her legs, a numbness that seemed to be rising up through her whole body.

The serpent exploded from the pool ahead of her, its ugly fanged countenance screaming and spitting. Lilith stood before it as if facing into a breeze rather than the storm it truly was. Her expression remained unmoved, her heart steadfast. She could not stand unaffected before the power of its tail though; the creature lashed her side sending her hurtling onto the wall of the chamber. Lilith crumpled into the water but burst immediately from it, kneeling in the freezing liquid she stared fixedly at each point of the room but the creature had gone as quickly as it had appeared.

Mikael stood and was ready for when the creature returned, his shield warily held before him, tightly fastened to his arm, as he took a step forward from the wall. Its writhing form materialised in the darkened room, for one brief second its ghostly shape was translucent and unreal and then the solidity of its evil presence impacted on the space and water around it, displacing water and air outward with almost explosive power.

Prepared for the lunge of the creature's massive head and gaping jaws he dodged to the left slamming his right arm and the shield into the side of the snake's face with a flash of pure light. It screamed from the impact of the holy weapon. Mikael leapt at the thick body of the creature, just behind the head. It reared as he clung to it, clambering to get astride its neck he raised his shield, clamping his thighs around the scaly sinews – he brought the shield's rim down on the serpents forehead, just above and between the eyes. The blinding flash dazed the creature, it writhed and screeched in pain spitting at the room.

Mikael and the giant snake suddenly faded from the pool like chamber, locked together in a deadly struggle. The waters were smooth and stagnant, as if they had been undisturbed for centuries.

Arkturon led the group from the water logged room, Juwniper brought up the rear with an arrow ready poised in her longbow. Just as she entered the passageway down which Arkturon was leading them a thunderous crash erupted behind her with a cry more terrible than any she had heard. She turned, looking back into the chamber she saw a huge serpent crowned with a blinding light, and she saw Mikael, he was riding the creature, as if breaking a wild stallion. The image faded and died before she could even think of releasing the arrow in her hand.

"Arkturon!" she shouted, "Quickly!" She crouched with one knee to the ground, her arrow still pointed to the room. He and Rebekah were already on their way back, having heard the commotion for themselves.

Lilith stood determinedly, her sopping white shift clinging to her uncomfortably, and she passed into the centre of the chamber once more. Violently the serpent appeared but with a shining burning light atop of it, Mikael... Mikael was battling with the beast... Mikael was there! Lilith fearlessly ran and leapt at the serpent's head, she had to be with Mikael – she must not lose him. She clung to the snake's lower jaw, desperately digging her fingers and nails – that grew into long, sharp claws – into the soft flesh inside the lips of the horrid screeching and hissing mouth, kicking at the hard and unyielding scales of the wide neck she tried to wrench its lower jaw from its upper.

"It was an illusion... to hold us back!" said Arkturon emphatically. "You can trust nothing that you see within this domain." They stood at the far doorway of the water logged chamber.

"But what if it was not an illusion." countered Juwniper. "What if it was real?"

"We must wait... to be sure." said Rebekah, "and then resume the search."

With resignation in his tone he said "Very w-" but before he could finish the serpent appeared before them. Mikael's shield giving off a blinding light as it seared and burned into the creature's skull. It reared up out of the water dragging the desperately clinging form of Lilith and an ear splitting shriek reverberating about them. Juwniper loosed her arrow directly at the monster; its course ran true and pierced the slitted orb of its eye, sending violent spasms through its long foul body. The creature, Mikael and Lilith all faded as if they had never existed.

"We must bind it to our reality; it seems to be flitting in and out of existence," said Arkturon now convinced, "it's like it's moving from one reality to another."

"But how?" exclaimed Juwniper. "And if any of us touch it, they will be dragged along with it... like Mikael and Lilith."

"We could be split up forever!" said Rebekah alarmed.

"We must all be linked together... then I will bind this creature to us, to our reality. But if one of us goes with it then we all must go. Come; grab my belt with you free hands, keep your weapon hands free."

They did as he had instructed and Arkturon stood with his staff, held vertical in both hands, before him.

The creature came again, as if it were summoned.

"Serpent hold!" shouted Arkturon with absolute authority, his voice booming above the deafening hissing cries of the snake. "Hold to me, I command you!" The wizard thumped the base of his staff down onto the ground beneath the water and a yellow white light reeled out from the crown, like a thick almost solid rope the light twisted from staff to creature and spread shining tendrils all over the giant snake. It was ensnared. Arkturon now held the creature with his will and he brought it down. Already weakened by the wounds inflicted by Mikael, Lilith and Juwniper it could not find the strength to resist. Its sinuous form faded and disappeared, its illusion lost and broken. Mikael and Lilith fell to the pool like floor.

They emerged coughing and spluttering, Rebekah rushing to their side, the others closing round and drawing them on, back toward the end of the passage way. Onward they ran – daring to hope that they might escape – back through the immense hall full of columns and drapes and on into another sunken passage, the floor of which was again hidden beneath dark impenetrable water.

The waters churned before them though, and an imposing figure rose to block their way. It was Bäliyl himself, twisted and distorted into a rough semblance of Hlewid but even more grotesque; he had the curved antlers that rose and arched forward from the back of his head but also there were large curling and twisted goat horns at his temples and two long thin spirals that jutted above his protruding brows. Slowly the menacing bulk of the new Kernunnos Inversus, the Lord of Deceit, arose from the water. Its hideous visage was still recognizable as that of Bäliyl but bloated and bulging, it snarled at them with an angry grin. He held Sumbrandr in his left hand as his new cloven-hoofed form, red-hued and raw, warped and overdeveloped by the demonic essence now present in him, stood proud and exultant.

"SO MERDHIN..." the demon voice, even more grating than Hlewid's, reverberated in their minds as well as their ears, "THIS FEEBLE FEW IS THE BEST BAND OF WARRIORS YOU COULD MUSTER? THE BEST YOUR TRUMPED UP POWERS COULD DRAW TO YOURSELF?"

The demon's voice grew louder as he spoke. "A LITTLE GIRL, A SEX OBSESSED FAY AND A LOVE LORN CALLOW?" He escalated to a scream as his awful gaze fell on Lilith, "ALL HERE TO RESCUE AN UNGRATEFUL WHORE?!"

"DEAR ME!" he continued, suddenly calm, shaking his massive head in mock disappointment. "HOW THE MIGHTY FALL – THE OBSOLETE TITLE OF A DECAYED AND PRIMITIVE IDEAL CAN BRING NONE OF ITS FORMER GLORIES TO BEAR. HOW MEANINGLESS THE OFFICE OF MERDHIN HAS BECOME."

Arkturon smiled, ignoring the attempt to goad him. "We have got this far." he simply stated.

The demon laughed. "TRUE, TRUE... AND I COULDN'T HAVE ACHIEVED ALL THIS WITHOUT YOUR HELP – BUT THIS IS AS FAR AS YOU GET – I HAVE UNFINISHED BUSINESS WITH MY

LITTLE TOY," the demon smirked at Lilith, "I CAN NOT ALLOW YOU TO LEAVE WITH IT."

Juwniper swiftly drew her bow and an arrow, letting it fly straight for the demon's face.

Bäliyl swatted the missile away with a laugh. "COME ON, LITTLE HARLOT OF ARIYANRHOD. COME TO ME... I'LL SHOW YOU WHAT REAL LOVE IS." He sneered, holding his fat long penis toward the faery, vigorously pumping the length of its stiffening shaft.

"The only love you could hope to get here is from that overgrown hand of yours!" shouted Juwniper scornfully.

Unable to contain himself, Arkturos laughed aloud at the retort.

"SILENCE!" raged Bäliyl.

"DO NOT MOCK ME MERDHIN, THE ONLY FUCK YOU COULD FIND WAS A CHILD – A GIRL BARELY OLD ENOUGH TO WIPE HER OWN ARSE – SHAME ON YOU!

"WHAT'S THE MATTER," the demon condescended, "COULDN'T FIND A GROWN WOMAN WILLING TO LAY WITH YOU? DID YOU THINK AN INEXPERIENCED CHILD WOULD HAVE NOTHING TO COMPARE YOU WITH – WOULDN'T BE SO UNIMPRESSED WITH YOUR PITIFULL MANHOOD?

Again Arkturon ignored the demon's jibes; they did not affect him so Bäliyl moved his attention on.

"LITTLE REBEKAH... FUCKING AN ANCIENT OLD FOOL WHEN SHE KNOWS SHE SHOULD BE FUCKING MIKAEL... OR TRYSTING WITH HER OWN YOUNG SISTER – SWEET BUT NOT SO INNOCENT LUWSIY... OR IS IT BOTH THAT SHE WANTS TO FUCK – TOGETHER?

"WOULD YOU LIKE THAT, BECKY?" his eyes turned directly to stare into hers, "WOULD YOU LIKE TO SEE MIKAEL SHAFT YOUR YOUNG SISTER. I KNOW LUWSIY WOULD'VE LIKED HIM INSIDE HER – HOW SHE BEGGED TO BE FUCKED WHEN I HAD HER TIED AND NAKED ON MY ALTAR."

"At least anyone I fuck will be willing, you ugly bastard!" derided an increasingly impatient Rebekah, "I wouldn't have to bind and bewitch them like you!"

"YOU INSOLENT BITCH!" fumed Bäliyl, his anger now raging he took a step toward Rebekah.

"You dare touch her..." shouted Mikael, stepping forward, "I'll rip your foul heart out!"

The demon's laughter erupted with fresh glee. "AH, THE PARAMOUR SHOWS A BIT OF SPUNK, HOW ENTERTAINING MISPLACED LOVE CAN BE. THE POOR LITTLE FOOL WILL RISK HIS LIFE – AND, IT SEEMS HIS VERY SOUL – FOR ANY YOUNG AND FUCKABLE WENCH THAT COMES ALONG – YOU'VE LET THAT SHINING ARMOR GO TO YOUR HEAD."

Mikael took another stinted step forward, straining to hold himself back, gritting his teeth.

The demon's eyes blinked rapidly at the shining light from Mikael's shield and armour. "IT IS NOT LIKE YOU HAVE BEEN FAITHFUL TO LILITH'S MEMORY NOW IS IT? FUCKING EVERYTHING YOU COULD GET YOUR HANDS ON." then, glancing at Rebekah, he said "OR AT LEAST TRYING TO."

Rebekah could feel her face flush with both anger and unreasoned embarrassment. Unthinking she drew her red glowering buckler back as if to punch him, brandishing it with cold hate in her eyes.

Bäliyl's laughter erupted once more. "YOUR LITTLE COCK GLOVE SHOWS SPIRIT ARKTURON. HAS SHE NOT GROWN BORED OF YOU YET? NO? WELL YOU BETTER WATCH HER – WATCH THAT SHE DOES NOT GROW TIRED OF YOU FOR SHE SEEMS TO ENJOY MANY DIFFERENT FRUITS... MAYBE SHE'LL SEEK A YOUNGER MORE HEATED LOVE, BACK WITH HER SISTER OR THE DELIGHTFUL JUWNIPER HERE... IT WOULD NOT BE FOR THE FIRST TIME."

Arkturon showed a slight flash of anger, but kept himself controlled.

Juwniper, as always with her bow ready to fire, aimed the arrow tip at the centre of the demon's forehead and said steadily. "He is simply trying to turn us against each other, he fears us."

The demon's dreadful gaze turned angrily to Juwniper. "SILENCE YOU WHORE!" He yelled.

Frustrated, Rebekah shouted back sarcastically "Oh, silence yourself, you ugly, perverted bastard. Your endless drooling and droning is boring us!"

"YOU INSOLENT LITTLE BITCH!" fumed the demon as he perceived that any control he thought he had over the situation was slipping through his taloned fingers.

Bäliyl resorted to roaring at them. Straining and flexing his muscular but grotesque frame and fanning out his huge demonic bat-like wings to fill the width of the passageway. With petulant ferocity he suddenly conjured a flaming ball of phantasmic energy with his right hand and slung it right at Rebekah's startled face.

Rebekah instinctively raised her buckler to block it and the phantasmic pulse struck – but was repelled by the adamantine defence, ricocheting right back at he who threw it, it burst upon the demon's shoulder and caused him to stagger back, stunned.

"Juwniper is right." said Arkturon. "He fears us – it is our love and fellowship that holds us together, giving us strength. He is trying to undermine that for he knows we can defeat him."

Arkturon then shouted "Mikael!" and threw his sword to the weapon-less young man. As Mikael turned to the wizard's call, he caught the blade by its hilt and immediately readied himself to attack.

Arkturon raised his staff, pointing the crown at the still stunned demon, and quickly fired a big phantasmic plasma ball right at his chest.

Juwniper pulled her bow as taut as can be, with arrow still in place, and loosed it at the furrowed brow of the multi-horned demon while Lilith quickly fashioned a small but blinding and brilliant white phantasma ball of her own and propelled it with a wave of her hand, directly into Bäliyl's eyes – blinding his already blinking eyes.

Mikael then rushed at Bäliyl, crashing his blazing shield into the demon's bulk moments after each of the various projectiles had hit their mark. The demon reeled from the multiple onslaughts. "Go – all of you!" shouted Mikael as he pushed Bäliyl aside with all the remaining might given to him by Sumbrandr while it was in his possession, and stabbed the wizard's long sword violently up into the demon's broad, muscular abdomen.

Arkturon ushered Lilith, Rebekah and Juwniper past the struggling demon and shining knight then backed out behind them with staff ready.

Letting go of both the blade and his shield, taking a deep breath, Mikael dropped to the waterlogged floor, wrapping the cloak of invisibility tightly about himself.

Bäliyl bellowed his rage at the sudden attack. Confused by the blinding and burning lights and the piercing, stabbing pain of sword and arrow he attempted to shake the discomfort and disorientation from himself. Stumbling forward he tried to blink away the obscuring glare burned into is vision – again and again he blinked rapidly, straining to see the cool gentle darkness once more.

With still blinking and blurry eyes he finally saw the empty waterlogged room before him. His furious roar was heard throughout the castle.

Mikael crawled below the water line, trusting in his cloak of invisibility to conceal him from the demon's furious gaze. Still holding his breath he crept up and out of the water as slowly as possible so as not to disturb the pool surface sufficiently enough to draw attention to his escape.

"DAMN THOSE CONTEMPTUOUS WORMS!" Bäliyl screamed. *HOW DARE THEY DEFY ME!* His crazed roars echoed and soared into the high twisted towers that now belonged to him.

The demon became a raging fury, splashing and searching with one clawed hand and waving the sword Sumbrandr in the water about him with the other.

"WHERE ARE YOU, YOU LITTLE MAGGOT!" Bäliyl called hysterically.

Passing through the doorway from the waterlogged passageway Mikael desperately exhaled – quietly and slowly – then inhaled careful sweet air into his aching lungs.

Almost an afterthought, Bäliyl pulled the sword from his chest – as if it were just a thorn from a finger – and slung it aside, then swatted the arrow embedded in his forehead to the ground. "FIND THEM!" He then bellowed to the castle at large.

Steadily Mikael mounted a sweeping staircase then moved down the dark corridor he found himself in, the others were nowhere to be seen, cautiously looking to and fro his steps increasing till they soon became a run. A run for his life – for a splashing, howling curse erupted behind him as Bäliyl furiously gave chase.

The demon's thunderous hoof steps pounded on the stone stairs and then the corridor's floor, seeming to shake the very walls around Mikael as he fled. The pounding thumped up into his soul, a confusing beat exacerbating his fear and exhaustion. Mikael ran and turned down a corridor blindly.

He could feel the foul hot breath of the demon at his back. He sensed the powerful, clawed hand that reached out for him. A dead end loomed before him in the darkness; Bäliyl's oppressive and angry presence pressed him from behind.

He looked back to see the demon's right hand – reaching out to him – about to grab his shoulder. Ahead, a spectral image rushed suddenly toward him, panic invaded his determined thoughts but the recognition of his own appearance calmed and lifted his desperate spirit, almost tumbling with joy he leapt impetuously head first at the mirror image of himself, eyes closed – heart thumping – muscles burning.

The demon's savage claws lashed his back, ripping and gouging through his cloak and armour. Mikael hit the mirror, presenting no hindrance at all it distorted and moulded around him and then he passed through; with a bone crunching thump he rolled and skidded across the floor in agony on the other side.

The mirror flexed and started to settle back into shape but then the form of Bäliyl suddenly lunged from the black surface, twisting and pulling the mirror but incapable of breaking through, stretching it out over Mikael's prostrate form, the demonic shape of a multi-horned head with fanged mouth agape, the semblance of wide shoulders and muscular arms appeared – one hand clawed, the other still holding the sword Sumbrandr as if ready to strike. The demon's black image held for the briefest of moments before being whipped back with a thunderous crack, expelling the threat of his darkness from the light of Kear Pedrivan.

Sumbrandr fell to the floor with a clang and clatter while the Black Mirror flexed back and forth again before fully settling to its normal smooth and reflective facade.

Mikael laughed with contempt at the thought of Bäliyl being thrown backwards into the shadows of his own cursed realm from this blessed and bright one.

"The dark cannot exist in the light." said Matt, the Divine Lord Kernunnos, as he approached down the corridor from his lofty throne room. "Only by invitation could he hope to enter here."

A distant scream of impotent rage could be heard from the other side of the mirrored portal – it faded to nothing.

"Mikael!" Lilith shouted with relief and concern as she rushed to him. Crouching by his side and hugging him carefully. Arkturon, Rebekah and Juwniper all stood panting by the side of the mirror, relief grinning on each of their faces – they had made it through barely seconds earlier.

Mikael hugged Lilith back. "My love," he said, grimacing through the pain of burning claw marks down his back, "whether in life or in death – I knew our love would see us together again."

Chapter Twenty Eight – Sore Wounds and Bitter Hatred

Aggareth had the undead Acolytes bring Wellnap, dazed by the blow to his head and entranced by her enchantment, to her and her sisters' chamber half way up the central tower of the keep. There Maqlath was waiting, weak and injured – Aggareth had stitched the gash across her abdomen and had removed the two arrows that had pierced her – but she was in dire need of blood. Only with fresh blood could she hope to regain her strength and have the power to heal herself more fully.

"I bring a present, sweet sister." said Aggareth as she had the Ranger laid out beside her sister. Aggareth ripped his sleeve open and bit into Wellnap's forearm with her canines, then offered the welling wounds to her sister, pushing the arm to Maqlath's lips and letting the blood flow and spill onto them and between them.

The feverish and semiconscious Maqlath reacted with an instinctual predatory impulse that latched her mouth to the wounds on Wellnap's arm and she drew his life's blood voraciously into herself. Her health and strength started to return almost immediately, Maqlath took hold of Wellnap's arm herself and drank deeply of him.

"Do not drain him entirely, sister." said Aggareth. "I have plans for this one – we are going to leave him here for the soldiers to find when they come hunting us. They will not find us, dear sister, but they will find him – he will be the start of our revenge against them. We will avenge our father and we will avenge Igymeth – all those who took them from us will pay, my sister. They will pay dearly."

Maqlath continued drinking her fill.

Corporal Villovürt, with Luwsiy, and Rigormort, with a still passed out Pendal, had rode for the rest of that night and then kept going well beyond dawn without rest. Exhausted and hungry, it was approaching noon when they came upon the first Rangers from their station fort coming the other way. There were four of them, reconnoitring the track ahead from a camp that was being established by Captain Hammett as a forward operations post a few furlongs back up the track. Villovürt told them that the Lieutenant, the Sergeant and Corporal Lannik shouldn't be far behind them with three of the men, and then with a heavy heart she informed them that the three others in her troop were dead. She also warned them that at least one vampire sorceress, probably two, were still at large and also of the undead outbreak – "The gods alone know what might have been reanimated back there in the deep of the Old Forest!" she told them.

Luwsiy, mute and sullen, was clearly suffering from shock but, Villovürt figured, her condition was probably as good as could be expected. Pendal, on the other hand, was barely breathing and his chances of making it much further had to be pretty slim, he must have lost so much blood that she was surprised he had made it this far. Never the less they had to keep going, at least a little further till they could rest and eat in the relative security of the Ranger camp.

Lieutenant Lethbridj, Sergeant Rinawn, Sinkhoal and Lickety came upon the same four Rangers about thirty minutes later and arrived in the forward operations post barely ten minutes after that. The camp was a hub of frantic activity, all being directed by Captain Hammett, the commanding officer of the Meadengiat Ranger station. About twenty Rangers were busy felling trees, widening the small clearing that was already there, and quickly establishing a palisade perimeter. The Sergeant could see that a few canvas bivouacs had already been erected and that under one of which was Surgeon Donaldson, their station's head medico, tending to Pendal and the girl. He quickly dismounted and helped the very pale and weak looking Lieutenant to do likewise. The Lieutenant refused to go straight to the medico though and insisted on reporting to the Captain first, he limped painfully over to meet the commanding officer – even though he was already coming their way – and briefed him on all that had happened.

The Sergeant had no trouble persuading Sinkhoal to report to the Surgeon, so he accompanied him over there to see how Pendal was doing. A downcast Villovürt came out from under the canvas shelter as they approached.

"How's Pendal?" asked the concerned Sergeant, "Is he alright?"

"I'm sorry, Sarge," she said despondently, "Pendal didn't make it – he'd lost too much blood."

Sergeant Rinawn stopped and looked up to the sky in exasperation, gritting his teeth – wanting to shout and rage – but he contained his anger and grief. "The girl – Luwsiy?" he finally asked after taking a moment, "How's she?"

"Physically she seems fine, just a few abrasions and minor knocks, but mentally – well, she's pretty traumatised by the whole experience, hasn't said a word since the keep."

Rinawn nodded to the Corporal's words. *At least we saved her – and that damn sorcerer is dead*, he thought, *but at such a price – was it all worth it?* He dispelled the notion though; it's exactly what they all signed up for and he reminded himself that – *you don't become a Ranger if you're not willing to take the risks.*

"Rigormort," said the Sergeant, "get yourself to the Surgeon, I'd better go over and tell the Lieutenant about Pendal."

Luwsiy – now dressed in some Ranger clothes that Elliy had produced from her pack and some boots that she'd manage to scrounge from somewhere – stared at the blanket that covered the body of the young Ranger; from head to foot it covered him. She couldn't believe that he was dead – he was so young, not much older than herself; *he died because of me*, she could not help herself thinking, *as did the others – at least three others had died, four including Mikael, and the rest had been willing to.* She knew she was not to blame, but she could not prevent the gnawing guilt from eating away at her.

Luwsiy had thought she'd done with crying but, there and then, she cried for the young soldier. She cried for all of them, for all of those that had been willing to risk themselves to save her – none of them had to do it, come to her aid, but they did, unquestioningly. The Rangers, Mikael, Lilith, Arkturon and Rebekah, they all had come. Although Luwsiy had seen the worst in people over the last few days, she had also – she now realised – seen the best.

After a good feed and a few hours rest, Sergeant Rinawn led Villovürt, Rigormort, Sinkhoal, Lickety and Luwsiy, all on fresh horses, onto the track from the palisade camp and back toward the village of Meadengiat. Surgeon Donaldson had been forced to order the Lieutenant to stay in bed rest there at the camp, even then it was only the threat that "You'll lose that leg if you go on!" that made Lethbridj listen and agree to stay. "Damn it man but you're a stubborn one," the Surgeon had said, "but you'll never be as stubborn as me – stubborn is my bread and butter – so lay yourself down and give that wound time to heal or I swear I'll take that leg off, just to spite ya."

As the Rangers in charge of Luwsiy wound their way back along the forest track they were met intermittently by various troops, some leading small trains of pack animals carrying supplies, coming the other way. Sergeant Rinawn knew they'd be massing at the forward operations post, ready for a full sweep and clear out of the sorcerer's castle and its environs – *they'll be tied up tracking down wilding goblins, rogue trolls and a menagerie of undead for weeks. The two witches though*, he thought, *they won't be dumb enough to hang around – they'll be long gone, or well hidden. Too clever by half, they were.* Deep down he knew they would be back, *they wanted the girl* – he was sure, and he'd be waiting for them. *Sooner or later they'll come for her and then I'll have them!* They personally killed three of his men – that he knew of – and he was going to make damn sure that they paid for those men with their lives.

After about four hours travel down the track they came to the first of a series temporary staging posts set up along the forest path by Captain Hammett as he had come the other way. They were small manned camps providing a place to rest, eat and a change of horses so communications could be more easily sent back and forth. Each staging post was about four or five hours ride from the next. Sergeant Rinawn was impressed – *The Captain certainly didn't do things by halves*, he thought approvingly, *he must have mobilised Rangers from multiple stations up and down the line to get all this in motion.*

Buy the time they got to the next of the small staging camps, the sun had well and truly set. They stopped to eat a meal then sleep through the short midsummer night. The oppressive heart of the Old Forest had been left behind a few hours earlier but they still had a fair distance of the Great Forest to trek through. Corporal Villovürt reckoned they'd be back at Meadengiat well before the sun would set on them again. Luwsiy was relieved, she already felt so much better and with each meal and rest – no matter how short – she felt her vitality and spirit grow stronger as the distance between her and that castle increased. She was apprehensive about getting home though, her father was dead and Rebekah had gone – who knows where. She'd have no family to greet her, only memories of how her life had been and of how it could never be again.

Luwsiy felt safe and secure with the Rangers but still had not spoken a word, not even to Elliy, and the guilt over those that had died continued to gnaw at her. She didn't know what to say to those she rode with. Luwsiy wanted to thank them, but couldn't think of the words that would adequately express how she felt, so she said nothing, adding to the sense of guilt that tore at her heart.

Early the next morning, while they were readying to move out, the dark-elf Corporal asked her if she was feeling any better. "Yes," said Luwsiy quietly, then blurted out "thank you for coming for me, Elliy – thank you for everything." Once she started talking she found she could not stop and, a little louder, she went on, "I'm so sorry – sorry for what happened... and for the soldiers that died – you must all hate me." She started to cry and pleaded "Please forgive me?"

"Luwsiy," said Villovürt, putting her hand on the girl's shoulder "you're not responsible for that – there's nothing to forgive."

"You've nothing to be sorry for, lass." said the Sergeant over the saddle of his horse, his smile and expression of concern was a revelation that took her somewhat by surprise – she had assumed that gruffness was his nature. "We all signed up for this, but you were an innocent dragged into it against ya will – you're not to blame for any of it." He then continued as he mounted his horse, "You showed some real mettle back there, after what ya did to that sorcerer I'd be proud to ride with ya and fight by ya side any day of the month..." then he laughed, "certainly wouldn't wanna get on your bad side though."

Luwsiy allowed herself a grin of relief, felt both at his approval and at the fact that the guilt had started to lift from her heavy soul.

One second Rebekah and Arkturon were standing before the throne of Matt in Kear Pedrivan, with Mikael and Lilith on one side and Juwniper on the other – and the next, after Matt had waived his hand ceremoniously before them, they were back in the magik circle up in the glass observatory of Rose Mansion. The sun was high and shining in through the broken panes above them. For a brief moment it felt, to Rebekah at least, like they had never left – but so much had changed since they were last there. Mikael and Lilith were both of the Otherworld now, while Rebekah herself felt like a different person entirely; older, wiser and more confident. Rebekah realised that she had grown up.

"We must go to the Inn," she said suddenly, "I need to see Luwsiy, to check that she is alright – she must be so worried about us." Rebekah was mortified at how they had parted, Luwsiy had seemed so betrayed... then, wondering if Luwsiy would even be back yet, she said "How long have we been gone?"

Arkturon wandered from the circle and seemed to think a little, sniffing the air. "Well, it's noon," he said confidently and added, a little less so, "probably a day or so after the summer solstice. So we've been gone about a day and half – two at the most." But he didn't seem entirely convinced by his own deduction.

"Really?" said Rebekah, somewhat doubtfully – not least because of the wizard's apparent bemusement. She knew that time passed differently in the Otherworld but they seemed to have been gone an age, she would have thought it had to be much longer than a day or two.

"I'm pretty sure;" he said, "I think Matt must have done a little magikal fixing when he sent us back – usually when you spend any length of time in the underworld realms a much greater amount of time has passed back in the real world." Arkturon seemed to think a moment. "Of course it's possible that we've been gone a whole year."

"What!?" said a startled Rebekah as she followed him.

"But I think that highly unlikely." he assured her as he started going down the stairs into the house. "Let's see if there are any horses in the stable and if they haven't starved to death – well, we'll know it's only been a couple of days then won't we."

There was one horse safely stabled in its stall and three others ambling about outside, all very much alive and well fed. The loose horses were the three they and Mikael had ridden into the Forest Saveadj – the two that had been left with Afagddu and the other they had lost in the tunnels of Uffren, the Cold Place; they seemed in fine fettle and were still tacked and saddled as if they had just wandered there direct from the Otherworld. All three came over and greeted the two sapiens as if they were long lost friends.

By the time Luwsiy and the Rangers finally broke from the cover of the forest and rode across the familiar open fields that sprawled around the village of Meadengiat, the afternoon sun, still hot and blazing, had started on its journey toward the western horizon. The village and its environs bustled with the to and fro of villagers, Rangers and Watchmen; the odd cheer rang out as they caught sight of the kidnapped girl being returned to her home. As the riders approached the inn, Luwsiy was delighted to see that Rebekah and Arkturon were outside the front entrance – apparently just alighted from the two horses at their back – and were deep in conversation with two green robed Truth Seekers there.

In the shade of the inn's doorway Bodkin hovered behind the two officers of the Priory; he was trying to eavesdrop on Arkturon's account of where he and Rebekah had been and what they had been up to. Bodkin was overjoyed that Miss Rebekah was safe and well but he burned with questions he wanted answering, not least, *why was Arkturon looking so young all of a sudden* and *where exactly was Luwsiy – had she been rescued or not?* Straining to listen in on them he was distracted by a couple of hurrahs from various villagers nearby and saw that a bedraggled and rather tired, rough looking group of Rangers were coming down the main road toward the inn. In amongst them was a girl in a red riding cloak... it was Rebekah's red riding cloak. Bodkin stepped forward into the sunlight.

"It's Miss Luwsiy!" he shouted and pointed, a big relieved grin on his face.

Rebekah looked instantly to Bodkin who seemed to have appeared from nowhere and then she turned to follow his shaking hand that pointed up the road.

Sergeant Rinawn led what was left of his troop up to the threshold of the inn and they all, Luwsiy included, dismounted in unison.

The two sisters rushed to each other, both with tears in their eyes, and hugged. Their last, bitter parting now forgiven and forgotten, they were just relieved to be home and together again – neither wanted to let the other go.

A thickset, stalwart looking man he'd never seen before came up to the Sergeant with a big grin on his face; the stranger grabbed his hand and shook it vigorously. "Well done, Sir." he said.

Bodkin then started slapping the others across the back, Sinkhoal winced after his turn but took it good naturedly, as Bodkin continued, "You all look like you need a stiff drink – and probably a good old-fashioned home cooked meal too? Come inside, it's on the house."

The Sergeant looked to his comrades, "Well, I can't argue with that." he said with a grin of his own, and led them into the inn.

Deep within the black pool of the old Romannik baths beneath Rose Mansion something stirred. Something that had been bound to the utter darkness within the pool many years ago, a something bound by a sorcerer who was now gone from this world. With his passing the spells he had wrought were untangled and their power faded away to nothing. The sorcerer had been powerful indeed, he had fashioned that something as a rare and difficult form of golem from slick and viscous pitch. He had animated it with the demonic shade fractured from an ancient demoness – summoned and infused by sorcerous spells that stretched the limits of even his artifice – then he had used that something he created, used it in an unspeakable way. When he had finished with it, all those years ago, he cast it to the bottom of the fouled polluted pool from which it was fashioned. He bound it and imprisoned it there; forever separated from the daughter he had begat upon it, that was brought to term unnaturally swift within it and that was then born out of it and cruelly snatched away.

Something stirred and arose from the black pool of the old Romannik baths beneath Rose Mansion. It was cold and it was hungry this fractured shade, a demonic anathema loose in a world where it did not belong – searching for a daughter that was already dead.

Moon Shade

Book Two of the Phantasmagoriad

Coming Soon...

Peter Guy Blacklock

About this Publication and it's Publisher

The Anti-Verse Tales are an ongoing series of short stories, novellas and novels from Peter Guy Blacklock - set within the Anti-Verse that is **Gaea Parallaxis**. The Anti-Verse is not another universe, it is simply the flip side of ours, equal and opposite... a dark Alternative World, intrinsically bound to ours, that mirrors the myths, legends and folklore of our own. These tales, set in different times and technological periods past, present and future, but firmly within the same universe, will invariably contain extreme themes and situations of a profane, violent, horrific or sexual nature. Expect adult language and situations as well as overt violence and gore!

You have been warned.

The 451 ePublishing Haus is the book publishing arm of Harbinger451.co.uk - we will soon be publishing the Dark Matter Series of eBooks, a FREE periodical collection of the most influential contributions to the darker side of genre fiction featuring classic works from the pioneers of dark speculative fiction.

We also publish new and original dark alternative genre fiction to buy, as well as our *Anti-Verse Tales* series we have the *Dollar Dreadful* and *Adult Fairy-Tales* series and soon many standalone titles too. We hope to soon be publishing detailed guides expanding the *Anti-Hero RPG* rules, the *Universal Mythos* system of occultism and the *ABYSS* Jack the Ripper Timeline.

Peter Guy Blacklock

About the Author

Peter Guy Blacklock was born and raised in an unremarkable town in the north-east of England by a remarkably supportive and well adjusted working-class family. After 14 years of ineffective education he found himself in Art College, which led to twenty years employment as an Archaeological Illustrator in which he produced a wide variety of technical illustrations for publication as well as more general illustration, design and copy work on educational and display materials intended for schools and the general public. Eventually the hunt for a half decent salary within that occupation led him to the Museum of London and a move to the capitol where he still lives today in happily married bliss.

He is passionate about genre fiction, film and games, has a fervent interest in history, mythology and folklore and is fascinated by the deeper meanings behind ritual practice, ceremonial magic and occult lore. He is a keen Ripperologist, a devout Lovecraftian and a determined new writer of dark-genre fiction and non-fiction books. A good deal of his spare time is spent online where, under his user-name of choice 'Harbinger451', he is creating a website and writing a blog that explore the alternative worlds that encompass his passions.

Peter Guy Blacklock

Legal Notice

This Paperback Edition 2018
First published in Great Britain, Europe and the World by
Peter Guy Blacklock
Harbinger451
451 ePublishing Haus
London
England
2017
Copyright © Peter Guy Blacklock 2017

Peter Guy Blacklock

Printed in Great Britain
by Amazon